Han Kŭt

Critical Art and Writing
by Korean Canadian Women

Han Kŭt

Critical Art and Writing by Korean Canadian Women

EDITED BY THE KOREAN CANADIAN WOMEN'S
ANTHOLOGY COLLECTIVE

INANNA PUBLICATIONS AND EDUCATION INC.
TORONTO, CANADA

Copyright © 2007 Inanna Publications and Education Inc.

Individual copyright to their work is retained by the authors. All rights reserved. No part of this book may be reproduced or transmitted in any form or by any means, electronically or mechanically, including photocopying, recording, or any information or storage retrieval system, without prior permission in writing from the publisher.

Published in Canada by Inanna Publications and Education Inc.
210 Founders College, York University
4700 Keele Street, Toronto, Ontario M3J 1P3
Telephone: (416) 736-5356 Fax (416) 736-5765
Email: inanna@yorku.ca Website: www.yorku.ca/inanna

Canada Council   Conseil des Arts
for the Arts   du Canada

The publisher gratefully acknowledges the support of the Canada Council for the Arts for its publishing program.

Printed and Bound in Canada.

Front Cover Design: Anne-Marie Estrada
Interior Design: Luciana Ricciutelli

Library and Archives Canada Cataloguing in Publication:

Han kŭt: critical art and writing by Korean Canadian
women / Korean Canadian Women's Anthology Collective

Includes bibliographical references.
ISBN 978-0-9736709-8-1

1. Canadian literature (English) – Korean Canadian authors.
2. Canadian literature (English) – women authors. 3. Canadian
literature (English) – 21st century. 4. Korean Canadian women.
I. Korean Canadian Women's Anthology Collective

PS8235.K67H36 2007   C810.8'09287089957   C2007-903595-7

For our mothers:
Lee Myung-Suk, Lee Hyung-Ja, Huh Jung-Hee and Park Soo-Ja

Contents

Acknowledgements
ix

Introduction
Korean Canadian Women's Anthology Collective
1

I. Learning to Fall

How to Make *Pogee Kimchee*, Or
Ingredients of One Korean Canadian Woman
Helen H. Kang
15

Halmonee
Jean Yoon
18

The Education of Misses Kim
Elaine K. Chang
23

Falling
Jane Park
29

Lost
Jin Huh
39

"Coming Out" as a Queer Korean Woman in Canada:
A Personal Cultural Narrative
Ruthann Lee
41

The Funny Looking Dress
Jane G. Kim
58

Regret
Jin Huh
67

Learning to Walk
Ann Shin
70

II. Lost Homes and Founded Nations

Incorporating Ji-Won Park into the Canadian Nation:
The Good Girl, the Monster and the Noble Savage
Hijin Park
77

Our Bodies Are Battlefields
Una Lee
94

Back Home?
Nuri Kim
96

Here, at the Seams
Julie Kang
99

The *Mudang*: The Colonial Legacies of Korean Shamanism
Merose Hwang
103

TABLE OF CONTENTS

Irony
Elaine K. Chang
120

III. Bodies and Beyond

Identities
Suzy Yim
125

A Peculiar Sensation: A Personal Genealogy of
Korean American and Korean Canadian Women's Cinema
Helen Lee
129

The Picnic
Melissa Kim
153

Ontario Lottery Corporation
Min Sook Lee
155

On Lotus Blossoms, Rice Kings, and Riot Grrrls
Gloria U. Y. Kim
159

IV. Disrupting Tongues

White Life
Jean Yoon
165

Can the Desert Change?
Michelle Cho
167

Un/becoming Jonquil
Julie Kang
171

Snake
Hana Kim
174

Cold Comfort: Sex Slaves for the Japanese Imperial Military
Sylvia Yu Chao
175

Madwoman
Gloria U. Y. Kim
186

You
Hana Kim
190

Breaking Boundaries: Bringing Communities and Unions Together
Jenny J. H. Ahn
191

V. Junctures

Ajuma: The Third Gender
Helen H. Kang
199

Mom's Dream and Ginger Man
Far-San
204

Skilled Korean Women on the Move: Becoming Transnational Migrants
Young-Hwa Hong
207

TABLE OF CONTENTS

1997
Juliana Choi
229

Fallen
Juliana Choi
231

Dear X
Isabelle Kim
233

Korean Drummers
Ann Shin
241

Contributor Notes
242

Acknowledgements

We wish to acknowledge and thank past editorial collective members Jennifer Chang, Helen H. Kang, Yukyung Kim-Cho, and Jesook Song for their work at the early stages of this project.

Also, we wish to acknowledge our families, friends, and allies who have supported and inspired this project.

Special thanks to: all our contributors, Anne-Marie Estrada for her kick-ass cover design, Luciana Ricciutelli and Andrea Medovarski of Inanna Publications and Education Inc., Anna Camilleri, Clara Ho, and Hon-Yee Choi.

Thank you also to the Toronto Women's Bookstore, Han Kŭt Collective, Asian Community AIDS Services, Ontario Public Interest Research Group-Toronto, Heads Up Collective, Centre for Women and Trans People at the University of Toronto, SistahFire Writing Collective.

KOREAN CANADIAN WOMEN'S
ANTHOLOGY COLLECTIVE

Introduction

"Han": A play on "*Hanguk*" which means "Korea"; also refers to a history of suffering among Koreans. It can also mean "big," "some," or "one."

"Kŭt": Can mean agitation, grassroots ritual, political art, collective action, or noisy, also describes a type of spiritual exorcism conducted by a *mudang* (female shaman).

Han Kŭt: Critical Art and Writing by Korean Canadian Women is an anthology of writing and visual art that asks *what are the creative possibilities of being Korean, Canadian, and a woman at this particular historical moment*? This book offers a variety of meanings and perspectives on how the identities of race, gender, sexuality, class, ability, religion, and nationality shape and inform the ways in which Korean Canadian women are seen, and more importantly, see themselves. By naming our anthology *Han Kŭt*, a newly created phrase, we hope to impart a challenging and imaginative vision of Korean Canadian women.

The publication of *Han Kŭt* uncovers some of the unique and largely undocumented creative works by emerging and more established Korean Canadian women artists, activists, and writers. Partial as all texts are, we aim to begin the process of addressing some of the complex and multiple viewpoints, stories, and challenges facing Korean women in Canada. We do not claim to speak for all Korean Canadian women but hope that the works contained in this anthology resonate, at least in part, with the various parts of ourselves.

The Story Behind the Stories: How *Han Kŭt* Began

One summer evening in 2002, three young women met at a downtown Toronto bakery to discuss the possibility of working together to edit an anthology highlighting the work of politicized Korean women in Canada. We had met one another through feminist and anti-racist student activist networks at the University of Toronto. Each of us was beginning to think more seriously about issues of identity and our personal and political relationships to the phrase "Korean Canadian women." During this meeting, we lamented that we did not know of any existing collections of writing or artwork by Korean women in Canada.

As we became better acquainted, we found that many aspects of our histories were strikingly similar and we felt strongly connected as Korean women engaged in social justice struggles. This was really exciting! We no longer felt a need to deny different parts of ourselves; in fact, by getting to know one another we began to feel more complete. For the first time, being Korean didn't feel separate from other aspects of our selves, especially from our political activism. Additionally, externally imposed, and in turn, our internalized stereotypes of what it meant to be Korean women in Canada—Christian, straight, model minorities, depoliticized, subservient, compliant, *yamchŏnhae* (gentle)—could finally be turned on their heads.

This connection with one another inspired us to find others who felt the same way. Gradually, the editorial collective expanded as other Korean-identified women who were interested in this anti-racist, feminist book project joined the group. Through our discussions, we repeatedly noted how we have all longed for books, films, and cultural role models that reflect our personal and political experiences of living in Canada. Additionally, we agreed that it would be most valuable to pay homage to our mentors and the creative cultural work that already exists. The collective has since worked to organize the compilation and publication of this anthology.

Our first call for submissions went out in 2004 and at least three subsequent calls were sent out on various lists and networks after that. One of the main reasons it has taken us five years from our first meeting to the publication of this book has been due to our time constraints as workers, students, teachers, artists, and activists. At these meetings, we would not only go through our new submissions, but also discuss our political and ideological aims for the book; for example, who our target audience would be. Early on, we had challenging conversations about what we meant by "Korean Canadian women"; that it was not race, ethnicity, gender, and citizenship per se as much as it was the experience of being racialized, gendered, and heterosexualized in Canada that we wished to explore.

The size and composition of the collective fluctuated since that first meeting in 2002. By the summer of 2005, the collective expanded to include eight women. At the time of publication, we were back down to four members. While it has been mostly exciting to forge ahead with our book project, the process of working as such a large editorial collective has also been difficult to negotiate. Although it was our commonalities that brought us together, we eventually realized that if we did not confront our internal differences, we would continue to struggle to coordinate and proceed with our work as editors. At present, we continue to work through the challenges of acknowledging and accounting for our relative positions of power and privilege. Yet each of us involved in the project would agree that it has been a useful political, intellectual, and emotional journey.

Locating Koreans in Canadian Multiculturalism

Koreans are now one of the fastest growing racialized communities in Canada (Statistics Canada). Prior to the 1970s, the Korean community in Canada was extremely small and comprised mainly of temporary residents seeking employment and educational opportunities. While there has been a long history of immigration from other countries in Asia, particularly China, Japan, and India,[1] little is known about early Korean migration. At various points, Canada's immigration system has been more open or closed depending on a number of competing factors; namely the desire to populate Canada with white Europeans, particularly British settlers, and the need for cheap migrant labour in the service of economic expansion and nation-building (Thobani). Nationalist ideologies informed by colonialist practices and narratives have constructed the Canadian nation as a white settler society. In other words, the ideal Canadian citizen is white, male and heterosexual (see Razack).

In 1967, changes to the Canadian *Immigration Act* introduced a "colour-blind" points system,[2] leading to dramatic increases in migration from parts of Asia, Africa, and South America, including a sharp rise in Korean settlement in Canada. Correspondingly, a number of state-sponsored projects were initiated throughout the 1970s and 1980s, which helped to implement a system of "official" multiculturalism in Canada. However, rather than working in the interests of immigrant and racialized groups, several critical feminist and anti-racist scholars have argued that Canada's multicultural policy maintains the status quo by silencing protest (Bannerji). For instance, rather than addressing why people of colour and Indigenous nations continue to have limited access to political and economic power, we are more likely to see cultural festivals that affirm Canada as an open, tolerant, and meritocratic society in which all peoples are welcome. In this manner, multiculturalism conceals systems of white privilege, ongoing colonialism of Indigenous peoples, and racism against people of colour.

Throughout the 1970s, thousands of Koreans immigrated to Canada each year. Most were working and middle-class families from Korea's urban centers who arrived as part of the family reunification program. Many Koreans built their livelihoods through corner stores and restaurants as communities formed themselves across Canada. For many first-generation Koreans, their hard work as self-employed businessmen and women in Canada has been a stepping-stone to creating a new, more prosperous life for their children. Newly arrived immigrants were able to get support from more established community members, particularly in urban areas, as the Church provides a locus around which people congregate, meet, and develop community. In the 1980s and 1990s, as the focus of national immigration policy shifted to further reflect Canada's global economic interests and Korea became more of an international economic power, there was a further rise in Korean migration to Canada. Eventually the composition of Korean migrants changed from working-class and middle-class workers to predominantly wealthy entrepreneurs with a marked increase in the number of temporary residents and international students (Kwak 2004).

Ironically, despite the growing numbers of Koreans in Canada and the upward mobility of its second-generation and newly immigrated populations, Koreans remain an under-represented minority group in Canada. Representations of Koreans in North America have shifted dramatically over the past few decades. The majority of mainstream older Canadians may continue to understand Koreans primarily in the context of the Korean War. In the popular media, for example, older American television programs such as *M*A*S*H* depict Koreans as inferior and needing to be saved by the West—the Americans in particular. More recently, following the 1988 Seoul Olympics, cultural signifiers of Korean food such as *kimchee*, products such as Hyundai cars, cultural icons like Korean American actor and comedian Margaret Cho, and top-ranked golf players Se Ri Park, Grace Park, and 17-year old Michelle Wie, as well as the more recent controversial discourses about North Korean leader Kim-Jong Il, are increasingly recognized and consumed by the Canadian mainstream. Additionally, widely sensationalized U.S. media reports of the 1992 Los Angeles riots, which emphasized racial conflicts between black and Korean communities, may still resonate with Canadian audiences.

At this particular historical moment, Koreans in Canada appear to possess a certain kind of cultural currency that may indeed render the "Korean Canadian woman" visible in particular ways. However, by attempting to develop a more complex understanding of "Korean Canadian women," we must be wary of any overly-celebratory presentations of cultural difference that are integral to the Canadian project of nation-building in a global economic context. In a related way, Nandita Sharma and Himani Bannerji have argued that immigrant communities most often engage in class politics with the intention of upward mobility rather than in the interest of social and economic equality. The Korean community in Canada is no exception.

Koreans have migrated to the West for various reasons but the history of Christian proselytizing in Korea and of Japanese and American military, economic, and cultural imperialism cannot be ignored. We can only begin to speculate on how the impacts of these different but related forms of religious fundamentalism and imperialism on Korean (im)migrants have informed and secured Canada's own nation-building project. Certainly, they have worked to obscure any similarities arising from long histories of colonialism as well as other potential solidarities between Korean and Aboriginal communities.[3] As long as the construction of the category "Korean Canadian" continues to stake its claims to citizenship and refuses to acknowledge the ongoing colonization of Indigenous peoples, it serves to consolidate rather than challenge the project of settlement and colonial relations. It is therefore important to consider opportunities that examine how (im)migrant policies are connected to the continued colonization of Indigenous peoples in Canada as a way to buttress white nationalist projects of capitalist expansion.

Finally, we must consider the political implications and consequences of (re)articulating diasporic affiliations when differences (of migration history, geographic location, sexuality, class, religion, and language) are too easily obscured or ignored. We must challenge the prevalence of heterosexual notions of family and normative gendered identities within the Korean Canadian community that erase the existence of queer and trans Korean women. Overall, we've come to understand the necessity in tracing various modes of Korean women's resistance to heterosexist forms of Korean nationalism and hypermasculine, imperialist, and racist Canadian nationalisms.

Presenting the *Han Kŭt* Anthology

To date, there have been few published works on the Korean Canadian community or Korean Canadian women in the English language.[4] This book is thus the very first of its kind. In *Han Kŭt: Critical Art and Writing by Korean Canadian Women*, we aim to achieve three goals: first, we hope to add to the limited selection of cultural resources that explore Korean women's stories and perspectives in Canada; second, we reflect on our relationship with Korean nationalism and Canadian multiculturalism; and third, we complicate what it means to be "Korean Canadian women."

From deeply personal vignettes to broader critiques of Canadian society, this anthology provides a diverse collection of short stories, prose, poetry, visual art, academic and personal essays that contribute to building a more complete landscape of published works by, for, and about Korean women in

Canada. Starting in Section One, "Learning to Fall," the contributors share important narratives on some of the life lessons 1.5 and second generation women are learning from girlhood to adulthood and motherhood—centered around some familiar themes such as identity, language, sexuality, relationships, and death. The pieces focus on the kind of life lessons that can only be learned by "falling," by making mistakes and learning from them. This section also explores the relationships that second generation children have with older generations, illustrating the powerful socio-economic, political, and psychological processes that have shaped their understandings of self and community.

Helen H. Kang's "How to Make *Pogee Kimchee,* or Ingredients of One Korean-Canadian Woman" offers a playful rebuttal to a recipe for *kimchee*. By injecting her own personal commentary, Kang makes adjustments to the traditional recipe for *kimchee*—and, ultimately, to the components of what it means for her to be a Korean woman. Jean Yoon's "Halmoni" is a touching and at times humorous tale of a young granddaughter exploring her similarities to her dying, strong-willed, and melodramatic *halmoni*. Elaine Chang's "The Education of Misses Kim" is an ironic and deftly written poem that challenges the use and the ability of the English language to frame the complexity of the diasporic experience. Jane Park's short story "Falling" also takes up struggles around language as she artfully recounts a daughter's quest to understand what it was like for her late father to adapt to life in rural Alberta. In "'Coming Out' as a Queer Korean Woman in Canada," Ruthann Lee explores the impact of "coming out" to her mother and how this links to broader issues of gender and nation. Lee raises critical, often unchallenged, issues of heterosexism and homophobia in the Korean community in the context of Canadian multiculturalism. In the short story "The Funny Looking Dress," Jane G. Kim provides a humorous and painfully honest account of a young Korean girl who learns how to grapple with the pressures and contradictions of adolescence in small town Alberta. Jin Huh's poem, "Lost," shares what a healthy romantic relationship might feel like when it is being experienced for the first time. Her second poem, "Regret," speaks of a daughter's regret towards her dying mother and reflects how displacement, racism and Christianity affect her understanding of self and her relationship with her mother. Finally, Ann Shin's fictional piece, "Learning to Walk," renders a portrait of intergenerational understanding between mothers and daughters from the perspective of a new mother as she cares for her own aging mother.

In Section Two, "Lost Homes and Founded Nations," we wish to present some preliminary insights on Korean Canadian women's vexed relationship to both Korea's postcolonial nationalist project and Canada's superficial tolerance of racialized communities. We present pieces that explore displacement, militarism, racism, and sexism in the context of Canadian nationalism and some of the legacies of colonialism on Korea's nationalist project. Several pieces look at how Korean women are contradictorily positioned within dominant constructions of Korean and Canadian nationalism. To elaborate, in Korean communities in Canada, Korean women are expected to build and preserve "Korean culture" as a way to protect their communities from assimilation. At the same time, we are limited by the patriarchal and heterosexist models of Korean nationalism, which impose conservative structures of family and community. In the context of the dominant Canadian society, Korean women face both exclusion and token inclusion as "model minorities."

Hijin Park's critical essay, "Incorporating Ji-Won Park into the Canadian Nation: The Good Girl, the Monster and the Noble Savage" provides an analysis of citizenship in her account of a recent attack on a Korean woman residing temporarily in Canada to study English. The images in Una Lee's "Our Bodies are Battlefields" draw correlations between women, war, and militarization. Of particular significance is the centering of the nation in her artwork. Nuri Kim's written reflection, "Back Home?" is a personal story of longing for a home. She expresses feelings of displacement and dislocation common to many diasporic Korean women. In the moving short story, "Here, at the Seams," Julie Kang captures a similar sentiment of loss and (re)building identity and community by chronicling the routine of an aging Korean woman as she travels the Toronto subway from work to home. Merose Hwang's essay, "The Mudang: The Colonial Legacies of Korean Shamanism," provides a detailed and critical historical analysis of the figure of the *mudang*—a Korean female shaman—in the context of Korean nationalism and colonial relations. Examining the ongoing history and treatment of the *mudang* is particularly important in relation to contemporary Korean feminist movements. Finally, the compelling stills taken from filmmaker Elaine Chang's "Irony" provide a challenge to projects of white nationalism and capitalist development.

In our aim to complicate existing notions of what it means to be "Korean Canadian women," we present Section Three, "Bodies and Beyond." In this chapter, we confront stereotypes commonly attributed to Asian women, such as the meek and docile "lotus blossom" and the overly aggressive "dragon lady," which reflect the sexual dehumanization of Korean and Asian women. This chapter continues to illustrate Korean women's resistance to sexism, racism, and other forms of oppression and misrepresentation. Various contributors question the prevalence of heterosexual notions of family within the Korean Canadian community and a larger society that erases the presence and realities of queer Korean women. In particular, contributors in this section explore themes of bodily representation and resistance through different forms of cultural production, including photography, creative prose, film, and comic strips.

Suzy Yim's striking photographs and revealing personal essay, "Identities," convey a powerful message about how the intersections of gendered, racial, and sexual identities are lived and produced. Yim offers an honest and in-your-face response to the ways that she has been (mis)read by the people she encounters in everyday situations. Melissa Kim's "The Picnic" similarly offers a glimpse into the pain of cultural misinterpretation by describing an incident in which a white Canadian onlooker comments disapprovingly on her family's memorial ritual. This story reflects how Korean cultural "traditions" are often heralded as static and backward in the context of Canadian, or western, cultural racism. Through illustrations, Min Sook Lee depicts with wit the experiences of a second generation Korean Canadian in a family-owned and operated business with the "Ontario Lotto Corporation." These families strive for economic mobility and status through different types of self-employment and the establishment of small businesses in Canada. Helen Lee's landmark essay, "A Peculiar Sensation: A Personal Genealogy of Korean American and Korean Canadian Women's Cinema," provides a seminal analysis of the role of Korean North American women in the realm of filmmaking. Lee remarks on the privileged position that these growing numbers of Korean North American women independent filmmakers occupy and investigates the relational aspects of identity formation and the ways in which Korean women are positioned vis-à-vis other racialized, immigrant, and Indigenous communities. Finally, in this section Gloria U. Y. Kim makes explicit the experience of racial and sexual stereotyping as a Korean Canadian woman in her critical essay, "On Lotus Blossoms, Rice Kings and Riot Grrrls." Kim is adamant about the responsibility of Korean Canadian women to recognize, challenge, and respond to sexual and racial oppression in order to (re)claim power for themselves.

The fourth section, "Disrupting Tongues," continues to disrupt simple and static understandings of "Korean Canadian women." We present pieces that highlight resistance and political activism by Korean Canadian women. The chapter begins with Jean Yoon's short story, "White Life," which brings to light some of the subtle and not-so-subtle forms of Canadian racism experienced by a Korean woman who has married into a white Canadian family. In "Can the Desert Change?" Michelle Cho provides a self-reflexive essay detailing her experiences of alienation within white mainstream political activist communities. Cho talks about intersecting oppressions and calls upon racialized communities to "claim space" as a political act. In her personal essay, "(Un)Becoming Jonquil," Julie Kang reflects upon finding a voice as a Korean Canadian woman writer by thinking through ideas around cultural authenticity. For Kang, cultural identity does not have to limit one's creative vision as an artist. Sylvia Yu

Chao draws on her recent encounters with former Korean comfort women in her essay, "Cold Comfort: Sex Slaves for the Japanese Imperial Military," to describe the system of Japanese military sex slavery in Korea, which existed from 1932 to 1945. Yu Chao pays homage to the survivors she interviewed, led by her belief that speaking publicly about the brutal system of military sexual slavery is an act of political resistance. Hana Kim's poem, "Snake" (originally written in Korean and translated into English), speaks to residual emotions of suffering and raw pain, while her poem, "You" (also translated), addresses feelings of anger and ambivalence regarding the end of a relationship. The series of photographs presented in Gloria U. Y. Kim's "Madwoman" subvert and disrupt dominant representations of Asian women. Kim's photographs recognize and honour the power and magic of Korean "shaman-priestesses." In the final piece, labour activist Jenny Ahn writes about her political journey and involvement with the Asian Canadian Labour Alliance in "Breaking Boundaries and Bringing Communities and Unions Together." Ahn describes how her understanding of social justice has been shaped by her "roots," which also fuels her commitment to labour activism both within Korean Canadian communities and with broader communities.

In the fifth and final section, "Junctures," we bring our readers to a crossroads, where we hope to show that these conversations by and about Korean Canadian women — with themselves, within the Korean community, and with other racialized communities in Canada, and with mainstream Canadian society — continues on in complex and multi-layered ways. Helen Kang's "Ajuma: The Third Gender," offers a personal reflection that uncovers entrenched perceptions of the sexuality of older Korean women based on the author's experiences as a young sexual health educator. In Far-San's "Mom's Dream and Ginger Man," a daughter and mother attempt to communicate long-distance via telephone, which hinders the daughter's desire to tell her mother about her new romantic relationship with another woman. Young-Hwa Hong's scholarly essay, "Skilled Korean Women on the Move: Becoming Transnational Migrants," provides a sociological analysis of interviews with professional immigrant Korean women who negotiate difficult challenges of racism and sexism in the Canadian labour market. Hong argues that for many of these women, global mobility has not been accompanied by a corresponding economic and social mobility due to systemic barriers concerning race and gender. Julianna Choi's two poems, "Fallen," and "1997," evoke the contradictions of filial duty and self-love. In a poignant letter written to her young son, Isabelle Kim's "Dear X" eloquently speaks to the concerns and complexities associated with mixed raciality and differences in language. Finally, Ann Shin invokes vivid and powerful images of women in her poem "Korean Drummers" that affirm and celebrate our collective identity as women.

Han Kŭt as a New Beginning

The title of our compilation—which draws upon and combines the multiple meanings of "*han*" and "*kŭt*" to create a new phrase—denotes our desire to engage meaningfully with questions of social justice and anti-oppression. With this anthology, we hope to contribute to past and future discussions of how racialized women can dismantle systems of oppression and contribute to a more just society. As both colonized subjects *and* citizens or immigrants in a white settler state that perpetuates ongoing colonialism against Indigenous peoples and racism against people of colour, Koreans are simultaneously oppressed and privileged in complicated ways. We are concerned about the limits of constructing diasporic communities in isolation from other communities. It is important for us, as women of colour, to engage not only with our own cultural community and mainstream Canadian society, but also with other racialized communities. Additionally, we need to examine our privileged position in relation to Indigenous communities and confront how we as citizens participate in Canada's ongoing violence of colonialism. Bonita Lawrence and Enakshi Dua remind us that we must be mindful of how to frame claims for antiracism in ways that do not ignore the struggles of Indigenous people. By examining these complicated and often tenuous dynamics, we can better understand and find ways to engage in political solidarity with one another.

The naming of "Korean Canadian women" remains an important political intervention and response to oppressive systems. As co-editors of this book, we have been active in constructing and producing the category of "Korean Canadian women." We have endeavoured to trouble and complicate any static and taken-for-granted understandings and attempted to move beyond lamenting the problems of representation. Rather than merely rejecting stereotypes that are commonly attributed to Asian women, we have offered up some new and multifaceted stories, essays, poems, and artwork that challenge such racist, sexist, and one-dimensional representations. This is merely the beginning of a much needed and long-term dialogue amongst ourselves and with other communities.

The Korean Canadian Women's Anthology Collective
Jin Huh, Patricia Lee, Ruthann Lee, and Hijin Park
June 2007

[1] The history of Chinese immigration to Canada is more widely documented, particularly when migrant workers from China were needed to help build the Canadian Pacific Railway (CPR). After 1885, when the CPR was completed, Canada closed its doors to Asian immigrants through a number of overtly

racist means. The Chinese Head Tax was introduced in 1885 after those working the railway were no longer needed. The *Chinese Exclusion Act* of 1923, Canada's Gentleman's Agreement with Japan in 1907, and the Continuous Journey Stipulation of 1908 that effectively kept immigrants from India out of Canada, all worked to bar entry of Asians into Canada. See Jakubowski for further details.

[2] The *Immigration Act* of 1967 is considered a turning point in the history of Canadian immigration policy. While overt racial discrimination was removed, more subtle forms of discrimination took over (Abu Laban and Gabriel).

[3] There is, however, some promise of collaboration in the realm of cultural production. For example, Korean Canadian filmmaker Helen Lee's short film, *Prey* (1995), starring Korean American actor Sandra Oh and Native Canadian actor Adam Beach, briefly but cleverly explores the contemporary relationship of a young Korean Canadian woman and Native man in Vancouver.

[4] Exceptions include Min-Jung Kwak's more recent academic work on the Korean Canadian community in Vancouver (2004) and on Korean immigrant women entrepreneurs (2002) and Yi Sun-Kyung's memoir, *Inside the Hermit Kingdom* (1997). Over the past several years, studies and scholarly collections of Korean American feminist writings have emerged, such as Ji-Yeon Yuh's *Beyond the Shadow of Camptown: Korean Military Brides in America* (2002); *Dangerous Women: Gender and Korean Nationalism*, edited by Elaine H. Kim and Chungmoo Choi (1998); and Young I. Song and Ailee Moon's *Korean American Women: From Tradition to Modern Feminism* (1998). While in some cases, Asian American women's texts and anthologies have also included Korean Canadian women's writings, the historical specificity and unique context of Korean Canadian's women's experiences have not been adequately addressed. Additionally, there has been some work by Korean Canadian women published in two of *Fireweed's* special-themed issues: *Awakening Thunder: Asian Canadian Women* (1990), and *Rice Papers: Writing and Artwork by East and Southeast Asian Women* (1994). *Fireweed* was a quarterly journal published in Canada that focused on feminist writing, politics, art and culture. It is no longer in print.

References

Abu-Laban, Yasmeen and Christina Gabriel. *Selling Diversity: Immigration, Multiculturalism, Employment Equity, and Globalization*. Peterborough: Broadview Press, 2002.

Bannerj, Himani. *The Dark Side of the Nation: Essays on Multiculturalism, Nationalism and Gender*. Toronto: Canadian Scholars' Press, 2000.

Fernandez, Sharon, *et al.*, eds. "Awakening Thunder: Asian Canadian Women."

Fireweed: A Feminist Quarterly 30 (1990).

Fireweed Collective, eds. "Rice Papers: Writing and Artwork by East and Southeast Asian Women." *Fireweed: A Feminist Quarterly* 43 (1994).

Jakubowski, Lisa. *Immigration and the Legalization of Racism*. Halifax: Fernwood Publishing Co., Ltd., 1997.

Kim, Elaine H. and Chungmoo Choi, eds. *Dangerous Women: Gender and Korean Nationalism*. New York: Routledge, 1998.

Kwak, Min-Jung. *An Exploration of the Korean-Canadian Community in Vancouver* (Working paper series No. 04-14). Vancouver: Vancouver Centre of Excellence: Research on Immigration and Integration in the Metropolis, 2004.

Kwak, Min-Jung. "Work in Family Businesses and Gender Relations: A Case Study of Recent Korean Immigrant Women." Unpublished Master's Thesis. Toronto: York University, 2002.

Lawrence, Bonita and Enakshi Dua. "Decolonizing Antiracism." *Social Justice* 32 (4) (2005): 120-143.

Lee, Helen. "A Peculiar Sensation: A Personal Genealogy of Korean American Women's Cinema." *Dangerous Women: Gender and Korean Nationalism*. Eds. Elaine. H. Kim and Chungmoo Choi. New York: Routledge, 1998. 291-322.

Razack, Sherene. "Introduction: When Place Becomes Race." *Race, Space and the Law: Unmapping a White Settler Society*. Toronto: Between the Lines Press, 2002. 1-20.

Sharma, Nandita. *Home Economics: Nationalism and the Making of Migrant Workers in Canada*. Toronto: University of Toronto Press, 2006.

Song, Young I. and Ailee Moon, eds. *Korean American Women: From Tradition to Modern Feminism*. Westport: Praeger Publishing, 1998.

Statistics Canada. *Population Projections of Visible Minority Groups: Canada, Pro-vinces and Regions*. Ottawa: Statistics Canada, 2005.

Thobani, Sunera. "Benevolent State, Law-Breaking Smugglers, and Deportable and Expendable Women: An Analysis of the Canadian State's Strategy to Address Trafficking in Women." *Refuge* 19 (4) (2001): 24-33.

Yi, Sung-Kyung. *Inside the Hermit Kingdom: A Memoir*. Toronto, Key Porter Books, 1997.

Yuh, Ji-Yeon. *Beyond the Shadow of Camptown: Korean Military Brides in America*. New York: New York University Press, 2002.

I.
Learning to Fall

HELEN H. KANG

How to Make *Pogee Kimchee*, or Ingredients of One Korean-Canadian Woman

1. Cut the *baechu*[1] in half or into quarters, depending on the size.

    First generation, second generation, 1.5 generation. Depending on how long you have lived outside of Korea, you are a number. Someone said I'm a 1.75 generation for having lived in Canada for so long. As time passes I'm divided into increasingly smaller decimal points.

2. Let the *baechu* sit in 15 percent brine until the leaves are limp.

    When my sister first went to school in Canada, she started to lose her Korean within a matter of months. She was five years old. My parents made sure to reverse that process, for which she and I are both grateful. But even now, when I don't speak Korean for lengths of time, my tongue gets "curly," to use the Korean expression, which means that I tend to slur my Korean pronunciation.

3. Rinse thoroughly, making sure to get all the dirt out of the crevices between the leaves, and strain.

    After we ate *kimchee*, or any Korean food that was strongly flavoured, my parents would have us brush our teeth thoroughly before leaving the house. "It's not polite to smell garlicky," they said. "You have to remember that you're in someone else's country." I doubt my parents ever meant the First Nations people of Canada.

4. Cut *mu*[2] and spring onions into thin strips at about 4 cm in length. Set them aside.

    Someone spread a rumour that Asian people are naturally thin and small, especially women. By genetic chance I fit that image. I've had people suspect that I was anorexic when I was a teenager. My parents own a health food store and while working there I've had many unpleasant opportunities to sell weight loss products to women. "You're so thin! I want to look like you." "Asian girls are so lucky. You're naturally skinny." Set them aside.

5. Wash oysters in lightly salted water. Strain and set them aside.

I once dated a lanky white vegan boy who studied philosophy. I told him about *kimchee*, the most cherished of Korean foods, and how it can't be made vegan. He claimed that any food could be made vegan, explaining that his Greek friend had been able to stay vegan while eating traditional foods. Back then I lacked the language to explain why I thought he couldn't say that. But I knew I felt uneasy about him showing footage of animals being slaughtered by people of colour in meat packing factories as he flashed his blue eyes handing out brochures to students on campus. Strain and set him aside.

6. Finely chop garlic and ginger. Set them aside.

"Do you have a boyfriend?" "When will we see you get married?" I recently attended a childhood friend's wedding and was showered with questions like these. Without a man at my side, in a few years I'll be considered a *nochonyo*, an old maid. I envision a different type of partnership, an alternate form of family. Garlic with garlic. Ginger with ginger.

7. Soak *gochugaru*[3] in warm water then chop it finely.

"You're Korean? Oh, then you must like spicy food." Somehow I've become a fake Korean for having only a moderate tolerance for heat. There are times when I catch myself trying extra hard to impress people with my limited heat tolerance, as if to prove that I have the Korean-spice gene. Actually, my favourite type of cuisine is Mediterranean—olives, herbs and cheeses.

8. Mix together *gochugaru*, *mu*, spring onions, oysters, garlic, and ginger. Add shrimp *jot*[4] into the mixture and salt to taste.

I am Korean born. I am a bio-woman. I am queer. I am a daughter. I am a sister. I am a friend. I am a feminist. I am a student. I am a writer. I am an ally. I am an activist. I am a Canadian citizen. These are only some of the ingredients. Mix them together and season to taste. To whose taste? I want to be salty, sour, bitter. Compassionately sweet, pensively mild, abrasively spicy.

9. Take a section of the *baechu* and spread bits of the above mixture in between the leaves. Pack the folds carefully so that the entire *baechu* holds together.

My life is a story, written leaf by leaf, built on one experience after another, one memory upon another. It weaves through my body, all the different lengths and colours of my hair, my walk, my scars, memories of loving or hating my face, my skin colour, the shape of my eyes. The progressions and contradictions somehow all hold me together, sometimes solidly but most of the time only precariously.

10. Place the *baechu* into a large jar, pack it down tightly. Repeat steps 8 to 10 with additional *baechu* sections. Seal the jar and store until the flavours have soaked through. Enjoy.

This book, this collective, my group of Korean women friends all form a jar of *baechu kimchee*. All precariously formed life stories placed side by side, the memories of one seeping into another. Salty meets sweet, bitter meets sour, mild meets spicy. The *kimchee* has ripened over the years and its flavours will continue to change in the times to come. Enjoy.

[1] A large leafy vegetable, similar to Chinese cabbage or nappa. Isn't it funny that one exotic food is defined here by comparing it to another exotic food?
[2] A white root vegetable with a crispy texture.
[3] Dried and ground red hot chili peppers.
[4] A pungent sauce or side-dish made with fish or seafood aged in salt.

JEAN YOON

Halmonee

Halmonee is lying in bed, half-smoked cigarettes planted like spokes in a wide seashell that she uses as an ashtray. She is resting on her elbow, thick glasses sliding down her nose. Her hair is perfectly white and thinning on the very top, just where she can't see it herself with a mirror. She used to make my mother brush her hair carefully each night and pluck out the white ones until finally my mother refused because there were more white hairs than black. She is used to it now but every now and then she still begs my mother to help her dye her hair. My mother always refuses. Now her hair is short and so soft that when you run your fingers through it, it feels like spring grass. It is hard to believe she is so old.

There is a book in her hand with very large print. The pages are thin and elegant so you can see, like veins in the skin, the words on the opposite page. I think it is the bible she is reading, but maybe it's a book of hymns. She doesn't sing herself but she enjoys calling the preacher and telling him that she is dying, soon, oh how her body aches, please speak up, there are bees in the air, oh please come soon, she had to phone herself because her terrible daughter doesn't believe her pain.... And when the preacher comes, he brings his wife, a neat lady with shoes that match her pale peach dress. They hold her hand and sing energetic hymns. Halmonee reads all these hymns over and over so when the preacher and his wife do come, she knows exactly which ones she wants them to sing.

Her skin is without spots, like those I see on the faces of some other old people, and it is deliciously soft. Under her bed, she has a great brown purse with a gold clasp that is shaped like a daisy. Here and there the gold has rubbed off, leaving a dull grey finish. In her purse she has skin cream, powder, and a long rectangular tortoise shell comb. I like this best. The teeth of the comb do not bend like the plastic comb I carry in my knapsack. They are stiff like wood and when you hold the comb to the light, it is like looking through a venetian blind, half-opened, made of earth marble.

There are other things hidden in her bag. Some candies, a case for her dentures, a tarnished silver spoon wrapped in a piece of Korean newspaper, some elastics and a package of long black hairpins. Sometimes she stows her jewelry in her purse, too. Her most treasured piece is a wide gold ring, notched in a familiar pattern of stars. About once a year she hands this ring over to my mother saying that since she's about to die soon, her only daughter should have it. My mother takes the ring with solemnity and cynicism. A few days later, when my grandmother is feeling better, my mother returns the ring and whatever else my grandmother has bestowed upon her.

She was so pretty when she was young, my mother tells me. She was so pretty and spoiled. All her sisters pampered her and she was so strong-willed and stubborn that she could never learn anything from anyone. There is resentment in my mother's voice. She looks at me and holds her stare for a moment. You are a lot like her, she means to say. You are a lot like her.

I remember once imitating my grandmother. My father was sitting on the sofa, his belly taut like a drum from over-eating. He hadn't yet learned how to fend off my mother's appeals that he eat this and try that, just a bit more, honey, or it will have to be thrown away. His eyes were sleepy. He rubbed the stubble on his chin with one hand and held his stomach with the other. "*Aigoo, noh-moo mah-ni mogoh-soh-yo.*"

My mother was in the kitchen, walking quickly but ineffectively from one end of the kitchen where the sink was to the other end where the stove and all the dirty pans were. My grandmother was leaning one elbow on the table, smoking a cigarette, talking in her cranky and insistent tone. Mom had obviously done something wrong. I watched as my mother grew increasingly agitated and my grandmother finally stopped talking, opened her purse, pulled out some pills and popped them in her mouth. She held the pills under her tongue, her cheeks puffed with air so that the bitter white taste wouldn't spread through her mouth. She walked slowly to the sink, her hands level with her elbows, sawing gently back and forth as she took each delicate step. She stepped up on the two inch platform that Dad put in front of the sink so we could all wash dishes without discomfort. (The sinks in every house we have ever lived in were just slightly too high.) She tossed back a glass of water and screwed up her face as she swallowed. You could see the tension exaggerated in her neck, the almost mimed gulp. She saw me watching her and quickly glanced away.

I knew then that she needed an audience. Every actor needs an audience. I could understand that.

She was sitting again, but now my mother was locked up tight. She refused to answer. I guess that's when I decided it was time for action.

"Look at this, Mom!" I said.

I sat opposite my grandmother, mirrored her smoking, her posture, the light groans as she shifted in her seat to relieve the pressure in her hip that was putting her foot to sleep. I stood slowly, pushing against the table for support, adding an extra moan for effect. I hobbled to the sink, popping pills as I went. I was extra slow turning the tap. It was so hard to do with an eighty-two year old wrist. Cheeks puffed, face squinching just so. Swallow. Finally a sigh that shudders through old old bones. *"Aigoo, mom-mee ulma-nah ahpoh-soh, chook-kae-soh-yoh!"*

I looked through the corner of my eye to see my mother frozen, like an animal that is seeing double and doesn't know which way to run. I saw my father standing at the doorway now, suppressing a laugh, panic in his eyes. I saw my grandmother, her mouth open just about to cackle.

"Aigoo, aigoo, aigoo, aigoo, aigoo," I sighed. Hurt tumbling downhill in a breeze. That's how she used to show she was tired. That's how my mother sounds now. That's probably how I'll sound at the end of a day, when and if I ever get as old as she did.

One thing I liked about my grandmother was that she could take a joke. She had lousy taste when it came to playing jokes on other people. She often told stories, marvelous dangerous stories about her deeply felt sufferings, the less truth the more convincing. She created constant havoc. She didn't seem to know when she was going too far, but she had a laugh that was healthy and selfish.

"Godammy" she used to say. "Godammy you!" Later I taught her "son of a bitch," which through her lips came out something like, "son oba beach." A wicked smile used to flicker across her face when she swore in English. I loved that look. "Puck-ah! Puck-ah! godammy son-oba-beach!"

When my grandmother finally died, it was a relief for everyone. She had been sick for a long time, but no one knew she was as sick as she was that summer of '83. She had been threatening death for almost twenty years. No one believed her anymore. I was working as an actor that summer and for some reason I just knew it was that day. All morning it had been raining, the sky was neurotically sunny and thunderous. By three o'clock it was clearing up but the ground was still wet and in the park where we were playing, the ground would be muddy and dangerously slippery. By five o'clock I was ready to hit the subway and get to work but I stalled, waited by the phone and at five-thirty I called the theatre. The show was cancelled. I rushed to Doctors' Hospital, still carrying my bag with all my warm-up clothes, some make-up that I needed for the show, a book to read on the train. I was worried because if the stage manager noticed I wasn't there when he made the cancellation official to the cast, I might get into a lot of trouble. But somehow I knew something was happening.

HALMONEE

Halmonee had been in the hospital for two weeks, growing weaker each day. Her weight had dropped to almost eighty pounds. The doctors didn't know what it was but they were making us wear masks when we went to see her. Tuberculosis was whispered in my parents' bedroom. Tuberculosis, not of the lungs, but of some other internal organs. A tuberculosis which could not be detected by x-ray.

Doctors' Hospital is on Brunswick, just north of College. The hospital is small and made of yellow brick, the kind that was in style in the fifties. It has that flimsy ugliness of buildings put up in haste and optimism. My grandmother was on the eighth floor. There were two elevators. There were about five people waiting. Behind the silver triangular button was a red glow. Good, I thought, it can't be long.

I waited eight minutes. I could have walked up in that time. For the first few minutes I was anxious. I drummed my fingers on my shoulder bag. I walked back and forth. The floor was grey tile marked off in square yards. I pressed my toes into the intersection of the tiles. Pirouette. The elevator still hadn't arrived. Several more minutes would pass before the door would open but I knew then that she had died.

My mother was crying and holding my grandmother's hand. My father was not there. He was talking to the doctors and would be back soon. "You just missed her," my mother sobbed in Korean. I nodded. "I know."

Later my mother stepped out for a minute and I was left alone with my grandmother. She was still warm. Or at least, her face was. But she was so thin now it was awful to look at her. Her lips were dry, as dry as the skin on your feet after you've been walking barefoot. There were deep cracks at the corners, a thin layer of red underneath. I pulled aside the sheet, gently, and looked at her feet. They were purple and swollen. Her flesh was filled with water wherever circulation was limited: her hands, her feet, the side of her hip. Her hands, her beautiful hands, were curled so tight, close to her face, and yet inside her thumb, across her palm, her flesh was black. She had such beautiful hands. She used to cream them gently and her nails were always perfect and unadorned.

There was a white plastic tube that had been inserted in her nose and I had seen it feeding her air; it was lying now on her pillow, no longer necessary. The intravenous tube was still in her left arm, the tape not covering the huge expanse of skin bruised and broken from so many needles.

She shouldn't have died like that. She was always setting the stage for a grand exit. Hymns, friends around her, the wailing of daughter and son, their vocal remorse, too late. She should have died at home, with a descending *aigoo, aigoo, aigoo...*, a softening whistle through her lips, her eyes open and knowing.

My three cousins, my brothers and I carried the coffin. We hadn't seen each other in several years. We traded sober compliments on how we'd all changed. My uncle stood by in a stiff new suit. My mother wept uncontrollably. I remember her hands trembling as she struggled to replace my grandmother's thick gold ring on the finger where she had worn it for so many years. My father protested that it was foolish to bury an heirloom, but my mother insisted. I think she was afraid my grandmother might return from the dead and ask for it back.

I still own some of Halmonee's old clothes, a grey coat of quilted silk to be worn on weddings and grand occasions. It is made of heavy cloth embroidered with silver. There are carefully hidden pockets inside the folds of dark purple lining. The coat still has the stale smell of baby powder, the acid tinge that hung lightly on her skin towards the end, a faint cigarette burn on the right cuff. And inside a pocket I had never noticed before I found a square wooden comb that I remember she said she couldn't find. Fine white hairs and dust as pale as breath.

ELAINE K. CHANG

The Education of Misses Kim

1.
essay, miss kim, means to try

in a monograph, manifesto world she
would be an essay. short
on aspiration she could not hope
to be tall but reach for the top
nevertheshorter of breath 400 m.
behind the others.
essais-toi mlle. try. despite all that
you don't know it can't hurt to.

2.
english lesson

no. an afternoon
is not delicious. only
lunch breakfast supper
the things you eat dear. yes oh my.
Mrs. Ross laughing says this then
burbles like stew
all through the first knitting class.

not delicious,
that night she doesn't sleep.
number nine needles

are fine silver chopsticks
or firebrands clacking
contrapuntal music
for four hands. or
a conversation. converse
ants cross words till morning.
citizen sam awakes at six
to westclox and wearable
vengeful delectation.
his wife's first statement
in this country:
a sweater. v-neck
for victory.

3.
chemical warfare

it's a marshmallow mommy
you eat it.
it won't hurt you

4.
polymorphous

polly more for us
per verse

prolly less for us
per hour

semiotic chora hey
hooray mamamamotion
popopoetic popo language   rides waves   we   (the password is freeeee)

priapic

onomatopoeia ick thick symbolicking prick
someone hit me with a stick   of some type

but I regress
I forget   (*l'hommelette* [*qui m'oublie*])
I revolt
I repeat (lather rinse)   poly wants a poly wants a

5.
amerirang

arirang arirang koh sayee nee wah [. . .] arirang
arirang koh say can you see by the donzerlee light
[. . .] by the try right's last gleaming [. . .] and the rockettes read grayer [. . .]
that our frag was still there [. . .] or the land of the flea and the home

6.
the mother was a fugitive from a chain gang

and the daughter would pretend she'd always already
been kissed. always already been tampered with. she was already
tampered with all right, sent downriver to good schools and
not the home for wayweird girls or the correctional
women's facility where she could have been turned all right. she would
expand looking for clues in all the wrong places: in
sand dunes, cowichan sweaters, last duchesses on walls.
mysteries nowhere and everywhere, like god's non-existence
in the open secret of rolling Rs pounding the pacific coast,
sound of dissipated foam in the fillings among the chattering
residents of toothache inside out halfway homes for this one
wayweird girl and her buzzing wordless terror of what would
become of her. ariringing in her teeth, always already in her
mentada nervosa dentata.

send for a dentist? the penman might do in a pinch.

7.
haiku-arizona

light palpitates dark
with white plastic forks leaving
no marks on tear ducts
pressed to granular
hiss, issue faint steam in shapes
of hammers or stars.

feet first she falls on
his tongue, taut landing curling
up round her ankles.
filigree cracks climb
freeze-dried high arches, send thrills
metatarsal to rocking skull, cross-hatch
up a likeness to trees or
fishbones. nothing hurts

despite what marrow
might say. arid abysmal
adulthood crumples
air above snakes that
lash limbs and weave brittle
slippery mirages
of human women
who look humid but sound hoarse.

their stiletto breath
taps holes in hot sand.
his words sizzle, dissemble
when they land, form
pearl bead pools she now dabs
behind as many undulating knees, on pulse
points wrung uncertain.

8.
miscegenation: a two and a half-paragraph essay
(by miss h. k. kim)

One often sees people drawn by Disney with other people drawn by Disney. This can hardly be surprising, the D.B.D. constituting roughly eighty percent of the general population. More and more, however, one seems to find people drawn by Disney with people drawn by Groening, or by Modigliani, and with some of these pairs sweet-tempered, rambunctious offspring yet to sprout telling teeth one way or another. This procreative activity alone might be read as a sign of greater social acceptance for interphysiognomical couples, and the often unreadable results can indeed be revealing. For many years (mind you) it has already been the case that the product of a by-Groening-by-Groening match can look exactly like a by-Modigliani, and a purebred D.B.M. at that, thanks simply to a skilled orthodontist. And what with the wonders of tanning beds and plastic surgery, whereby anyone with the money can look like post-op Pinocchio, Ashton Kutcher or Kimora Lee Simmons, the *reductio ad absurdum* of physiognotype is rendered that much more absurd.

With the admittedly qualified advantage of hindsight one could by way of further illustration regard Dopey and Goofy as D.B.G. *avant la lettre*. Perhaps this was why they were sterilized without their consent, my guess would be sometime in the late 1940s or early '50s, when electroshock therapy was also perfectly legal and widely employed. Such practices persist in some places to this day (as noxious as that is for compassionate thinking people to imagine) as do theories of genetic inheritance and national or ethnic-cultural character which survive, nay thrive, in some of the market logics of mail-order mating, transnational adoption, and bad schools.

Agreed: there are three kinds of people. But does it matter who drew us? So long as we are all drawn into the same vast Circle of Life, all drawn generous draughts of one multiculti love?

9.
picnic

kim bap, a d.m.z., a red plaid blanket

under that a world not more colourful but
more complicated.

the mother
descends from menders and healers, gamblers,

deserters, addicts, lapsed buddhists, ruiny loony
tunes. a broken line with needles and insufficient
iron in its veins and in its stopping in its

// the 38th //

the daughter
tries to represent

twilight's next gleaming?
this a part from her self
her aforeffort.

JANE PARK

Falling

While the pages burn, I sit by the fire, surprised by my calmness. I have waited twenty years and now I watch as the fire consumes the paper and transforms my father's scribbled words into ash. I know every page. It has taken me twenty years to learn his language, to read these words. And in ten minutes, nothing will remain but a pile of ash.

I will say these words from memory while I sleep, or so my husband says, though he does not know Korean. Sometimes when I wake on these mornings I will panic. To stop the panic, I will say a prayer and then make coffee, feed Charlie, and get ready for work.

Make coffee, feed Charlie, and get ready for work. A few months ago an old man came into the clinic and sat in the reception area eating a pear. The way he chewed his food reminded me of my father. I didn't cry at his funeral, so I was surprised when I had to excuse myself. "My contact lens," I said, blinking ferociously, hating myself for crying now.

My father chewed his food slowly, whittled twigs, and wore a brown wool worsted cardigan. This is how I remember him. He used to find twigs or branches near his "office" and carve imaginary princes, princesses, and monsters—toys for Thomas and me. Now, I realize that he made these toys because he could not afford to buy them. But with the twigs he would transform our living room into far-off villages, battlefields, heaven and hell.

His office was in the woods, a fifteen-minute walk from our store and house. For a desk, he placed a plank of wood between two branches, and used milk cartons for his seat, and went to work before the break of dawn, before the store would open. Sometimes he would write well into the day, and my mother would shout from the back of the store, or the front of our house, "Elly, get dad, the dairy order is here and I have customers."

I would run to his office and find him writing, forgetting that today was the day the dairy order arrived. I hated interrupting him. Sometimes I would quietly walk up behind him, hoping that he would see or sense me first.

"Elly, is that you?" he would say without turning his head.

"Yeah, dad. It's milk day today."

He would turn off his portable radio, gather his papers, his pens, and pack everything into the milk crate he used for his seat.

Come rain, come shine, come snow, come sun, he would go off into the woods with his milk crate to his office. It wasn't really so much in the woods as at the base of a forested mountain. Though it wasn't really so much a mountain more than the last whimper of the great Rocky Mountain Range.

We lived in Pincher Creek, a town just off Highway 21, which used to be a booming mining community. When the coal disappeared so did the men and we relied on the highway to bring in a lonely truck driver, a wandering tourist. We lived in a house attached to the store at the back, so the front of the house faced the woods. Before us the Kroshinskis lived in the house—three generations of Ukrainian grocers until the great-great-grandson, Bill Kroshinski, died an aged bachelor, a notorious profligate. Our store was still called "Kroshinski's General Store" although on our store sign somebody had painted a *t* over the *n*: *Kro–shit–ski*.

Thomas and I attended school in the next town. A school bus would pick us up from the store every day and take us to Crow's Feet Elementary School. If we ever complained about the forty-minute bus ride, the bullies who called us the "Kro–SHIT–ski kids," or the teachers with their stale saliva breath, or our parents would remind us that they had never received a formal education and neither had our grandparents.

My parents revered education like religion. They had grown up poor and could not afford to go to school and, ironically, only when my father immigrated did he formally begin to learn Korean to place structure into his speech. He was constantly practicing his reading and his writing.

Before every parent-teacher interview, my mother would wear a smart dress ordered from the *Sears Catalogue* and my father would wear his only suit, and they would close the store early—for that night only—to visit my school, to visit my teachers. Afterwards, they would come home with their eyes sparkling as they reported to us what our teachers said about our progress and our potential.

I can imagine them in front of our teachers nodding their heads, saying nothing, doing nothing, because they were so cautious about unknown codes they might violate. Once, during our Christmas Concert, I was playing a piano solo. My parents closed the store early to attend the concert. My mother wore a fuchsia dress to match the poinsettia pinned onto her lapel and my father wore—for the second time that year—his suit. They entered the school the way the Ukrainians in that town entered a cathedral: silently, solemnly, and with their hands hanging awkwardly. They walked down the halls not knowing if they should be walking straight or holding plastic punch cups or speaking with somebody, anybody.

Mr. Stevenson approached us.

"It was good of you to come."

"Yes."

"I did not know you lived in Pincher Creek."

"We do."

"How are you doing?"

Miss Shell, another teacher, interrupted us to flirt with Mr. Stevenson—my parents not knowing whether to be relieved or offended. I always enjoyed watching Miss Shell with her drawn out laughter and her hot-pink fingernails which ran through her teased hair, her words making Mr. Stevenson blush. I have often wondered if my mother was ever like her: brash and sexy.

My father told us that he married my mother because of her rice cakes. In Korea, during the Chusul Thanksgiving Festival, he tasted "the most delicious rice cakes in the world." Later on that evening, he met their creator and was stunned that a beautiful fifteen-year old girl had enough "wisdom"—as he called it—to make these rice cakes. He was nineteen at the time. They married three weeks later. There is a photo of my mother in a short skirt and with long hair holding my father's hand the evening after their wedding, though I cannot imagine them in love. I imagine my father recited his poetry into her unschooled ears. My mother was easily impressed by anyone who knew anything. They came to Canada immediately after their wedding.

I was born prematurely eight months later, in Crow's Feet General Hospital. Two years later my mother sponsored her eldest brother and his wife. They bought a busy supermarket in Crow's Feet which enabled him to afford a son, a daughter, three dogs, and a trip to Disneyland for the entire family—including the dogs—every summer vacation.

We called my mother's brother Uncle Sam though he did not officially have an English name. Later, when I was learning American history, Thomas and I chuckled as the angular Uncle Sam pointed to us from my textbook and said I WANT YOU.

"I WANT YOU!" and I placed my father's white calligraphy brush against my chin.

"I WANT YOU!" and Thomas put on my father's straw fedora.

My Uncle Sam sat solemn and stoic like an Indian Big Chief. My father laughed and tried to explain to him what the hilarity was all about. My father loved stories like that. He loved whittling his twigs. He loved calling me the Princess of the Orient. He loved to tell Thomas that snow fell because the gods were eating porridge for breakfast that day.

He loved winter best with the snow falling down gracefully, whitening the world. He would disappear then, both in his office and at the store. At the store, he would sit behind the counter beside the glass window and watch the sun stream, the snow fall, and the wind blow. Some customers commented that he was "a dreamy old man." Others got impatient and banged their cola cans or tapped their fingers on the counter to get my father's attention.

He read his books, his English books, which were carelessly tossed and forgotten around the store. Sometimes he would place his book on top of a counter, a shelf, a barrel of loose beans, and forget about it until a passing customer would pick up *War and Peace*. "Does Tolstoy make the beans heartier?" a customer once asked, impressed.

As in Korean, he was self-taught in English. He began by reading my schoolbooks. I was angry that my father would take my books when I had a book report due the next day. Books were constantly disappearing from my schoolbag. In the winter the snow discouraged me from venturing into my father's office. So the next day, when I could not submit my book report, I would lie: "Not enough time" or "Lost my book." Mr. Stevenson wouldn't understand, and I was ashamed.

Soon he graduated to the classics. Monthly, a hardbound classic novel would arrive in our mailbox: Simpson Publishers' World Masterpiece Series. Because the postal office was in Crow's Feet, I was the mail deliverer. Every day after school before the school bus came I collected our mail from the post office. At the beginning of every month, as I came home from school, my father would ask me casually, as if it were a passing thought rather than an obsession, "So, did anything arrive in the mail?" When the book finally arrived, my father would disappear for a day or two into his Reading Room—a spare room where my father lay on the bed and read. Later, he would emerge and act as if he'd just remembered he had a wife at the store and children to feed; though he never apologized, he was always embarrassed. My mother, also, was embarrassed for him and asked him how he could selfishly sit and read all day while there were milk jugs arriving, customers buying, tomatoes rotting, and only my mother to "work like a dog"—as she would phrase it in perfect English.

I tried to help. After school, whenever the Reading Room was locked or my father's milk crate was gone from the closet, I would go immediately to the store. My mother would often place me behind the counter so she could check food inventory, spray vegetables, dust shelves. My cheeks would burn if someone I knew came in: my friends, boys in my class, Mr. Stevenson.

"Oh, hello there, Elizabeth."

"Hello Mr. Stevenson."

"I didn't know you lived in Pincher Creek."

"I do."

"How are you doing?"

"Fine, and yourself?"

"Fine, just fine"

And we would talk about the snow, or the sun, or the school, as he walked down the aisles, filling his basket. I hated having to take his money, pack his groceries, and say "have a nice day" when I secretly wanted to dishevel my hair in the hopes that he would pack me into his basket, load me into his Buick, and drive me away from Pincher Creek.

There were many times I wanted to run away. Once, after a particularly cruel fight between my parents, I slammed the door and ran as fast as I could, as far as I could, which was about half a mile before the snow began freezing my toes, my nose.

When I turned around I saw my father walking towards me.

"Why do you make mom work like a dog?" I yelled, crying. "Why can't you be like Uncle Sam so me and Thomas can go to Disneyland?" and I started asking him many more questions that all began with *Why do you?* or *Why can't you?*

It's funny the way my father was so obsessed with words, and yet he could never use them when they were most necessary. He was silent, stunned, and stood in front of me as I threw these darts at him.

The next week I saw a book lying on the bed in the Reading Room entitled *Fatherhood: The Journey*. The week after that it was replaced by *How to Love Your Wife*. Soon my father cleared a shelf and devoted it to the literature of self-improvement. Books like *I'm OK, You're OK,* or *Making Your Millions Begins with Your Mind* began arriving in the mail.

During this time, my father insisted that Thomas and I should eat dinner with him. Usually at dinnertime, my mother and I would stay at the storefront so my father and Thomas could eat first. However, my father arranged it so my mother tended the cash register while he ate with us. During dinner, he would straighten his posture, rest his index finger on his knife, and ask, "So, Thomas, Elly, tell me how your day went."

"Fine."

"Good."

"Anything happen at school?"

"Nope."

"Nah."

"Any funny stories you want to tell Daddy?"

Silence.

I dreaded these dinners because I dreaded the silence that I could not break and the words I could not say. My father would ask the same questions over and over and Thomas and I could not answer them. We felt as if answering his questions were a sort of betrayal of the way things really were.

Soon these dinners stopped. The book collecting also stopped. I noticed that more than half his self-improvement books still had their spines uncracked, their glossy dust covers still shining.

The fights between my parents continued, although they weren't really fights, because my father was a passive man, and he would just listen as my mother shouted her complaints. Once a man came into our store drunk. He asked my mother for some pussy, and when she didn't understand what he wanted, he began fondling his groin. "Pussy," he said over and over, and she did not know what to do except scream. My father, who was stocking shelves at the time, ran to her, saw the man, and stood there shocked.

My mother, acting on instinct, jumped over the counter and began pushing the drunk man out of the store. He thought these were embraces and held my mother fast and kissed her neck with his moist lips. Still, my father stood there shocked. It was only when my mother began yelling at my father that he pushed her away from the drunk man—who was almost double my father's size. "Go home," my father said in a tone which may have sounded mild but was quite violent coming from him. Throughout all of this my mother continued yelling at my father, saying how could you let this man disgrace your wife? How could you just stand there? And only because the drunk man felt humoured did he leave the store, slapping my father on the back and telling him, "Your wife needs to get laid."

I felt bad that my mother felt bad because my father was a coward. Thomas, when he heard this story, punched the wall and said if he were there the man would have had his fuckin' balls punched out.

My father would not make eye contact with me or anyone else that night, or the nights following. It was as if he was a child and we were the judging parents: it was that type of fear. And I hated hating my father for not being able to punch out that man's balls.

This incident happened at the beginning of the coldest winter ever recorded in Crow's Feet County. I remember in late November the insides of my nostrils froze as I collected the icicles hanging beneath our van. Inside the house we listened to the radio as the announcer announced, "CLOSED, Crow's Feet elementary and high school. CLOSED, major banks, stores, and hospital. CLOSED, Highway 21 and 14 until emergency troops can clear the roads. Please stay home. Please stand by."

The snow continued to fall for two weeks as the school and the store remained shut and even the icicles disappeared, for nothing melted. The snow only collected and grew. My mother could do nothing except drink tea at our kitchen table and worry about the fruit, vegetables, milk, and meat rotting in our store. The bananas rotted first. Even in the cold, fruit flies managed to breed. The first day there were no flies. The day after, and the succeeding days, they bred and multiplied and soon danced their way into the other aisles and then into our home.

One night my mother sat staring at the wall.

"Look Mom," I said as I began trying to kill the fruit flies, clapping and dancing and leaping like the flies, at the flies.

"Elly, don't do that."

So I sat across from her, putting on a solemn face.

"We will be with Uncle Sam next week."

"Uncle Sam's visiting?"

"No, we will move in with Uncle Sam and work for him."

"But we have our store."

"No. Not anymore."

I remember the cold, which you could not escape. It frosted your fingertips, chilled the windows, and entered your mind, numbing it from sense. Despite the record-breaking cold, my father still woke early every morning, filled his mug with hot tea, layered his body with wool, cotton and down, and collected his milk crate to go to work.

He would not stay long. He would arrive back in the house an hour later and use his icy fingers to shock Thomas and me into waking up before he disappeared into the Reading Room for the day. Then again, late at night, he would refill his mug, put on his clothes, and walk out the back door with one arm clutching his milk crate.

The night my father was to leave for Uncle Sam's supermarket, he visited me before going back to his office.

As my father cracked open the door and crept into my room I pretended to be asleep. As the hinges squeaked and the floors creaked, I tried to compose a sleeping face even though my muscles twitched.

He slid my head gently into his lap and caressed my hair and he whispered words in Korean. I do not know what he said, only that it was difficult for me to pretend that I was sleeping. He probably knew, I thought, that I was faking my sleep though I could not open my eyes.

I wish I had opened my eyes. I wish I knew what he said. He used a strong quiet voice and hushed out words as rivers pour forth water, meandering anywhere, seeping into the soil, the soul.

I fell asleep while pretending to be asleep.

I wish I had opened my eyes.

My father died twenty years ago. The next morning my mother was packing at the store, and my brother was still sleeping, so I was the one who answered the *knock knock knock*. I went with my mother to identify the body.

A dead man looks like he's asleep only his skin glows flesh green. My father froze, and was still frozen when I came to him. There were red and black blotches melting in his skin. They found him a quarter of a mile away from his office. The avalanche, they said, fell on him, and rolled him down the slope.

I didn't cry at his funeral: I do not know if this was right or wrong. All I remember were the cabbage rolls brought by the Ukrainian Orthodox Church for a consolation of grief. It was my first time eating cabbage rolls, and I felt guilty for eating three-quarters of the pan while Thomas and my mother were properly mourning.

I do not know how people are supposed to grieve. My Auntie cooked a dinner for a hundred people the night before my father's funeral. My mother prayed alone, in her locked room, many nights afterwards. And my brother wept aloud, and made others weep with him, when he kissed my father's closed coffin and proclaimed "I love you, daddy" to the entire congregation.

My mother, a few days after the funeral, collected my father's clothes, books, twigs, anything flammable, and burned them behind our store in an empty oil drum. She told us that our ancestors burned the possessions of the dead to purify their souls so their spirits could journey on.

The smoke rose and created a screen which tinted the moon a dark yellow. I remember the face of my mother watching the clothes, books, and twigs turn into ash. I had stolen a pile of pages from my father's Reading Room, without telling my mother, in the hopes that I would one day read its contents. I do not enjoy lying or hiding but I did not want to tell my mother that there were still possessions of my father lingering on. Nor did I tell her or Thomas about the dream, or the reality, of my father visiting me before his death, for I was ashamed of pretending to be asleep.

The ash blew and mixed with the falling snow.

***

Sometimes my mother will visit me at the clinic, unannounced. The receptionist will interrupt a session and politely whisper, "Mrs. Lee is waiting for you," and I will excuse myself and see my mother waiting on a chair, swinging her legs like a little girl.

These are never emergencies. They are silly visits to ask me if I need more *kim-chee* prepared or if the Reverend's wife received the lemon loaf recipe. My mother enjoys periodically dropping by the clinic—as opposed to my house—to ask about these non-emergencies. She is getting old and looks hurt when I ask her to wait until I finish with my patient. But she will wait and may even mention to those waiting in the reception area that I am her daughter, how are you, why are you here, and make other small conversation.

Her period of mourning is over. The photos of my father lie with the dust in the attic and she is currently dating a Korean widower. She is old and should no longer be living alone. She is nearing blindness though she watches television to pass her days. Last Christmas Thomas took a vacation from his accounting firm and came home. We discussed my mother's living situation.

"How is she doing?"

"Fine, Thomas, fine."

"Does she still receive those checks?"

"Yes. I'm paying half of her rent, but don't tell her. She doesn't need to know."

"You don't need to Elly, she receives *a lot* from the insurance company."

"How much?"

"*A lot*. When dad died he was in their premium plan."

"He was?"

"Those checks saved us from being dead poor."

"I did not know that."

Later, much later, in fact, only two weeks ago, Charlie invited a linguistics professor over for dinner. Although Charlie teaches in the physics department, he knew how badly I wanted another person to read my father's manuscript, and so he befriended Dr. MacLennan—who was also married to a Korean woman. After tea, I casually asked Dr. MacLennan if he would read over some Korean work. He agreed and his eyes quickly scrolled down the pages.

"Elizabeth, are you learning Korean?" he asked.

"Yes, yes, how did you know?"

"Funny, I used these exact exercises when I began learning Korean."

He then told us about his fascination with *Hangul*, and the phonetic nuances of the Korean language, and then about his current project, which was to record the oral languages of the North American Aboriginals, for their languages would be lost forever, since, in many cases, this was the last, literate, legitimate generation. I kept silent throughout the night as the revelation slowly unfolded: this was not my father's work but his exercises copied and memorized to learn and perfect. They were stories about cats and dogs and children playing on the river banks and nothing more.

The only work of my father's that I have ever really known was a poem about the falling snow. He read it to me eagerly one night because, I believe, he needed to air his creation and I was the only one home when he returned from his office. As he held the page his hands shook and his voice fell like the snow outside. Afterwards he translated the words into English.

The poem was about the comfort of falling snow, which falls carelessly and covers the earth and makes people forget the dead grass underneath. And the snow symbolized words because just as no two snowflakes are alike, neither are the words we say, which also fall and melt into oblivion.

At the time I could not appreciate the meaning of the poem and I kept silent after his explanation.

Some nights I wonder how it was, the last moment of my father's life. I wonder if he died first from being so cold, or from the lack of air, or from the shock. Afterwards, I may think of why he died, and then my mind becomes blank, as blank as the colour of snow, and I will try falling asleep though my eyes will not close.

Originally published in Echoes Upon Echoes: New Korean American Writings *(Asian American Writers Workshop, 2003).Reprinted with permission.*

JIN HUH

Lost

We have been crunching through the snow for hours
neither of us
wanting
to say the word
lost

                lost
in the spaces between
our fears
unable to find
the way

So used to walking this path
  a different way
with someone
     so unlike you,
Learning now
     for the first time
a lover
  walking beside me
does not always lead to
  closed doors
collapsed
     expectations
sharp-toothed
words
that are the only
bridge

that connect our tattered selves

You
are
unfamiliar

sometimes I want to hide
run back to what I know

a solitary room
pale blue walls
a window facing brick
where I sit on a bed
alone
and beyond the padlocked door

                    It's you there now

It's you here today
And we walk this path
side by side
your hand fits
perfectly in mine
we are
lost and not-lost
Afraid,
   to speak of it
     will break the spell
but I gather all my strength together so
that I do not lose myself again
do not lose us.

RUTHANN LEE

"Coming Out" as a Queer Korean Woman in Canada
A Personal Cultural Narrative

I came out to my mom like a white person.

I sat her down on a bench in a park and said, in English, "Mom, I have something to tell you. I am a lesbian."

I planned the announcement the summer I turned 23. I made it into a huge, dramatic deal. At the time, I felt it was the right thing to do. I felt it was something I *should* do. There was urgency. There was pressure. To be authentically queer, I believed, was to disclose my sexual identity to the person I trusted, loved and felt closest to—my mother. Even though the word "lesbian" wasn't something I felt entirely comfortable labelling myself with, I felt it was a word *she* might be familiar with and somehow understand.

As if!

If the word lesbian didn't even fully resonate with me—how could I expect it to resonate with my mother?

Instead, hearing her daughter claim herself to be a "lesbian" caused my mother much grief and confusion. In Korean, she exclaimed, "No, no you're not! You're just lonely. Is it because of your father?" She immediately urged me not to tell him. Later, my mother told me I could do anything I wanted once she was dead. That, ultimately, has been the most difficult thing I've ever had to hear—understanding that this aspect of my existence could bring my mother that much shame and fear.

While it is apparent that my mom "just needs to work through her homophobia"—with the blatant lack of support and discussion there is amongst the Korean community in Canada regarding issues of homophobia—I wonder just how long this process will take. I've spent much time distressing and debating whether I should have gone about my "coming out" in another way. Perhaps if my mother and I shared a common language (and not a mixture of broken-English and fragmented, awkwardly-phrased Korean), things would be different. Perhaps if I had known that there were alternatives to the prescribed narratives I'd gleaned from the few coming out books I'd read, or the scripts I'd heard on television and the narratives of my white queer friends, I might have saved a lot of emotional pain and frustration. Perhaps my mother's sentiments would be different if she didn't already feel acutely aware of being different and "other" as a racially marked Korean woman in Canada. Perhaps she would feel differently if she saw more Asian[1] queers on television.

In addition to the desire to be honest with a person I love dearly, I continue to speculate on the reasons why I felt such intense pressure to tell my mom I was a lesbian. This is, professedly, the driving force behind this essay—to explore what "coming out" means. Coming out to whom and for what purpose?

I have gathered that for my mother and many others in the Korean community, same-sex relationships and gender transgression are repudiated under the guise of Korean or Asian "tradition." But I think it is important to locate this perspective within the larger neo-colonial context of Canadian racism, heterosexism, and discourses of multiculturalism. I wish to contextualize the way in which racialized communities try to shield any signs of deviance as a manner of "saving face" and upholding notions of respectability in an attempt to preserve their already-limited social status.

On "Coming Out"

I began this essay thinking about the ways in which I have come to identify as "queer." For a number of reasons, I have always felt uncomfortable with the term "coming out." Firstly, if I were straight, I'd never have to "come out" as heterosexual. Secondly, my own "coming out" story never feels complete.[2] I "come out" in different ways, to different constituencies, communities, and individuals—all the time. Yet, I can also choose to "hide" my sexuality to protect myself from homophobic ostracism, stigma, and the burden of having to explain—I can "pass."

In contrast, being identified as different and subordinate in the racial sense feels familiar to me. I am more prepared to encounter and contest racist epithets like the ones I heard in my childhood—remembering the white school boys chanting the unforgettable rhyme: "Chinese, Japanese, dirty knees, look at *these!*" coupled with the gesturing of large breasts (an expression that indicates, I believe, the way in which Asian identities have been constructed to exclude lesser-known nationalities and an illustration of how racist ideas are frequently linked with sexist ones). By and large, queers become visible through *acts* of queerness; queers can choose to "hide" the sexual parts of their identities—their desires—an option that is not possible in face-to-face interactions for racialized persons. Put more simply, I have never had to "come out" as "Asian."[3]

Disturbingly, homophobia in Asian communities is sometimes explained through modernist discourses of Asian "culture." For example, in a Toronto-based study on HIV/AIDS prevention and education for lesbian, gay, and bisexual Asian youth, Maurice Poon and Peter T. Ho contend that "[h]omophobia is particularly prevalent in Asian cultures; the intensity of heterosexism and homophobia is much stronger in Asian cultures than in the U.S. culture" (54). While the article is targeted toward other (mainstream) social service providers as well as government funders, the explanation for homophobia asserts essentialized and reductive understandings of "Asian-ness" and fails to acknowledge that the Asian community exists within a dominant white Canadian context.[4] Thus, racism is not named and the Asian community is posited as inherently "more homophobic" than western society.

However, in writing about homophobia and heterosexism in the Korean community, I fear reinscribing the idea that Asian families are more squeamish about sex and sexuality than any other group. At the same time, homophobia is sometimes felt most intensely within our immediate families, where we have claimed "home." As Richard Fung has described:

As is the case for many other people of colour and especially immigrants, our families and our ethnic communities are a rare source of affirmation in a racist society. In coming out, we risk (or feel that we risk) losing this support, though the ever-growing organizations of lesbian and gay Asians have worked against this process of cultural exile. (184)

Far too often, I have heard sentiments that Asians are "traditional" and hence Asian "culture" is deemed "sexually repressed." Repressed according to whom? Paul Gilroy, among many others, warns against the appeal of the idea of tradition, stating that "the defence of tradition can ... open a door to ultraconservative forms of political culture and social regulation" (13-14). Particular meanings of "tradition" and "culture" circulate in what can be called a neocolonial context in Canada. Similarities can be drawn between colonial racism and Canadian racism. Thus, elite Asian community members may uphold homophobic beliefs in efforts to secure heterosexual privilege within a white supremacist society.

The Korean community can, in distinct ways, represent an Asian nation-state. Specifically, the "Korean community" can be constructed as masculine and heterosexual, which sanctions and enforces patriarchal norms and codes of behaviour. Homophobic, sexist, and other oppressive ideologies are justified under cultural nationalist arguments. By deploying discourses of tradition and modernity, elite members of the Korean community attempt to uphold social status by securing heterosexual privilege that connects to notions of respectability in a Canadian context. As a result, hierarchies of gender, sexuality, class, and others are reproduced within the Korean community. Jeeyeun Lee succinctly clarifies this colonialist understanding of homophobia and heterosexism within the context of U.S. racialized communities:

> People in Asia, the Third World, or racial minority communities are not *more* homophobic; they are *differently* homophobic, in ways conditioned not only by beliefs, values, and circumstances but also by histories of Western imperialism and U.S. racism. (196)

Here, I want to emphasize the different psychic and material costs of "coming out" to families, different communities, and the nation itself. By "coming out," queer Korean women confront and respond to an overarching context of Canadian racism and homophobia, *as well as* the reconstitutions of racism in the queer community and heterosexism and homophobia in the Korean community in various ways.

Disrupting Cultural Nationalism in the Korean Community

As mentioned previously, homophobic, sexist, and other oppressive ideologies are justified under cultural nationalist arguments. By deploying discourses of tradition and modernity, elite members of the Korean community attempt to uphold social status by securing heterosexual privilege that connect to notions of respectability in a Canadian context. As a result, hierarchies of gender, sexuality, class, nationality, language, and others are reproduced within the Korean community.

Families are linked to ideas about nations—feminist theorists such as Anne McClintock have extensively discussed the trope of the nation as "family." McClintock has argued that the significance of the biological family trope has been "an indispensable figure for sanctioning social hierarchy" (65) throughout nationalist projects. In particular, "women are typically construed as the symbolic bearers of the nation, but are denied any direct relation to national agency" (McClintock 62). The family trope continues to function in the present context and works to solidify cultural nationalist ideologies of race. As Rhonda Williams describes:

> In the ideologies of contemporary cultural nationalism, families are *the* sanctioned site for the reproduction of authentic racial ethnic culture. Healthy families are monogamous, dedicated to masculine authority, and affirm traditional gender roles; unwell families include sexually promiscuous adults and foster female dominance. (144)

Williams critiques the cultural nationalist tendency to mirror and embrace Euro-Western models of nationalism by pointing to its colonialist basis: "nationalists who embrace the autonomous, monogamous, conjugal heterosexual family as the domestic ideal suppress their indebtedness to European and Euro-American nationalist notions of proper family life" (145). Diasporic communities can therefore be located as the source of ideological and political support for nationalist movements that reinscribe patriarchal hierarchy.

Bearing these points in mind, I have made certain connections between my relationship with my father and what this relationship might reflect in a broader context of the Korean community. In my own experience, my mother's insistence on hiding my "deviant" sexuality from my father signifies how upholding the status of a respectable family within the Korean community is dependent on heterosexual conformity. Breaking away from these ascribed sexual and gender roles constitutes a betrayal to my father, the community, and the nation. This investment in heterosexism relies on the model of nation/community as family. The stability of the Korean community is marked through institutionalized heterosexuality, conjugal relationships and biological reproduction.

Unfortunately, such notions of stability conveniently align themselves with dominant Canadian "family values" ideologies, thereby replicating gender hierarchies and the regulation of sexuality. Furthermore, this ideology maintains normative and binary assumptions of gender, ascribing set roles and codes of masculinity and femininity.

Normative codes of gender are largely enforced through dominant representations of men and women. In particular, dominant representations of Asian women in North America have been informed by gendered and racialized colonialist ideologies that construct a kind of hyper-heterosexuality. Historically, sexist and racist ideologies articulated through Orientalist discourses have shaped such understandings by portraying Asian women as vapid and sexually submissive. As Said describes, "women are usually the creatures of a male power-fantasy. They express unlimited sensuality, they are more or less stupid, and above all they are willing" (1996: 35). Nira Yuval-Davis terms this exoticized understanding of women in the Middle and Far East an "orientalist culturalist tradition" in which sexuality is placed at the heart of identity construction such that "dreams of forbidden pleasure and fear of impotency" (51) are placed onto the racialized "other." Fung summarizes, "[b]ecause of their supposed passivity and sexual compliance, Asian women have been fetishized in dominant representation" (183). Central to this construction is the idea that Asian women are at the service of white men.

Exclusively heterosexual portrayals of Asian women centre the idea that Asian women are reproducers of the nation: "the historical legacy of racialized gender roles has created a cultural nationalism that in seeking to challenge white constructions of Asian, may inscribe sexism and heteropatriarchy" (Atluri 53). This particular understanding of Asian women's sexuality can account for the invisibility of queer Korean women's identities in North America, particularly when contrasted with colonialist stereotypes of the feminized Asian male. As David L. Eng and Alice Y. Hom have pointed out, "where dominant images of emasculated Asian American men and hyperheterosexualized Asian American women collide—the Asian American lesbian disappears" (1). Invisibility and exclusion for Korean lesbians is thus connected to dominant stereotypes, understandings and representations of Asian women in Canada.

Colonial discourses about Asians continue to enforce and inform notions of cultural difference. What is perhaps most disturbing, however, is the way that the Korean community can maintain investments in these same ideas. However, the very presence of queer Korean women challenges the Korean community to explore its investments in heterosexism and expand heteronormative definitions of the family and community.[5]

Queer Community: Culturally Exclusive, Politically Inclusive?

When I think about my connections and experiences with the "queer community," I recall my early quests for support and information about sexuality and sexual identity. As a queer youth, I approached a few mainstream queer organizations and hung around the gay district of Toronto. Generally, my experiences with mainstream queer organizations in terms of seeking support and information around issues of sexuality were unhelpful. I often experienced feelings of exclusion and discomfort and an inability to relate to the experiences of the other group members. The first queer youth organizations that I connected with felt very clique-y, consisting mostly of white gay-identified males and very few people of colour. At gay clubs and at gatherings for queer youth, I often felt out of place, particularly due to my appearance.

Fashion and aesthetic for youth is a contested site because it has multiple meanings in different contexts. They are a mark of status—and determine who is "cool," accepted, and belongs. Within a dominant white Canadian framework, fashion can be considered a marker of class and respectability (Frolic). In the dominant queer community, fashion can be also a mark of "in" and "outness" (Frolic 261). While for queer youth, fitting in may not be tied to conventionally "respectable" aesthetics, it is likely to be highly racialized. There are pressures to conform to a certain aesthetic of whiteness in the queer community. Thus, when surrounded by many white queer youth who were very "in" with the community, I usually felt as if I didn't exist.

Queer Asian men often deal with overtly racist stereotypes that exist in the queer community—of the submissive, smooth "bottom" who is looking for an older, white Sugar Daddy. This is otherwise known as the "Rice Queen" phenomenon. A "Rice Queen" is a gay Caucasian man primarily attracted to Asians. This is similar—although not quite equivalent—to the "Yellow Fever" concept in heterosexual couplings. As David Eng explains, using psychoanalytic paradigms:

> The concept of Yellow Fever exists squarely within the approved norms and acceptable knowledges of a conventional colonial order, working to buttress white male heterosexuality through the possession and exploitation of the native brown woman. Conversely, the suppressed equivalent of this phenomenon is the homosexual Rice Queen fantasy. This Rice Queen fantasy—entailing attachment to and desire for the Asian male body—exists squarely within the tabooed regions of symbolic prohibitions against homosexuality and nonwhiteness. Its emergence into the domain of visibility would thus shed light on the abject underside of the symbolic order, an order whose stability is contingent not only the disavowal but also the violent suppression of homosexuality and nonwhiteness. (158)

Eng thus points to the potential subversiveness of white male, Asian male pairings in contesting normative, heterosexual constructs of desire.[6] Yet he is also careful to note how the stereotype of submissive gay Asians has emerged and is reproduced through a colonialist framework: "the cruel white man and the submissive Oriental lotus blossom mark a narrative of imperial knowledge that is assiduously cultivated and rescripted by the colonial order" (158). Fung has likewise linked this racist construction of gay Asian men to nineteenth-century western scientific discourses of social Darwinism and eugenics, which were crucial to the operation of colonialist projects (182).[7] Thus, queer Asian males face a sense of racial hyper-visibility and exoticism in the mainstream queer community. The stereotype of the youthful, gay Asian coupled with the white, older rich man can be linked to pressures on younger gay Asians to fit particular aesthetics. Moreover, there is a distinct relationship between gay male capital and visibility in the queer community.

Cherrie Moraga has argued that "queer is not cultural. It's not cultural in the sense that it is not an identity emerging from a culturally ethnic group. It's an identity that can encompass many, many cultural groups" (Moraga and Weatherston 73). Because queer identities are not unified under material experiences, Moraga contends that "queer" can be more of a coalitional term: "queer identity suggests some point of connection and holds strong potential for coalition, but it can't be a cultural movement in the historical sense" (74). Along related lines, my more recent link to the queer community has largely been based on politics. The queer community can be defined in terms of its political vision, which is often based on ideas of inclusion and tolerance. The mainstream queer youth organizations I once frequented prided themselves on operating from some form of open-minded and/or progressive ideology.

However, the notions of tolerance and inclusivity, in particular, stand out for me—they encapsulate the paternalistic, multiculturalist national rhetoric that helps to erase Canada's ongoing history of colonialism and exclusion of racialized minorities that continue to pervade its legislative policies and practices. To what extent does the "queer community" align itself with discourses of liberal multiculturalism? On whose terms are people being tolerated and included—and to whose benefit?

Moraga has further stated that she refuses to align herself with Queer Nation or feel much affiliation with the gay movement, noting that she has more in common with straight Chicanos than gay white men because "money protects" (Moraga and Weatherston 68). Like Moraga, I find that the queer community in Toronto is representative of white gay male culture and is in agreement with the values of western culture at large. My connection to Toronto's queer community as a queer Korean woman is fraught with ambivalence due to historical and persistent conditions of invisibility and exclusion. It is the context of white-dominated queer culture that makes the "queer community" a place of not belonging for queer Korean women. My place in it is largely unacknowledged, ambiguous, or pigeonholed. Survival, the dominant queer community teaches me, is tied to capital and being able to "pass."

But Asians Are Cool Now:
Generational Identity Politics, Multiculturalism and Hybridity

In *Against Race: Imagining Political Culture Beyond the Color Line*, Gilroy gives a provocative critique of racial identity politics by examining its relationship with fascism post-World War II. One of his arguments is that because racial identity politics rely on the concept of authenticity or an undisputed origin, it has the dangerous tendency to reproduce forms of authoritarianism and leads to homogenizing effects where "the political language of identity levels out distinctions between chosen connections and given particularities: between the person you choose to be and the things that determine your individuality by being thrust upon you" (106). Gilroy argues that the demand that is placed on individuals to identify is driven by a commodity-driven culture.

Rosemary Hennessy has offered a similar argument in her book, *Profit and Pleasure: Sexual Identities in Late Capitalism*. Hennessy argues that the emergence of sexual identities can be linked to the advent of late capitalism, wherein modern states encourage forms of identity politics in ways that obscure class inequalities. As a result, Hennessy contends, class-based alliances have become increasingly difficult to organize and even imagine.[8] Both Gilroy and Hennessy connect identity-driven culture to the commodification and "branding" of identities. Now, identities can be bought, sold and purchased and hence linked to certain modern "lifestyles."

Drawing on these insights, I argue that acquiring and/or taking up certain identities in modern Western societies holds different social, political and economic currency. This seems particularly relevant to Canada's socio-political context where marginalized groups gain recognition through national ideologies of multiculturalism. In order to attain civil recognition and rights—political, social, or economic—individuals must seek out services based on groups or organizations that have been named under specific cultural identities (see Bannerji).

As argued earlier, the perpetuation of patriarchal, sexist, and heterosexist views in the Korean community can be attributed to arguments based on "tradition" and "culture" and are often expressed as ideological conflicts between generations of parents and children (e.g., my mother and myself). Yet more recently, I have begun to question the idea that Korean parents are tightly holding onto notions of "tradition" and culture, thereby maintaining conservative ideologies about who and what the Korean community should look like in Canada. I want to contextualize this understanding because it seems unfair to claim that heterosexism and homophobia within the Korean community is sustained by an older, immigrant generation. It reaffirms a self-serving myth by once again positing the first-generation immigrant as stereotypically "backward" and not as politically progressive as those of us who were born and raised in the West.

The political struggles faced by second-generation Koreans in Canada differ significantly from those of our parents' generation. In particular, language barriers and the subsequent lack of access to social services and employment as a result of both overt and systemic forms of racism challenge many first-generation and/or immigrant Korean Canadians. By contrast, those of us in the second generation who have been raised in Canada rarely grapple with language barriers; our challenges tend to revolve more around issues of cultural dislocation and identity formation. Such issues structure and inform our material opportunities in dramatically different ways. This may include the constant negotiation of "assimilatory" pressures that are informed by our relative familiarity with the Canadian system—as our ability to access and navigate this system is largely facilitated by our fluency in the English language.

Other important aspects to consider regarding generational differences between Koreans in Canada are the issues of commodification and cultural appropriation and how they have impacted the formation of identities. For example, my own sense of connection to the Korean community often emerges when visiting places like Koreatown, both in the downtown core of Toronto and in the newly-gentrified areas of North York, Ontario. In these locations, there has been a marked increase in the number of Korean groceries and food chains, banks, restaurants, bars, clubs, and businesses such as clothing stores, bookstores, and other retail establishments. In particular, the commodification of Korean culture and commodities in the form of signifiers such as food (e.g., *kimchee*, Korean barbecue), Hollywood celebrities and American sports icons (Margaret Cho, Sandra Oh, Se Ri Park, Grace Park, to name a few) have shaped definitions of the Korean community.

The gradual commodification of Koreanness in North America has been somewhat disconcerting to me. For example, I feel very proud of Korean American comic and pop culture icon Margaret Cho for breaking all sorts of boundaries and rules and ideas about Asian women. At the same time, it has been extremely frustrating and strange to be compared to her all the time ("you look just like Margaret Cho")—most notably by a large contingent of gay white men![9] While on the one hand, I am glad to be associated with such a strong, kick-ass Korean American woman, on the other, I believe such comparisons disturbingly reflect the endurance of racism in the contemporary moment.

In her essay, "Eating the Other: Desire and Resistance," bell hooks has talked about cultural commodification in which whites fetishize an authentic otherness. Focussing on youth cultures in particular, hooks argues:

> The contemporary crisis of identity in the west, especially as experienced by white youth, are eased when the "primitive" is recouped *via* a focus on diversity and pluralism which suggests the Other can provide life-sustaining alternatives. Concurrently, diverse ethnic/racial groups can also embrace this sense of specialness, that histories and experience once seen as worthy only of disdain can be looked upon with awe. (25-6)

In the North American context, Korean culture is becoming increasingly commodified, involving new and/or transformed racist and highly gendered stereotypes of the Korean "other." To a certain extent, "Korean-ness" is trendy and our own authenticity has become an object of desire within dominant white culture. As a result, political strategies of resistance employed by second-generation Korean Canadians may involve complex and contradictory negotiations of identity that are related to aspects of performance and pop culture, which include the myriad examples of creative work found in this anthology.

Some Final Reflections on Invisibility, Silence and "Passing"

I continue to think about invisibility and race a lot—about how invisible I feel in the queer community. A white dyke once told me, "If I saw you on the street I would in no way think that you were queer," and recently, a gay Asian boy said the same thing to me! I also think about all the times that I've "passed" knowingly as straight and how I'm not out to my dad. I know this passing is tied to being Korean.

In conclusion, I wish to reflect upon a few final themes regarding the apparent disparities between queer and Korean communities. As a queer Korean/Asian woman, I have often distinguished these communities as distinct entities. I have felt simultaneously included and excluded from these communities. I believe that this disparity is maintained through fears that have generated silences about differences in power and privilege.

In the same way that Japanese Canadian academic Mona Oikawa has professed, "I want to look at my own self-silencing practices in sites that are of crucial social, political, and emotional importance to me" (267), being racialized as "Asian" complicates my relationship as a queer Korean woman to notions of silence and acts of self-silencing. Subsequently, when I think about "coming out" in different spaces I often feel ambivalent, which reflects this contradictory positioning. My reluctance to become an "in your face" queer conflicts with the "mysterious, silent and passive" Asian stereotype and reflects my struggles with internalized racism. As Oikawa writes: "the tension between the lived realities of oppression and the threat of loss, on the one hand, and the internalization of this oppression, on the other, is something I continue to live with and negotiate in my work" (268). At the same time, it is important to recognize that not challenging heterosexism in the Korean community and not exposing practices of heteronormativity (no matter how naive or benign) can have dire costs. The silence surrounding the homosocial/homoerotic works to justify hegemonic relationships and maintains the disavowal of queerness in the Korean community.

Dana Y. Takagi has described the fraught relationship that Asian Americans have with the concept of silence. She argues that in popular understandings of Asian American identity, silence has functioned as a metaphor for the assimilative and positive imagery of the "good" (model) minority. However, "analysis of popular imagery of the 'model minority' suggests that silence is understood as an adaptive mechanism to a racially discriminatory society rather than as an intrinsic part of Asian American culture" (26). I wonder, how do notions of silence, acts self-silencing and silencing practices inform political claims to the category of "queer Korean woman"? Takagi has astutely noted: "while silence is a central piece of theoretical discussions of homosexuality, it is viewed primarily as a negative stereotype in the case of Asian Americans" (27).

Oikawa similarly remarks on the contradictory position of "visibility/invisibility" that many racialized queers experience in different spaces. She contends that "identities become fragmented and marginalized in settings when they are treated as minority, exotic, unique, even perverse. This is done through processes that either render them invisible or render them as larger than life, where only part (or parts) of us are called upon to be seen or to speak" (265). Consequently, this fragmenting can affect how racialized queers discuss certain parts of our identities in different contexts. For example, a queer Korean person may not feel safe to address heterosexism and homophobia in the Korean Canadian community and resent the expectation that a queer person of colour should instruct white queers with a comprehensive analysis of gender, race, class and sexuality.

In the course of my research, I have concluded that "passing" as heterosexual is tied to gendered and racialized stereotypes. I have found that there are still profound disconnections between ideologies of racial and queer identity. In the mainstream queer community, I am invisible because I am not read as "truly" queer. In the dominant Korean community, I am also denied because Koreans "can't" be queer. In this peculiar and tenuous positioning of impostor/not-impostor, I am unwillingly granted heterosexual privilege unless I choose to speak up. It is a fragmented positioning that has led to competing pressures in the face of homophobic challenges and questions of social and political responsibility.

These are only some of the difficulties in accounting for multiple oppressions and addressing intersectional identities by acknowledging difference in a truly comprehensive way.[10] As a queer Korean woman, I am fragmented in the eyes of others when forced to talk about certain parts of myself at the exclusion of others. In a related way, Eric Reyes has written about the conflicts experienced by queer Asians as they construct and claim identity:

> To be Queer-identified forces us to confront the privileged white gay male position of power. To be Asian-identified is to confront the power of a racist society. For Asian Queers this produces the contradiction of choosing space over place. To claim Queer is to de-locate oneself from the place and rootedness of home, family and community to the idealized space of a "Queer community." Creating memory, ideas, and space, we have had to learn the process of locating and dislocating not the physical place of continent but the spatial sites of desire. (255)

There are all sorts of power dynamics that exist amongst my mother, family, partner, friends, colleagues, co-workers, and myself that are representative of much larger constituencies. We are all part of different "imagined communities" (Anderson 1983: 15-16)—Korean, Asian, queer, Canadian—that are defined by and in relation to one another. If identity is about belonging and marks what we have in common with some people and what differentiates us from others, the way we relate to different communities—and to each other—reflects the vexed, complicated, uneven, and unequal ways that power functions within them. The formation of queer Asian communities has inspired me to claim an identity as a queer Korean woman living in Canada. The process of "coming out"—has been described as "the ways in which social groups and categories organize, stage, and discipline the naming of our desires" (Eng and Hom 16). Asian queers may choose to "come out" to different communities. By declaring who we are, we are trying to express what we are, what we believe and what we desire. However, these beliefs, needs and desires are often contradictory—not only amongst different communities but also within our selves.

What are our desires as queer Korean women? To what communities do we want to belong? What future communities do we seek to create? In the course of my research and reflection, I have come to understanding that we don't need dichotomously defined communities to have identities. We can actively create new communities by naming ourselves before someone else names us. In the process of claiming an identity of "queer Korean women," we may claim what we believe belongs to us.

This essay is a modified version of my Master's research, "Coming Out" as Queer Asian Youth in Canada: Examining Cultural Narratives of Identity and Community, *which was conducted at the Ontario Institute of Studies in Education at the University of Toronto in 2003. I wish to thank my thesis supervisors, Alissa Trotz and Rinaldo Walcott, in addition to my queer Asian youth participants, friends, and allies for their much-needed support and encouragement throughout the process of writing this project.*

[1] For the purposes of this essay, the category "Asian" includes but is not limited to descendants of Cambodian, Chinese (Hong Kong, Taiwan, China), Japanese, Korean, Filipino, Laotian, Singaporean, Thai and Vietnamese nations. I also consider the concept of "Asian-ness" to be a socio-historical construction of the Western imagination, albeit with real and pervasive material effects.

[2] Nayan Shah has written about the ways in which South Asian queers have used coming out narratives "to make sense of their feelings of difference from mainstream society" (143). He describes two general patterns in these narratives, the first explaining sexual orientation as originating in adolescence with awareness of attraction to members of the same sex. The second pattern, which he argues is more prevalent among women, illustrates desire developing out of politics and describes the movement from political consciousness to sexual identification. I often connect my understanding of "queerness" to

what I learned in university, in particular through women's studies courses and my exposure to (white) feminist, lesbian and gay theory. While I still say that I "came out" as queer when I was 23, I continue to hold reservations about this fixed manner of articulating identity in that it often only seems to produce new forms of scrutiny rather than understanding.

[3] Of course, not all queers have the power or choice to "hide" their sexualities. They are "out" by virtue of not fitting into traditional expressions of gender identity and norms. Similarly, there are mixed-race individuals who may "pass" as white, a point that Takagi also makes: "Of course there are exceptions, for example, blacks that 'pass' and this is perhaps where homosexuality and racial identity come closest to one another, amongst those minorities who 'pass' and gays who can also 'pass'" (Takagi 34, fn 8).

[4] The study outlines three reasons why homophobia is heightened in Asian cultures, citing various "traditional" belief systems that are claimed to be intrinsic to Asian cultures, such as: "homosexuality is against nature," "homosexuality works against economic traditions," and "homosexuality is in conflict with the traditional gender role and family structures, which tend to be well-defined in Asian cultures" (Poon and Ho 54). Interestingly, the authors frame these justifications for homophobia as unique to Asian cultures as if these values and belief systems are not also constitutive of western, Canadian thought.

[5] See Shane Phelan's related argument on the relationship between North American gay/lesbian movements and challenges they have posed to notions of citizenship. Phelan contends: "the most significant challenge to privatized/ naturalized family has been the response of gay communities to AIDS. Gays and lesbians around the world have created organizations that extend the caring function of family to those in need, which has in turn produced changes in participants' ideas about who is family" (159).

[6] However, as Tim McCaskell has noted: "[t]hose of us who have been assigned to the category of "white" share in the benefits of a culture that has dominated the globe for the past five hundred years. Ethnocentric notions of beauty have dominated our culture and the cultures we dominated historically ... in spite of the optimistic theory that people with more interracial contact are less ethnocentric, it is the power imbalance in those relations that organizes how much anyone learns. The rice queen isn't necessarily less racist than the white boy who likes white boys because he has more contact. His power can insulate him from the feedback he needs to unlearn it. And the intimacy of a relationship may provide him with even more opportunities to display his racist presumptions" (46-8).

[7] Fung argues that the stereotype of submissiveness and subservience of gay Asians is reflected in North American commercial gay pornography, which appears to be geared towards a white viewer since Asians are perpetually

portrayed in roles of sexual servitude.

[8]Hennessy thus argues for a historical materialist perspective "which understands social life to be historically and materially produced through relations of labor through which people make what is needed to survive" (59). Hennessy contends that the politicization of capitalism would reorient the politicization of identities to begin with human needs and would "make visible the strategies of displacement that have helped remove class from view and that have abstracted identities from their social conditions of existence" (Hennessy 224).

[9]For an insightful, contextualized analysis of comedian Margaret Cho and her relationship to gay white communities in North America, see Atluri.

[10]This research has pointed to the limitations of, in particular, queer theory in addressing issues that pertain to transgendered and transsexual communities. The theoretical and practical tools that have attempted to address the realities of transgendered and transsexual experiences have largely been additive and inclusive in approach. As Inderpal Grewal and Caren Kaplan contend: "the binary gender model is so pervasive and universalized that it has become naturalized. In most queer studies in the United States [and Canada, as I have argued], destabilization of gender binarism seems to remain in the zone of gender permutation or diversity" (667). My study has not sufficiently acknowledged nor challenged these limitations. I thereby posit that future research must deepen our understanding of the ways that sex and gender binaries operate and the ways in which they intersect with and are simultaneously constituted by and through racial categorizations. In addition, my study points to the need to theorize and research processes of racialized and sexualized identity formations beyond the limits of the nation-state. Grewal and Kaplan have pointed out, for example, that the nationalist basis of academic disciplines in "articulation" theory and "intersectionality" approaches have participated in producing sexual subjects as nationalist subjects or as cultural-nationalist subjects. They contend that scholars have attempted to resolve this limitation by arguing for complex or hybrid subjects, somewhat inadequately (669). While my study has examined diasporic queer Asian identity and community formations in Canada through a queer, postcolonial framework, I make note of Jasbir Puar's important observation that "the genealogies of 'queer' and 'diaspora' share a particular absence: neither foregrounds complicities with the concepts of the nation-state" (407; see also Lee 1998). In its larger format, my study points to formations of a radical queer Asian cultural politics and a social movement in Canada; however, this preliminary investigation warrants further research on the ways in which a queer Asian social movement in Canada may be shaped by issues of transnationalism and how racialized sexualities are being shaped by contemporary processes of globalization. This seems imperative in light of the global HIV/AIDS epidemic and the ways in which First World and Third World

sexual subjects are being produced through globalized HIV/AIDS discourses (see Puar). Future research must therefore address how queer Asian activists in Canada are implicated in these processes in order to challenge these newer forms of racism and homophobia.

References

Atluri, Tara. "Lighten Up! Humour as Anti-Racism in the Work of Asian American Comic Margaret Cho." Unpublished Master's Thesis. Toronto: Ontario Institute for Studes in Education at the University of Toronto, 2002.

Bannerji, Himani. *The Dark Side of the Nation: Essays on Multiculturalism, Nationalism and Gender.* Toronto: Canadian Scholars' Press, 2000.

Eng, David L. *Racial Castration: Managing Masculinity in Asian America.* Durham and London: Duke University Press, 2001.

Eng, David L. and Alice Y. Hom, eds. *Q & A: Queer in Asian America.* Philadelphia: Temple University Press, 1998.

Frolic, Andrea N. "Wear it With Pride: The Fashions of Toronto's Pride Parade and Canadian Queer Identities." *In a Queer Country: Gay and Lesbian Studies in the Canadian Context.* Ed. Terry Goldie. Vancouver: Arsenal Pulp Press, 2001. 257-284.

Fung, Richard. "Looking for My Penis: The Eroticized Asian in Gay Video Porn." *Asian American Sexualities: Dimensions of the Gay & Lesbian Experience.* Ed. Russell Leong. New York and London: Routledge, 1996. 181-198.

Gilroy, Paul. *Against Race: Imagining Political Culture Beyond the Color Line.* Cambridge: Belknap Press of Harvard University Press, 2000.

Grewal, Inderpal and Caren Kaplan. "Global Identities: Theorizing Transnational Studies ofSexuality." *GLQ: A Journal of Lesbian and Gay Studies* 7 (4) (2001): 663-679.

Hennessy, Rosemary. *Profit and Pleasure: Sexual Identities in Late Capitalism.* New York: Routledge, 2000.

hooks, bell. *Black Looks: Race and Representation.* Boston: South End Press, 1992.

Lee, Jeeyeun. "Toward a Queer Korean American Diasporic History." *Q & A: Queer in Asian America.* Eds. David. L. Eng and Alice. Y. Hom. Philadelphia: Temple University Press, 1998. 185-209.

Lee, Ruthann. *"Coming Out" As Queer Asian Youth in Canada: Examining Cultural Narratives of Identity and Community.* Unpublished Master's Thesis. Toronto: Ontario Institute for Studies in Education at the University of Toronto, 2003.

McCaskell, Tim. "Towards a Sexual Economy of Rice Queenliness: Lust, Power and Racism." *Rice: Explorations Into Gay Asian Culture and Politics.* Ed.

Song Cho. Toronto: Queer Press, 1998. 45-48.

McClintock, Anne. "Family Feuds: Gender, Nationalism and the Family." *Feminist Review* 44 (1993): 61-80.

Moraga, Cherrie and Rosemary Weatherston. "Queer Reservations; or, Art, Identity, and Politics in the 1990s." *Queer Frontiers: Millennial Geographies, Gender and Generations*. Eds. Joseph Allen Boon *et al*. Madison: University of Wisconsin Press, 2000. 64-83.

Oikawa, Mona. "Locating Myself Within Histories of Dislocation." *Privileging Positions: The Sites of Asian American Studies*. Eds. Gary. Y. Okihiro, Marilyn Alquizola, *et al*. Pullman: Washington State University Press, 1995. 265-270.

Phelan, Shane. *Sexual Strangers: Gays, Lesbians and Dilemmas of Citizenship*. Philadelphia: Temple University Press, 2001.

Poon, Maurice and Peter T. Ho. "A Qualitative Analysis of Cultural and Social Vulnerabilities to HIV Infection Among Gay, Lesbian, and Bisexual Asian Youth." *Journal of Gay & Lesbian Social Services* 14 (3) (2002): 43-78.

Puar, Jasbir Kuar. "Transnational Sexualities: South Asian (Trans)nation(alism)s and Queer Diasporas." *Q & A: Queer in Asian America*. Eds. David. L. Eng and Alice Y. Hom. Philadelphia: Temple University Press, 1998. 405-422.

Reyes, Eric E. "Asian Pacific Queer Space." *Privileging Positions: The Sites of Asian American Studies*. Eds. Gary Y. Okihiro, Marilyn Alquizola, *et al*. Pullman: Washington State University Press, 1995. 251-259.

Shah, Nayan. "Sexuality, Identity, and the Uses of History." *Q&A: Queer in Asian America*. Eds. David L. Eng and Alice Y. Hom. Philadelphia: Temple University Press, 1998. 141-156.

Takagi, Dana Y. "Maiden Voyage: Excursion into Sexuality and Identity Politics in Asian America." *Asian American Sexualities: Dimensions of the Gay & Lesbian Experience*. Ed. Russell Leong. New York: Routledge, 1996. 22-35.

Williams, Rhonda M. "Living at the Crossroads: Explorations in Race, Nationality, Sexuality, and Gender." *In the House that Race Built*. Ed. Wahneema H. Lubiano. New York: Pantheon Books, 1997. 136-156.

Yuval-Davis, Nira. "Cultural Representations and Gender Relations." *Gender and Nation*. London: Sage, 1997. 39-67.

JANE G. KIM

The Funny Looking Dress

I recall a story my mother used to tell me near bedtime, told as though it was a remarkable tale that I would cherish throughout my entire life. A classical "how you came to be" story, to be kept as a trophy tale to impress someone on a first date, or to, at the very least, attract the spotlight in a group conversation.

The story always began with a predictable melodramatic sigh as my mother explained the significance of the date of my birth. The date was July 21st on a night as black as my first full head of hair, and it happened directly on the bottom steps of the poor, stone housing complex where my parents first lived. My mother had given birth too early, according to the soothsaying cards read out to her nine months prior. I was precisely three days premature, and exactly three days short of being born with so-called notorious luck and beauty. Sookyun, the community's spiritual advisor and my mother's confidante, predicted that I would be born the same day as my great-great-grandmother, who had lived until she was 104, and that she had envisioned in a lucid dream, where I, too, was present, blessed with silky fine hair, slender thighs, and long graceful arms dancing on stage, eliciting desirous gazes from spectators below.

Crying out in excruciating pain, my mother held her oversized belly with her petite hands as she leaned against the peeling wall in the narrow hallway of their home. Refusing to believe she was in labour and in denial of the jabbing pangs in her lower abdomen, she stood there hunched over and praying methodically in monotonous and uneven tones. Warm, transparent liquid oozed down her trembling legs as she recalled what Sookyun had repeatedly told her. "Your baby mustn't be born before the 25th. She may start pushing and crying to be freed, but it is important that you hold on."

She let out a piercing scream and dropped to the hardwood floor.

"Or be prepared ... for an unexpected curse."

Unable to change the inevitable, my mother and my jittery father, who had already grown impatient with her superstitious behaviour, tried to head to the hospital but they only made it as far as the bottom steps leading to the parking garage. It was on those steps that my mother finally gave birth to her prophesized baby girl.

Exhausted, she then gently lifted me into her outstretched arms and caught her breath, suddenly expelled in one long swoosh. There I lay in my mother's arms, the execration Sookyun had forecasted, quietly mewling underneath a surprisingly giant mess of unruly, curly black hair—the first incident ever in Korean history!

Hence, my nickname – Step! Not just because I was born on one, but also because my parents had a difficult time pronouncing Stephanie, my real name, the "ph" sound non-existent in the Korean spoken language. Shortly after immigrating to Canada in the early '70s, my parents figured they would also change their names, perhaps to socialize better or to gain greater job opportunities. Conveniently, they set their hands on a thin book of names while, at the time, unenlightened of the fact that it was of Italian domain. So, my father, whose real name is Jung-Ho, legally changed it to Stefano, my mother was given Francesca, and my poor brother, Gino. Not only did we appear comical with Italian names, but they didn't serve any purpose for our minority status. Our last name, Lee, gave everything away anyway.

None of that really mattered afterwards. By the time I was nine years old we had moved to a small town called Lamont, located just on the outskirts of Edmonton, Alberta. Our family stuck out noticeably as we intruded on a segregated and already established community. The town was predominately filled with Ukrainians and white Canadians who owned farms just a short distance from the town itself. It was here that I began to notice my physical differences but, more importantly, where the myth of my birth began to slowly unfold and subtly terrorize me.

The population of Lamont consisted of approximately 1,000 residents all cooped up together. Privacy was limited. Situated side by side were one elementary school, which I attended, and one high school where my older brother Gino went. Up the street, which we had named Uptown, lined one after the other was the town's drugstore, the supermarket, a small hardware store, a video/arcade unit, a barber shop, a couple of restaurants, a Catholic church, and one convenience store, which was proudly owned by my parents. Initially, this store, brimming with candy and popsicles, was the major factor in both my brother's and my own quick adjustment to our relocation. We had sacrificed our home and birthplace of warm Vancouver, B.C., for the promise of an eternity's worth of free sweets and chocolate anytime we wished. The bribery was difficult to resist. We entered Lamont weary and watchful in midwinter, snow piled high above our knees and snowflakes thick with ice crystals melting on our tongues.

My brother and I made friends quickly as people flocked toward us, interested and enthused more than anything that something new was happening in town. It was very rare that new kids would spring into Lamont, let alone yellow ones. I lucked out and became best friends with Fiona Sanders, the most popular and well-liked girl in school. We shared a common fashion sense as both our parents were pretty well off and took us shopping at the grand West Edmonton Mall in the city a couple of hours away. Truthfully, my clothes were slightly better than hers, more because my mother had expensive taste and spoiled me with the latest labels and trends at the time. Even more so, I personally thought, it was because my parents owned the only store in town, while her parents owned a mere dairy farm. We sought each other out from across the field. It seemed like she had spotted a kindred spirit: a girl who had also tasted the luxury of Guess jeans and Adidas running shoes. We got acquainted immediately. Fiona was definitely more beautiful though. Her golden brown tresses were her best asset, flowing soft and straight down her long spine, stopping just above her bottom. Her face consisted of delicate features and fair cheeks that turned a slight crimson when she laughed, magically drawing attention to her whole face as she scrunched her features together in laughter, loosening only after regaining the poise she seemed to have naturally mastered. I recall many times catching boys and girls in our class staring at her, exuding slight envy. She was near perfect, especially next to my short, petite body, in stark contrast as a discoloured and curly-haired misfit.

There was an article in the *Toronto Star* that I read recently about Korea being one of the top plastic surgery capitals in the world. It didn't surprise me at all that this tiny peninsula would be awarded such dubious distinction. At night when my mother would reiterate her tale, she would gently pinch at the corners of my eyes proclaiming that it was necessary to do this in order for my eyes to grow to their optimum potential, preceding the surgery I would supposedly have when I got older. When I questioned such absurdity, my mother would say in a cool and nonchalant manner that it wouldn't be right if I kept my eyes the way they were and that, in fact, adding the eyelid crease would bring me a better husband and a more satisfying life. I started to believe her as I became convinced that my life was hexed, comparing Fiona's face with her large hazel eyes to my tiny slits, thick eyelashes hovering over them like prickly shades. I conceived an image of her straight silky hair, the hair Sookyun had envisioned for me, and began feeling sorry for myself, claiming that my life was unfair when all I desired was to be normal and jinx-free. Unable to sleep, I would straighten my curls viciously with a large paddle brush, obsessively counting the strokes, imagining that if I brushed hard enough, I might successfully reverse the curse myself. I became just as superstitious as my mother.

The summer after my first year in Lamont, I discovered two things. One was the rosary and, with it, the Virgin Mary. The other was my sprouting body. At the beginning of July, my mother bought tickets for my brother and I to fly to Korea. The sole purpose, I thought, was to exorcise this curse as my seven aunts all crowded around me when we arrived, clicking their tongues at my misfortune. The first place they took me was to a hair salon in downtown Seoul. The stylists chattered in Korean while I sat timidly in the styling chair endeavouring to digest this outlandish setting. I responded to the stylists in both broken Korean and English, suddenly uncertain of my ability to speak, adding *ed's* to past tense my verbs and *ing's* randomly. I was embarassed as they laughed out loud, annoyingly poking around in my hair as though there was something good to eat in there.

This miraculous procedure of attempting to straighten my hair involved hours of having to endure putrid odours and noxious chemicals while simultaneously listening to the high-pitched whistling and whirling sounds of their state-of-the-art hairstyling equipment. I became light-headed and fell into a hazy reverie. The room became blurry as I blinked rapidly, suddenly unable to distinguish where I was. The people all smelled funny and a strange figure in the mirror peered back at me. I saw an image of my face, but my hair was suddenly fine and straight, safe to say even silky and iridescent under the fluorescent lights. I remember waking up in the chair, startled by the ice-cold water being splashed on my face and the uninviting loud foreign sentences aimed at rousing me.

"Wake up, Step," my aunt said with a thick accent. "It's time to go home."

Sweating and still slightly dizzy, I mumbled, "Is the curse gone? Did you get rid of it? Is it gone?"

I was handed a portable mirror that allowed me to admire all the different contours of my head. I witnessed a total transformation of once puffy wild tresses, to luxurious and glossy blue-black hair, pin straight, slick, and sticking flat against the sides of my rosy cheeks. It worked! With newfound energy, I held the mirror tight in my hands and pranced around the room giddy with delight. The stylists allowed me to keep the mirror as a token of their generosity, and I examined my reflection narcissistically all the way home to Canada. The rest of that trip was a blur, as the most significant and memorable part of my trip had passed. I couldn't control my eagerness to go home and show off to my mother and my friends. I couldn't wait to stand next to Fiona.

My good spirits were short-lived, however, as I stepped off the plane into Edmonton's untimely hot and humid summer weather. Within seconds, individual strands of my hair began to coil together, springing upwards in a singular pattern. By the time I had reached my house, the curls had gathered into a giant mop on top of my little head. I sped directly to my room, heading to the rosary hanging from the cross over my bed to pray to the Virgin Mary as I had seen my aunts doing in Korea. Gripping the pearl beads in my hands so hard that my knuckles turned white, I squeezed my eyes shut and chanted, "Hail Holy Queen, mother of mercy—please, oh, please, let these curls fade away!"

* * *

Summer was ending, and routine began to take hold as the weather cooled down and the sun dulled near evening. I had just come back from the park with some neighbourhood friends when I noticed an unfamiliar car parked in our driveway. A visitor. It was a rare occasion because we seldom had people come over. I crept in quietly, suddenly uncomfortable entering my own home, putting on a falsely shy demeanour yet hopeful that I would find a playmate my age. Instead, in the centre of our living room sat Sookyun, the witch from our old community, chewing on apple slices my mother had prepared neatly on a tray.

She wore a thick multicoloured cardigan sweater over a low grey V-neck sweater that exposed her sagging breasts when she bent forward. Her stockings were thick and itchy looking, lint balls hanging loosely at the feet, underneath an outdated green skirt that reeked of stale closets. She scanned me from head to toe in a deliberate, almost eerie manner. Her beady eyes were so piercing they paralyzed my body. I suddenly felt bare-naked and entirely misread, agitated more than nervous as she *tsk-ed* her dry tongue at me. Raising her wrinkled finger she motioned for me to come toward her. Despite the wonderful, chunky jewellery she had on her wrists that I couldn't help but notice, I shook my head disobediently, staying attentive to my stubby toes digging into the thick carpet. She spoke to my mother as if my presence was of minor importance.

"Disobedient and not blessed with beauty," she said, emphasizing the "and" as if she was surprised at her conclusion.

She spoke in Korean, but I could still understand. My Korean was actually pretty impressive, especially after all the slang and new lingo I had picked up from my trip that even my mother was unaware of. Nevertheless, I gasped at her remark, which my parents overlooked, allowing Sookyun to continue.

"See what I told you" she scoffed. "That hair…" and, after working her way toward me, she began patting my chest and rear as if she was frisking me for some hidden goodie and exclaimed, "Oh! She will develop big breasts, too, and a hideous round bottom!"

My mother muffled her breath as I stood still, naïve about what all this meant or would mean. Sookyun, however, kept shaking her head while blatantly pointing out yet another adversity that would befall my life.

"She will never look right in a *hanbok,* I am certain. She will never marry."

A *hanbok* is a traditional form of dress worn by Koreans for special occasions and, as I learned later, the ideal body for such an exquisite gown is flat-chested with narrow shoulders, devoid of any voluptuousness let alone a fully-rounded butt.

I hated Sookyun that day, and every other day that followed for her stupid predictions. And I hated my mother that night as she failed to defend me, hopelessly drawn in by superstitious nonsense.

In a heated fury, I huffed around my room, throwing useless ornaments against the wall, stomping loudly, and testing my parents' limits with company in the house. Getting no reaction, or rather attention, I flung myself onto my bed and accidentally bumped my left nipple against the edge of my bedpost. I cried out in searing pain, unable to compare such a feeling to any previous injury, and clutched my breast for several long minutes. The throbbing produced curiosity in me, goading me to lift my t-shirt above my chest. In a stiff position, I bit my lower lip as I observed a slight bruise beginning to swell on top of my pink nipple. My heart palpitated as my thoughts centred on Sookyun's horrific words. I lifted my shirt again and saw the other side slightly swollen as well. How could that be when I had only hit one?

I couldn't bear this question any longer and frantically scurried into my parents' room, naked from waist up, cupping my budding nipples. I called my father aside and confided in him, stressing that I must be taken to the doctor. A faint pinkish glow washed over his face as he covered me up with my pyjamas. He said it was a sign that I was too frivolous with my time and should be concentrating harder on my studies. That night I held on tight to my rosary and recited the *Apostles' Creed*. When it was time to make my wish, I asked for my nipples to stop growing. I promised to memorize all my multiplication tables as fair exchange for my wishful proposition.

"Amen," I whispered as I secured scotch tape I had found in the bathroom drawer directly over the tiny protruding bulges, hoping they would flatten somehow.

The torment I felt that summer became full-fledged by the time school started again. We began learning about living organisms in science class, and were assigned projects on specific creatures. I had to research the tapeworm and grew to understand that these long, meticulous worms fed off your body, growing rapidly and up to twenty feet long. I was excited to complete this assignment feeling extremely independent and scholarly.

Sookyun had overstayed her welcome that month. She lived with us for several weeks and began making sarcastic remarks about my eating habits. My appetite had grown larger those days as I wolfed down ten perogies at a time, loaded with sour cream and fried onions, which my mother had learned to make from her Ukrainian friends.

Sookyun spat out, "No man will take her for a wife with that gluttonous behaviour," as she sneered and looked at me with pity.

I matched her look and stared daringly into her eyes, taking a deliberately oversized bite from a fat perogy, letting remnants of sour cream slide down the side of my mouth. I ignored her new assumption, all the while detesting her and her wicked premonitions.

"You should check her for worms," Sookyun stated. "Either that or you have little hobos living in your stomach," she teased, turning to me.

Worms? Little hobos? That night, I felt funny, literally feeling the tapeworm I had convinced myself was growing in my stomach, battling with the hobos that had also taken refuge in my belly. Suddenly, I felt a rumble of scary living organisms, multiplying and adapting within the walls of my intestines. I resorted again to my rosary, begging the Virgin Mary to rid me once and for all of this wretched curse Sookyun had cast upon me.

My prayers seemed to have faded away in midst of my delusional state, as I began dreaming of tires rolling one after the other, expanding and booming louder as they rotated closer toward me. I woke up sweating, hot, and sticky and my throat felt clogged and sore as I ran to my father again in absolute panic. I was convinced that the worm was trying to crawl out of my mouth as I revealed to my father the secret of the new inhabitants in my stomach. My dad sighed, exasperated at my irrationality and fierce imagination. He squinted his tired eyes, slightly wrinkled at the corners, when he discovered I had developed a fever and took me to the town doctor a couple of blocks away.

The doctor made me gag two times and offered me candy in return, then announced to us both that I had tonsillitis. I begged to differ.

"Stephanie, there are no worms in your stomach, and certainly no tapeworm. These things just don't happen in Canada, especially in healthy little girls like you."

I shook my head in defiance, claiming that I had done research on them. "They *do* happen," I insisted. "It's just *rare* that's all."

He humoured me and prescribed the antidote, but with consequences. He drew the procedure on a piece of paper, detailed diagrams which explained the method used to expel the worms: something called induced vomiting. To everyone's surprise I instantaneously felt much better. I nodded my head obediently when he explained that my enlarged tonsils were responsible for the odd feeling at the back of my throat, and that I was going through a growth spurt, solving the mystery of my growing appetite. I was convinced that the worm had mysteriously dissipated after, of course, devouring all the hobos with it. I completed my science project and received an "A" for "great creativity," then stored it in an old shoebox, afraid of its influence if I ever read it over again.

* * *

October was coming to an end, and kids began to rave about Halloween, secretly whispering to each other their ideas for costumes. Fiona and I had our own secret, planning to create something spectacular together with the idea of making a grand entrance. We decided that she would be the evil witch dressed in black and I would be her opponent dressed in white, with an agreement that we would have equal powers marked by identical wands we had seen in a *Sears* catalogue. Excited to start on my costume, I raced home to find Sookyun and my mother waiting impatiently for me in the kitchen. Having always had a strong instinct for trouble, I started to feel tiny butterflies in my stomach as I attempted to read my mother's facial expressions. They were both sitting down on the floor cross-legged around a big brown package already opened. A present. The fluttering butterflies turned alive with sudden excitement, as I loved, as any other kid loves, gifts of any kind.

"Open it," my mother goaded as her face began to brighten.

My smile widened as I flung my backpack on the floor, and greedily plunged into the box.

"Wow..." I drawled as I lifted the garment out of its wrapping, my voice fading with obvious disappointment. "What is it?"

"A *hanbok*," Sookyun stated with a condescending tone, notably unimpressed with my ignorance.

"Oh," I muffled, "thanks."

My thoughts had already reverted to my costume as I got up quickly. However, before I could even reach the door to exit, Sookyun and my mother began to speak in unison about how expensive the gown was and to have shipped from Korea. Then they began to exaggerate Sookyun's sister's great efforts and special care in seeing that I got the *best* one possible. I knew I should have trusted my first instinct as they stripped my clothes off, replacing them with the funny looking dress that I thought looked inappropriate for any occasion.

Inevitably, on Halloween day, I showed up at school in this very vibrant, oddly-shaped and, for me, humiliating gown. I was forced to wear it so that I wouldn't disrespect such a kind gesture from Sookyun's family. My mother had even slicked my hair into a tight bun making my eyes appear more slanted than they already were, and decorated my face with bright red lipstick, exaggerating the lines so that they looked permanently pursed, exactly the way I would have drawn them in a picture book. The dress was splashed with a mixture of greens, yellows, and reds, trimmed with gold lining, and a blue satin sash extending across my chest. The sash was pulled tightly into a thick knot, pushing my lungs inward so that I could hardly breathe. On my feet, I had on white, pointy, elf-like cushion socks with rubber soles, made so that I could walk on them outdoors. I felt silly, even for Halloween, and my brother made me feel even worse as he snickered and poked fun at my strange appearance.

The first person I saw was Fiona in her gothic witch gear, looking amazing with her face painted green, artificial warts pasted across her cheeks. She muffled her laughter when she caught sight of me as I stood there with clenched hands glued to my sides, looking miserable in such an outrageous outfit. Tara Thompson, another one of our friends, skipped into the room dressed as an angel, and gasped when she saw me, not knowing whether to laugh or stay silent. I ignored them both and huffed away, angry that Fiona had given Tara my original role and extremely jealous of the identical wands positioned in their hands, as opposed to my floral printed fan, a supposedly great addition to my *hanbok*.

The only people who appreciated my costume were my teachers, who never really mattered anyway, as they *oohed* and *ahhed*, taking me into different classrooms to show me off to their colleagues. I felt uncomfortable as they set me apart from everyone else, curiously examining and admiring the intricate patterns on my dress. That day the teachers came up with a new prize on account of me, awarding me with the "best ethnic costume," whatever that meant. As I got up to claim my prize, I secretly wished for Sookyun's death and fantasized myself dressed as something other than what I was—a clown or a ghost or even a pumpkin. I didn't know what I was dressed as so I lied up on the podium and said I was a witch in disguise. I think I overheard my teachers say something about a *Geisha*.

Either way, the day was coming to an end as my makeup streaked and my hair became loose from its thick bun. Fiona, who had grown tired of Tara, sauntered home with me, and as a peace gesture let me carry her sparkling, silver-tasselled wand. From across the street a boy in the one of the younger grades called out to me, "Hey Chink! Where're ya' going China doll?" The boy howled with laughter letting his friends join in on the fun as they continued their mocking.

Fiona and I exchanged scowls as I bravely turned around and retorted, "I'm not Chinese!" I paused and placed my hands on my hips in a defiant gesture. "I'm Korean!" I shouted, knowing how to distinguish myself only by knowing what I was not.

We proceeded to my house, anticipating big pillowcases full of licorice and candy, when Fiona began to ponder, "What are you anyway, Step?"

"Huh? What do you mean?" I asked, sincerely baffled.

"I mean, you're not black obviously ... and you're not white..."

I paused, unsure on how to respond and shrugged. "I don't know..." I said, dumbfounded. "Pink?"

We then giggled, bursting into the girlish laughter only best friends share, skipping the rest of the way home, my fluffy, curly mane bouncing side to side in the brisk fall wind.

JIN HUH

Regret

Morning light seeps through
broken blinds and dust bunnies
I wake up
knowing
what morning it is

Guilty words
ready
to burst forth in holy confession
Words that have built their strength through
years of defiant rebellion
delineated by
distances
in space and time
    that span oceans
sparked by
  centuries of colonialism
  western imperialism
  men crusading for power
all of this: forming its imprint on my yellow skin
all of this: internalized

Years of unformed feelings
ready
to be named

Heart pounding
regret compounding
I could tell her
       I see you now as a woman

Not just as
the one who told me
    to make my bed or it would be thrown out with tomorrow's garbage
I could speak the unspoken
Tell her who I really am
Open doors
build bridges
over deep
schisms filled with
    secrets   and   silences

But my tongue grows thick
with milk and butter
Unable to wrap around words
ohm-ma could understand

Words
what I want to say are just
mere words
that on this morning
cannot adequately convey the
depth of my regret

How to make up for a lifetime of mistakes in
one
moment?

This cliché of a moment
when prodigal children come home
express everlasting love to their parent,
this moment of forgiveness
before death

She sits across from me
hands loosely clasped on lap
Her sweater hangs limply on her
emaciated shoulders
I take her cold hands into my own
These two sets of hands
once identical
in shape and appearance
hers so often
marinating kimchee
peeling sa-gwa

REGRET

Now
weak, wrinkled
Old hands
The hands of someone dying.

Morphine swims
through her
cloudy eyes
But a clear outline of
something
there
   maybe
that my life is my own
not hers
   or anyone else's to lead
that she's sorry too
that hope is elusive
    hard to grasp at the end
but passed on
from mother
to daughter
        it lives on

This moment of
regret
I was aware of its coming
resolute to clipping the bud before its bloom
but it continues to
live vividly
and I must choose
what
to
glean
from
it

ANN SHIN

Learning to Walk

Fog creeps onto the Don Valley Parkway, shouldering in among the trees and settling in. Windshield wipers smear the glass. It is 5:00 A.M., dark, and the orange highway lights are haloed by mist. I know this road well, this drive up to my parents' place. But it's been a while since I've had to do it so regularly.

In the back seat my daughter stirs in her sleep, her face splitting into a wide grin. Seven months old and still a toothless wonder, she looks like a senile old man. Shifting my hands on the steering wheel, I focus on the road, sleep glowering behind my eyes. It is ungodly to be doing this at this hour. Worse, to be doing it for the next two weeks.

I hear whimpering from the back seat and I hunker down, praying it will go away. There is the telltale swish swish of Zara's head shaking from side to side and a sob. She is waking up. I reach behind and wave a toy in front of her face. Zara rubs her eyes and bats the toy away, her sobs gaining momentum. It's a losing battle, this drive home. If she wakes during the drive she'll start wailing. I have to steel myself against her shrill cries. By the time we pull up to my parents' place, I'm shaking. I jump out of the driver's seat and run around to the back, unbuckling Zara and picking her up.

In my arms Zara is delicious; I could eat her in one swallow. I kiss her repeatedly on her lips. She coos, patting my face in a reflexive response we share together as mother and daughter. It is a pure, visceral joy I can't remember experiencing with my own mother. But it must have happened, there are photos that suggest it.

The years telescope and I stand as an adult in front of my parents' new wheelchair accessible home.

Walking into the house, I lay Zara down in the spare bedroom. I stick a bottle in her mouth and make my way across the hall, opening the door onto my mother's room. The air is stuffy, heavy with sleep. Next to my mom's hydraulic bed are two noisy wall clocks whose ticks are off just enough to create an eternal echo of ticking in the room. My head resounds with the clocks' ticks as I wheel my mother's chair to her bedside.

My mother stirs, calling, *Yobo, yobo, is that you?* She is calling for my father who is away at a conference.

Wake up, I tell her, *time to wake up*. I switch on the light and her hand shoots up to shield her eyes. She gazes at me confused, apologetic — a familiar expression.

Lifting the covers, I place my hand on her right leg and try to lift. The calf muscle turns rigid and goes into spasm. I have to wait a moment and in that moment I consider why my mother wears this expression so often. My mother is sorry that I have to help her, yet again. She is apologizing for being handicapped for 27 years.

When I was nine years old she had a near-fatal accident. She fell head-first from the second storey of our mushroom farm. My father found her hours later, lying in a pool of blood. There were surgeries. Relatives flew in. My brothers and I were sent to stay with an aunt. My mom survived the surgeries, but remained in a coma for three months.

When she awoke all she could do was open her eyes. Then close them again. It would take close to a year before she could start moving any of her limbs, let alone speak.

My mother says, *I haven't been a proper mother to you.*

I am indignant and insist, *You have been my mother, just by being alive, you are my mother. I am grateful for it.* But neither of us is altogether convinced. As a statement it is true, but there are so many other truths about our relationship that are omitted from that statement. I am only now trying to recover them one by one.

When my mother had her accident, I fell ill myself. For days I was ferried back and forth from the doctor's office to the hospital, undiagnosed, and in constant pain. When they finally operated on me they found my appendix had ruptured. So while my mother lay in a coma in a Vancouver hospital, I spent Christmas recuperating in the children's ward of a hospital in Langley. In some ways this is symptomatic of how I deal with all trauma. Things rupture inside me and go unnoticed for a while.

I lean over my mother's bed, grabbing hold of her left calf. Her foot lifts six or seven inches off the bed and then hangs there hesitantly. I tuck my hand into her curled toes, feeling their callused rigidity. I push her whole leg up to complete the move.

One, she says, and we wait for the foot to fall back to the bed. I wonder if she is as aware of her foot as I am. Her thigh muscle releases slowly and her foot comes down as if being lowered by hydraulic suspension. There will be a "two" followed by a "three"; she will count her way to "twenty." After this exercise she will go to the bathroom. She watches the clock, waiting for the minute hand to reach 12:00, at which point it will be 7:00 A.M. Only then will she get up to go to the bathroom.

It has been years since I've had to help my mother so intimately. Even longer since she extended herself for me. She used to be the kind of mother who did everything to say "yes" to her kids. When I invited my first friend to our Langley farmhouse, I told my mother that we had to serve apple pie—my five-year-old logic being that you couldn't serve Korean food to a white friend from school. My mother had never baked a pie, and the farmhouse only had a woodstove oven at the time. Still she made apple pie from scratch, leaving a full Korean dinner on the stove. I was ecstatic that we could serve Laurel "normal" food.

The list of things my mother did for us was endless—everything from driving us to soccer practice and piano lessons, to sewing figure skating costumes and reading stories to us. She was also a full-time registered nurse and a working partner in the new family business, the mushroom farm. This is the mother I remember from before the accident, whom I still long for even as an adult.

I am a mother myself now, and it's stirring a new longing in me. As if by having my own daughter I am re-awakened to all that has been missing in my relationship with my mother. I have a bond with my baby that is complete in its physical and emotional gratification. As I help my mother bend her leg, I realize that the only physical intimacy I share with my mother is about her handicap. I let her leg drop to the bed. My arms hang heavy and dull at my sides.

Koreans say you can tell a person's disposition by reading their facial expression at rest. It's called *insang*. You could say a person has a warm *insang*, or a nervous *insang*, or an *insang* that shows they've been through a lot of hardship. My mother's face settles into a flat, almost stern look. It is the face of someone who doesn't normally face others. I imagine I wear that face when I am in front of the computer screen at night. One might call it apathy or stoicism. One might say there has been damage to the cerebral cortex affecting the emotions. Or one could say it is a well-managed denial of loneliness. I watch my mother and I long for her to say something to me, anything. My affections send their little minions to her door and stand there, waiting expectantly. But her door has been shut for years, covered with a heavy overgrowth of ivy.

This door remained closed throughout my childhood. I lived in my own world of books and writing, and it's a world into which I still wish to retreat. Travelling into my head, immersing myself in writing, I obliterate her and all others from my mind. There is relief there, being alone, but also feelings of guilt for having abandoned those dependent on me. As a child, this inner world enabled me to be self-sufficient enough to survive. But now as I contemplate my daughter, I question if I am truly "sufficiently" an individual, a mother, a partner, a daughter. Am I really, fully any of these if part of the reason why I work is to escape? To escape from feeling lonely? To escape unfulfilled desires?

It is a minute before 7:00 A.M. I check on Zara in the other room and find her sprawled on the double bed with her arms flung out, her curly hair sweaty with sleep. Babies are so wanton with their body heat. She might go into a fright, her hands shooting up in some vestigial instinct like a primate grabbing for its mother's belly. But usually she sleeps like this, completely open and fearless, staking claim to that small piece of real estate beneath her body.

The world is my daughter's and our relationship reflects that sense of unmarred potential. I understand her various needs, that is: "I am hungry," "I am bored," "I am sleepy," "change me," "look at me." We have complete communication. I'd like to keep this simple arrangement, preserve this sense of unlimited potential. I don't want to fail her or for either of us to be disappointed in one another. Better then, for her to remain in infancy where the world of potentiality outballasts any possible disappointments or sorrows.

My daughter will start walking before my mom can walk again. That is, my mother will never walk again.

My mother's world has shrunk down to this living room with its exercise rail, the kitchen, and her bedroom with the hydraulic bed and the two noisy clocks. She funnels her industrious spirit into an intricate schedule of activities that accounts for every solitary minute of her day. Ten minutes at the bar, fifteen minutes doing knee bends, twenty minutes of deep breathing, twenty minutes walking at the bar, thirty minutes lying down, ten minutes for the bathroom, then lunch. But only thirty minutes for lunch, because there are exercises after lunch.

This is the life of a self-winding watch, a woman with a heightened dependence on ritual that was developed over years of time spent alone. Becoming physically needy has made her wont to ignore her emotional needs, such as "I am lonely," "look at me." She has crafted a life where those needs are never addressed, a life dictated by schedule. It's a strict schedule that doesn't allow time for hanging out and chatting. I've had few conversations with her that weren't interrupted by an exercise or a trip to a washroom. When I ask her if she felt lonely today she says no, and laughs ruefully. She is too busy to be lonely.

I shift my mother's legs down from the bed and help her pull herself onto her wheelchair, my hands on her hips, holding her flannel pajama bottoms up.

Thank you Annie, she says as she wheels herself to the bathroom. Swish swishh, her fingers slide over the wheels.

I am trying to reconcile this woman in the wheelchair with the mother of my past. I have this fantasy that she used to be a supermom who worked two full-time jobs and cooked for the family and still had time to read us stories and kiss all our boo-boos. Indulging in this fantasy is easier than feeling my grief today. It's also easier than considering that my mother may have always been a little too busy, too overworked, a little too distant.

I stand with her in the bathroom, my hand guiding her feet back into her pant legs. I tug the waistband up to her knees so that she can stand up and pull up her pants with one hand.

I have no memory of what her body felt like before the accident, how she hugged. But I am re-learning what it is to accept my mother's body for what it is. I am trying not see it as an embodiment of clues and hints to that other body, the perfect body that was my mother before the accident—the perfect mother, whom I barely remember and who probably never existed, but whom I willfully reconstruct.

In front of me is not the perfect mother. There is simply my mother. I cannot design nor select a different mother. She cannot return me and request a different daughter. We are bound by blood in a relationship strung together by a series of tentative agreements. I answer if you phone me. You fret if I'm sick. I come when you need help. You want me to be your daughter. I want you to be my mother. So we try, each in our own language, we try to be these—mother and daughter. And this is our love. The acceptance that what we each offer falls short. We fumble, signaling with hesitant gestures our damaged love.

I ask her to call me when she's bored, and she does, several times a day, the conversations so formulaic we could record our responses and play them back to each other with similar effect. Except there would be one main difference. The fact that my mom picked up the phone to call me, and I answered.

Annie, is that you?
Hi mom.
Are you still at work?
I'm just finishing up. How was your afternoon?
Fine. I did the walking exercise four times today.
Great. Good for you.
How is Zara?
I don't know yet, I have to pick her up at daycare.
Oh. (a pause) *I miss her.*

You know mom, Zara misses you too.

II.
Lost Homes and Founded Nations

HIJIN PARK

Incorporating Ji-Won Park into the Canadian Nation

The Good Girl, the Monster and the Noble Savage

In the summer and fall of 2002 the assaults of six Asian women and girls temporarily studying English in the Greater Vancouver Area (GVA) garnered significant attention. Beginning with the attempted murder of Korean national Ji-Won Park in May 2002 and ending with the murder of Chinese national Wei Amanda Zhao in October 2002, the attacks on Asian females sparked a national debate about the vulnerability of non-Canadian Asian females in Canada and in British Columbia in particular. Elsewhere[1] I have examined how the violence inflicted on these women and girls became of concern because the women and girls were nationals of Asian countries, who were associated with Asian economies, and not Asian Canadian women. An economics of compassion and specifically the intersection of race, gender, nationality, and class was central to the production of the violence as a collective issue deserving of attention. Rather than concern over the safety of Asian women and girls, the construction of the attacks served as a vehicle to address anxieties and fears about the GVA's courting of, and dependence on, Asian migration and capital.[2]

This paper argues that an understanding of the events of 2002 must go beyond an analysis of the economics of Asian migration to Canada. It does so by focusing on how dominant narratives of Canadian citizenship were written over the violence done to Asian women's bodies. In particular, I limit my examination to the first and most prominent attack, that of Ji-Won Park. Through an analysis of Canadian media, government and judicial documents on the attack of Park, I hope to reveal the conditions under which those deemed "foreign" are incorporated into the Canadian nation as "one of us."

Compassion as Canadian Identity

In May 2002 Ji-Won Park, a 23-year-old Korean national studying English in Vancouver on a student visa, was attacked while jogging in historic Stanley

Park. Authorities state that Park was randomly chosen and strangled until unconscious by 24-year-old local resident Robert Wallin. The attack left her with permanent, severe brain damage. In a coma after the attack, Park eventually regained a limited ability to hear, see, and communicate by blinking her eyes. Although she has exceeded all medical expectations for recovery, she is still dependent on others to care for her needs and will most likely be so for the remainder of her life.

Deemed a tragedy for Park, her family and the city of Vancouver, politicians, the media, members of the public, English as a Second Language (ESL) schools, and community organizations discussed what Canada's responsibility was and should be to Park and her family. At issue was whether British Columbia should pay for Park's lifelong care and whether Park and her family should be allowed to permanently stay in Canada. Prominent within these debates was the effect Park's attack would have on Vancouver's English as a Second Language industry and the tourism industry. Debated on radio and television call-in shows and newspapers as well as in local, provincial, and federal government offices, most Canadians were said to be in favour of full financial support for Park and her family (Canada 2209; British Columbia 4257-4258; Armstrong).

In January 2003, the province of British Columbia announced that Park's medical bills and a living allowance would be provided by a provincial fund created by the newly passed *Victims of Crime Act* (Morton). Subsequently Park and her family were granted permanent resident status on compassionate grounds in December 2004 (O'Neil). Upon the announcement of the Park family's permanent residency status, the story of the brutal beating that tarnished Canada's reputation faded away as Park's dream of staying in Canada was accomplished. Often defined as the right and only thing to do, this narrative followed the case from the beginning to the end.[3] Shortly after the attack, Rex Murphy of the Canadian Broadcasting Corporation's evening national news program, *The National*, argued:

> She was here to learn one of our languages, experience one of our cities and by her own initiative and industry, begin to build a life. And now, she's in a coma, in a vegetative state. Her mother is in anguish. It was an obnoxious piece of this country's refuse that caused this tragedy. Merely then as a signal that when a manageable misery is presented to us, we accept its management, this country, without delay, without any teasing of the bureaucratic regimen or any throat clearing by hesitant politicians, Canada should say yes to Ms. Park and yes to her mother. She should be allowed to stay.... She should, if she escapes the coma, be offered rehabilitation here for as long as it takes as well. I'd guess that most

of the people in Vancouver now feel very much the same. It was their beautiful, safe city that was stained by this act. It can to some degree be redeemed by another. Let her stay. Not out of charity but because it's the right thing to do.

Reporting on the Minister's announcement of residency status, the *Vancouver Courier,* in an article aptly titled, "Welcome home Ji-Won Park," commented that:

The wheels of bureaucracy turn very slowly in this country, but Immigration Minister Judy Sgro finally decided that Park and her family can stay in Canada. It was the decent—and only— choice to make. What kind of country would this be if we didn't take care of a person who was attacked in Canada by a lunatic Canadian? (39)

Lawyer Michael Hwang, who often spoke for the Park family, called the attack, "an offence against society" (qtd. in Fong 2002a: A3). Similarly Fong (2002a) reported on British Columbian Member of Parliament Lorne Mayencourt's views that, "…his gut tells him that caring for Park for the rest of her life is, "…the right thing to do. It's a real critical question for us as a nation. We have to believe we are the kind of people that believe we have obligations" (A3). This sense of obligation and doing the right thing is said to be intrinsic to Canadians. In discussing fundraising efforts to pay Park's medical bills, Myers argued, "British Columbians are responding to a random act of violence in the only way they know how—with random acts of kindness" (A8).

The above statements reveal that in addition to the economics of international education and tourism, the construction of the attack of Ji-Won Park was framed by narratives of who "we" are as a people, community and nation. Park's desire to live in Canada and Canada's taking care of Park and her family represents the success of the Canadian dream. In addition to the national-capitalist fantasy of economic mobility, Asian bodies who desire Canada represent the Canadian national-capitalist fantasy of greatness, of moral and cultural superiority. Park has been taken care of not only to present the message to Asian international students and Asian countries that their business is welcome and they will be protected, but to present the message to Canadians and to others that Canada is a just, peaceful and compassionate country that does the right thing. The story of Ji-Won Park became as much about the story of what David Jefferess refers to as "Canadian compassion as Canadian identity" as it did about the economics of the ESL industry (44). Thus the moral panic was one of the preservation of the Canadian national imaginary as well as about maintaining an economic status quo.

In defining Canadians as compassionate, ethical people, Park is defined as the sufferer in need of compassion. Analyzing the history of the meaning of compassion, Marjorie Garber contends that from the fourteenth to the seventeenth century, compassion was increasingly understood as hierarchical and as existing between disparate people. It is something that is "shown towards a person in distress by one who is free from it, who is, in this respect, his superior" (20). Compassion, then, was closely tied to charity and condescension. In the 1800s the rubric of compassion often focused on the spiritual benefits to the one giving compassion. The pain of the sufferer was said to provide a vehicle of pleasure for those who were compassionate. As Garber cites from a sermon in 1876, "Compassion … gives the person who feels it pleasure even in the very act of ministering to and succouring pain" (20). Compassion and charity were also central to the development and justification of colonialism and empire building. The civilizing mission was pivotal to the conquering mission as the west was defined as the "custodians of civilization" (Paddle par. 21). In a postcolonial context, compassion is increasingly tied to social issues like human rights and multiculturalism (Garber 19).

Not surprisingly, a number of authors argue that acts of compassion often reinscribe relations of power and social inequities rather than diminish or dismantle them. Elizabeth Spelman contends, "…compassion, like other forms of caring, may also reinforce the very pattern of economic and political subordination responsible for such suffering" (7). Sara Ahmed concurs and reminds us that: "Being moved by the other's pain elevates the Western subject into a position of power over others: the subject who gives to the other is the one who is "behind' the possibility of overcoming pain (36)." Ahmed goes on to state:

> The over-representation of the pain of others is significant in that it *fixes* the other as the one who "has" pain, and who can overcome that pain only when the Western subject feels moved enough to give. The transformation of generosity into an individual and national character involves a form of "feeling fetishism": feelings of compassion are fetishized by being cut off from histories of production (36, emphasis in original).

For example, the colonial histories that structure the dominance of the English language as a universal global language required for international business and communication are veiled by discourses of globalization (Buttigieg). Masked is, as Gregory Hadley argues, the degree to which English is studied in various places and contexts because it is the language of the lone remaining superpower, the United States (2), and the language in which international bodies often decide the fate of people's lives. Nonetheless, Park is by no means an oppressed "Third World" migrant forced to move for economic survival. Jeong-Eun Rhee and Mary Ann Danowitz Sagaria state:

> ... international students, even within a context of U.S. imperialism, are hardly the "oppressed." Some international students voluntarily reconstitute their identities across national borders to actively engage in and enrich global capitalism. Thus, they are consenting participants who subscribe to global capitalism. (91)

Although relatively privileged and intentionally mobile, migrants such as Park still remain embedded in the practices of global capitalism that primarily serve the interests of elite men in the west. Furthermore, the construction of the attack of Ji-Won Park reinforces orientalist, sexist and ableist representations that affirm histories of western modernity. The next section analyzes the constructions of the main characters in the attack of Park: Ji-Won Park, her family, Park's attacker, Robert Wallin, and one of Park's "heroes," John Lightowlers. It emphasizes how these narratives reinscribe hegemonic scripts of race, gender, nation and disability.

The Good Girl, the Monster and the Noble Savage

In analyzing contemporary media representations of Asian women in the west and in Asia, L. H. M. Ling divides the representations into three categories: Good Girl, Bad Girl, and Unwanted Girl. Good Girls vary from the safe, familiar, domestic "good wife, wise mother" to perky singles to bow-tied middle-management to gracious, servile "Singapore Girl" to "hot single babes" (146). Bad Girls are hyper-heterosexualized and sell sex, often to western men, as prostitutes, entertainers, party girls, and mail-order brides. Examples of Unwanted Girls include single "superwomen," grating "domestic workers," and humiliated "comfort women." Viewed with a combination of contempt and pity, Unwanted Girls are unwanted because they fail to devote themselves to the betterment of the hypermasculine family, economy, and nation. Ling emphasizes that these categories are not mutually exclusive and Good passive daughters can become Bad Girls when they seek the comforts of western men and nations. Similarly the Good Asian Girl may be defined in the west as Good precisely because of "bad"/deviant sexual submissiveness. Ling highlights these categories not because they are comprehensive but because "[t]hey illustrate merely a general pattern of gender representation for the Asian woman that caters to both the Western Valiant Prince ... and the Asian Warrior Prince" (146).

Although Ling argues that the Bad Girl dominates western representations of Asian women, Park was constructed by the Canadian media and government elite as an exemplary Good Girl. This is in keeping with Yasmin Jiwani's (2005) recent work on the television show *Relic Hunter,* which argues that contemporary representations of Asian women in western film and television differ significantly from historical representations (185). Historically Asian women appeared as exotic and erotic objects of the white heterosexual male gaze; however, Asian women now appear in the starring role of heroine, a role previously reserved for the white male hero (182). Seemingly "positive," Jiwani contends that these roles exist due to contemporary forces of globalization that aim to manage multiculturalism and capture the burgeoning Asian American market (189). Although Asian women, whether good, bad, or unwanted, are often hypersexualized, Park is not constructed in relation to heterosexual men. In large part due to her disabled body, Park appears to be desexualized as an innocent, idealic victim.

During Robert Wallin's sentencing hearing, Justice Dillon in her "Reasons for Sentencing" described Park as thus:

She was a petite, twenty-three-year-old student who had come from Korea in her fourth year of studies. She wanted to further her English in pursuit of a degree eventually towards a master in international conferencing. She was fluent in Turkish, French, and English as well as Korean. By her mother's account, she was a wonderful daughter, talented at many things including piano and flute, and active in sports. (*HMTQ v. Wallin* par. 6)

This construction of Park is similar to those contained in media reports. Classmates described her as "vivacious and athletic" (Armstrong A8). She was particularly fond of tennis, racquetball, swimming, skiing, and jogging. Close to her family, Park spoke to her mother daily. Through an interpreter her mother, Chun-Ram Lim, said that, "She was liked by everyone, was bright, positive, outgoing and always had a smile on her face.... She had lots of friends, lots of spark. She was a leader" ("Ji-Won Park's mother reads impact statement" B7). Generous and kind, Park began volunteering at a seniors' home shortly after she arrived in Vancouver.

Park and her family are also devout Christians. The media reported on how her mother read the bible to her daughter while she lay in a coma for six weeks. They believed in the power of prayer and the church (Fong 2002b). One of Park's dreams was to meet the Queen of England, Canada's head of state. Upon hearing of the Queen's visit to Canada in the fall of 2002, the pair prayed daily for Park to fulfill her wish (Lazaruk). Her wish was granted with the assistance of public relations officials and the then Prime Minister Jean Chrétien's wife, Aline Chrétien (Fraser). Several media outlets reported on the

Queen's statements praising Canada for, "crafting a multicultural society that provides a model for the rest of the world" (Mickleburgh and Valpy A5) and for "a particular Canadian genius for altruistic openness and reconciliation" (Steffenhagen A1). The Queen's celebration of Canadian multiculturalism was juxtaposed with stories of the Aboriginal woman who waited to give the Queen an eagle feather, the largely Chinese and South Asian crowd that applauded her speech in Vancouver, and the disabled Korean woman who wore pearls, held a lily, prayed for days and waited for four hours to see the Queen.

Park was central to many of the reports on the Queen's visit to Vancouver. As reported in *The Globe and Mail*:

> The Queen has touched Canadian hearts wherever she has gone during her four-day visit to British Columbia. But it is safe to say that no heart was touched more deeply than that of a young Korean student yesterday as the Queen passed through the lobby of the Hotel Vancouver. Last May, Ji-Won Park suffered severe brain damage ... For the past month, since she heard about the Queen's visit, Ms. Park had been set on meeting the monarch, her face wreathed in smiles whenever she heard the word "Queen." (Mickleburgh and Valpy A5).

The *CTV News* highlighted Park in their telling of the story on its nightly national news program. Correspondent Vennavally-Rao stated:

> And for Jiwan [*sic*] Park, this day would bring a much-needed lift. The Korean exchange student was strangled by a stranger and left for dead in a city park earlier this year. Recently out of a coma, she was given a few moments to meet her Majesty. Still unable to talk, her face said it all.

The disabled Korean woman's dream to meet the symbol of white Britishness and of Canada's history as a white settler state appeared to be a newsworthy story desirable for its "feel good" qualities. It exemplified the story of Canadian progress through the inclusion of minorities that the Queen and the mainstream media attempted to tell.

Ji-Won Park is constructed as an extroverted, active, stable, moral, single, family-oriented, Christian, socially-conscious, ambitious, hardworking, worldly, educated, talented, and focused, upwardly mobile individual who had immense potential. What makes Park a perfect subject to rescue is that she was all this prior to her disabling attack by "one of us." She was an ideal, model citizen and possessed the characteristics of someone worthy of rescue. Historically Asian women who were defined by the west as in need of saving were primarily women constructed as destitute, uneducated women who were prostituted and enslaved by Asian men and cultures (Paddle; Lessard). International students have also been constructed as objects of rescue (Rhee and Sagaria 89). Ji-Won Park, however, is not an uneducated, destitute woman unfamiliar with western cultures, languages and morals. She can be seen as a domesticated Other consuming western education, languages, and cultures as she mimics the western liberal subject. On the other hand, the very act of consuming western culture emancipates her and turns her into an active, rather than passive, subject.

In keeping with historical representations of Asian women needing to be saved, Park is constructed as suffering. Dissimilar to representations of Asian women in Canadian history, Park's affliction is due to the savagery of "one of us" and not due to the barbarity of Asian culture and men. As a symbol of "one of us" and the daughter we should adopt, Park is described as "vibrant" (*HMTQ v. Wallin*, 2003 BCSC 809) and "active" (Bermingham 2003: A4) prior to the attack. Park is silenced by Wallin rather than by Asian men. In other words, the construction of Park draws on both historical representations of disempowered Asian women and of empowered white women. Analyzing western women's campaigns of the 1920s and 1930s to save China's "slave girls," Paddle argues that:

> The image of the silent, suffering and childlike figure became the image and symbol of Chinese womanhood for the West. Set alongside the emerging figure of the modern Western girl, healthy, active and independent, the Chinese slave girl remains silenced, mute, passive and childlike, linked in the Western archives to a traditional culture and the practices of antiquity. (par. 1)

Within this dichotomous construction of passive east and active west, Park exists as a hybrid subject who occupies both positions. She is a symbol of what Jiwani (2005) refers to as "an emancipated femininity and an assimilated ethnicity" (182). Consistent with western discourses of modernity, Park is valued as an migrant who turns "her back on her own kind to grasp freedom and opportunity in the United States" (Kelsky 244). Lauren Berlant reveals that it is migrant women in particular that are valued for "having the courage to grasp freedom" (195). The violence done to her body was defined as significant in part because her body stands in for Asian nations and economies. It is clear, however, that Park also represents the Canadian nation. The violence is committed against the Canadian national imaginary that defines these acts as an aberration that must be recouped. Situated as an outsider and an insider, Park represents the promise of Asian capital as well as a sign of Canadian morality and greatness.

In a reversal of roles, it is the Asian woman who is welcomed into the nation as a symbol of all that Canada aspires to be and the white man who is abjected and incarcerated as a "refuse" of the nation (Murphy).[4] As two disabled subjects, albeit one disabling the other, discourses of disability shaped both of these representations. In addition, the constructions of the Chinese "slave girl" and the active western woman, as provided by Sarah Paddle, are infused with ableist discourse that constructs the norm as "healthy, active, and independent" and the abnormal as "silenced, mute, passive and childlike" (par. 1). Historically disabled people are often constructed as childlike objects of pity and charity. Simi Linton maintains that people with disabilities have generally been constructed within dichotomies of either pity and contempt and as heroes or monsters. Constructed as opposites, Ji-Won Park and Robert Wallin occupy either side of the disability dialectic.

Robert Wallin is everything Park is not. While the able-bodied Park is active, stable, and selfless, Wallin is constructed as lazy, volatile, and self-absorbed. Park is ambitious, hardworking, worldly, educated and upwardly mobile. Wallin is floundering, unable to work, uneducated and on a downward spiral. Rex Murphy (June 11, 2002) referred to Wallin as a "sadistic moron," a "thug," and a "vicious mutant." Park, on the other hand, is "an innocent young woman" and "bright, industrious, athletic, cheerful." Justice Dillon portrays Wallin as thus:

> Robert Wallin was a pathetic character of twenty-five years at the time of the offence. He lived with his parents, spending his days watching TV, playing on the computer, and bussing around town. He described himself in his police interview as a spoiled, lazy, middle class computer geek who lives at home, smokes marijuana, and sleeps in late. He has never been given a grade equivalent at school, and has always been in special homes or classes for the learning disabled. He has never had a driver's licence. He is unemployed, perhaps unemployable, as he has never held a job and is described as having few measurable skills. (*HMTQ v. Wallin* par. 12)

The judge goes on to describe in great detail court ordered psychiatric reports that outline a long history in the mental health system. Diagnosed with several mental disorders as early as age six, Wallin continued to be diagnosed with numerous and varied psychiatric conditions. Medicated for much of his life, Wallin is noted to be aggressive, anxious and paranoid without medication (*HMTQ v. Wallin* par. 13). Reporting on court proceedings, the media documented the findings on Wallin's psychiatric condition (Hall; *Crawford*; Bailey).

Contrary to the construction of Wallin as an uneducated, violent, alienated monster, the disabled Ji-Won Park is constructed as a heroine who aims to overcome her disability. Disabled people are accepted in so far as they affirm the normalcy of able-bodied people. Much like the figure of the innocent smiling child in a wheelchair who is exhibited on television telethons imploring for money (see Phillips), Park is a childlike figure admirable for her resolve and deserving of charity. Hogben (2004a) informs:

> She must use a wheelchair and is dependent on her mother and brother. She communicates with sounds she cannot yet form into words, by raising her left arm, or with an infectious smile that stretches from one side of her face to another. It's a smile that defies the sadness of her struggle. She dreams of the day when she can inspire others. She wants to be like recently deceased actor Christopher Reeve, who inspired others by battling to overcome spinal cord damage, her dedicated brother David explained. "If she can speak again by herself, she wants to give hope to people who are the same," David said haltingly, struggling occasionally with the unfamiliarity of English. "She has a dream to tell her story. How she overcame everything from almost being killed, almost dead, but she lives." It is a long way back for Ji-Won. Before she was attacked, she was in her fourth year of university studies. She was happy, outgoing and athletic. She spoke Turkish and French as well as Korean and English. (B5)

Whereas Wallin is described as a hopeless figure living off others and contributing nothing to the community, Park's recovery is defined as miraculous (*Bermingham* 2003: A4). Her expressive eyes are said to shine and her body to radiate joy as she battles to become a semblance of her former self (*Bermingham 2002*; Berry 2003a). David Hogben (2004a) titles a subsection of his article that outlines the chronology of the Ji-Won Park case, "Crippled Victim's Brave Fight" (B5). Crawford Kilian depicts an exaggerated heroic figure when he states that "[s]he is not confined to her wheelchair, but enthroned in it." Illustrative of the paternalistic and orientalist ways that Kilian constructs Park, he describes her as having a "karate punch of a smile." Those who critique the support of Park are said to do so because of a devaluing of disabled people (Mayencourt cited in Hogben 2004b).

Able-bodied or disabled, Park is positioned as a potential ideal citizen and an ideal figure of rescue. She is so since she is constructed as continuously aiming to strive to be the western liberal able-bodied subject who overcomes oppression and violence. Her desire for the west and her desire to overcome her disability represent the capitalist masculinist fantasy of "triumphant individualism" (Wang 267). Robert Wallin, on the other hand is a home-grown monster who must be segregated for the well-being of the nation. Justice Dillon agreed with the Crown and Defense that Wallin's nine-year prison sentence should be served at a regional health centre in order to treat his mental illness. Both narratives of the Asian Good Girl who strives to overcome her disability and the disabled, hopeless monster affirm ableist discourse of the normalcy of western constructs of health, ability, accumulation and consumption.

In addition to Ji-Won Park, another racialized body was implicated in Wallin's act of violence and saved through Canadian generosity. John Lightowlers came upon the unconscious Park when he was riding through Stanley Park on his bicycle to pick up a bag of cans he had previously left behind. The 26-year-old unemployed Ojibwa from Ontario collected cans for income. Lightowlers saw Wallin leaving the scene and detained Wallin until authorities arrived. Initially Wallin drew upon the stereotypical figure of a criminal and told Lightowlers and the police that he was running after a "giant, tattooed Black American ex-serviceman" he saw "straddling a Chinese female" *(HMTQ v. Wallin* par. 3; Proctor A3). Wallin later admitted that he did so because it was a convenient stereotype (Bailey A5).

Rather than being attacked by a fictitious savage Black male criminal, Park was saved by an heroic Aboriginal figure. Similar to most heroes, Lightowlers is described by the police and the media as a selfless hero who thought little of his own safety, who simply "did what he believed was right" and who does not consider himself to be a hero (Lazaruk A4). Described as gentle and soft-spoken, Berry (2003a) goes on to state that:

> Lightowlers is a bright, articulate man with a well-honed wit and easy-going demeanour. An Ojibwa, he was adopted at age three by a white family and grew up in Ontario. Currently on the hunt for a job, he's worked on farms and ranches and has worked as a volunteer with the disabled. (A6)

The portrayal of Lightowlers may be consistent with depictions of white heroes, however, as a racialized subject within a space made possible by the disavowal and selective commodification of Aboriginal peoples, the construction of Lightowlers cannot escape this legacy of colonial rule (see Mawani 2003b: 126).[5] Likewise, the construction of Wallin as a violent monster is not comparable to the construction of the Black male as the exemplary figure of violence and criminality. Within a white settler state structured along racial lines, Wallin's acts are the acts of an individual and exceptional to white males. Conversely, Black males are the symbol of degeneracy within a racialized logic that restricts their representation to fixed categories that uphold histories of slavery, colonialism and white supremacy. The predominance of this narrative of Black male criminality enabled Wallin to name the Black male body as the perpetrator of violence.

Historically Aboriginal men have largely been constructed as blood-thirsty savages and enemies of civilization or as noble savages and friendly sidekicks of the white male hero (Rollins and O'Connor). Lightowlers is a noble savage: A gentle, soft-spoken, easy-going, selfless man, untainted by western wealth and present in the "virgin" lands of Stanley Park. Shortly after the attack, the bike Lightowlers was riding the day of Park's attack was stolen. After the media publicized Lightowlers deeds and plight, an outpouring of generosity ensued with numerous offers of a bike. Lightowlers also received offers of employment inside and outside of British Columbia (Hall; Berry 2003b). Thus, the Aboriginal man who saved Ji-Won Park was ultimately saved by Canadian goodness. This erases the history of white settler violence that shaped Lightowler's economic poverty in the first place and restricts him from benefiting from the labour of his ancestors.

The representation of Aboriginal men as noble savages erases the violence of colonialism by reducing Aboriginal people to idealic, spiritual caricatures fixed in history. Referred to by Park and her family as, "an angel sent from God" (Berry 2003a: A6) Lightowlers remains an otherworldly figure untainted by white settlement. The simultaneous erasure and presence of Aboriginal people in Canadian history is evident in the history of Stanley Park. At the same time that Aboriginal people were being evicted from their land in the 1920s and 1930s, totem poles and "Indian villages" were being erected in Stanley Park as a symbol of Vancouver's identity (Mawani 2003b: 102). This deep ambivalence towards racialized bodies and of difference in general is an integral component of contemporary multicultural Canada. It informs the construction of Asian women in the current historical moment. While violence against those deemed "foreign" may at times be recognized and retributions made, the dominant narrative surrounding the violence routinely masks the histories that produce eastern desire for western modernity. The economic and political structures that generate the conditions for violence, and have been produced through violence are erased by narratives of Canadian goodness.

---

[1]This paper is a part of a chapter from my doctoral dissertation entitled *Constituting "Asian Women": Canadian Gendered Orientalism and Multicultural Nationalism in an Age of "Asia Rising."* The dissertation examines how the Canadian nation state in the late twentieth century and early twenty-first century produces itself as both global and national through the bodies of Asian women.
[2]The education and training of international students in Canada is estimated to have a CDN $4 billion impact (Holroyd 1). The English Language Teaching (ELT) industry accounts for more than 25 percent of this amount. Unlike other English language teaching countries, such as Britain, the Canadian ELT market

is heavily dependent on students from Asia, particularly South Korea, China, and Japan (Hiebert and Kwak; Canadian Association of Private Language Schools November 1). Vancouver is Canada's largest ELT market with over 60 percent of the market share. Over 75 percent of students studying English in the GVA are from Asia (Vancouver Economic Development Commission 7-8). The rapid growth of the GVA's English industry and the increase in percentage of foreign students who choose to study in British Columbia (rather than other provinces such as Ontario) is said to be due to the fact that foreign students are increasingly from Asia and Asian students tend to study in British Columbia (Iturralde and Calvert 3).

[3]Endorsement of lifelong financial support for Park was not unanimous or uncontested. Several letters and editorials published in British Columbia newspapers highlight the need to take care of our own and to stop giving special treatment to foreigners because they are foreigners. On January 26, 2003, *The Province* published a series of twelve short letters (A19) commenting on the government's decision to pay for Park's lifelong care. Of these twelve letters, five wholeheartedly supported the government's decision with no qualifications (McCarthy, George, Massignani, Bennett and Hansen), four were supportive and sympathetic but contained suggestions and qualifications (Brooker, Cardona, Holtby, Hopkins), and the remaining three letters did not support the government's decision (James, Rae, Larson). Nonetheless most public discourse on Park advocated Canadian life-long support for Park. In addition, both the comments that support Ji-Won Park and define her as representative of the Canadian nation and those that denounce elite acceptance of Park as one of us both contribute to the nation building process of defining the boundaries between desirable citizens and undesirable citizens. As Ang cites Hage, divergent opinions in public debates on the position of racialized minorities in white settler states do not disrupt power differentials which define white settlers as those entitled to define who and what is tolerated and racialized minorities as the ones being tolerated (39-40). Significantly, the self/other divide is reproduced through these deliberations.

[4]Throughout Canadian history, Asians have been routinely constructed in opposition to white subjects as representing all that was undesirable in building a model settler colony. From the late 1800s onward the Asian presence in Canada was often associated with a decline in Canadian standard of living based on narratives of cleanliness and disease (Mawani 2003a), crime (Anderson), national security (Oikawa), and miscegenation (Jiwani 2006). The exclusion of women and the separation of men and women was seen as crucial in inhibiting the development of Asian communities in Canada (Dua).

[5]See Culhane for an analysis of Aboriginal invisibility through the production of spectacles of consumption.

References

Ahmed, S. *The Cultural Politics of Emotion.* New York: Routledge, 2004.

Anderson, K. J. *Vancouver's Chinatown: Racial Discourse in Canada, 1875-1980.* Kingston: McGill-Queen's University Press, 1991.

Ang, I. "The Curse of the Smile: Ambivalence and the 'Asian' Woman in Australian Multiculturalism." *Feminist Review* 52 (1996): 36-49.

Armstrong, J. "Korean student in coma after attack in park: Her parents are asking that she be allowed to stay in Canada for rehabilitation." *The Globe and Mail* June 11, 2002: A8.

Bailey, I. "'Put me in jail,' begs man who beat jogger." *National Post* May 1, 2003: A5.

Bennett, R. "'Beautiful way of showing we care': It would be nice to do this for BCers as well." Letter to the Editor. *The Province* January 26, 2003: A19.

Berlant, L. *The Queen of American Goes to Washington City: Essays on Sex and Citizenship.* Durham: Duke University Press, 1997.

Bermingham, J. "Student's eyes flash new hope after attack." *Times-Colonist* August 11, 2002: A1.

Bermingham, J. "BC gov't will care for beating victim for life." *The Province* January 24, 2003: A4.

Berry, S. "'You are like an angel sent from God'." *The Province* May 4, 2003a: A6.

Berry, S. "Unemployed Stanley Park hero getting offers of jobs. *The Province* May 7, 2003b: A7.

British Columbia. *Legislative Assembly. Debates. 37th Parliament, 3rd Session.* Vol. 9, No. 16, 4 November, 2002.

Brooker, W. "'Beautiful way of showing we care': It would be nice to do this for BCers as well." Letter to the Editor. *The Province* January 26, 2003: A19.

Buttigieg, J. A. "Teaching English and developing a critical knowledge of the global." *Boundary 2* 26 (2) (1999): 45-57.

Canada. Parliament. *House of Commons. Debates, 38th Parliament, 1st Session.* Vol. 140, No. 37, 2 December, 2004.

Canadian Association of Private Language Schools. *Improving Canada's Competitiveness in Private Language Training World Markets, Policy Position Paper.* November 2003. Retrieved January 11, 2005, from http://www.capls.com/English/about/policy_position_paper_nov_03.pdf.

Cardona, G. "'Beautiful way of showing we care': It would be nice to do this for BCers as well." Letter to the Editor. *The Province* January 26, 2003: A19.

Crawford, T. "Vancouver man apologizes for choking Korean student, leaving her disabled." *Canadian Press NewsWire* May 9, 2003.

Culhane, D. "Their Spirits Live Within Us: Aboriginal Women in Downtown

Eastside Vancouver Emerging into Visibility." *American Indian Quarterly* 27 (3/4) (2003): 593-606.

Dua, E. "The Hindu Woman's Question." *Canadian Woman Studies/les cahiers de la femme* 20 (2) (2000): 108-116.

Fong, P. "Support grows for Ji-Won Park: Politicians, citizens, experts agree that Canadians should provide perpetual care for injured Korean student." *The Vancouver Sun* June 15, 2002a: A3.

Fong, P. "Stanley Park assault victim wakes from coma: Ji-Won Park, 22, has been taken for short day trips and recognizes family members." *The Vancouver Sun* August 12, 2002b: B1.

Fraser, K. "Patience, good PR pay off for Ji-Won." *The Province* October 8, 2002: A4.

Garber, M. "Compassion." *Compassion: The Culture and Politics of an Emotion*. Ed. L. Berlant. New York and London: Routledge, 2004. 15-27.

George, J. "'Beautiful way of showing we care': It would be nice to do this for BCers as well." Letter to the Editor. *The Province* January 26, 2003: A19.

Hadley, G. "ELT and the New World Order: Nation Building or Neo-Colonial Reconstruction." *TESOL Islamia* 2004: 1-25.

Hall, N. "Reluctant hero meets victim at attack site." *Times-Colonist* May 10, 2003: A3.

Hansen, B. "'Beautiful way of showing we care': It would be nice to do this for BCers as well." Letter to the Editor. *The Province* January 26, 2003: A19.

Hiebert, D. and M.-J. Kwak. *Transnational Economies of Export Education*. Working paper series No. 04-15. Vancouver: Vancouver Centre of Excellence: Research on Immigration and Integration in the Metropolis, July 2004.

HMTQ v. Wallin 2003 BCSC 809. Supreme Court of British Columbia. Docket 21618-3, May 23, 2003.

Hogben, D. "Choking victim's family wants an end to the threat of expulsion." *The Vancouver Sun* December 2, 2004a: B5.

Hogben, D. "Beating victim, family can stay in Canada: Mother, brother and sister shed tears of joy." *The Vancouver Sun* December 3, 2004b: A1.

Holroyd, C. *Canada Missing Opportunity in the Booming China education Market*. Vancouver: Asia Pacific Foundation of Canada, January 2006.

Holtby, L. "'Beautiful way of showing we care': It would be nice to do this for BCers as well." Letter to the Editor. *The Province* January 26, 2003: A19.

Hopkins, D. "'Beautiful way of showing we care': It would be nice to do this for BCers as well." Letter to the Editor. *The Province* January 26, 2003: A19.

Iturralde, C. and C. Calvert. *Foreign Students in Canada 1980-2001*. Ottawa: Citizenship and Immigration Canada, January 2003.

James, R. "'Beautiful way of showing we care': It would be nice to do this for BCers as well." Letter to the Editor. *The Province* January 26, 2003: A19.

Jefferess, D. The borders of compassion: The Canadian imaginary and its external others. *International Journal of Canadian Studies* 25 (2002): 43-67.

"Ji-Won Park's mother reads impact statement." *The Vancouver Sun* May 1, 2003: B7.

Jiwani, Y. "From Dragon Lady to Action Hero: Race and Gender in Popular Western Television." *Asian Women: Interconnections*. Eds. T. Hellwig and S. Thobani. Toronto: Women's Press, 2006. 161-182.

Jiwani, Y. "The Eurasian Female Hero[ine]: Sydney Fox as Relic Hunter." *Journal of Popular Film and Television* 32 (4) (2005): 182-191.

Kelsky, K. "Gender, Modernity, and Eroticized Internationalism in Japan." *Cultural Anthropology* 14 (2) (1999): 229-255.

Kilian, C. *Ji-Won's Progress*. May 26, 2005. Retrieved July 25, 2005, from http://www.thetyee.ca/News/2005/05/26/JiWonsProgress.

Larson, T. "'Beautiful way of showing we care': It would be nice to do this for BCers as well." Letter to the Editor. *The Province* January 26, 2003: A19.

Lazaruk, S. "Ji-Won's big wish: Student disabled by brutal attack longs to meet monarch." *The Province* October 6, 2002: A13.

Lazaruk, S. "Citizens, police officers honoured for bravery." *The Province* April 28, 2004: A4.

Lessard, M. R. "Civilizing Women: French Colonial Perceptions of Vietnamese Womanhood and Motherhood." *Women and the Colonial Gaze*. Eds. T. L. Hunt and M. R. Lessard. Washington Square: New York University Press, 2002. 148-161.

Ling, L. H. M. *Postcolonial International Relations: Conquest and Desire between Asia and the West*. New York: Palgrave, 2002.

Linton, S. *Claiming Disability: Knowledge and Identity*. New York: New York University Press, 1998.

Massignani, B. "'Beautiful way of showing we care': It would be nice to do this for BCers as well." Letter to the Editor. *The Province* January 26, 2003: A19.

Mawani, R. "'The Island of the Unclean': Race, Colonialism and 'Chinese Leprosy' in British Columbia, 1891-1924." *Law, Social Justice and Global Development* (1) (2003a). Online: http://elj.warwick.ac.uk/global/03-1/mawani html.

Mawani, R. "Imperial Legacies (Post) Colonial Identities: Law, Space and the Making of Stanley Park, 1859-2001." *Law Text Culture* 7 (2003b): 98-141.

McCarthy, L. "'Beautiful way of showing we care': It would be nice to do this for BCers as well." Letter to the Editor. *The Province* January 26, 2003: A19.

Mickleburgh, R. and M. Valpy. "A regal knack for making fondest dreams come true." *The Globe and Mail* October 8, 2002: A5.

Morton, B. "New home will help her healing: Assault victim, family move into new apartment." *The Vancouver Sun* January 24, 2003: B3.

Murphy, R. "Point of view." *The National-CBC Television* June 11, 2002.

Myers, C. "Students rally around Ji-Won." *The Province* June 19, 2002: A8.

Oikawa, M. "Cartographies of Violence: Women, Memory, and the Subject(s) of the 'Internment.'" *Race, Space and the Law: Unmapping a White Settler Society*. Ed. S. H. Razack. Toronto: Between the Lines, 2002. 71-98.

O'Neil, P. "Assaulted student won't be forced out." *The Vancouver Sun* June 20, 2002: A2.

Paddle, S. "The Limits of Sympathy: International Feminists and the Chinese 'Slave Girl' Campaigns of the 1920s and 1930s." *Journal of Colonialism and Colonial History* 4 (3) (2003).

Phillips, C. "Re-imagining the (Dis)abled Body." *Journal of Medical Humanities* 22 (3) (2001): 195-208.

Proctor, J. "Victim's family relives agony following Stanley Park attack." *Victoria Times-Colonist* May 1, 2003: A3.

Rae, H. "'Beautiful way of showing we care': It would be nice to do this for BCers as well." Letter to the Editor. *The Province* January 26, 2003: A19.

Rhee, J.-E. and M. A. Danowitz Sagaria. "International Students: Constructions of Imperialism in the *Chronicle of Higher Education*." *Review of Higher Education* 28 (1) (2004): 77-96.

Rollins, C. and J. E. O'Connor, eds. *Hollywood's Indian: The Portrayal of the Native American in Film*. Lexington: University Press of Kentucky, 1998.

Spelman, E. *Fruits of Sorrow: Framing Our Attention to Suffering*. Boston: Beacon Press, 1997.

Steffenhagen, J. "Queen pays tribute to BC's diversity: She enjoins Canadians to 'stand on guard' in the face of fresh challenges." *The Vancouver Sun* October 8, 2002: A1.

Vancouver Economic Development Commission. *Vancouver's English Language School Sector*. Vancouver: Vancouver Economic Development Commission, 2003.

Vennavally-Rao, J. "Queen wraps up visit in BC." *CTV News* October 7, 2002.

Wang, C.-M. "Capitalizing the Big Man: Yao Ming, Asian America, and the China Global." *Inter-Asia Cultural Studies* 5 (2)(2004): 263-278.

"Welcome home Ji-Won Park." *Vancouver Courier* December 5, 2004: 39.

UNA LEE

Our Bodies Are Battlefields

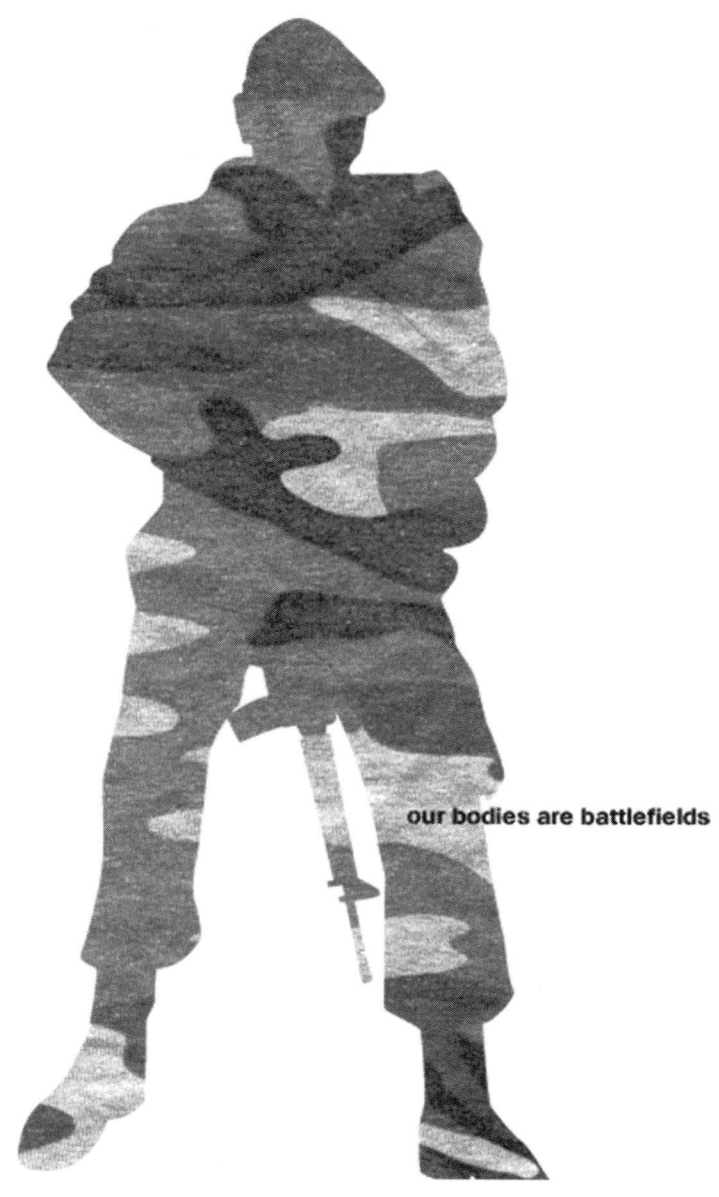

OUR BODIES ARE BATTLEFIELDS

NURI KIM

Back Home?

When I lived in Canada, English speakers talked about Korea as "back home" for me. Now that I am living in Korea, I sometimes feel Toronto is my "back home."

"Going back home" was never relaxing for me, nor really comforting. After a few weeks of staying at my parents' home when I returned to Seoul after having been away six-and-a-half years, I started looking for my own place. I worked on this urgent project for days.

My mother: *Why don't you stay at home?*

My father: *Take your time. Get some rest first at home.*

I told my father, *I can't get a good rest here.*

My sister Number Two, who lives away from my parents with her husband and kids, was sad when I said, "my parents' apartment is not my home."

At the time, I found an "officetel," a one-room studio with all appliances including a washing machine and an air conditioner. It had everything I needed in a tiny space. Seoul Forest was nearby but it was not really a forest and the officetel was not really homey.

Recently, I moved into a two-bedroom apartment surrounded by mountains. I have a veranda, a bedroom, and an office, but no living room or sofa. I didn't buy much furniture as I was worried about what to do with it when it comes time to move again. I never seem to have enough money to invest in nice furniture anyway. It is convenient to be a minimalist.

My friend Rosa calls herself a minimalist. She moves frequently with her cat, Mao. We used to live together and we were more or less a family. Like sisters, we often fought, but we also took care of each other. We even had a long distance fight through e-mails between Toronto and Seoul. Rosa used to be a successful fundraiser for a big international NGO. But as an eco-feminist, non-structuralist, and artist now, she does not find having a full-time job attractive. "I am not able to anymore," she says. "And I can live cheaply."

Rosa hasn't had a regular income for many years and, therefore, cannot show enough monthly income to even apply for alternative housing like a co-op, which is generally less expensive than other rental arrangements. Her recent art work focuses on homeless people.

Homelessness is very familiar to me. A friend who was in Toronto at the same time as I was, and now lives in Cuba with her sweet Cuban partner, also says she "does not know where her home is." We talked about the feeling of homelessness in Toronto.

The men sleeping in the City Hall subway station in Seoul are seemingly good at making their temporary home there comfortable. I always see them on the way home after working late. I see my friend and myself beside them.

Temporary home … I am used to it. I never know where I will go next or what I will do. Maybe I am a real "global citizen."

A good thing to learn from Buddhism and environmentalism is that this world is a temporary home to all living lives. We are just borrowing this world while we live here.

Thinking positively, I have many homes— at least two or three. Seoul, Toronto, and Busan, the harbour city where I was born and grew up, getting ready to become a migrant. Many faces pop up when I think of Toronto but only a few when I think of Seoul, Korea.

I thought I would free myself from the biological and psychological ties to my parents when I left "home" ten years ago, but I could not really do that. I think this is because I owe them—they gave birth to me, and they rasied me.

I cannot forget about my parents, especially my mother. My mother represents my worries, regrets, resentments, home of the gene for my scatteredness and forgetfulness, and … love. The poor social services for seniors in Korea adds to my worries when I am away.

I often think of Toronto and miss the city, the people, and the social environment in which I lived for more than six years as one of many outsiders living there. I thought I was starting a fresh new life.

Perhaps I felt Toronto was "homey" because there are so many outsiders—immigrants, refugees, sexual minorities, homeless people, and psychiatric survivors—out in the public receiving care from social workers and health professionals, and organizing themselves. I am not the only one who looks odd. There are many "odds" and together they make up the majority although they do not possess much power.

In Korea, the majority of people look the same and I am one of only a few "odds." As a Korean who has lived abroad, I am often categorized as a "foreigner." But, I was never called a foreigner in Toronto. I was Chinese, Japanese, Korean, an "international student" in the beginning and a "permanent resident" later on, but never a foreigner. Where do I belong more?

***

Phone rings.

"I am on ichat. Are you there?"

As always, without exception, it is Bona who is trying to wake me up in the morning. My eyelids are heavy but I am looking hard at my computer screen and the small round lens to show my face to him.

He is with his mother setting up a new computer for her. He asks me about what I plan to do for the day. I ask him how his day is going.

He calls me two or three times every morning to wake me up.

Soon, Bona will be in Korea with me for the third time since I left Canada. Although I look like a Korean in Korea, Bona does not, so he will be an obvious foreigner.

When he comes we will discuss whereabouts he and I might live. I have to think hard on where I will next call home.

I found the best solution though. My home is myself. It is inside me. Hopefully.

JULIE KANG

Here, at the Seams

This is the way that Mrs. Lee walks to the station on Tuesday afternoons at four o'clock. She leaves Kyung Min Lee his late lunch, getting cold now, on the counter of their store, and for the first few steps down Bloor Street, worries that she has forgotten something. A clean fork. A ready soy sauce packet from Lucky Restaurant. It is her routine. Remembering to consider what she may have forgotten.

 The late August weather has brought with it some relief from the heat of the summer. The fall-coming breeze, unfamiliar returning friend, breathes alongside her. She walks a little faster, hastening to beat the rush that is the end of the working day for, it seems, nearly half the city.

 She used to like to walk slowly. She imagines that if she just closed her eyes to just a little less than half shut, she could be that girl again, walking home on a gravel country path in tennis shoes. She imagines that this is a memory that could be walked through again, by this narrowing of the eyes. She saves this potential, like the extra lives seven-year-old Han Min Lee would exclaim distractedly about, playing his video games. Her son, now 27, going back into the line of fire again and again, maneuvering all these lives with just one hand.

 In that other land, Mrs. Lee walked with her eyes lifted high, high above the horizon, believing in the more-than-extra-life-giving power of Tomorrow. The only exception being the week when she got her first pair of tennis shoes at fifteen, new enough to have a rubbery smell, and spent the next two weeks looking down at them, at the way her feet put them into motion, as she walked and walked, and walked, forward.

 Bathurst Station is warmer than the air outside, and Mrs. Lee puts down her two canvas bags to find a tissue to wipe her forehead. The ingredients for homemade beef *mandoo* are bulky in the two bags. Three packages of flattened circles of egg pastry, long crisp sheaves of green onion, two packages of tofu. The ground beef is wrapped in paper and cellophane for preservation. This

Sunday is the east division's turn to serve at church, and they will begin preparing the *mandoo* early that morning. *Gyo-hae*, church translated into Korean. When Linda, her youngest, was five and learning everything in twos, she said "Go *hae*," and asked if people called it that to tell people to "go here," and then asked, when she learned in school about the difference between "here" and "there," when they would be visiting this other place called "Go there." At this, she'd given a stern correction, for principle's sake. "The Other place is not somewhere we want to go," she'd declared in perfect Korean, two lessons in one. It's a mother instinct within her, she figures, dividing the Good from the Bad, though behind the steady-voiced declaration are questions she used to ask herself.

It is nearing four-thirty, so Mrs. Lee gets her bags together, one on each side, plus her handbag, a Gucci knockoff her younger sister brought on her visit in '89, and heads towards the mouth of the stairs to the northbound train.

Wintertime, they came. Young ju and Ki ju thrilled to meet the "San-ta-Keu-Ra-seu Hal-abogee" at the mall, with Real Blue Eyes and Pink Cheeks, producing red-and-white candy canes from his big red stomach, like magic. Like in all the storybooks.

She arrives at the subway platform. It has been re-painted this summer. The warm orange that was the colour of walls when first she came here, before this store and the New life, before she had ever dreamt a dream in English, has been painted over a grey-blue, with a mural of graphics and stripes. As she waits for the rumble of the eastbound train, she tries to remember that colour.

In the old country, her mother had been a seamstress, and when Mrs. Lee came to this station for the first time in December 1976, this colour had struck her, reminding her of the shade of a dress that had hung in the house for a prolonged time; a customer had forgotten to claim it. They later found out that it belonged to a woman of high social class, daughter of a *yangban* class that could be traced from the Koryo era. She had died of tuberculosis and so her maid had not come to pick it up in the upheaval over the death of a woman with child.

That first year in Canada, Mrs. Lee, newly named, reacted almost physically upon seeing the variations on things she had known. They enchanted the young Mrs. Lee. She wanted to touch, taste, feel, *smell,* everything, disbelieving that she was really here. It was like finally living a tomorrow, before it could run away and become today or yesterday. She felt light and hopeful, perhaps in love. She laughed at the shapes of bottled drinks—"the Real Thing" it said in curliqued letters on one of them. Kyung Min read out the names to her in his English, much better than hers, and this one he read out like a present, like a promise made good on. She kept noticing the difference of the shape of electric sockets, the look of the dogs that people walked with and seemed also to talk with, the shapes of trees, barren, leafless, but the shape of a mysterious freedom and wideness when embraced and embracing such white, white snow. And then there were these orange subway walls in what was called "Little Korea." A sameness and a difference put each object in relief from its distant cousin.

With passing years, she has gotten used to the objects and ways around her, of course. It is the change of the landscape of the cities and even the country, and the way it is represented that she sees in the pop technicolour of Seoul-imported mini-series, now, that is startling to her. Surface as it is, she thinks that it must be reflection of things changing.

The first time she saw it, the news anchor in cream suit and impossibly large, doe eyes, and then read the article in the Korean newspaper, of the many women choosing to get "the double-lid operation" done, she could not believe the irony. That she did not have to leave her country to become an Other. She had laughed bitterly, but her heart was heavy and she could not quite explain why. She thinks that it is not out of sadness for them, but because of the feeling that something is shifting, changing there, moving forward without her. She feels unsteady. It is like one's memories changing with the things that happen in the present; do they not lose their essence in this change? She is sad. For the young girls in the article who say that they feel incomplete as they wait for their eighteenth birthdays, when they will finally be able to get it done. Like waiting to see through different eyes.

The train has arrived, and Mrs. Lee is surprised to find it almost full. There are no seats in sight, so, finding a spot by the doors, she tries to balance her bags in a comfortable enough posture.

"Today, I have been too slow," she thinks. "Why are my thoughts like this? Scattered and searching, like thoughts without a home?"

Her stomach tightens now. "I should have thought of what to make for Kyung Min to eat when he returns at eleven, and have I forgotten what the kids might need me to do…"

Suddenly she is reminded of Han Min's distant voice, calling from the probation office. "Driving under the influence," they called it. "It is this *Canadian* influence," she had wailed back, "what good has it done you? We came to this country for you, don't you know that? How could you? Take everything for granted!" And when there was no answer, "How did this happen-ed to us? What I did wrong?" her English broken in such crescendos of emotion.

A crisp official voice on the other line responded, "Mrs. Lee, will you or will you not be available to bail your son, Han Min Lee, out?"

Linda had stood silently, watching her mother on the phone, and then had begun clearing *banch'an* off of the table, transferring the condiments from the delicate serving plates to tupperware containers for the fridge. She had looked at her mother, her 57-year-old body overwrought with emotion, and walked out of the room, hugging her arms, letting the tears roam her face, soundlessly. This silent Linda, her closed mouth betraying nothing of the gushing phone conversation that trickles out, muffled, from behind her bedroom door at night. Mrs. Lee has gone downstairs to check the laundry a few nights in a row, unable to sleep, and has heard it. Too tired to be angry, and realizing it is not what has woken her up, and hearing Linda sound so happy, she tiptoes back to bed. "Is she in Love?" she thinks, a deep crease forming between her brows, wavering between relief and acute worry. *Who, who could it be?*

The doors of the train opening up with a low bell sound interrupt her thoughts. A Korean woman—her small face and features have that distinctive look, Mrs. Lee is pretty sure—and her husband?—a tall, red-haired man with pale skin, squeeze into the train beside Mrs. Lee. It isn't until there is a little more movement as people settle into standing positions around her that she sees the little face of a boy about the age of four or five peering up at her, and realizes that his little arms are clasped around the back of her legs. Her handbag and one of the canvas bags is grazing his bright auburn hair. The woman and red-haired man, settling in their spots, now turn to him and realize his mistake. "Ah! Yonggi-ah! Come here! Don't bug the nice *ah-jumma*!" the woman says in broken Korean-English. Yonggi's brown eyes widen and he blinks twice very fast, looking curiously at Mrs. Lee's face.

"I'm sorry! *Jesong hae yo,,*" the woman apologizes, "He thought you were his grandma," she explains.

"Didn't you, Yonggi, did you think she was *Halmoni*?" She smiles down at him, taking his hands. Her eyes are playful as she smiles, dark and bright crescent-shaped imprints. All this time, the red-haired man has been smiling apologetically towards Mrs. Lee. Now he draws closer and puts his arm around the woman and speaks, "*Jae ssong hae yo*," he says, bowing slightly. Mrs. Lee can't hide her shock at his near-perfect Korean. She replies, "Okay, okay. Thank you, thank you," speaking English instinctively. Before turning back to face the subway window, now out of the tunnel, she beholds the little one's face again and in beholding the simple wholeness of life that is in him, she is compelled and something breaks the cast of her thoughts, their sifting and searching for what things really are, their divisibility into memory or future.

With this, she turns, remembering that she is but a stranger on the subway, an aging woman starting to sweat from the weight of her bags. The train stops and she hears the family get off, their laughter, light as summer, trailing after them.

Soon it will be her stop. She watches with eyes hurting from the brightness of the sun, still aloft in the sky, as again the train moves forward, putting the landscape of Scarborough's graffitied playgrounds and backyards into motion.

MEROSE HWANG

The *Mudang*
The Colonial Legacies of Korean Shamanism

Fifteen years ago, if someone would have asked me what I thought of Korean shamanism, I would have had to plead absolute ignorance.[1] As an undergraduate Religious Studies major, studying Native American shamanism at the time, I understood shamanism to be a primordial religion similar to animism, practiced only by indigenous communities in a type of contradistinction from the governing state. It was then that a fellow student first revealed to me the existence of Korean shamanism. I was confused and captured by the possibility that Koreans identified with being "modern" and "indigenous" at the same time (but I was yet to make the important connection between the ideology of "indigenous" governance and colonial history until much later). In less than two decades, Korean shamanism went from being a virtually non-existent topic in Korean studies to making familiar appearances in many East Asian studies arenas. It has been examined through a wide spectrum of empirical and methodological research ranging from recording liner notes to ritual songs (Howard) to exploring consumer patterns for shamanistic services on the internet.[2] Most of the 1980s and '90s research on Korean shamanism were in the spirit of preservation. Field researchers went through great lengths to record and document *mudang* physiognomy, cosmology, epistemology, etc. But recently, with inspiration from post-colonial historians, shamanists have begun to question the very notion of "shamanism" in Korea (see Ch'oe; Han). Some scholars began to explore the nomenclature of "shaman" and of *mudang* (where previously, it was taken for granted that they were synonymous; see Kim, T.).[3] A few historiographers have concluded that the Japanese colonial government used Korean shamanism to serve imperial interests (Kim, S.; Walraven). Such patterns in scholarship have caused shamanists to deal with issues of race, gender, colonialism, and nationalism.[4] The conclusion post-colonial scholars have claimed is that "…the indelible Japanese imperial legacies of conquest and racism that were integrated into precolonial traditions of lineage-identity politics continue to dominate contemporary Korea's nationalist reconstruction of Korean ancestors and founders" (Pai, H. 20). To understand the mystique of Korean shamanism, it is necessary to trace its academic genealogy in Korea.

Mudang, Colonialism and Notions of Modernity

The emergence of shamanism in Korea is best understood by identifying it within Korean colonial history. The shaman subject was equated to a native female subject known as *mudang*. The first people to document *mudang* as "shamans" were British and American travel writers and Christian missionaries in Korea in the 1890s (Walraven). At first, westerners characterized *mudang* as female shamans who practiced "devil-worship" or who spread "superstition" (Bishop).[5] This *mudang* subject serves as a lens through which it is possible to assess the intellectual field of this period. *Mudang* have appeared as a vehicle to discuss an array of "modern" topics such as national history, science, technology, military, economics, etc. By studying the ways in which Korean intellectuals discussed *mudang* during the colonial period, it becomes apparent that most people writing about *mudang* saw them as a menace to the nation. They saw the nation (named variously as *kukka*, *urinara*, *uri kukmin*, *chosŏn*) in peril.[6] The nation retained agency insofar as it could be afflicted. *Mudang* explicitly antagonized the nation.[7] Most journalists that had anything to say about *mudang* during the colonial period saw *mudang* as the anti-nation. And in the most popular and political sense, writers who were invested in modernizing the state presented *mudang* as disturbing the nation's well-being. *Mudang* were said to contaminate the nation by generating and spreading diseases, illnesses, depleting national resources, and generally wreaking social havoc.

Mudang had an inherent impact on notions of the modern. This modernity discourse was the paradigm by which to discuss all things Korean in the early twentieth century.[8] To view the emergence of this discursive subject within a historical moment like the colonial period, it is worthwhile to situate it within a larger historical framework. A few of those profoundly influential historical incidents will be laid out here: Korea was coerced into an unequal trade treaty with Japan in 1876, which many historians have dubiously equated with the necessary enforced "opening" of Korea to the rest of the world, introducing the country to "modernity" (for a couple historiographical treatments of this issue see Deuchler, Kim, K.).[9] Japan's victories in their wars against China in 1895 and against Russia in 1905 allowed them certain leverage in negotiating political and economic territories throughout Asia. In 1905, Japan pressured Korea into signing Japan into a protectorate treaty. Five years later, on August 29, 1910, King Sunjong was forced to abdicate his throne making Korea an official colony of Japan. Japan continued to expand their colonial boundaries throughout Asia over the next 35 years until they were taken over by the U.S. on August 15, 1945. Japan surrendered itself to the U.S., and all of its colonies were divvied up between U.S. versus Soviet allegiances, also splitting the Korean peninsula between Sino-Soviet versus American military occupations.[10] Even today, the *mudang* discourse continues to be a part of the state project in South Korea.

Links have been commonly made between colonialism and modernity. The assumption is that colonialism, foreign aggression, and domestic insecurities caused colonized people[11] to "wake up" to the dangers of not being modern. Locating the "un-modern" subject—the shaman, the *mudang* (the Korean name that has become the most common equivalent to "shaman")—is a test of this theory. It is certain that the first time *mudang* were relegated to "shamans" was by foreign missionaries who wrote about devilish findings in Korea in the 1890s (Bishop; Landis; Wells). But, the discussion to chastise *mudang* was in existence in the Korean courts hundreds of years prior to these missionaries (Yi).[12] Without using the actual term "un-modern" the subject was treated as "un-civilized," "heterodox," and treated as subversive obstacles for the state.

Some major developments occurred just prior to and during the colonial period, affecting the discussion of the "un-modern" subject. The most important development was the emergence of popular presses in late nineteenth century Korea (Anderson).[13] In 1896, the first Korean/English bilingual newspaper, *The Independent*, frequently wrote about the problems around and ways to ban *mudang* from society (Schmid).[14] Also beginning in the late 1800s, the Meiji government erected academic institutions and commissioned ethnographic studies of their newly acquired archipelago territories and continued issuing state scholars to study the race and indigenous cultures of colonized subjects.[15] Through this colonial initiative, Korean "shamans" became case-subjects for Japanese imperial anthropology, ethnology, ethnography, and folklore studies. Another notable shift to the *mudang* subject during the colonial-era was that they became codified as women. Newspaper editors and ethnologists alike construed *mudang* as a flawed female gender. Korean nationalists were aligned with Japanese colonialists by correlatively discerning *mudang* as un-modern.

During the colonial period, the modern was unquestionably a part of the national project. If it was not explicit, it was always of inherent importance.[16] It also seems to have been implicit through notions such as *munmyŏng* (civilization), and *yamanin* (uncivilized people) (*Taehan maeil sinbo* 1910a: 2).[17] *Mudang* did not so much terrorize the "modern," as they were a reverse to the "modern." The threat was not so much to the "modern" itself, but rather, to the people and the nation that needed to "modernize." Popular press intellectuals used concepts like *minkuk* to inarticulately summon Korea as a national geo-political body, a local government under the Japanese empire, a common people and a population. This nebulous geo-political body was composed of people. When people were vulnerable or contaminated, the national body was weak. Colonialists and nationalists alike pushed for the *minkuk* to become modern and for people to do this by severing themselves from a part of themselves—the part that supported *mudang*.

By no means was this *mudang* discourse a subject that stood on its own. Many of the sources that touched on *mudang* during the colonial period were those that dealt with a larger problem of *misin* (superstition).[18] *Misin* was an abstract phenomenon that permeated society and was a much larger issue than *mudang*. Under the sanctions provided by the Government General on "official religions" (Chang), various religious sects voiced their concerns over *misin* and straying from "true" faith/ritual, to avoid being tagged as sacrilegious or otherwise "unloyal" to the empire (Park, K. 84).[19] Religious leaders served as nationalist and colonialist agents as they asserted that their religions/faiths were "modern" (Pak). They positioned their faith on a hierarchical model of reason and logic that assumed "superstitious faiths" (like those carried by *mudang*) contained no tenets or moral epistemologies and would hinder people's abilities to "spiritually advance." Writers wrote to publically pressure *mudang* and their followers to cognitively, spiritually change. When evangelism failed, criminal correction was enforced. Colonialist and nationalist writers assumed to plea for all Koreans but in singling out people like *mudang* they pitted individuals against each other. Writers wrote to criticize a Korean racialized identity. The narrative was wrought with ambiguities and contradictions while the *mudang* remained a steadfast enemy.

Gender Implications of *Mudang*: Constructing the Modern Korean Woman

Tension over individual rights and legislation were managed under a public program that allowed privileged male intellectual Korean subjects to govern their own affairs, by specifying the domains in which the local elites must initiate social institutions and help set the basic moral parameters and criteria. Discussion about the configurations and the boundaries of woman-ness were expressed through bi-monthly popular women's niche magazines like *Sin'gajŏng*, *Sinyŏja*, *Sinyŏsŏng*, and *Yŏsŏng*,[20] but the bulk of discussions around the "woman" problem—like *mudang*—were found in the general dailies and journals that were speaking to a male reading audience (*Tonga ilbo* 1933a).[21] These intellectuals urged the government, colonial "thought" and "hygiene police," alongside colonized communities, to hunt down these socially aberrant women (*Kaemyŏng sibo* 1935: 1).[22] *Mudang* were accused of inhibiting public peace, order, and regulation and were charged with adversely affecting public health and hygiene (*pogon uisaeng* [*Tonga ilbo* 1939]).²³ They were blamed for disregarding "modern" notions of "order and efficiency." *Mudang* were often described as young children, and sometimes, explicitly as girls, that needed to be taught a lesson or reprimanded through severe beatings. Such beatings were either relayed through police reports or were requests made by the intellectuals for the police to properly punish these evil women.²⁴

The social implications of *mudang* as women incriminated all women. The discursive *mudang* treated as a negative agent enabled a misogynist discussion about women as *punyŏcha* (married woman; lady; women and girls; women-folk [*Tonga ilbo* 1933a: 3; 1939])²⁵ in order to segregate and control womanly behaviour and activities. *Mudang* needed to be controlled for their trickery over ignorant, uneducated, illiterate women (*musikhan punyŏ* [*Tonga ilbo* 1933b; 1939]). Women at large were charged with enabling and promoting these *mudang*. Men set the gendered benchmark and under misogynist normative discussions where women became the deviants. Women were seen as the ones most closely tied to "old customs," with a natural affinity for things un-modern. They were blamed for supporting these enemies of the state just as *mudang* were used as a device to pressure, regulate, and control women. Women-at-large were implicated in jeopardizing the nation.

Women were a concern for the nation because they were seen as having the social duty to be competent bearers of future generations and mothers of the Korean people. Not only were *mudang* depictions of "wrong" women, but they were also discursive designs to create and manage gendered behaviour. Women were cast into the periphery of "modern civilization" by associating their gender to *mudang*. The displacement of *mudang* subjects was part of a masculinist model to categorize and totalize a multitude. These male-oriented writings consistently identified women in association with *mudang* as foolish, silly, stupid, simple, half/slow-witted, dull-headed (*musikhan, ŏrisŏk* [*Tonga ilbo* 1939]) presenting a public need to excise or cultivate parts of the population.

Mudang were entrenched in male intellectual prejudices against unregulated women's social spheres and boundaries. They were chastised for openly banging on drums and for disturbing public morals in broad daylight. They were accused of littering public spaces with ritual paraphernalia and berated for haplessly throwing precious food out onto the streets. They were seen as a nuisance to public safety, cleanliness, and order. They became trespassers and loiterers of the conceptual "modern space." They were often described as hiding and lurking in the dark. They were everywhere, yet suspiciously out of place, untraceable, and contagious. *Mudang* were unruly and wild. When the colonial space was a rare and coveted commodity meant only for people who could be properly confined, uniformed, and designed for proper behaviour, there was no place for women like *mudang*.

This premise was clearly laid out, not only in women's journals, or niche magazines, but in daily papers from this period. Through such writings, mothers were rallied to properly educate their children. They were also coached in respectable self-governance, among which included repelling *mudang* and *misin*-related activities. Urging these women to break from their "old habits" and to gain new knowledge, training, behaviours, etc. ... assumed that Korea's past generations were somehow insufficient or unproductive in the past. This coincided with larger discussions that grew especially towards the latter part of the colonial period, on "new women" and the "modern girl." Women as representatives for the nation played tenuously against a nation that was seen as too feminine. Colonial-era writers identified the national problem by rendering Korea as a weak and un-masculine nation (*Taehan maeil sinbo* 1910b).[26]

Cleansing the Nation: *Mudang* and Hygiene

A part of the "good mother" mobilization project included tutoring women on proper health and hygiene. This discourse was a common way of depicting the un-modern. Women were held responsible for dirtying and cleansing the nation. Again, *mudang* were typecast as obstacles to public health. They were seen as inherently dirty, foul, or otherwise unclean and unhygienic. Their "filth" was considered communicable, endangering the public. The *mudang* and hygiene connection revealed a relationship between controlling the physical and the spiritual bodies commonly found in modernity discourses (Foucault).[27]

One Christian journal, the *Kyŏnghyang chapchi*, captured this moment brilliantly in 1915. The writer juxtaposed a backward and non-believing *mudang* against a soon-to-be-Christian subject. In this story the writer claimed that a *mudang*, who had kept two bibles in her toilet stall, stumbled upon a soon-to-be-Christian proselytizer who asked her to give them to him, which she eventually did. There was no mention of why the *mudang* kept the bibles in the toilet but one can conjecture that these bibles were not only being neglected, they were being misused. Kept in the foulest part of the *mudang* residence, the bibles were defamed in the foulest way, making her actions and herself, not only sacrilegious, but also altogether contaminated. For the unknowing outsider, by keeping the bibles in her toilet stall, the *mudang* could have been seen as an oracle of defecation and her sanctuary a space that collected bodily waste. But, from the *mudang* perspective, the toilet stall was a space where dangerous and powerful spirits presided and the *mudang* could have deliberately placed the bibles there to rid the bibles of their spiritual efficacies (Kendall).[28] Although the original text did not describe the motive/reason behind the *mudang* actions, it was clear that it revealed an antagonism between Christian and *misin* epistemologies. The writer associated her actions with her toilet that made her private, un-clean, and dangerous. The *mudang* was clearly the antagonist who starkly contrasted the Christian protagonist.

This article further mentioned that after the man received the bibles, he was baptized and became fully converted and fully Christian. He later converted several members of his family. Once the man had the bibles out of the *mudang*'s possession, they were saved from defilement and destruction. The man became a hero for standing in harm's way by asking for, receiving, and using objects that could have been contaminated. Furthermore, not only were the bibles not wasted (figuratively and literally), they were constructively used to create new spiritual beings. The rightful, wholesome bearer was able to recover the bibles' productive potential. At the same time, this story reveals a moment when *mudang* and her actions (whether they were unwitting or deliberate) were inefficacious in transmitting filth. This type of story also successfully outlines a pattern in colonial-era discourses where the negative subject is treated as both a real and dangerous threat versus an immaterial and inconsequential nuisance.

Undermining the Power of Western Medicine and Science: *Mudang* as Threats to Physical Health

The portrayal of the unclean, unhygienic *mudang* worked in conjunction with *mudang* who created an environment of physical danger. Health issues, such as preventative medicines/practices, potential diseases, deaths, epidemics, and even uncleanliness (issues that may now be thought of as innocuous) were topics that were pervasive throughout the early twentieth century. The basic argument was that believing and participating in *mudang* services was a liability to one's health. One daily newspaper put it this way, "... when one's family is ill, they wander about not taking medicine until it becomes serious, and they go find *mudang* and *p'ansu* and buy ginseng medicine" (*Taehan maeil sinbo* 1908). *Mudang*, and those that sought them out, hindered the promotion of proper health care. These writers assumed that *mudang* and their patrons were opposed to "modern" forms of medical science. They depicted *mudang* as superstitious and "un-scientific." *Mudang* were depicted as disseminating wrongful and harmful information about preventative and curative procedures/medicines to the masses. A popular journal stated:

> ...when a superstition believer comes down with an illness, despite their symptoms, usually they first plead and ask the *mudang* or *p'ansu*, and after that process, go to get medicine. The fact exists that severe cases, that should be caught in the nick of time, are delayed, and innocent lives are lost.... We gravely regret these supposed medical cures' ill effects

that secretly seem not to cure people's illnesses and obliterates people's notions of science (*Kaemyŏng sibo* 1935).

Such writers advocated western-style hospitals and, on rare occasions, promoted licensed Chinese medicine (Shin).[29] Meanwhile, this meant that medical practices that were not publically recognized were totally inefficacious, if not dangerous. It could be further argued that these anti-*mudang* medicine writers were actually concerned with what they considered unsystematized, unregulated, uninstitutionalized and untraceable methods/products of health care.[30]

No Profits for the State: *Mudang* and the National Economy

Japanese colonial administrators worked alongside Christian missionaries to systematize, institutionalize, and centralize medicines and medical treatments throughout the colonial era. The Government General made this decision in order to back their "political ideology of the time as Western medicine was not just considered to be simply a form of medical treatment, but was also part of an ideology which justified Japan's rule over Korea" (Park, Y. 174). State advocates of western medicine did not merely criticize *mudang*-related health care as an alternative to other forms of health care. What was inherently at stake for the government was that such *mudang* services were a source of untapped capital. Nationalist writers also relayed the need to extinguish *mudang* practices for the interests of the national economy. It was understood that, "... *mudang*... wished on outcast people's good or bad fortunes, to swindle them out of their money" (*Taehan maeil sinbo* 1910b: 1). And, the reason that people relied on and supported *mudang* was because the masses were ignorant and bound by *mihok* (confusion, bewilderment, delusion, infatuation [*Taehan maeil sinbo* 1910b: 1]). Just as people were accused of wasting their precious resources, *mudang* were chastised for swindling. *Mudang* were also accused of illegal money-lending.

Mudang stood in the way of developing the state economy. The colonial government made the centralization of Korea's banking system a primary object for state agenda. But before the colonial period, many people in urban and rural areas of Korea participated in informal *kye* (rotating credit) systems.[31] Some notable characteristics of the informal *kye* was that they were mostly run by random groups of women as a means of savings, loans and investments — often for women who wanted to invest in small ventures or for family emergencies. The *kye* system usually operated on small-scale financial investments/returns and offered women credit alternatives independent of their husbands/in-laws decisions and without state-controlled centralized banking systems.

Mudang was intimately involved and invested in *kye*. She counseled and mediated on behalf of a *kye* recipient in a crisis situation. *Mudang* involvement in *kye* is best illustrated through the funerary or widow's *kye* (*sangbogye*) in which a community invested in mutual aid and reciprocity over a crisis situation. When widows became the primary decision makers over their homes, they were responsible to negotiate and cover costs for emergency household expenses like funerary processes (i.e., *mudang* charges to prepare and mummify the body and to conduct rituals for the deceased spirit and the surviving family). Women sought out *mudang* advice and services over their familial and communal crisis. Women participated in *kye* as proactive measures to secure and save their monies independent of their family's dictates. They voluntarily invested in *kye* associations through word-of-mouth and they were meant to operate collectively but because they were based on the good faith of each of its members they were not without risk.

Mudang thus directly challenged such state-governed public initiatives. Colonialists recognized that they were overlooking useful resources through such undocumented workers. They found it in their best interest to spearhead the *mudang* project. Under the guise of cultural tolerance, the Japanese colonial government enstated "The Regulations of the Preservation of Korea's Ancient Remains and Relics" in 1916 and erected Korea's first colonial museum in the following year. The colonial government started the tradition of preserving *mudang* as shamans (Pai and Tangherlini; Pai). *Mudang* were registered as colonial relics. They were then recognized by the state, granted special tax exemptions, and given license to conduct official "indigenous" ceremonies (Siddle).[32] The Korean dailies reported exclusively on unregistered *mudang* as criminals (rather than as women whose work was not good or useful enough for colonizing purposes). While this registry was presented as a part of the government's endeavour to appear culturally sensitive and accepting of "things Korean," it enabled the government to further control its colonial subjects by identifying *mudang* and their associates whereabouts, tracking their activities, income, etc. to bolster the state. But the preservation project did something even more powerful for the colonizer—it enabled them to unify and personify a Korean racialized subject through the negative depictions of *mudang*.

Criminalizing *Mudang* and Strategies of National Revival

Korean nationalists believed that unregulated bodies meant a loss of resources and a loss of production for the country. The concern to accumulate wealth was shared by colonialists and nationalists alike. A *Taehan maeil sinbo* editorial traced the wasteful life of a *mudang* named Suryun. In one issue, the editor implied that Suryun continued to throw away her money on *mudang* activities while the editor was, "left eating cold rice" (1910c: 2). One pervasive theme throughout the colonial period was that *mudang* caused national waste. A *Kaemyŏng sibo* article estimated the total amount of money lost to *mudang*. They claimed that there were approximately 18,000 *mudang* in Korea.[33] The conclusion was that over 4,471 schools could have been built in the amount of money that was wasted on *mudang*. This article lamented how rice was so scarce and yet so much of it was being wasted on and by *mudang* (1934: 6). Rice was wealth and *mudang* represented the hole in the national basket through which it was lost. From the 1930s onward, the Korean population underwent grave rice shortages and famines as a direct result of the Japanese mass war mobilization policies. This crisis caused many colonial era writers to use the rice shortage issue to rally public concern. The conclusion here was that the economy that circulated around the *mudang* was a useless and calamitous burden on the nation and its people. The waste of rice often arose in these arguments, not only to recall the tax burden issue in people's minds but it was often used metaphorically to provoke a sense that the nation and its people were being starved out in order to feed greedy and selfish *mudang*.

The solution to this problem was to criminalize *mudang* in order to suppress and eventually eliminate their activities. While a few *mudang* were made to officially represent the Korean race, others were fined, beaten, incarcerated, or continued their work under the radar of the state and police. This animosity towards *mudang* continued after Korea was liberated from Japanese colonial rule but it did not succeed in ridding the nation of them. Instead, the Korean cultural revisionism project in the form of a Cultural Protection Policy that started in the 1960s (Yang) borrowed directly from the colonial preservation project. President Park Chung-hee adopted colonial era techniques and strategies to design and mobilize a hyper-industrialized Korea (Choi). Still today, *mudang* represent the nation, to rally and orchestrate the Korean citizenry around a primordial mother. The current Korean shamanism field is a cultural relic of Korea's dynastic, colonial, and post-liberation statecraft and continues to be a technology of national governance (Choi).

Un-hinging *Mudang* from Colonialism

This paper has attempted to deal with the movement to expel *mudang* in Korea during the colonial period. My goal was to raise issues that would offset our current images of Korean shamanism as a naturally recognized Intangible Cultural Property (Yang). Shamanism, as I understood it several years ago, was an alluring image that represented national pride (primordial, indigenous mother). It was during my senior year at the University of Colorado that I studied my first image of a *mudang* on the cover of "The Shaman's Drum." I was mesmerized by the possibilities and significance of this "modern indigene" in Korea. Several years later, I learned to credit the popular narrative that glorified this tradition back to the so-called "ethnic nationalists" of the colonial era, such as, Yi Nŭng-hwa, Son Chin-tae, Ch'oe Nam-sŏn, and even Sin Ch'ae-ho. These scholars envisioned shamanism as Korea's philosophy, epistemology, and origin.

The modern South Korean state's promotion of shamanism has untraceably purified the unclean body of an earlier discursively "contaminated" *mudang*. This post-colonial state project has subsequently erased the fact that nationalists under the hegemony of "colonial modernity" once urged Koreans to expunge all traces of *mudang* from the nation at the same time the Government-General was displaying them as icons of their indigenous Korean colonial subjects. The far more pervasive notion that "*mudang* contaminated" the nation (which was a concern for local intellectuals for the larger part of the twentieth century) has just begun to gain attention in contemporary shamanism studies. A few historians have recently explored the collaborative efforts of Korean intellectuals and Japanese colonial administrators to repress shamanism in Korea. But in order to step back through the process of uncovering how an abhorred "indigene" becomes a symbol of a "glorious" nation, I have attempted to look at the ways in which *mudang* were used to identify notions of "indigeneity" for the purposes of the state

Throughout Korean history, *mudang* were subjects that put the country at risk. The dialogue was largely internal, involving Korean authors and subjects. These writers were connected to their "indigenous" subjects, raising the stakes in the mission to "other" these subjects. They lambasted *mudang* in order to overcome their own selves, to create newer subjects for a foreseeable modern nation. This focus has allowed a glimpse into the complexities around these early twentieth- century Korean intellectual debates. Nationalists envisaged a homogenous modern nation while they were immersed in colonial ideologies in a copasetic struggle to become a modern Asian race, capable of overcoming colonialism and gaining "independence." Via the assistance of shamanism scholars, the South Korean state has regulated *mudang* and their practices/ services in such a way that has aided nationalist projects and further excluded an already disenfranchised and alienated population of "indigenous" spiritual experts, calling "liberation" from colonialism into question. The current national celebration of *mudang* reveals the amnesia of the earlier colonial project that inspected, categorized, criminalized, and ostracized *mudang*. This national ideology is uncritical and non-reflexive of how and why they use "culture." While the South Korean government continues to sponsor *kut* (*mudang* rituals) to promote cultural nationalism, they need to first summon their own colonial legacies, and reconcile the violence and oppression Koreans continue to experience under the post-liberation "indigenous" government in order to ultimately exorcise the ghosts of colonialism.

[1] Shamanism might be defined as "a religion practiced by indigenous peoples of far northern Europe and Siberia that is characterized by belief in the unseen world of gods, demons, and ancestral spirits responsive only to the shamans; *also*: any similar religion" (*Merriam-Webster Dictionary* 2001: 1073).

[2] Google provides over a million hits under the search: "Korean shamanism" and is featured on the Korean Tourism Board (see, for example, <http://mudang.view.co.kr> and <http://shamanism.view.co.kr>).

[3] Tae-kon Kim was among the first modern scholars to question the legitimacy of *mudang* and the application of the term "shamanism."

[4] What continues to be missing from this discussion is the relationship between class, economy and shamanism—this is telling to the fact that the ones that write about shamanism in Korea continue to be the educated middle-class, unable or unwilling to discuss the problems of being self-appointed ambassadors for the often poor, rural, and otherwise disenfranchised women they are meant to represent. I am also implicated in this.

[5] These days, it might be less objectionable to characterize *mudang* as spiritual mediators who intervene in family and community crisis by being mediums and intercessors between disgruntled ancestor spirits and their living descendants. Laurel Kendall has conducted the most prolific research on contemporary western understanding of *mudang* (or what she more respectfully calls *manshin*).

[6] These obfuscated concepts of the country have been interpreted into present notions of nation.

[7] At times some other subjects were categorized alongside *mudang*, such as the *p'ansu* and *chŏmchaengi*, but the most commonly accused were *mudang*.

[8] Because of the limits of the scope of this project, this essay can only lay out a very superficial outline surrounding this historical period. The moments that are highlighted here have been commonly seen as some of the most important moments in Korea's modern history but should not be interpreted as comprehensive in any way nor should they be understood as ruptures in Korean history.

[9] This teleological understanding of Korea's "awakening to modernity" problematically privileges western imperialism and Meiji Japan's adoption of western "gunboat diplomacy" while ignoring Korea's long history of active non-western trade relations with Tsushima, Ch'ing, and Southeast Asian countries in the "late pre-modern" period.

[10] Some modern Korean historians have argued that Korea was never released

from colonial rule — and that even today, South Korea suffers from an American form of economic and military colonialism.

[11] This typically referred to non-white nation-states, where the power divide was clearly demarcated between white and coloured race-based nations. But in the Korean case, it was between Japanese and non-Japanese. A similar kind of logic was used during the colonial period where Japan fluctuated between distancing themselves as *the* "westernized" Asians one the one hand, while claiming themselves as the pioneers of "pan-Asianism" on the other, in order to assert their racial authority and to foster their expansionist endeavours in Asia.

[12] In 1927, Yi Nŭng-hwa, accompanied by Ch'oe Nam-sŏn were the first scholars to trace the historical roots of *musok* ("shamanism") in Korea's pre-modern Chosŏn period.

[13] Benedict Anderson popularized the theory that nationhood and nationalism derive from the development of print capitalism.

[14] The Korean language version of this paper, entitled *Tongnip sinmun*, was published strictly in vernacular *han'gŭl* without the use of Chinese characters, which was a radical literary innovation. This press was shut down in 1899. For an in-depth look at the controversy around early pre-colonial presses, see Schmid.

[15] For an in-depth treatment of the Meiji government's race-research projects on its "internal colonies," see Siddle.

[16] I am interpreting ideas of the modern from words that I have found from this period, such as *kŭndaesahŏe* and *hyŏndaesidae*.

[17] A good illustration of the impacts of *mudang* on the "modern" can be seen in this article in which a Japanese man ias alleged to have requested permission from the government to worship *mudang*. In a later article, the same man allegedly encourages the works and worship of *mudang*. The editor suggests that this was unthinkable in Korea when Korea was a more civilized (*munmyŏng*) country than Japan — a country of evil spirits (*makui*).

[18] During the Chosŏn dynasty, the term was used to equate "heterodoxy" as a challenge to Confucian state ideologies of "orthodoxy" (see Han; Walraven). This discussion became especially pronounced during the colonial period where people were writing about proper types of religious faiths as they were juxtaposed to *misin* under the restrictions of the Government-General's religion policy (see Chang). A good example written during the colonial period can be found in religious journals such as the *Chŏndokyo hŏewolbo*.

[19] During the colonial period, two major streams of debates around religion flourished. The first was the "discourse of religion as a sign of civilization: which asserts that religion can control and lead the development of civilization." The second was the "discourse of religion as a tool of edifying people: which

holds that religion plays a central role in establishing national identity and edifying people."

[20] Women's magazines were mostly in publication from the mid 1920s through 1940. Nearly 90 percent of the Korean population was literate in the 1920s. Of this group, literate women comprised a very small and nearly negligible percent.

[21] This article entitled, "Controlling *Mudang*: Deceiving Rural Women in Namhaesŏ District" effectively illustrates the misogynist paternalistic concern over the female population.

[22] This editorial states that *mudang* were "violating public order and good customs ... we sincerely hope that social oppression and government will be more strictly enforced."

[23] This particular article comments on the "appropriate" incarceration of *mudang* in the Sŏdaemun office — a colonial-era prison known to be the closest proximity to the capital city centre.

[24] However, it would be misleading to say that the female subject was the only gender that was "divisive," especially when, as noted above, *p'ansu* were commonly named alongside the *mudang*.

[25] Sometimes spelled: *punyŏ* (abbreviated form).

[26] In this newspaper article, the editor explains that the weak Korean nation can become strong if they do things such as abolishing *mudang* and building up the military. The editor foresees this as the method for Korea to become a strong twentieth century nation.

[27] Michel Foucault details this theory and its application in much of his work, but can be seen especially in his book, *The History of Sexuality*.

[28] This second interpretation was explained to me by Dr. Laurel Kendall (a leading Korean shamanism expert) while she chaired our panel at the Women's World Congress in Seoul, 2005.

[29] Standardizing western medical practice versus Chinese or "Eastern" medicine was a much-contested issue under Japanese colonialism.

[30] During the Chosŏn, there were also discussions to discourage *musikhan* ("ignorant" referring to unregulated medicines), in favour of Chinese medicine. Such discussions did not include notions of modernity per-se, but were nonetheless "pre-modern" state objectives to centralize medical practices.

[31] This system has commonly been used in pre-modern China, Korea, Japan, Taiwan, and Indonesia. It is still very common practice throughout South Korea. It is a system of mutual aid and cooperation through a social mechanism that effectively draws unrelated women together for a common financial purpose of lending and borrowing money from amongst each other.

[32] Long before the colonial period, *mudang* were considered illegal and were forbidden within the limits of the capital city. Such restrictions were not heavily

regulated and many instances were found when *mudang* appeared within the Chosŏn courts. Generally speaking, *mudang* had a long history of condemnation where their work was not secured in private nor in public. So, there were often stories about how *mudang* were caught and incarcerated for disguising themselves as other professional trades in order to earn their keep. When *mudang* were unregistered they were invisible, and due to the lack of such records, it is difficult to know for certain what their numbers were. The important shift that occurred with colonialism was not in officiating and criminalizing *mudang*, but rather in the importance of "indigenizing" this process to localize a "foreign" colonial government. Richard Siddle makes a persuasive argument on how a similar method was used to mobilize the Ainu community.

[33]The editor states that the estimates and figures were originally printed in the *Asahi* newspaper (no date or issue) and does not explain how these numerical figures were originally calculated.

References

Anderson, Benedict. *Imagined Communities*. 1983. London: Verso, 1991.

Bishop, Isabella Bird. *Korea and Her Neighbours*. 1898. Seoul: Yonsei University Press. 1970.

Chang, Pyŏng-kil. "Chosŏn ch'ongdokpu chonggyo chŏngch'aek" (Religious Policy of the Chosŏn Government-General). *Hanguk chonggyo wa chonggyo hak*. Seoul: Ch'ŏngnyŏnsa, 2003. 217-233.

Choi, Chungmoo. *The Competence of Korean Shamans as Performers of Folklore*. Unpublished doctoral disseratation, Indiana University, 1987.

Ch'oe, Sŏk-yŏng. *Ilje ha musokron kwa shingminji kwŏllyŏk* (*Discourse on Shamanism in Colonial Korea*). Seoul: Sŏgyŏng munhwasa. 1999.

Deuchler, Martina. *Confucian Gentlemen and Barbarian Envoys: The Opening of Korea, 1875-1885*. Seattle: University of Washington Press, 1977.

Foucault, Michael. *The History of Sexuality: An Introduction*. Trans. Robert Hurley. New York: Random House, Inc., Vintage Books Edition, 1990.

Han, Do-Hyun. "Shamanism, Superstition, and the Colonial Government." *The Review of Korean Studies* 3 (1) (2000): 34-54.

Howard, Keith. *Bands, Songs, and Shamanistic Rituals: Folk Music in Korean Society*. Seoul: Royal Asiatic Society, Korea Branch, 1989.

Kaemyŏng sibo. "Chŏnjosŏn ŭi mudang i sipp'alchŏn sŏk ŭl mŏkŏpse: ilnyŏnkan ŭi t'onggye" (Chosŏn's mudang consume 180,000 sŏk of rice: Statistics over one year). 6 July 1934: 6.

Kaemyŏng sibo. "Misinpangmyŏng ŭi undong ŭl ch'okham" (Demand for movement to exterminate superstition). 15 May 1935: 1.

Kendall, Laurel. *The Life and Hard Times of a Korean Shaman: Of Tales and the Telling of Tales.* Honolulu: University of Hawaii Press, 1988.

Kim, Key-Hiuk. *The Last Phase of the East Asian World Order: Korea, Japan, and the Chinese Empire 1860-1882.* Berkeley: University of California Press, 1980.

Kim, Seong-nae. "Hanguk ŭi syamŏnichŭm kaenyŏm hyŏngsŏng kwa chŏnkae" (Development and Foundation of the Basic Concept of Korean Shamanism). *Hanguk syamŏnichŭm hakhoe.* Seoul: Syamŏnichŭm yŏngu, January 2003. Unpublished.

Kim, Tae-kon. *Korean Shamanism: Muism.* Seoul: Jimoondang. 1998.

Kyŏnghyang chapchi. "Mudang syŏngkyochaek ŭl chŏnhayŏk: tyŏnchu kyohŏeb" (A Bible that was Given to a Mudang: Roman Catholic Church Report). 9 (326) (May 1915): 221.

Howard, Keith. *Bands, Songs, and Shamanistic Rituals: Folk Music in Korean Society.* Seoul: Royal Asiatic Society, Korea Branch, 1989.

Landis, E. B. "Notes on the Exorcism of Spirits in Korea." *Journal of the Buddhist Text and Research Society* 3 (3) (1895).

Merriam-Webster. *Collegiate Dictionary, Tenth Edition.* Definition entry page 1073. Springfield, Mass.: Merriam-Webster, Inc., 2001.

Pai, Hyung-Il. *Constructing Korean "Origins": A Critical Review of Archaeology, Historiography and Racial Myth in Korean State-Formation Theories.* Cambridge: Harvard East Asian Monographs, 2000.

Pai, Hyung Il and Timothy R. Tangherlini, eds. *Nationalism and the Construction of Korean Identity.* Berkeley: Institute of East Asian Studies, University of California, 1998.

Pak, Sa-chik. "Ch'omisinchŏk yŏ ŭi chonggyokwan" (The Religious View of Transcendental Superstition). *Chŏndokyo hoewolbo* 179 (August 1925): 5-8.

Park, Kyutae. "Religion, National Identity, and Shinto: A Comparative Study on State Shinto in Japan and Colonial Korea. *The Review of Korean Studies* 3 (1) (July 2000): 76-92.

Park, Yunjae. "Anti-Cholera Measures by the Japanese Colonial Government and the Reaction of Koreans in the Early 1920s." *The Review of Korean Studies* 8 (4) (December 2005): 169-186.

Schmid, Andre. "Censorship and the Hwangsŏng Sinmun." *Korea Between Tradition and Modernity: Selected Papers from the Fourth Pacific and Asian Conferences on Korean Studies.* Ed. Institute of Asian Research. Vancouver: University of British Columbia, 2001. 158-171.

Shin, Dongwon. "'Nationalistic' Acceptance of Sasang Medicine." *The Review of Korean Studies* 9 (2) (June 2006): 143-163.

Siddle, Richard. *Race, Resistance and the Ainu of Japan.* London: Routledge, 1996.

Taehan maeil sinbo. "Kyŏngdyech'yŏcha pyŏnginamyŏn" (When one's family becomes ill). 30 August 1908: 2.

Taehan maeil sinbo. "Ilin chyungmok iranchya nŭn" (A Japanese person by the name of chungmoku). 19 February 1910a: 2.

Taehan maeil sinbo. "Isipsyegŭi sŏmun" (Twentieth-century nation). 26 February 1910b: 1.

Taehan maeil sinbo. "Mudang yomul syuryun i" (Suryun, a wicked mudang). 10 March 1910c: 2.

Tonga ilbo. "Kiinp'yŏnmul ŭl jŏnŏpŭ ro mudang dobae rŭl ŭngjing" (Mudang who did deceptive work). 2 March 1939: 2.

Tonga ilbo. "Mudang ŭl ch'uich'e: nongchon ŭi punyŏ rŭl soki nŭn haeng ŭi namhaesŏ esŏ" (Controlling mudang: deceiving rural women in namhaesŏ). 24 June 1933: 3.

Tonga ilbo. "Sahoe rŭl tokha nŭn mudang" (A mudang who is poisoning society). 29 October 1933.

Walraven, Boudewijn. "Popular Religion in a Confucianized Society." *Culture and the State in Late Chosŏn Korea*. Eds. Jahyun Kim Haboush and Martina Deuchler. Cambridge, Mass.: London: Harvard University Press, 1999. 160-198.

Wells, Kenneth M. *New God, New Nation: Protestants and Self-Reconstruction Nationalism in Korea, 1896-1937*. Honolulu: University of Hawaii Press, 1990.

Yang, Jongsung. *Cultural Protection Policy in Korea: Intangible Cultural Properties and Living National Treasures*. Seoul: Jimoondang, 2003.

Yi, Nung-hwa. "Chosŏn musokko" (A Study of Korean Shamanism). *Kaemyŏng sibo* (*Enlightenment Bulletin*) 19 (1927): 4-85.

ELAINE K. CHANG

Irony

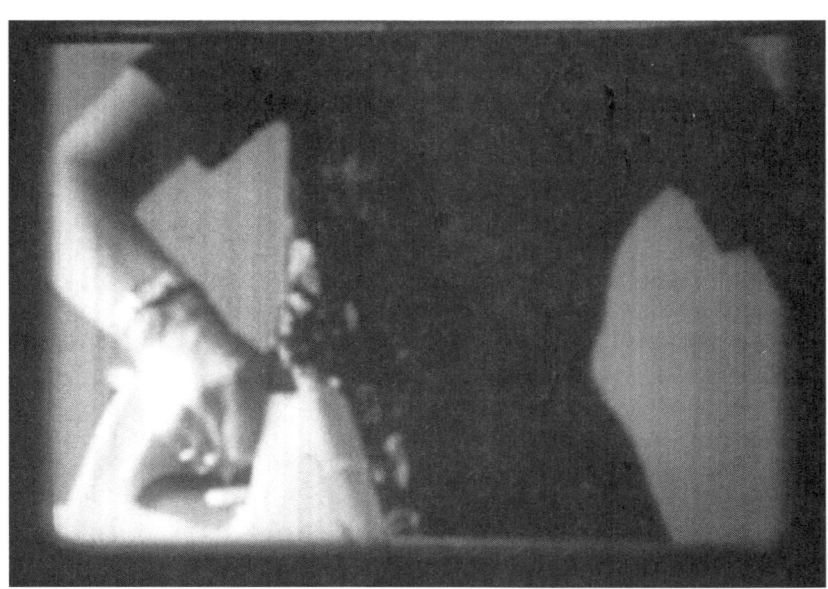

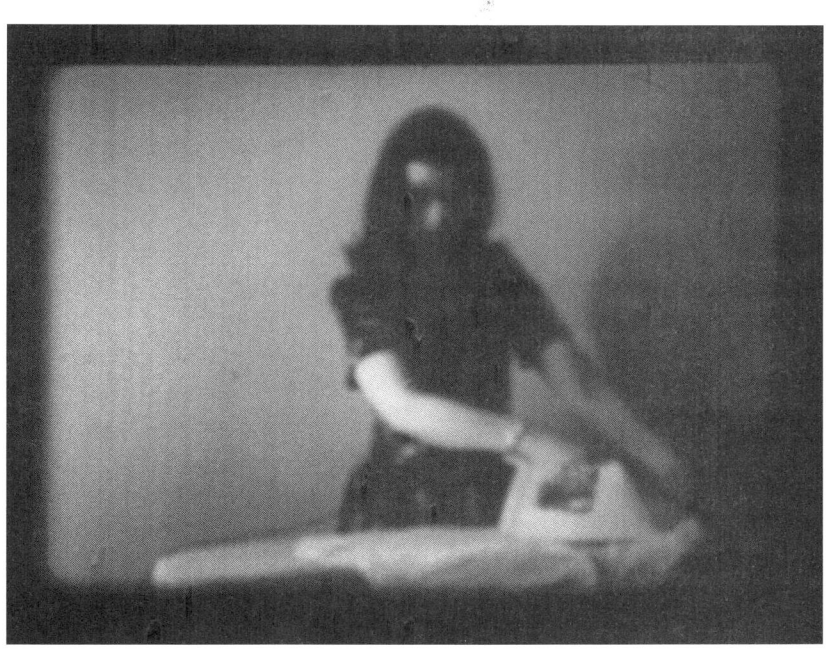

Still 1:

Trained hands, metal and steam sing songs of freedom…

Still 2:

…Not to mention progress!

Still 3:

Press to impress, onward, upward, to the summit of Mount Everpressed!

Still 4:

Laundresses of the world, unite. You have nothing to lose but your stains.

Elaine K. Chang's recent work bridges the creative and the critical, taking a playful approach to persistent, at times painful, questions of identity and place, memory, desire, and progressive politics. "The Education of Misses Kim" employs modified forms of written expression—faux variants of the essay and memoir, what she calls the "crushed haiku"—in a meditation on imperfect translation between Korean and English, and between a Korean immigrant mother and her Canadian-born daughter. In the experimental short, "Irony," a woman, a steam iron, and a wrinkled shirt collaborate and clash in a satirical parable of power, subordination, and imposed uniformity.

Thanks to Kevin Lim, for capturing and editing these photographic images.

III.
Bodies and Beyond

SUZY YIM

Identities

Learning as an Ongoing Process

I believe that learning never stops, no matter how well you've been "educated" or how old you are. I am forever learning and I still have a long way to go. This is my disclaimer.

"Is That a Girl or a Boy?"

Neither. Both. My gender is fluid, I have many genders and I present them both on stage and in everyday life. I am a drag king, a burlesque dancer, and an overall gender-bender. Binaries make me sad because they exclude all of the beauty that lies between; they suggest that you should be one or the other, not both, not neither, and you definitely shouldn't move around.

To me, being a gender performer is a way of celebrating the many colours of gender while entertaining. It's an opportunity to tell a story, fight oppressive stereotypes, or simply mock their ridiculousness. I want to be a rugged king who isn't misogynistic and a fierce femme who confidently embraces her sexuality.

"Are You a Lesbian?"

No, I'm queer, and no, it's not the same thing to me. Labels pose constraints because of all the language and assumptions that are tagged along with each word. People call me a lesbian but I do not fit the stereotype of a white middle-class womyn living with her partner and sixteen cats, who makes love wearing a flannel shirt as k.d. lang plays in the background. When people find out I have relationships with men they often assume I'm bisexual, but I believe there are more than two genders and I also don't identify as a confused, sex-craved femme who sleeps with her neighbour so her boyfriend can watch. This is absolutely not intended to be judgmental or phobic, or to devalue those who identify with the words "lesbian" or "bisexual;" rather, it is meant to acknowledge that stereotypes exist and while some people may happily fit these descriptions, I do not.

I love the word "queer" because although it too is a label, it's one that acknowledges the problems of labeling and expresses things in a more inclusive and fluid manner. To me, one of the most beautiful parts of the word "queer" is that what was once used as a form of marginalization is now reclaimed as a form of empowerment. I love that I am not "normal." My sexual orientation is queer, my sexuality is queer, my gender is queer, my politics are queer; I am queer.

"Where You From?"

I often find myself tokenized as a member of some sort of ridiculous pan-Asian, taste-of-the-orient group that consists of little bits of distinct cultures that people seem to think are all the same. Then there are those who are too smart to pool all the cultures together, so they ask "where are you from?"

I reply, "Toronto."

Shaking their head they say, "nah, I mean what are you?"

What are you trying to ask me? Are you really trying to gain a better understanding of who I am, or are you trying to place me into neat little boxes by asking me questions like what my "race" is. Identity is not neat, nor, in my opinion, should it be. I, for one, am fucken messy and I like it that way.

Sometimes, when I'm feeling generous I'll say, "I was born in Canada but my parents emigrated from Korea." Sometimes I stubbornly dance with my opponent and repeat the word "Toronto" until they sigh and give up. Yes, I'm Korean, but that's not all I am, and why does it matter so much anyway? If I tell people I'm Korean they ask, "North or South? Should I be scared? Hey, do you people have toilets yet, or are you still using holes?" If I tell people I'm Canadian then they look at me and nod, "yeah, you're pretty white-washed. Are you ashamed of your heritage?" If anyone is ashamed about their ethnicity it's because systemic oppression has told them they should be, not because there's anything to be ashamed of.

I am a Canadian-born Korean with integrated cultures and I'm not interested in picking one over the other.

"Slut!"

You're damn right I am. This, too, is my reclaimed language, a word I use to celebrate my sexuality. There's so much non-consensual sexualization, so much stigma, and so many stereotypes attached to sex and who has it. Sex is something beautiful that is not always used in beautiful ways. For me being sex-positive goes much further than just giving the thumbs up to a good time: it's political.

Here's a good example of intersecting oppressions. Many people know that Asian womyn have a history of being sexualized in abusive ways, but let's take it a bit further. Womyn, ethnic minorities, sexual minorities, sex workers, persons of lower socioeconomic status, transpeople, people with ability concerns, and other disenfranchised populations are more likely to experience non-consensual power dynamics in sex while at the same time be given no space or visibility for their sexualities. The more categories you fill, the more marginalized you'll likely be.

I've spent a lot of my time advocating for sex-positivity and healthy sexuality. Sex is not just for the pleasure of straight white males; fucked-up power dynamics need to be struck down and more visibility and space needs to exist for others. I am not Korean to play the role of a submissive Asian. I am not queer for the male gaze.

"Hey, are you lesbians?"

"We're not going to fuck you."

"Aw, why not?"

Because I find you disgusting. My sexuality is for me and my lovers and the voyeurs that I welcome to watch. You didn't make the cut. Just because I have an active sex life with many lovers of all genders, that doesn't mean I'm easy and it most certainly doesn't give you the right to touch me.

Intersecting Identities

No one aspect of my identity can solely define me, nor can the collective of individual identities; it is the intersection of all my identities that speaks my experience. I believe that individuals of multiple minority groups experience oppressions much greater than the sum of the individual parts. Being queer leaves me subject to homophobia and heterosexism; being Korean leaves me subject to racism, but being a queer Korean means that I have even less space. Where is my visibility? Who are my allies? How can I find my community? My experiences are very different from the average straight Korean womyn or the average white gay male. Neither Korea-town nor the gaybourhood are really my home. I'm not just Korean, I'm not just queer, I'm not just any one thing; I'm a lot of things, and that's how I experience oppression. But it shouldn't end there. Although I have many intersecting avenues to be marginalized, each one provides me with new opportunities to challenge social norms and fight these oppressions and it's up to me to use them.

Each fight has its limits, however, and it is important to acknowledge these. At first glance I saw this anthology as an avenue for me to express my understanding of multileveled oppression and I was excited at the liberating opportunity to write freely, without fear of judgment. Conceptualizing identity in a holistic approach, I wanted to discuss critically the problems of multiple marginalization. Often, when one identity takes precedence in a situation, other identities are compromised. This book is about Korean-Canadian women, each author's shared identity. Being queer, gender-deviant, and sex-positive are less common and act as potential avenues to be othered and silenced. I have felt this weight and struggled through it while writing this short piece. Some felt I was too radical and should not be included in the book, but the support I received overpowered them. Others, myself included, feared what exposing my identities could mean for my family. Shock. Shame. Disgrace. How would their reactions be influenced by their Korean identity? This was more difficult to overcome. It became clear to me that even in a space where I was given the opportunity to speak honestly and freely I wasn't able to do so because I was submersed in many dominant cultures that did not embrace me. After much internal debate and deliberation I chose to censor myself, to present you with what you see here, no more, no less.

HELEN LEE

A Peculiar Sensation
A Personal Genealogy of Korean American and Korean Canadian Women's Cinema

Her hair is wrapped smoothly in a possibly comfortable bun, higher than seems right but that was the style then. She is perched on a rock, near flower bushes, smiling. My mother clutches a small handbag with gloved hands, her legs neatly arranged. Like my father, she wears a crisp suit. I don't know what colour because the image is from a black and white photograph, not a memory. They are about the same age as I am now.

As adults, I think we are haunted by an image of our parents in their youth, a time we never knew them. For child immigrants, these images of the past also come from another place. Not here. A place far enough away that a telephone call occasions worry first, not joy. My parents left Seoul when I was three years old. A year later, my sister and I joined them in Toronto, Canada. Our young tongues, trained in Korean food and language but unschooled and now unhomed, were soon eager for french fries and making friends in English. I think that age especially, around three or four (just prior to grade school, when private home life becomes formatively public), was critical when I try to recall where photographs end and memory begins. It isn't clear.

It is a kind of curse, I think, to leave your birthplace when you are young enough to lose your mother tongue but old enough not to forget the loss. For my generation, Korean American/Canadian women filmmakers who were born there but raised here, the utter contemporaneity of our experiences means "back there" and "back then" as much as right now. As someone who writes and makes images about such tongue-tying experiences, I would like to try to remember this particular haunting of representation and subjectivity, where language is the spine of memory. Through our images, the faded pictures of our mothers speak with new force, saying something about our lives here. I am certain we all became filmmakers as soon as we stepped off the plane.

For now, let's put away those childish wishes for assimilation and discover a new desire for affinity. This article represents the desire to look at the work of my peers, other Korean American women filmmakers,[1] and discover the connections among their work and also the films I have made. I wondered if there was anything specific about the efflorescence of media work over the past few years which represented commonalities of location. How did our experiences as *kyop'o* (overseas Korean) women inform our aesthetic practices? How did these works function from the perspective of cultural displacement and feminist intervention, where race and gender identifications were prominent? How did the imbrication of Korean diasporic sensibilities (our "*kyop'o*-ness or identities as overseas Koreans), and our multivalent positioning and constant negotiations as women and artists of colour in this new world, reflect in our work? What kinds of representational strategies were being deployed, and what did this new visual culture signify[2] — simply, what were we saying, and how were we choosing to say it?

First, I am quite struck by the fact that most Korean American filmmakers are, in fact, women. For a generation destined, according to classical immigrant narratives of social and economic progress, to be brilliant doctors and lawyers (and patriarchal imperative, good wives to boot), this is a startling find. Given the male-centered legacies of cinema history, theories of the cinematic apparatus, and the world of film production itself, it is also extraordinary. Was the desire for self-representation so intense as to supersede all the traditional barriers that usually placed women and people of colour as outsiders looking in? Or, in the case of Korean American women filmmakers, did our peripheral status accord a privileged view — a "double vision?"

I imagine a girl standing before a mirror, or a woman holding a camera to her eye. Slowly, she turns to behold her image reflected back at her, like a doubling or a twin. Not identical, different but same. She sees herself, as if for the first time.

A kind of "double consciousness"[3] is available to us, as minority women in the white-dominant culture of North American society. In an American context, we are Korean. In a Korean context, we are women. These media works embody an ambivalent and contingent status of American/Korean, white/other, here/there, and very often a place in between. Issues of race and gender are impossible to ignore when their privileges and oppression affect dimensions of everyday life, not to mention the critical and artistic expressions we try to bring to it. Aptly named a "triple bind" by Trinh T. Minh-ha (6), alluding to competing allegiances to different communities, this unique equation of subjectivity — Korean/woman/artist — can also prove immensely enabling. Could it be that patriarchal expectations for the son have, ironically, liberated the daughter? (Sometimes I do wonder if I would have engaged in such an unstable profession as filmmaking if I'd been expected to be the family breadwinner.) More likely though, the Korean daughter became a feminist with something to say.

Our issues are different from what I imagine our female contemporaries in Korea, immersed in anti-colonial, nationalistic discourse in conjunction with feminism in a neo-Confucion context, might take on. In the '80s, while Korean students were taking to the streets, the business of assimilation and dreams of professional prosperity were occupying Korean American youth. Immigrant success meant moving into ivory towers, not smashing them. But this is a crude simplification (especially now, with government gestures toward political reform stymieing former student movement members of the '80s, we are faced with a Korean society as economically stratified as ever in the post-Korean war era; as well, Asian Americans are coming to the economic and political fore as never before). Ultimately, for individuals and organizations devoted to progressive change, the question of what comprises socially committed, critically informed work is answered by where we are located. While cut from the same anti-imperialistic cloth as our Korean colleagues, I think we're more likely to critique ideals of western democracy and liberal society as illusions, than to claim them. Too many encounters with racism make it impossible to be a chest-beating American nationalist (and for a Canadian, it is downright anachronistic). Still, for mostly middle-class Korean Americans, the seduction of capital usually overrides considerations of class and sometimes even race. That's why when I speak of "identity," it is less a personal one (though it may be that, too) than a socially constructed, politicized identity which needs to be "earned" or declared. Although I have always been Korean, becoming "Korean American" or "Korean Canadian" was a longer, self-examining process. Acts of community in the context of racism and some marginality are, in this way, themselves political.

These films and videos by Korean American women are highly conscious artistically and theoretically mediated works (all produced by filmmakers with full benefits of college educations or art/film school, usually both). They are not "naive" in any sense, taking part in this highly politicized arena with strategies of reinvention and resistance. Much of the groundwork laid by feminist cinema and Asian American media has informed our filmic practices and we, in turn, extend those histories.[4] Fortified by debates around political and "third"[5] cinema (Pines and Willemen), the rigidities of realist filmmaking and pressures to produce only "positive images" of the community, we roundly reject the banality and victimology associated with "minority" filmmaking. Mere oppositionality, stereotype-fighting documentaries, or simplistic "identity" films ("I am Korean American, and this is a portrait of me") do not constitute this oeuvre. Like some nationalistic Koreans, I am proud of this. A fierce and prodigious discursivity is at work; like a persistence of vision, these plural or multiple forms of consciousness pervade our films. The combined forces of our immigrant family pasts, the lingering effects of Korean male patriarchal traditions, Korea's own colonial national history, they all feed into our contemporary North American perspectives. Sometimes there's time to kick at the can of postmodernity and cultural theory, too. As signposts of new knowledges and new subjectivities, these media works represent complex and personal articulations of race and gender, representation, and the politics and aesthetics of identity formation in film.

Born with a veil, and gifted with second-sight.
—W. E. B. DuBois

If there is a "godmother" to this recent flowering of work, it is the late Theresa Hak Kyung Cha. Her profound, luminous legacy of critical and poetic writing, performance art, and film and video work has left its traces. Although few of the film/videomakers discussed here would regard Cha's influence as a direct one (I knew only her name when making my first film), the themes and formal concerns of her media work during the 1970s and early '80s surface again and again in these contemporary films. Cha's semiotic explorations of language, memory, and subjectivity in the context of feminism and Korean colonial history are especially prescient. While the feminist, postcolonial writings and films of Trinh Minh-ha gripped me as a cinema studies undergraduate during the mid-'80s, I didn't yet know of Theresa Hak Kyung Cha before her. Like Trinh, Cha can be at once poetic and interrogative in her unusual forms of address, which are almost oracular. As a body, Cha's work rematerializes the site of Korea-as-cold-war-victim, and re-maps the emotional and cognitive terrain of "Korea" into something tangible for *kyop'o* understanding, a groundswell of critical fictions, diasporic imagination, and genuine political struggle.

Talk about marginal. Until a few years ago an identity as specific as "Korean American" filmmaker was an impossibility in the American cultural consciousness, even in its alternative quarters. When I made my first film, *Sally's Beauty Spot* (1990) and was living in New York, the prevailing term, politically and organizationally, was "Asian American." For someone from Canada coming to the States, even Asian American sounded great. To encounter organizations such as Asian CineVision in New York, Visual Communications in Los Angeles, and the National Asian American Telecommunications Association in San Francisco was a revelation. The history of Asian American filmmaking, I discovered, was predominantly Chinese American and Japanese American, and consisted primarily of documentaries. These organizations, devoted to supporting the production, promotion, and exhibition of media work by Asian

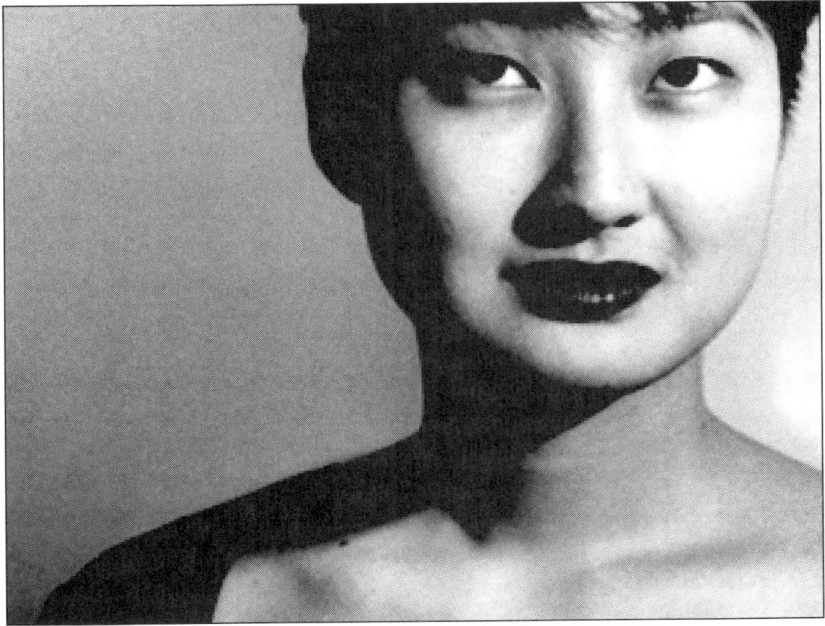

Sally's Beauty Spot, *1990, 12 min.*

American film/videomakers, also mounted annual film festivals. I decided I was going to make a film to show specifically at ACV's New York festival. The film wouldn't be documentary and wouldn't be earnest, but elliptical, theoretical, feminist, and hopefully, funny and accessible. This Asian American audience would be my primary audience. Besides, how could they turn me down; just how many Asian American filmmakers were out there, anyway?

Enough, I guess. I showed the selection committee a silent cutting copy, which kept falling apart in the projector. They turned down the film. Come back next year, they said, when it's finished. I did.

Sally's Beauty Spot is an image-and-idea driven film. Rather than focusing on character or story, the deconstructionist tendencies of the film and its hybrid aesthetics were inspired by a personal excitement with theory. Using a despised black mole on a young woman's breast as a metaphor for the threat of cultural difference, the film explores western notions of Asian femininity and idealized romance. Sally tries rubbing, scrubbing off, and covering up the skin blemish. Made without a script per se, the piece collages together my interest in postcolonial and feminist film theory with pop cultural elements. At the time, I was researching the representation of Asians in the history of American film and television. In the postwar period, a spate of Asian/white romances had emerged from Hollywood, what I call "miscegenation melodramas." Ubiquitous among them, and my clear favourite, was *The World of Suzie Wong*, starring William Holden and Nancy Kwan. Revisionistically speaking, I should spit out this bit of colonial candyfloss I know, but in truth I've loved eating it since childhood. The film was shown regularly on TV, and Kwan's prostitute was one of the few popular images of Asian women around. This kind of obsessive, acculturated form of spectatorship was interesting in itself: Korean girls in Canadian suburbs, glued to California sitcoms and old Hollywood movies on the tube, we were not exactly the intended audience for this once racy bit of entertainment. True, during all those times of looking rarely did any of these images look back at me. But this one did.

Kwan's Suzie Wong was dragon lady and lotus blossom rolled into one, but caught in a racist time warp, could you really blame her? She was beautiful, feisty, and deserved reclaiming. Homi Bhabha's seminal retheorization of the stereotype (66-84) was the trick. Instead of arguing the derogatory or false nature of racial and sexual stereotypes, Bhabha reconceptualized them as "arrested" forms of representation. Stereotypes should be viewed "relationally" according to other representations, he suggests, rather than held up to any picture of reality, thereby releasing it from burdens of truth or moralism. My "Suzie Wong" was a total fiction, pulp romance. As a Korean growing up in North America, it was impossible to be a real essentialist. No one knew where Korea was, so what could they really know about you, if they didn't even know where you came from? In this way, I became an Asian American before I became Korean American. Pillaging troves of Hollywood fare such as these "mixed race" dramas, I found all the Asian characters were Japanese or Chinese anyway (though I don't want to fight for Orientalist crumbs, this problem of the lack of a popular Korean signifier still dogs me to this day). Although Suzie Wong herself is from Hong Kong, the main character in *Sally's Beauty Spot*, while played by my sister, Sally, is not specifically named as Korean, Chinese, or Japanese, to underscore the shared dimensions of Asian American women's experiences.

Sally's Beauty Spot tries to give a pulse to these linchpins of racial and sexual identity, in tandem, as inseparable preoccupations. The discourse of race in the United States was, and still is, overpoweringly white versus black. If Asians are admitted into the dialogue, it is almost exclusively in relation to white-dominant culture. Such a status quo reinforcing focus on the white/other dynamic is not only supremely irritating, but it reflects the workings of power, not our multiracial society. Personally, I haven't been interested in representing Asian/white couplings. The predominant relationships in my films have been between Asian and other Asian, black or Native characters, and then only marginally, whites. In *Sally's Beauty Spot*, Sally's vacillation between white privilege and the prospect of a liaison with a black man (a pairing you'd be hard-pressed to find in Hollywood), reflects the tension of broaching an

Asian presence in the stratified minefield of American race relations. On the soundtrack, different musical idioms and numerous abstracted voices interrogate this terrain. Clips from *The World of Suzie Wong*, photographs and voices of other Asian women, and images of Sally's body punctuate this narrative of discovery and subjecthood. The film maps this progression of psychic and theoretical attachments to the body, spectatorship, and voice with a simple story about an unwanted mole.

When I showed the film to Homi Bhabha, one of the critical inspirations for the film, he remarked how the mole of "beauty spot" on Sally's breast functioned as the *punctum* of the piece. Roland Barthes used the term to describe how a peripheral detail in a photograph may "prick" or unsettle the viewer in ways unexpected from the photograph's more conventionally coded meanings. The *punctum*'s effect is startling, like a "sting, speck, cut, little hole." Registering a visceral effect, "It also bruises me," Barthes writes, "is poignant to me" (27). Such a compelling detail may give a clue to how we come to "remember" an image, or photograph, through the body. My sister, Sally (who by the way has no neurotic impulse toward her mole), had an immediate but different response to Bhabha's suggestion. To her, the *punctum* was not the mole but the stretch marks of her breasts. The film's final images are of a black man's lips dissolving into Sally's own, radiant smile.

> *She heard faintly the young girl uttering a sequence of words, and interspersed between them, equal duration of pauses. Her mouth is left open at the last word. She does not seem to realize that she had spoken.*
> —Theresa Hak Kyung Cha

During the mid-'70s, Theresa Cha began producing work as a student at the University of California, Berkeley. The sheer formalism, elegance, and occasional opacity of her text constructions, in writing and media, reflect an excitement and curiosity about French poststructuralist ideas, which were then gaining importance on this side of the Atlantic. For the theoretically uninitiated, Cha's work can be daunting. Embracing a conceptual indeterminacy characteristic of avant-garde performance aesthetics, their meanings are often created provisionally in the encounter between the text and reader. The specificity of the reader as a social subject is always a precondition of performing the meaning. But different from her Euro-American intellectual peers, her thoughts were as much about Korea, which was marginal even to a western understanding of "the Orient." Problems of language embody this sense of cultural displacement. The word, Cha implies, is not a universal or neutral signifier, not always in English or French. By a specific somebody, words are read, spoken, and breathed around, sometimes with considerable strain. In *mouth to mouth* (1975), the Korean language can offer the assurance and comfort of one's mother tongue, or is slippery as a cipher—depending on the viewer and her positioning. Cultural location, however, does not always guarantee a linguistic one. Language, once a repository and reliable signifier of culture, becomes contingent and fragile in the context of displacement.

mouth to mouth opens with a continuous left to right panning movement over a series of written characters: simple vowel letters from *hangul*, the Korean phonetic alphabet. The movement fades into black, then fades up to a video snow effect, accompanied by static noise. This is followed by an image of a woman's mouth framed in close-up, super-imposed over this snow/static. Her mouth widens ever slowly, but we don't hear her. Fade out. Fade in with another close-up of the same, her mouth forming a different, voiceless vowel. The video follows this pattern in a highly composed, almost ritualistic manner, with variations in sound treatments (static, water, bird sounds, sometimes silence) and the occasional camera movement. As in her other film and video work, the piece's formal austerity extends from the visual to the aural dimensions of the piece.

Although *mouth to mouth* references the populist, physiognomic origin myths of *hangul*,[6] the functioning of language for the *kyop'o* speaker is not nearly so transparent. The supposedly neutral text of written language is gradually overturned by the arduous, subjective aspiration of speech. This tension between the text and speech mirrors the disintegrating relationship between sound and image in the videotape. While the disembodied voice may function as a radical, even liberatory tool for her feminist avant-garde contemporaries (see Silverman),[7] Cha's voiceless body suggest other problems of cultural legibility and knowledge. Here, the disconnection of voice and body alludes to the oscillatory nature of native/non-native tongues where the transparency and certainty of language is suspended. The use of the vowel as a structuring absence of the word, as opposed to the positivity of consonants, underscores its supplementary but elemental nature. Significantly, two vowels are missing from the written text (compound vowels aren't even included here). The incomplete set suggests a child or beginner's first apprehension of the language, or the imperfect recall of a native speaker whose mother tongue is lost. Cha's mute mouth, forming familiar/unfamiliar vowels, "performs" the Korean language with a desire for speech. The vowels' "absent" nature indicates the materiality of language, as building blocks. Where language itself is homed, however, is another question.

Cha's long-standing interest in negative space and silence is shared by the work of more recent video artists, most directly in Yunah Hong's work. Hong's first videotape, *Memory/all echo* (1990), is based on Cha's seminal poetic text, *DICTEE* (168). The book itself is a complex document combining written text with graphic components, and covering topics ranging modern Korean history, Catholic ritual, and cinema spectatorship, to topographies of the human body. Hong's video gathers together archival material from the Korean war and dramatic reenactments filmed in Korea and the U.S., with visual montage elements such as computer-generated effects and photographic stills. Using *DICTEE* as a base text, the voice-over is comprised solely of selections from the book. But Hong's style is more allusive than illustrative of Cha's writing (see also Lew).[8] Rather than attempting an exhaustive, literal adaptation of the book, the video focuses mainly on themes related to Korean and American identity and issues of cultural and linguistic displacement, underscoring the interpretive possibilities and elliptical phrasings of the translation process itself.

Like the book, *Memory/all echo* attempts to engage the viewer in a self-reflexive, readerly relationship to the text. Hong tracks several discursive levels at once, extending the video's montage aesthetic to a multi-layered presentation of voice. Three narrators with different accents (signifying varying levels of acculturation to the English language), adopt several forms of address. In one segment, Cha's eyewitness retelling of her brother's decision to join a 1962 student demonstration against their mother's will is narrated in third person. The video dramatizes this sequence, collapsing Cha's real-life experiences with the story of a fictional character (played by the same actor). The use of the pronominal shifter (you/I; she/he) enables the subjective interplay between historical and autobiographical accounts locked by the accrual of time and memory. The sequence, although filmed in slow motion and extreme close-up, employs an arch, gestural performance style that drains the confrontation of any conventional dramatic intent or emotional identification. Linking her brother's anti-government position with a portrait of Yu Guan Soon [Yu Kwan-sun], the martyred nationalist heroine of 1919, the narrator/author/character traces the politics and history of modern Korean resistance to locate it within a personal, familial framework. The space between—tensions of nation and family, gaps between history and autobiography, the ellipses of story and memory—is transformed into a language of loss, displacement, and exile.

In Kim Su Theiler's *Great Girl* (1993), the haunting of cultural loss takes the form of a search for origins. The film's departure point is Theiler's own trip to Korea to find information about her birth mother. But this search doesn't function as a transparently autobiographical document or an effortless return of the subject to the mother/land. Laid out as a series of vignettes, the piece unfolds rather cryptically: a roomful of black hair, American dollar bills bandaged to a young girl's belly, an ambivalent childhood encounter with a U.S. serviceman (perhaps her father?), neutral adoption documents, uneasy travelogue footage of a hometown that existed before only in her mind. Like secret layers of a memory long repressed by familial and cultural silence, the discursive curiosity of this search unearths a place—Korea—sedimented by the absences and persistence of memory and silence in stark and unsettling ways.

Theiler's film begins with an extreme close-up shot of a black and white image, accompanied by music and a regulated scraping noise. The image is magnified to the point of illegibility. It is similarly difficult to locate the source of the sound, or its relationship to the image. This disjunctive relationship between the visual and aural is a primary stylistic trope of *Great Girl*, where sound is used contrapuntally, or non-synchronously towards a redefinition of the subject, who is variously named in the film ("K," Sun-Mi, Cho Suk-hi, and implicitly, Kim Su Theiler). This non-realist use of sound, including voice-over, represents an interventionist strategy which feminist film theorists such as Kaja Silverman and Mary Ann Doane have deployed against classical realist cinema's reinforcement of male subjectivity and the illusion of a unified coherent subject. The seamlessness of realist sound/image production masks "the potential trauma of dispersal, dismemberment, and difference" (47), and the spectator's imagined plenitude or insufficiency of the image/subject. As the mirror opposite of realist filmmaking, identity-production seeks to expose its material workings. In *Great Girl*, Theiler's deconstructive task is to uncover the past trauma of dispersal (adoption and immigration), dismemberment (separation and loss of the mother), and difference (the *kyop'o*'s return to Korea).

In a key scene of the film, "K" is being interviewed about the trip and her experience meeting hometown folks who can give her information. The sequence is reenacted by an actress (Anita Chao) wearing a suit and coiffed hairstyle, and sitting obediently behind a desk. Strangely, her lips move out of sync with the monologue, followed by a slight echoing effect. As she moves into a story about how a scar on her body could definitively identify her, "K" detaches the microphone from her lapel and leaves the desk, as the camera follows her walking into another part of the room. She talks about meeting a woman who "could be my mother." The beating noise (the dislocated sound from the film's opening) is almost thunderous. But no one provides the right answers ("I looked nothing like the pictures"). Engaged in what Cha has called a "perpetual motion of search," the film's discursive explorations of self-identity and self-knowledge render an asymptotic relationship to "truth": the closer she comes, the more inaccessible and irrecoverable her past is. The carefully staged testimony of "K"'s faked performance undermines the documentary-like presentation of a unified, spontaneous, "authentic" subject. The film's visual and conceptual fragmentation, and the interpolated nature of the filmmaker's investigation—chance meetings, faulty memories, nasty rumors (the townspeople's suggestion of her mother as a prostitute with no prospects but American adoption of her biracial, illegitimate child), and implied wishes for a happy ending—reveal the impossibility of a transparent search for cultural and biological origins. Later in the film, the initial, illegible black ad white close-up shot is widened to reveal the image's contents: sails of a bus curtain caught by an intense wind.

The effect of mass migrations has been the creation of radically new types of human being: people who root themselves in ideas rather than places, in memories as much as in material things: people who have been obliged to define themselves—because they are so defined by others—by their otherness; people in whose deepest selves strange fusions occur, unprecedented unions between what they were and where they find themselves.
—Salman Rushdie

The "in-betweenness" that characterizes films about immigrant experience, especially when faced with the physical or methaphoric possibility of return, is a persistent wound of the diasporic imagination. What is interesting is how these ideas take shape, depending on the form. The more free-wheeling language of experimental film and video can be immensely enabling in conveying a discursive complexity. It's possible to pack a film with dense ideas and a radical aesthetic, and be all the richer for it. The rules of narrative film, however, are far stricter. Still, the principle of diminishing audience (the more experimental your film is, the smaller your audience) plagued me as I contemplated a shift to narrative filmmaking. Why not try to communicate hitherto marginalized stories and characters through a more accessible form? At the same time, other models of contemporary innovative and subjective filmmaking that identified marginalized characters and the interplay of difference—cultural, psychic, sexual—showed it was possible to locate these ideas in a narrative context.[9]

My second film, *My Niagara* (1992), features a Japanese American/Canadian[10] protagonist, a 20-year-old woman named Julie Kumagai. In continuing my exploration of displacement and assimilation, and racial/sexual representation in film, I wished to collaborate with another Asian writer on a film about an Asian/Asian relationship. This didn't come about innocently. One of my guiding lights, video-maker Richard Fung, had an interesting reaction to *Sally's Beauty Spot* and the Asian/black dialectic it sought to set up. "So, you think that's radical, Helen?" he challenged (very gently, of course). "The Asian and black thing is provocative but you know what's really radical? Yellow on yellow." *My Niagara* is a story of maternal loss and intercultural discovery. Written with novelist Kerri Sakamoto, the film explores the inner world of Julie Kumagai who, on the cusp of adulthood, faces choices to move her life forward. At the film's outset, she is breaking off with a boyfriend and contemplating a trip to Europe with her best friend, Enza. Julie lives at home with her incommunicative father, and her life is shadowed by the death of her Japanese-born mother (who, on a return trip there when Julie was a small girl,

My Niagara, *1992, 40 min.*

died in a drowning accident off the coast). At Julie's workplace, a stately water filtration plant by the lake, she meets a young Tetsuro, who, recently emigrated from Japan but of Korean origin, is obsessed with all things American. They make a connection, but Julie ultimately cannot escape her listless state; life goes on. While this is the plot proper and *My Niagara* is a drama, the film is essentially minimalist and counter-dramatic in design.

The central relationship that Kerri and I wanted to portray was Julie and Tetsuro's, and their evolving realizations of cultural difference. To us, the picture of an assimilated Asian in America was a *sansei* (or third-generation) Japanese Canadian/American. But Julie's background also resembled my own upbringing in a predominantly white suburban environment. What were the differences between being a settled Asian person in North America, and a recent immigrant; what were the similarities? What kinds of dynamics and perceptions existed among Asians of differing nationalities living here? Also, how does the fantasy of Japan in Julie's idealized memories (as a place of origin and the site of her mother's birth and death), change when confronted with Tetsuro's experiences of discrimination as a Korean in Japan? Although these were our didactic considerations in creating the story and our characters, we were also dead-set against making an earnest "race relations" drama. Once established, cultural identity would be a given, not constantly "rehearsed" for an assumedly "white" audience: our audience would already be knowledgeable and informed. As well, there would be no obvious or Orientalist signifiers (for instance, although we assume Julie's father, as a *nisei* or second-generation Japanese, had an internment camp experience, this never comes up in the film, not as much because the story isn't his but that this would be the most obvious filmic representation of a *nisei* character. He was just an emotionally bottled-up dad, for personal as well as cultural reasons). Enza and Dominic (not coincidentally, both ethnic whites) have their own quirks, and Tetsuro his Memphis stylings.

Julie (Melanie Tanaka), Tetsuro (William Shin) and Mr. Kumagai (George Anzai) are played by non-professional actors, not because of the dearth of Asian actors, but because of a particular "non-performative" performance style that I had hoped to experiment with. Different from documentary-like naturalism, the style I was searching for was a convergence of real-life personas and scripted characters toward non-psychological portrayals. Reduced and flattened, they could suggest an inaccessible state of interiority. I thought their alienation wouldn't be properly served by gutsy, positivist performances. Muted or held-in, their canted expressions of emotional discord and cultural displacement alluded to theoretically based notions of absence and negativity. Suspicious of models of identification that relied on audience absorption, I hoped for some critical distance (was it possible to be both emotionally engaged and critically aware at the same time?). Similarly, the progression of the story is obliquely presented and ultimately subverted. Julie's own passivity is mirrored in the film's languid expository style. In the ending, Julie's momentary communion with her father (she finds a charged but constipated gift of a wooden box he's crafted himself—touching, but also oddly paralyzing), also denies specific narrative closure. But it is less a refusal than a deferral. The film's final notes, the daughter's dutiful gesture of filling her father's rice bowl, and an image of her mother's watery grave, suggest another chapter of a continuing story.

Also dealing with families and parent/child dynamics, other narrative films by Korean American women filmmakers avoid a deconstructionist approach in favour of a realist, reconstructionist tone and spirit. These works feature critical dilemmas faced by Korean American families with female protagonists, interestingly all daughters, at their center. While issues of national culture and the family still coalesce around language, critical discursivity is transformed into dialogue and dramatic conflict.

Problems of language and cultural difference encountered by second-generation Korean Americans, compounded by biracial identity, are the subject of Kyung-ja Lee's *Halmani* (1988). Kathy is born of a Korean mother and U.S. serviceman father. Her home life is an example of middle-class assimilation, idyllic and erased of any signs of ethnicity. Living outside of an urban center (and therefore outside a community of Korean Americans), Kathy's white-as-norm American comfort is uprooted by the arrival of her very Korean grandmother, Halmani. Oriental signifiers start to proliferate: gifts of a ceramic vase and traditional *hanbok* dresses, yucky foods, odd customs, and an unrecognizable language. Her mother's assurance that "Korea is a long way away" is threatened by Halmani's newfound presence, and a reminder of not the foreignness "over there" but of the difference within.

Kathy speaks only English, and Halmani only Korean, so grandmother and granddaughter literally cannot speak to one another. Halmani's Korean is left untranslated, reinforcing Kathy's sense of estrangement (and curiously, the viewer's; I craved for Halmani to be on equal footing but Lee decides not to subtitle Halmani's dialogue). Instead, their method of communicating transfers to the body, and oscillates between the physical connection/repulsion of Kathy's own biological and cultural ambivalence. Still, their bodies can correspond. The film's framing often places Kathy and Halmani within the same two-shot, emphasizing their shared physical stature. "Halmani noticed that you're left-handed, too," her mother says. It's when Halmani does something strange and visceral, like squatting on the earth, chanting while polishing the vase, or praying as she burns paper, that Kathy's alienated Americanness seeks to excise any display of alterity.

When asked to draw a self-portrait in class, Kathy models her fingers around her face and is stymied; the drawing's a mess, and she runs away. After her father brings her home, Kathy proclaims, "She's disgusting. I hate her," and smashes the precious vase to the ground. Halmani's reaction is swift and perfect: fury and true disgust. This a moment when Halmani's identity, throughout the film positioned as "authentic" and unknowable, won't be denied. The film's resolution, Halmani's forgiveness and Kathy's penance, plays out the banality of cultural compromise: Kathy eats her words after Halmani takes the blame for the broken vase, and dons the *hanbok* for her family. Through the verbal and nonverbal communion of the film's final scene, a long shot of Kathy and Halmani together against a desert sunset, Kathy willingly accepts not just the signs of cultural difference, but the language itself. "*Kamsahamnida*, Halmani," she thanks her grandmother, her tongue humbled by the native.

The desire for assimilation takes a decidedly adventurous, sardonic turn in Christine Chang's *Be Good, My Children* (1992). At the film's outset, Chang boldly asks of her character, "Why did you come to America?" A musical-comedy-drama, the film satirizes the saga of a struggling Korean immigrant family in New York City: Mom is a "Jesus freak" who works in a Harlem clothing store, Judy aspires to be an actress but tends bar on the sly, and Jimmy is failing out of school (the father is notably absent). Mom still hopes for mainstream professional success for her children, who opt for white boyfriends, and wished-for car dealerships in LA. Their entanglements and conflicts form the basis of the film's plot, but it is the extra-diegetic levels, in the form of two "narrators," which subvert our expectations of the conventional family drama.

The film opens with an Asian woman wearing impeccable make-up and a huge blond wig languishing on top of a bed, clutching a teddy bear. This is Snow White (played by Chang herself). She addresses the camera directly, introducing the family via a photo album and acerbically decrying this "mean world." Snow White functions as an omniscient narrator, like a guardian angel to the family, but more devilish than angelic. In an early episode with Jimmy, she dribbles chocolate candies to lure him, fairytale-like, into a lesson of simple economics, NYC-style ("These are pennies; we throw them away. These are nickels; we give them to beggars"), before releasing her authority as the film's driving force ("Say it! I have absolute power"). Another figure, Mae East, who is first introduced as daughter Judy's alter ego but soon enters the story as a character in her own right, provides the main musical numbers. It's high camp, with Mae East's torch songs and the sexually charged persona of Snow White, part sex kitten/part dominatrix, releasing the drama from the realist confines of the typical immigrant narrative.

Toying with conventions of a morality tale, Chang discards the myth of hardworking, model minority citizens in an explicit critique of the American dream and the white norm. Offset by the sheer jazziness of the musical interludes, the family's parables offer a deeply ironic perspective of Korean immigrant life (for me, marred only by some of the actors' inauthentic Korean accents). One of Mae's musical numbers is even set in a California drive-in theater in the middle of an earthquake. In another sequence where Judy recounts a dream to a psychologist, several Asian women with names like Cherry Blossom, Miss Butterfly, and Lady Dragon first display themselves as stereotypical submissives but end up beating up on the white males, yelling, "That's not my name!" Later, the same women, including Judy, rally together in a self-affirming musical number led by Mae East's rebel femininity. By presenting an unequivocally sexual image of the Asian woman in a campy musical or melodramatic context, the film avoids essentializing the Asian American experience or "fixing" the stereotype as false/true. The film's radicality lies in this refusal to reinforce dramatic realist presentations of what Korean women are "really like." Its parody of Hollywood happy endings similarly denies escapist tendencies of the immigrant narrative. When Jimmy and Judy steal the church offerings from their mother's church to hail a cab to "somewhere over the rainbow," and Mom launches into the show tune of the same name, you know that Snow White (and Chang herself) is smirking. "Oh my, just the lullaby I needed," she says. "But forget it. This ain't no time to dream."

The dysfunctional family and personal compromises made to sustain the illusion of perfect nuclearity also propel the narrative of Hyun Mi Oh's *La Senorita Lee* (1995). The film follows the choices made by Jeanie Lee, a vivacious young woman ending an affair with Tomas, a Mexican worker who has left her pregnant. She feels pressured to marry Harry Kim, a childhood friend and young doctor, in order to bail out her mother and grandmother. The backstory is the financial ruin of the family's business during the L.A. riots, and the father's subsequent abandonment of his wife, mother, and daughter (even in a houshold containing only women, patriarchal pressures still assert themselves). Oh presents Jeanie's personal crisis as an example of the complex positioning of this generation of Korean American women in Los Angeles, poised on the edge of a continent bordered by desiring bodies, clashing cultural realities, and a "prodigality of tongues" (Shohat and Stam).

The film's structure is circular, beginning and ending with Jeanie (also played by the filmmaker) lying on a highrise rooftop, moments after fleeing her traditional Korean wedding. The strains of a Korean folk song and the vivid colours of her *hanbok* and *chokturi*, set against the smoggy backdrop of downtown L.A. and the sound of helicopters in the distance, portray the conflict almost iconically. We enter the story through Jeanie's vision, a close-up shot catching her half-conscious state as she passes through dream, sleep, and memory. The film's flashback structure effectively internalizes the site of Jeanie's dramatic conflict into her body, so that the drama unfolds as part of Jeanie's consciousness and her subjectively-drawn world. Struck by pregnancy cramps in the bathroom of a hotel room she's sharing with Harry on a whim, Jeanie's thoughts move to an idyllic scene on the same rooftop where she and Tomas speak Spanish to one another, and share a night of lovemaking. Later, on the operating room of an abortion clinic, the threat of terminating her pregnancy conjures up an image of a small girl—Jeanie herself as a child. This jolts her into a moment of self-apprehension, and she runs. Jeanie's "wildness" and its repression are also reflected in the film's structure, a continuous sublimation of her sexual identity into the filial role of dutiful Korean American daughter and now, mother.

When Jeanie's feminist will and new world freedoms are overtaken by considerations of the family's future (ruled by the interdependency of different immigrant generations and, ironically, a continuation of patriarchal structures supported by women), her marriage to Harry is a sign of defeat. But Jeanie's radical decision to keep Tomas's baby shows the exact price of compromise. "I don't believe anymore," she tells a small Mexican boy on the rootop in one of the film's last scenes. The "cosmopolitanizing of humanity" in a place like Los Angeles (which Tomas calls "the loneliest city in the world"), can also signal what Rey Chow has named a "vanishing of human diversity" (137). Difference is subsumed by forces of urbanization, assimilation, and homogenization. At

Prey, *1996, 26 min.*

the film's closing, various spoken lines from the film create a voice montage over a single shot of Jeanie's quiet face, ending on a freeze-frame of her eyes opening, wide awake. Of the different languages that haunt her—Korean, Spanish, English—which will her child eventually claim?

Hyun Mi Oh's script was a kind of revelation when I first read it several years ago. Encountering its cultural sophistication and astute writing recalled a time years earlier, when I first saw Pam Tom's seminal film, *Two Lies* (1989), a beautifully made black-and-white film about two Chinese American sisters and the psychological aftermath of their mother's eyelid operation. With strongly enacted characters and a compelling story, it struck a perfect balance of cultural identity exploration and expertly crafted narrative. The film spoke to me, and it spoke well. The film also made me laugh, the better to spit out, not swallow, the bitter pill of racial assimilation. For a fourth-generation Chinese American filmmaker like Tom, the question of language isn't such an issue (all the dialogue is in English). But for 1.5 generation filmmakers such as Oh and myself, language functions as a kind of primal site of conflict, a site which signifies torment, misunderstanding or loss. Perhaps it is because I am now struggling with Korean language lessons, or crave certain foods for which I do not know the names, or cannot discuss intellectual topics in real depth with my parents, that I make the films I make, to recover this sense of loss.

The confluence of language and crisis surfaces in my third film, *Prey* (1995), a drama about a young Korean Canadian woman who falls for a shoplifter in her father's convenience store the morning after an overnight robbery. Taking place over the course of one day (but a day that will determine what the next days are like), Il Bae's everyday family routine is upset by this handsome Native stranger, Noel, who insinuates himself into her life and apartment. Is he to be trusted? A surprise visit by Halmoni, her grandmother who doesn't speak English, forces her to choose alliances, but Il Bae's defense is poorly negotiated by the fact of Noel's ethnicity and his disheveled, possibly dangerous appearance, as much as by Il Bae's unsure command of the Korean language. These problems of miscommunication and cultural perception are heightened by circumstance when Halmoni meets him not only post-coitally shirtless but also in possession of a gun (echoing a specter of violence familiar to Korean American store owners' lives). In the film's conclusion, a late-night confrontation set in their convenience store, Noel proffers this gun to Il Bae's father as a safeguard against future robberies. But to the father, Noel couldn't be anything but a robber, and her mistakes the gesture as a hold-up. Il Bae's final introduction ("Dad, this is Noel. Noel, this is my dad.") is in some ways just the beginning.

The meeting of Il Bae (Sandra Oh), a young Korean Canadian woman and Noel (Adam Beach), a Native man, creates an unexpected alliance. While they each come from totally different social spaces, there are also aspects that are shared—the same high school, a sense of cultural displacement, and lives shadowed by personal loss (the death of Noel's sister, Lucy: Il Bae's absent mother). I think of their relationship as a completely contemporary one, a phenomenon of the late twentieth century that allows such encounters between Asian immigrants and indigenous people to be possible. Since Koreans emigrated in significant numbers only in the past two decades, it's historically unlikely that Il Bae and Noel would have met until now. Native people, who suffer the same invisibility as Asians and other racial minorities in mainstream media, are practically unknown to the Korean American/Canadian community. It was important to me to explore how a Native character could impact on a Korean family who may have never before acknowledged the Native presence in their adopted land. Halmoni refers to Noel as a "foreigner," not suspecting the irony of her words. While Il Bae and Noel are familiarly cast as star-crossed lovers, this "new world" narrative also creates an emotional space where ideas around ethnicity and belonging can be as meaningful and dramatic as cinematically coded elements like trust, desire, and gunplay.

In conceiving the film, I wanted to avoid reinforcing certain dualisms that I thought typified some Asian American filmmaking. The binaristic opposition of tradition (old, backward "Orient") and modernity (progressive western ideas and attitudes) particularly unnerved me. Although traditional perspectives play a large role in our lives, I don't believe that Korean identity played in simple conflict with living in North America. It wasn't an either /or choice; we live an incredibly hybrid existence. In the film, both English and Korean co-exist, however fragilely, a balancing act of language and identity for 1.5 or second generation immigrants of any nationality. Hyphenated existence (Korean-Canadian, Korean-American) from an adult perspective as opposed to the assimilating impulse of childhood affords the distance and desire, and sometimes necessity, for both tongues to exist in simultaneity. A typical convenience store was the perfect stage to enact this drama, a place where so many Korean Americans have spent their lives (my own movie-watching hours are just recently outpacing my days behind a retail counter). Il Bae's father, circumscribed by this setting, is a barometer of this tongue-twisting dance of language and race. Even he, as imperfectly "bilingual" as his daughter, misunderstands—his daughter, Noel's intentions, the unending drone of labor at the expense of love. By the film's end, Il Bae does not make an either/or choice, but mediates her father's position into a place of forced compromise and personal release.

The script for *Prey* was originally written for Sandra Oh and my mother's sister, In Sook Kim, to play the roles of Il Bae and Halmoni. I knew this would be an interesting process of not only pairing a highly trained actor like Oh with my aunt, who'd never performed before, but also because Oh, like the character, didn't speak Korean and my aunt doesn't speak much English. Since I cannot really speak Korean either, a process of translation was integral to the project. At every stage, from rehearsal to shooting to editing, the interpreter, Jane Huh, stuck close and ready. I wasn't prepared for the cultural wrangling over specific attitudes and sayings that I thought were authentic or convincing, but Jane insisted were off-mark. True to form, my aunt, herself a prolific essayist and poet, refused to play the role of the grandmother (who was initially written as very accepting of Noel and Il Bae's liaison) and demanded changes. My aunt wanted Noel out of Il Bae's apartment and out of her life. While I never thought I'd take identity for granted, especially in a film about cross-generational differences, here I was making my own cultural assumptions. Ultimately, developing Halmoni's character was a collaboration between my aunt and myself, a creation of the Korean and *kyop'o* imagination. I doubt the film would exist without her.

No one today is purely one thing.
—Edward Said

From our "simultaneously split and doubled existence" (Jameson 51) as Korean American women, we have learned to become adept, sophisticated readers of images. From this minoritized position, we have learned to focus on subversive readings and peripheral details, seeing how the *punctum* satisfies. Now, we take up the whole frame; as writers and filmmakers, we have created new images, enlarged those details. Can the production of an image of identity lead to the "transformation of the subject in assuming that image" (Bhabha 40-65)? The representation of Korean women is complex, figured by and interpolated through a variety of discourses, but each frame of these moving images elucidates us, bringing the image of the colonial subject one step closer toward self-identification. The ideas of home, memory, language, and desire obsess us; we try hard to translate these collective thoughts in ways never imagined for us. These narratives of the tongue, voice, and body, they all speak with newfound specificity. The velvet grain of Mae East's voice, Sally's crooked smile, the flaring of Jeanie Lee's *hanbok*, Cha's silent lips — all engaged in a "perpetual motion of search," these explorations signal a kind of *kyop'o* arrival. While the question of identity is never guaranteed, this new clamoring of images suggests other, curiously beautiful ways of traveling in a strange land.

©*1997 from* Dangerous Women: Gender and Korean Nationalism *edited by Elaine H. Kim and Chungmoo Choi. Reproduced by permission of Routledge, a division of Taylor and Francis Group.*

[1]Although I refer to "filmmakers," videomakers are also included here. Also, I use the term "Korean American" although it is properly "Korean North American," which includes Canada as well as the United States. To talk about differences (and similarities) of Korean American vs. Korean Canadian identities and histories would comprise another article, so excuse my predominant use of the former.
[2]"New" is relative, and everything is context. While the "history of cinema" recently celebrated its centenary, the respective histories of Asian American and feminist cinemas date back only some twenty odd years. In this particular context, anything called "Korean American" would have been begging company, or collapsed into other definitions. Only in the last few years has this work reached a critical mass to be so named. In this sense, film and video work by Korean American women is still a cinematic project in its infancy, and this survey is provisional at best. For reasons of space and focus, this discussion centers around a selection of experimental and narrative works, not documentaries. Refer to the filmography for a more complete list of works by Korean American filmmakers.
[3]W. E. B. DuBois's concept of "double consciousness" is useful in cultivating possibilities for considering cultural difference in non-dualistic ways. Allow-

ing the co-existence of objectification and subjecthood, he writes about "this sense of always looking at one's self through the eyes of others." This turn-of-the-century model of decolonization for post-emanicipation blacks uncannily resembles the tricky balance between identification and alienation marking the post-colonial, migratory experiences of the late twentieth century.

[4]One striking note is the dearth of filmmaking by Asian American lesbians, including Korean Americans. I can't speculate why, but the absence is astonishing considering the strength of lesbian work in feminist cinema, especially in recent years.

[5]"Third cinema" (versus Third World cinema), was first coined by Argentinian filmmakers Fernando Solanas and Octavio Getino during the late '60s as a rallying cry for anti-colonial, revolutionary cinema. During the late '80s, a renewed concept of third cinema was debated, especially among black British theorists and practioners, to signify the work of diasporic, politically- and theoretically-minded filmmakers who were starting to see themselves increasingly in terms of a community (see Pine and Willemen).

[6]*Hangul*, developed under the reign of King Sejong (1418-1450), was designed to replace Chinese characters and achieve widespread literacy. The consonants are said to be based on the shape of the human tongue, mouth, and throat when forming these letters.

[7]Silverman examines the work of Yvonne Rainer, Sally Potter, Patricia Gruben, and Bette Gordon in relation to the asynchronous use of the female voice and female subjectivity.

[8]Walter Lew's book offers another example of a critical collaged based on Cha's *DICTEE*.

[9]Although I watched Korean movies whenever possible, they weren't a prime source of inspiration because, with the exception of a few works, the exported films I saw during the '80s and '90s were typically staid melodramas or slight comedies. Because I was interested in subjective cinema, middle-aged male perspectives (from which the directors invariably worked) about Korean women and their representation in Korean cinema struck me as idealized or, again, marginalized or tokenistic.

[10]Japanese American or Japanese Canadian, the interchangeability was intentional because the co-writer, Kerri Sakamoto, and I believed the social and political histories were so similar, so why not the personal ones? This story was meant to transcend an arbitrary national border and acknowledge the similarities between the experiences of people of Japanese descent in North America.

References

Barthes, Roland. *Camera Lucida*. New York: Hill and Wang, 1981.

Bhabha, Homi K. *The Location of Culture*. London: Routledge, 1994.

Cha, Theresa Hak Kyung. *DICTEE*. New York: Tanam Press, 1982.

Chow, Rey. "Where Have All the Natives Gone?" *Displacements: Cultural Identities in Question*. Ed. Angelika Bammer. Bloomington: Indiana University Press, 1994.

Doane, Mary Ann. "Ideology and the Practice of Sound Editing and Mixing." *The Cinematic Apparatus*. Eds. Teresa de Lauretis and Stephen Heath. New York: St. Martin's Press, 1980.

Jameson, Frederic. "Modernism and Imperialism." *Nationalism, Colonialism, and Literature*. Eds. Terry Eagleton, Frederic Jameson, Edward Said. Minneapolis: University of Minnesota Press, 1990.

Lew, Walter. *Excerpts from: Dikte, For DICTEE*. Seoul, Korea: Yeul Publishing Co., 1992.

Pines, Jim and Paul Willemen, Eds. *See Questions of Third Cinema*. London: British Film Institute, 1989.

Shohat, Ella and Robert Stam. "The Cinema After Babel: Language, Difference, Power." *Screen* 26 (May-August 1985): 35-58.

Silverman, Kaja. *The Acoustic Mirror: The Female Voice in Psychoanalysis and Cinema*. Bloomington: Indiana University Press, 1988.

Trinh, T. Minh-Ha. *Woman, Native, Other: Writing Postcoloniality and Feminism*. Bloomington: Indiana University Press, 1989.

Selected Filmography

This listing includes films and videos made by and about Korean American women, available through the following distributors or filmmakers:

Be Good, My Children, Christine Chang, 1992, 47 min. 16mm. Women Make Movies, 462 Broadway, #500, New York, NY 10012, 212-925-0606.

Camp Arirang, Diana Lee and Grace Yoon Kyung Lee, 1995, 28 min. video. Third World Newsreel, 335 West 38th Street, New York, NY 10018, 212-947-9277.

Comfort Me, Soo Jin Kim, 1993, 8min. video. 201 Wayland Street, Los Angeles, CA 90042, 213-550-1772.

Daughterline, Grace Lee-Park, 1995, 11 min. 16mm. Grace-Lee Park, 6104 N.E. Sacramento, Portland, OR 97213, 503-223-2243.

Distance, Soo Jin Kim, 1991, 13 min. video. Soo Jin Kim (see *Comfort Me*).

Do Roo (Circling Back), Soon Mi Yoo, 1993, 14 min. 16mm. Yellow Earth Productions, 3900 Cathedral Avenue N. W., #501A, Washington, DC 20016, 202-338-9577.

A Forgotten People, Dai-Sil Kim Gibson, 1995, 59 min. 16mm. CrossCurrents Media, NAATA, 346 9th Street, 2nd Floor, San Francisco, CA 94103, 415-552-9550.

Golden Dreams, Alice Ra, 1995, 9 min. 16mm. CrossCurrents Media.

Great Girl, Kim Su Theiler, 1993, 14 min., 16mm. Women Make Movies.

Halmani, Kyung-ja Lee, 1988, 30 min., 16mm. Pyramid Film & Video, 2801 Colorado Avenue, Santa Monica, CA 90404, 310-828-7577.

Here Now, Yunah Hong, 1995, 32 min., 16mm. Yunah Hong, 223 East 4th Street, #12, NY, NY 10009, 212-677-8980.

An Initiation Kut for a Korean Shaman, Diana Lee and Laurel Kendall, 1991, 37 min. video. University of Hawaii Press, 2840 Kolowalu Street, Honolulu, HI 96822, 808-956-8697.

In Memoriam to an Identity, R. Vaughn, 1993, 5 min. video. Katharine Burdette, 15308 Alan Drive, Laurel, MD 20707, 301-725-0472.

Korea: Homes Apart, Christine Choy and J. T. Takagi, 1991, 60 min. 16mm. Third World Newsreel.
La Senorita Lee, Hyun Mi Oh, 1995, 26 min. 16mm. Cinema Guild, 1697 Broadway, #506, New York, NY 10019, 212-246-5522.

Living in half tones, Me-K. Ahn, 1994, 9 min. video. Third World Newsreel.

Memory/all echo, Yunah Hong, 1990, 27 min. video. Women Make Movies.

Mija, Hei Sook Park, 1989, 30 min. 16mm. Visual Communications, 263 South Los Angeles Street, Suite 307, Los Angeles, CA 90012, 213-680-4462.

mouth to mouth, Theresa Hak Kyung Cha, 1975, 8 min., video. University Art Museum and Pacific Film Archive, University of California at Berkeley, 2625 Durant Avenue, Berkeley, CA 94720, 510-643-8584.

My Niagara, Helen Lee, 1992, 40 min, 16mm. Women Make Movies.

Permutations, Theresa Hak Kyung Cha, 10 min., 16mm. University Art Museum and Pacific Film Archive.

Prey, Helen Lee, 1995, 26 min., 16mm. Canadian Film Centre, 2489 Bayview Avenue, North York, Ontario, M2L 1A8, Canada, 416-445-1446.

Red Lolita, Gloria Toyun Park, 1989, 6 min., video. Gloria Toyun Park, 3064 Cardillo Avenue, Hacienda Heights, CA, 91745, 818-336-6141.

re/dis/appearing, Theresa Hak Kyung Cha, 1977, 3 min., video. University Art Museum and Pacific Film Archive.

Sa-i-Gu, Christine Choy, Elaine Kim, Dai-Sil Kim Gibson, 1993, 36 min., video. CrossCurrents Media.

Sally's Beauty Spot, Helen Lee, 1992, 12 min., 16mm. Women Make Movies.

Through the Milky Way, Yunah Hong, 1992, 19 min., video. Women Make Movies.

Translating Grace, Anita Lee, 1996, 20 min., 16mm. Nagual Productions, P. O. Box 364, Station P, 704 Spadina Ave, Toronto, Ontario, MSS 2S9. 416-588-6976.

Undertow, Me-K. Ahn, 1995, 19 min., video. Asian American Renaissance, 1564 Lafond Avenue, St. Paul, MN 55104. 612-641-4040.
Videoeme, Theresa Hak Kyung Cha, 1976, 3 min., video. University Art Museum and Pacific Film Archive.

What Do You Know about Korea? R. Vaughn, 1996, 7 min., video. Katharine Burdette, (see *In Memoriam to an Identity).*

The Women Outside, Hye-Jung Park and J.T. Takagi/Third World Newsreel, 1995, 60 min., 16mm. Third World Newsreel.

MELISSA KIM

The Picnic

August 15th, 1995: Korean Thanksgiving Day

The food preparations ended around one o'clock, and my entire family crammed into the van and piloted towards "Holy Spirit Cemetery." Arriving at God's gate, my family moved expertly through a labyrinth of tombstones, the engraved names enlightening visitors of past heroes, all proudly bearing bouquets of beautiful flowers. Delicate little patches of the Garden of Eden were everywhere; old ancestral trees were in perfect balance with the rainbow coloured flowers, beautiful in the winter, glorious in the spring. Coming upon my deceased grandfather's territory, my mother set the table with the rice cakes in the middle, the fruits owning the four corners of the table, the egg rolls and the fish hugging the East and West of the rice cakes, and *soju*, a Korean beverage, leaning against the leg of the table.

As a young child, it was explained to me that this feast was prepared for my deceased grandfather—it was our way of honouring him. This tradition occurred twice a year; once on Korean Thanksgiving and the second on the anniversary of his death. The table of food was always set at the foot of his small, rectangular plot. Forming a semi-circle around his plot, we would pay our respects by bowing.

Our traditional bow consisted of three fluid motions: First, our hands would pile gingerly on top of the other, then our foreheads would correspondingly touch our hands, and finally, our knees and palms would grace the soft green grass. As it was custom to respectively bow twice as a family, we prepared to start our second set. However, we were soon interrupted when an elderly white woman, holding a bouquet of flowers, spat heatedly towards us, "A cemetery is no place for a picnic!"

I wiped a bead of sweat off my forehead. My grandmother's face distorted with uncertainty. My father's hands fell limply to his side. My young brother whispered into my mother's ear, "You didn't tell me this was a picnic." My mother's eyes flashed with indignation, but her mouth remained silent. My family stood together, shocked into stillness by eight small words.

"A cemetery is no place for a picnic...."

MIN SOOK LEE

Ontario Lottery Corporation

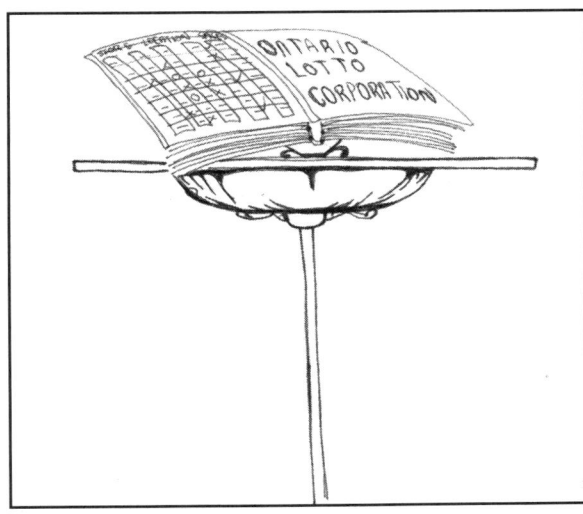

WE HAD THE DISTINCTION OF BEING THE ONLY STORE IN ONTARIO WITH TWO LOTTO MACHINES —

THIS MEANT THAT WE HAD TO KEEP UP WITH THE SALES THAT WARRANTED AN EXTRA MACHINE. ON BUSY NIGHTS, MY DAD, MY SISTER AND I WORKED THE COUNTER AS A TEAM. OUR MOTIONS WERE FLUID, SPARE AND REHEARSED.

IN WHAT SEEMED LIKE ONE LONG CONTINUUM OF ACTION, WE PRESSED
THE PADDED BUTTONS OF THE HUMMING BLUE MACHINE,
FED PENCILLED-PAPER INTO THE SLOTTED OPENING,
SWIFLY RECREASED JAMMED AND WORN PAPER INTO SHARP EDGES,
AND MADE CHANGE.

MY DAD HAD SET UP A SHELF AREA AWAY FROM THE COUNTER
WITH PENCILS, ASHTRAYS, LOTTO SHEETS, A CALENDAR AND A
649 ROULETTE WHEEL. THIS AREA WAS THICK WITH SMOKE,
CROWDED WITH ELBOWS AND HUNCHED SHOULDERS,
WAS THE MEETING PLACE FOR MANY NEIGHBOURHOOD PEOPLE.

OUR PROFIT MARGIN WAS ONE PERCENT OF THE TOTAL TICKET SALES. AT THE NIGHT'S END MY DAD WOULD TALLY THE SALES OF BOTH MACHINES, SIGH, AND DESPAIR AT THE FALLING RATE OF TICKET SALES.

IN SIX MONTHS THE LOTTO CORPORATION CONTACTED US AND INFORMED US THAT OUR SALES DIDN'T WARRANT THE EXTRA MACHINE. THEY CAME TO TAKE THE MACHINE AWAY ON A TUESDAY MORNING AND FROM THEN ON THE STORE'S HECTIC LOTTERY NIGHTS SUBSIDED INTO QUIETUDE.

GLORIA U. Y. KIM

On Lotus Blossoms, Rice Kings and Riot Grrrls

When I was a little girl, I used to lie in bed and caress myself absent-mindedly. In my innocence I never thought I was doing anything wrong. In fact, I delighted in discovering my body's response to itself. I even remember naively telling my little brother that if you rubbed yourself a certain way, it would feel good. Then, while I was still in grade school, my mother told me during bath time to be careful how I touched myself (with a waving hand motion) "down there" because I could get a disease. Imagine my daily terror after that when washing up! That was my introduction to sexual shame, understood, as if through osmosis, from euphemisms and gestures.

The absurdity of it strikes me now as a grown adult—but my path was set. My formative years consisted of my masturbating in the dark, all the while praying I wouldn't get caught by my mother, my father, or paradoxically, by God himself (as if he would be bothered by the onanistic concerns of a little Korean girl)! This shame inhibited my sexual growth and tinged my early sexual experiences with a certain fearful denial (oh, the memories of groping with boys in the basement dens of friends, pretending that the lump that I felt against my leg wasn't really there). When I got a little older, this naiveté contributed to the trauma of my lost virginity. I remember calling up a guy friend and sobbing, "Is that all there really is to it?" And, on top of that, add the sudden onslaught in my early twenties of a certain kind of attention from a certain type of man (shall we call them, *ahem, rice kings?*) who wanted my favours in a very specific way.

Needless to say, my early forays into sex were nothing if not ridiculous and somewhat traumatizing. If I had the language back then that I possess now, I could have laughed about it and seen my way out of my helpless fury at my early sexual experiences. But coupled with the early shame, the kind of attention I was receiving only reinforced my aggravation. Time and again I would rage at casual incidents I felt no control over. Walking down the street with

Asian girlfriends, we were assaulted with "Look at the China dolls!" or worse yet, "Chinky pussy!" Less in-your-face, but no less demeaning, were times when I was chased by toothy-faced *"Ko-nee-chee-wa's,"* or *"Nee-how-ma's."* I loathed these encounters yet, as a, *gently-mannered* Korean girl, I found it difficult to express how offended I was. In their misplaced way, the guys were trying to make me feel comfortable and start a conversation they thought I could participate in. Too bad they didn't realize from the flawless English of my responses, I had lived most of my life in Canada, and that I was neither Chinese nor Japanese. I finally learned to respond by shrieking, *"Get rost, you roser!"* in high-pitched falsetto to get my point across.

For a long time, I couldn't articulate what offended me so much about these men and their presumptions about me and my Asian-ness. I had only my instinctual anger. But when I started talking to other people about my encounters, I began to feel that yes, I was right in being offended, and it had something to do with being exoticized, in being seen not as a human being, but as a stereotype of my culture. The stereotype was very much about being a certain type of woman, a *hand-covered-over-the-mouth-while-giggling* nymphomaniac, and was attributed to my race rather than being a personality type that anyone of any race could be.

What is particularly interesting is that the two concepts of Asian womanhood, the Lotus Blossum and the Dragon Lady, or *geisha* and *harridan*, while deeply entrenched in western symbology, were completely unknown to me until my encounters with rice kings. It was their expectations that taught me what these stereotypes were—stereotypes that I believe have set the tone for the way Asian women and girls are perceived the world over, and have contributed to how they are marketed and exploited in the sex trade.

I felt as an Asian woman I needed to reclaim my voice and so with that intention I decided to make a documentary film on the way Asian women are fetishized. I thought, I'll make something that kicks ass, that tries in a punk rocker, riot grrrl sort of way to say, *hey, this is so not cool and we ain't takin' it no more!* I planned to apply for funding and ambitiously hoped to be able to make something that could be seen on television. After all, I thought, "diversity" was the new buzzword, and every funder and broadcaster wanted to get on that bandwagon. But several things happened that made me realize that we weren't as far ahead as I thought. Funders, while initially liking the story, didn't want to believe that the exoticization of Asian women was an everyday phenomenon as I was suggesting, but instead needed to think of this as an aberration in our multi-culti times. These funders were, for the most part, men, and I think for them to believe that these stereotypes were so common, led them to question whether they, as members of this white male-dominated society, could also be complicit.

Also, I found it strange that most of the Asian women I spoke to weren't as enlightened as I thought they'd be. Women that I thought of as smart and intelligent, when interviewed, said things to me like, "I get why men like Asian women. We're so much more delicate and we have such soft skin." The Asian women I knew who were in relationships with white men, as I was and am now, were confused about the political dynamics of the relationship and for the most part, reluctant to examine them. One Asian woman filmmaker confessed to me that "in the sack," she wasn't comfortable taking the lead, but instead, let her white husband (who was a self-confessed *connoisseur* of *women of colour*) do whatever he wanted. It almost helped me understand why one loathsome fellow said to me in a pre-interview, "Why do I like 'em? Because sexually, I can do whatever the fuck I want to them."

When I turned the lens on myself and looked at my own relationship I realized there are all sorts of things we take for granted in our roles as Asian women. For example, my boyfriend has always delighted in calling me "tiny" and "cute." Now, this may or may not be problematic for a woman of any other race, but for an Asian woman, this racial stereotype plays very much into our diminutive build and character-type, and therefore this is a loaded statement. Also, when I began to really scrutinize my sexual past, I couldn't say that I didn't in some way participate in my assumed "exoticism." As it is, women in general are socialized to respond to the world with a resounding "yes," and Asian women especially are raised to be self-sacrificing and obedient. As much as I'd like to claim differently, I know this to be true.

Cultures routinely participate in the continuation of their social values with some level of self-annihilation, but Asian cultures particularly have valued and systematically codified duty and conformity into their philosophies and their institutions. Confucius, one of Asia's greatest philosophers, emphasized the importance of social order and obedience, and influenced thinking and social behaviour for centuries in Asia. Recently, a Queen's University psychologist Mark Sabbagh found in a study comparing Chinese and North American pre-schoolers that Chinese pre-schoolers were better able to control impulsive attention and behaviour than their North American counterparts. Imagine my horror when Sabbagh explained this by saying that perhaps this had to do with genetics or perhaps it was because Chinese parents valued controlling impulses and following directions more than North American parents. The implications of this study, in terms of sexual behaviour and dynamics, make me cringe.

Society's romantic ideal that a woman is supposed to be swept off her feet by a man who is stronger, bolder, and more sexually experienced is taken to the *nth* degree when put in context of the Lotus Blossom stereotype. Many of my early sexual encounters played out some version of that fantasy in tone and attitude, with me as Asian sex kitten writhing in true porno fashion (for who doesn't somehow absorb pornography?—fashion, advertising, television, and cinema lives and breathes on such imagery) while the man would masterfully suck my breasts before moving on to diddle my clitoris in what he would imagine was erotic expertise.

All of this took me to the realization that perhaps this myth of the sexually submissive "Oriental flower" was, like all stereotypes, subconscious and ingrained in an almost primal way. And while no one wants to believe that they are so vulnerable to irrationality and unable to think beyond these stereotypes, least of all kick-ass riot grrrl filmmakers who have spent a lot of time thinking about race and sex and power, it seems that we are all sometime slaves to our limbic systems.

But my findings do not negate the fact that I and other Asian women are trying to do things to counteract stereotyping. And while the wider mainstream may not be ready for Asian women artists who say, "fuck it!" it is happening as we speak. I am not, of course, talking about the Quentin Tarantino-styled hyper-sexual Asian woman who is modeled on the Dragon Lady stereotype. I am talking about Asian women artists who are working their way out of these creepy "Memoirs of a Geisha"-like stories and attempting to just be—women like Jean Yoon and her *Yoko Ono Project,* a play that examines Asian women in relationships at their most human level. Or, Catherine Hernandez and her play, *Singkil,* which is based on a Filipino-Muslim dance that explores the mother-daughter relationship. While we may yet be in a position where we're damned if we do and damned if we don't, the perpetual Lotus Blossom or Dragon Lady, it's a matter of continuing to make the work and find our voices.

While I felt stymied for a while on my documentary, in the end, I have decided to go forward and just make the damn thing. Fuck shame, fuck embarrassment, fuck all the early well-meaning but ridiculous socialization about my sexuality and fuck other voices telling me that what I'm saying isn't relevant. Ultimately, my greatest strength in working out this project is in realizing that what I have to say isn't necessarily for mainstream audiences, but for people like me. While we may not yet have the numbers or the power, in acknowledging ourselves and our points of view by addressing ourselves without apology or explanation, we are slowly but surely clawing our way out of oppression and stereotyping and finding our way to empowerment.

References

Sabbagh, M. A., F. Xu, S. M. Carlson, L. J. Moses and K. Lee. "Executive Functioning and the Theory of Mind in Preschool Children from Beijing, China: Comparisons to U.S. Preschoolers." *Psychological Science* (in press).

IV.
Disrupting Tongues

JEAN YOON

White Life

Errol scoops boiled potatoes out of a pot and into a deep bowl. They look like huge eggs, what I imagine turtle eggs would look like if you could peel them. Bleached and tasteless, potatoes are the one dish that make me dread these family dinners. "You can't have dinner without potatoes," Errol says every time we sit down to eat. And they have to be mashed, pulverized, and further whitened with milk and a bit of butter.

There are so many names to remember. Ann, Jon's mother; Errol, his father. Ted, Errol's brother, therefore Jon's uncle. Ted's woman, soon to be his third wife, Melanie or Maureen or Margaret, some name that starts with "M." Bob, also Errol's brother, older than Ted and Errol and married to Janet, his second wife, or maybe his third but certainly not his first. The mysterious and absent baby brother Drew, who is an alcoholic. Linda, the only girl of the family and never mentioned.

Ann's family is on the West Coast. She comes from a family of nine.

I squeeze Jon's hand under the table. Jon passes me the carrots while his mother leans over solicitously. "Try some brussel sprouts, Sally. Parsnips anyone?" Jon pats my leg as if to say, "You'll be fine, Sal, it's just a meal, relax."

There are two forks. Two of them. Is one for the meat, and the other for the salad? Or is the second for desert and the spoon that lies like a headboard above my plate is to stir the coffee? Relax? I'm supposed to relax?

Errol says, "So tell us what a traditional Christmas is like in your family, Sally?" I put down my fork, swallow and think back. Traditional. Christmas. An oxymoron. Christmas in my family has always been a series of minor disasters with the occasional success in emulating the festivities we saw played out on television. We had almost all of it worked out, but it was never spontaneous. A tree, presents, stockings and even turkey dinner. I don't know how my mother managed that. She struggled to cook meals that didn't make sense to her, meals that never looked right, meals that tasted so bland that when it was all laid out she would say she wasn't really hungry, she'd just watch us eat. Christmas. A White Christmas. Now I have it. Snow drifting over the city, a white family, a white life.

I start trying to explain this to Errol, but realize that he is drifting away, losing interest. He wants details of "ethnic colour," odd traditions from the old country. He wants me to tell him that Korean-Canadians make turkey stuffing from *kimchi* and shrimp, that we have a version of Santa who wears silk and says, "*Eung Eung Eung*" instead of "Ho Ho Ho."

"More potatoes, Errol?"

Later Ted asks me how I, as a Korean, feel about the Japanese. I tell him about Dad who knows how to speak Japanese perfectly but refuses because of his deep resentment over the occupation. How the relationship between Koreans and Japanese has never been good, despite or perhaps because of the similarities between the two cultures. How the Japanese still refuse to grant full citizenship to those of non-Japanese descent, most of whom are Korean. The bitterness of it.

Ted says, "Oh yes, those Japs are so damn racist."

He goes on to say how the internment of the Japanese was therefore justified, especially if you consider the times. He says the Japanese were never really Canadians, they never really felt Canadian and there were, without a doubt, spies among those interned. "How would you know?" I bristle. And what about the children, the one's who had never been to Japan, the ones who were born in Canada and grew up reading *Anne of Green Gables* just like everyone else? How do you justify jailing a seven year old?

He says, "They were all Japanese."

"They were Canadian," I insist. "And what about the German-Canadians? Why weren't they *all* rounded up? Why wasn't all *their* property confiscated and sold off? What about German *aliens?* How exactly do you determine citizenship, Ted? By the colour of your hair? By how round your eyes are?'

Bob and Janet both pull away from the table. Errol stands and starts stacking dishes. "I'll go get the coffee," Ann says. "I'll help," says Melanie.

"If war broke out between Korea and Canada, what would my status be? Would you have me shipped off to the Northwest Territories?" My voice is very low. Almost a growl. The room is utterly silent.

"Of course, war with Korea at this time is ridiculous." Ted leans back in his chair, expansive and totally at ease. "The question is hypothetical."

I stand and realize I am shaking. I feel flushed and hot. Janet laughs nervously. Jon puts his arm protectively around my waist. Ann stands pale and rigid at the head of the table holding a coffee pot. Janet and Bob lunge for the table.

"We'll start taking these away," Bob says loudly. "Starting with the knives."

MICHELLE CHO

Can the Desert Change?

I've always felt like a penguin in the desert of Canada's Whiteness, where the myth of multiculturalism and tolerance masks the true experience of racialized minorities and Others who don't fit the mainstream definition of what it means to be Canadian. Despite Canada's attempts to celebrate cultural differences, why do I feel I don't belong? The desert does not sustain people like me where the ideal inhabitant has all of the markers of privilege: someone who is White, male, straight, middle-class, able-bodied, young, and Christian. Everyone needs more than food, shelter, and water to survive; we all need community. But what happens a when a person can't find a community to fit into?

I've met so many people wandering in the desert who are searching for their oasis, many of whom I assume experience similar feelings of alienation and a lack of belonging. But is it really about finding an oasis, or is it about transforming the desert to make it equally livable for us all?

Growing up in a white-dominated society, I was left parched and dehydrated by the effects of racism, classism, and sexism (although I didn't know it at the time). But when I tried looking for a place in the Korean community, it didn't quench my thirst either. My interaction with the Korean community was limited to Christian groups, which I found full of cliques, petty conflicts, and materialistic tendencies. Perhaps these internal power struggles are inevitable in a community rejected and devalued by mainstream society. The first generation longs for their children's stability and push them into professional, high-paying jobs in the hope that their children will gain the status that they never enjoyed. This was never my interest.

I went to a high school where the majority of students were from White, middle- to upper-class families. I felt like a complete anomaly in a place where everyone looked like they stepped out of a glossy magazine and where I was the token exoticized Other in a Benetton poster ad. My friends were well-intentioned and tried to understand me, but no one ever really got it. I was never sure what "it" was, but I knew that there was something inside me that had to get out.

When I was 16, I had a discussion with a White friend's dad about the Korean War. When it became clear that I didn't really know the history very well, he proceeded to tell me that I should learn my country's history. At first I was embarrassed, then angry. When my friend's father told me that I was uneducated about "my country," he implied that Canada was not my home and that I had failed as an ambassador for Korea, even though I had never pretended to be one. But looking back, I see that he was right. While I was defensive and wish he had been more sensitive, I did not grow up knowing the history of Korea and regret this.

As children of the diasporic experience, we have little control over what we learn about in school. I never learned about the histories of racialized communities in Canada, the true history of past and present experiences of colonization, nor was I provided the opportunity to explore them. This, in particular, includes the silencing of traumatic histories in Korea, such as the plight of Korean "comfort women." About five years ago, I stumbled upon some articles detailing the experience of approximately 200,000 women in who were kidnapped into sexual slavery in service of the Japanese military, which to this day continues to be denied by the Japanese government. It made me so angry to know that had it not been for the survivors that came forward to break the silence, this would have remained a secret never to be spoken of in the open. Looking back, I am stunned that the colonization of Korea by Japan, the trauma of the Korean War, nor their experiences of racism, sexism, or classism in Canada was, and still are, rarely mentioned by the elders in our community. Sometimes I wonder how my perception of self and community would have changed had I grown up with a deeper understanding of the political and historical context into which I was born.

When I got to university, I hoped that I would begin to find my place in the academic world, only to find again that this was another part of the desert of Whiteness. I was committed to the theory of social justice and decided to apply to the School of Social Work, thinking that it would be a place which would celebrate difference and where I could gain skills to work with people living on the margins like me. However, when I was accepted into the program I realized that what I had hoped for had been a mirage. There I was again, in a White-dominated institution, in a faculty where no one looked like me. Was I only there as a token? It seemed that way because I always felt called on to be a spokesperson for all people of colour.

Searching still for my oasis, I got involved in student activism. When I went to protests, people would chant, "This is what democracy looks like!" But when I looked around and saw no one that looked like me, I wondered, how this could be democracy when communities of colour weren't present?

Throughout my life, my interaction with people has often begun with the question, "Where are you from?" Many people seem to look at this question as an easy starting point to a conversation and perhaps as a way to begin a connection or get to know me better. Little do they know, I've already shut down and checked out, because I'm no longer interested in engaging in the same scripted discussion about how I'm different, or some long-winded anecdote about an Asian friend or previous lover.

Although I have not died in the desert, I definitely have not been unaffected. I've struggled with depression my whole life and while depression may have something to do with one's genetic makeup, dealing with the external realities of living in the desert doesn't make it any easier.

Sometimes people tell me that I overly politicize things and get too emotional. I think that the idea of making the personal political gets de-legitimated because it disrupts the idea that a well-formulated argument must be rational and even-tempered in order to be acceptable. But if people are dying in this desert, isn't it legitimate to say how I find it hard to separate what I think in my head from what I feel in my heart? In order to make sense of all of my lived experience, it's helped me to understand that all of it connects to a larger political reality.

Finding role models has always been difficult and it's only now that I'm beginning to make connections with people that can give me advice on how to resist different forms of domination and still be well. Recently I met a group of Korean women who believe in resisting racist, sexist, classist, and other forms of domination. I realized then that it had taken me 25 years to find people that looked and thought like me. And I wondered how different life would have been if I had people around me when I was growing up who understood what I was going through.

My own family has always been nurturing and if it wasn't for their support, I wouldn't have survived at all. Yet however much my parents encouraged me to be my own person, I still felt guilty that I wasn't doing my best to fit into Canadian society through the typical ways of getting a good job and enjoying the ride, rather than rocking the boat. I think it was difficult for them to understand at first because they didn't want me to put myself at risk.

One might say, "What's a penguin doing in the desert to begin with anyway? If the penguin doesn't feel like she belongs in the desert, why doesn't she return to the Arctic?" But what if you were born in the desert and you have no choice because it's your home? Sure, I may be able to find some Korean groups where I feel at home. And yes, I can enjoy the occasional cultural event or ethnic restaurant, but I need more than a few groups or events that dot the desert like occasional truck stops.

At the same time, when I call myself a penguin in the desert, I remind myself that Canada is a White settler nation, won through cultural genocide and theft of land. Our diasporic communities need to do a lot of work to recognize the way in which we are complicit in reproducing oppression. Surviving as racialized people in a capitalist, colonial empire is difficult when the elusive dream of success and privilege is so attractive to those that have suffered so much. Many of us have been forced to come here because of the social and political turmoil in our home countries. We have to also remember how much we benefit from being able to live here.

In order for us all to really belong we need to change the landscape of this country. We need to move beyond a two-dimensional way of human interaction determined by rigidity of social constructionist notions of race, class, gender, queer identities, dis/ability, and age. As a woman of colour, I refuse to be submissive and play into dominant notions of Othering. Now I just take space where I can, because I've realized that no one is going to offer it to me. I'm still not sure where my future is. I just know that whatever I do, I want to continue to challenge and deconstruct the complexities of oppression in our society.

I'm convinced now that it isn't about finding an oasis, but rather challenging the hegemonic structures in our institutions and the destructiveness of racism, sexism, hetero-normativity, and classism in our relationships with the people around us. In order to do this, racialized communities must claim the space we deserve. If we don't, we will never transform the desert into a place that we can live. It's easy to slip into a spiral of negativity and fatalistic notions that things will never change. But I have to believe that change is possible because if it isn't, then I have nothing left to hold on to and I will never belong.

JULIE KANG

Un/becoming Jonquil

How does one write as a "Korean-Canadian-Woman writer?" This is a question that impressed itself upon me, not only as I considered submitting a piece to this anthology on "art and writing by Korean Canadian women," but over the years as a reader and as I became increasingly convinced that a writer is what I hoped and had to be.

Growing up with "Anne with an e" as my penned heroine of choice, whose red hair and freckles made her "different" in her neighbours' estimations, the landscape of Avonlea's blossoming orchards and elegantly effusive characters and surroundings held me in rapture. On long summer days spent in the pink brick suburbs and with parents who considered the lament "I'm bored" a sign that I needed to be enrolled in summer math school, I wrote stories.

It was an exquisitely beautiful day in Beverly Creek ... Jonquil walked along the path from her visit for tea with Hyacinth, skipping the whole way, stopping at points along the way to admire the Magnolias and Pristine and Ballerina roses in Mrs. McDonald's' picket-fenced garden....

Looking back, I realize that I thought that this was the only way to write when putting pencil to paper—to draw a picture of an idyllic scene of beauty. I pored through my mother's garden books to find the most pleasing names for plants and flowers. For the name of the neighbour with the lovely garden, I chose our family's favourite drive-through restaurant at the time.

I wrote Jonquil just the way I thought she ought to be—with wavy hair the colour of wheat, and the most delicate angelic face. I wrote about Jonquil's adventures walking around the village of Beverly Creek, sniffing flowers and exclaiming how beautiful it all was. I envisioned completing the series, *Jonquil of Beverly Creek*, by summer's end.

Many seasons later, I left Jonquil to her flowers.

In Grade 10 English, I stumbled across a little book called *Dance of the Happy Shades*, and was never quite the same. There was beauty in the most ordinary movements and conversations, I discovered. Inspired anew, I wrote.

This time, all of my characters were girls and women whose "lives" seemed firmly planted on Canadian soil, as if it made their existence more believable and permanent, ignoring the lessons I learned in history class—that it would be truer to life if their ancestors had journeyed to this land from somewhere else.

By then, I was starting to realize that others identified me as Asian, sometimes to my surprise, as I had internalized the characters that I had grown up writing about and emulating.

The stories I wrote during this time were mostly about heartbreak and disappointment and broken relationships, "issues" that evoked all of my sympathy as a fifteen-year-old keenly aware that if I was in so much pain from my unrequited pining for a boy in an older grade, there must be others who felt the same pain. It was not until several years later, after some disillusionment with writing, that I realized that I simply did not identify with the characters I wrote into life.

One moment stands out in my mind when, as I was reading through the stories I had written in high school, I realized that at the age of fifteen I had been writing, quite passionately, about the life of a middle-aged anglosaxon housewife in the '50s! I had been so moved by the stories of love and despair set in the living rooms of women from that era, that I had assumed that there was something in the settings and characteristics themselves which established for them a literary monopoly over anything I had personally experienced.

This brings me to another important question: is it necessary for one to write about one's own experience exclusively? Is my writing only valid if I write from the distinct, identifiable perspective of a Korean Canadian woman? I don't think so. After all, in writing fiction there is an essential imagining, a donning of another's experience, to live out of the many textures unique to an imagined individual.

However, for me, the realization that my Korean heritage was "allowed" to come through on paper, brought me out of my disillusionment with writing.

But, even with this realization, as I attempted to write stories, my words were slow to come and heavy with meaning, the burden of writing the experiences of those who I thought had not, would not, or could not write their stories, upon my shoulders.

During this period, it is not surprising that every story I wrote ended up being about my mother, in one way or another. Her face was present in every story I wrote, perhaps because her life seemed so much a "life lived," because her identity as a woman who had grown up in Korea, a land with a seemingly endless line of ancestors, had that permanence and believability I had so wanted to convey in my earlier writing. I believe that writing about the uprooted quality of her life in Canada somehow gave her life here something of that permanence and believability. Recently, we both realized that she has lived more of her life in Canada than in Korea, and this confronted and challenged my view of her identity, and mine.

Still, it seemed strange to write about a life that looked or felt like my own experience of life, because as a "Canadian with Korean ancestry," or a "Korean born in Canada," I felt I had no roots in this soil or any other. I simply could not capture a life such as mine, in either world, I thought.

Later, I came to understand that if my voice was indistinguishable from those of the heroines I grew up with, or those of my Caucasian classmates, this did not mean that my work was merely a copycat version that required an apology. It was liberating to realize that the objects and meanings that have shaped my experience are no less mine because I do not fit the description of the dominant culture, and that I also do not have to be constrained to write as a representative of my ethnicity.

I realized that my voice did not have to stand for all things "Korean" or "Canadian," or even to dwell neatly in the hyphen in between.

I have begun to write again. On long summer days, I am again embracing the Jonquil in me that loves the beauty in this world, who knows the pain of picking the most beautiful rose. I am poring over my mother's garden book, naming the growth I see in the soil.

HANA KIM

Snake

Nobody sees the stains in my heart.
Nobody sees through the holes in my throat.
Nobody smells the stench in my stomach.
                Nobody knows about my past.

뱀
김하나
번역 김하나

아무도 내 심장의 얼룩을 보지 못한다;
아무도 내 목구멍 속의 구멍을 보지 못한다;
아무도 내 뱃 속의 악취를 맡질 못한다.
       아무도 내 과거를 모른다.

SYLVIA YU CHAO

Cold Comfort
Sex Slaves for the Japanese Imperial Military

I was the only Asian kid at my suburban elementary school in Vancouver. As a result, I keenly felt conspicuous and out of place. "Where's Korea? Is it in China?" my ruddy-faced Caucasian friends innocently asked. They didn't mean to make me feel like I had come from a country of little consequence. But our class history lessons focused on a Eurocentric view of world events, which didn't help my brewing identity issues. Nevertheless, at home or at great-uncle's house, I gathered up pieces of Korean history. I was piqued by the fact that my mother's uncle, Kim Tae-Houn, was fluent in Japanese because he lived in Korea under thirteen years of Japanese occupation that lasted from 1910 to 1945. He had always quietly shunned Japanese stereos and cars, instead drove a Cadillac and bought only American-made products. I learned part of the reason why he did that was because he was a firsthand witness to acts of oppression and abuse of Koreans at the hands of the Japanese durinig the colonial period. And he himself was, more than once, unfairly treated by Japanese teachers throughout middle school and high school.

What was shocking to me was discovering the story of the "comfort women"—young Korean women (as well as women from other Japanese colonies) who suffered unspeakable pain in Japanese military and government sanctioned rape stations. It's a terrible chapter of history that must not be forgotten. Between 200,000 and 400,000[1] women, 80 percent of them of Korean descent (Hicks 11), were kidnapped, deceived, and coerced into a system of sex slavery in East Asia from 1932 to 1945 (Coomaraswamy).[2] However, the Japanese government continues to deny their direct involvement (Yoshiaki 37).

The military sexual slavery issue, which still today is unresolved, propelled me onto a journey of research and soul-searching that has lasted for years. It has also led me to take several trips to Washington, D.C., to San Francisco, and to Seoul so that I could meet military comfort women survivors. I wanted to know how these women were able to survive unspeakable abuse and what their lives were like now. These women were taken at the prime of their lives. Those who made it home were subjected to lives of isolation, ostracism, and suffocating feelings of shame and guilt (Hicks 20). Many felt too defiled to marry. Quite elderly now, their suffering continues. The *halmonis* (Korean word for grandmother) I spoke with have complained of sleep disorders and terrible nightmares.

They have not received closure of any kind. To this day, the Japanese government refuses to acknowledge and accept legal responsibility for its "comfort women" system despite key historical documents proving they were directly involved (Watanabe 10). In a U.N. report in 1997 by Special Rapporteur Gay McDougall (1998), she calls Japan's enforced enslavement of the comfort women "one of the most egregious cases of wartime systematic rape and sexual slavery in history."

Japanese Government-Sanctioned Sexual Slavery System

The Japanese Imperial Military sexual slavery system was intended to boost the morale of the troops, and prevent them from raping local women (Chung). The women forced into this system were drawn from areas the Japanese considered racially inferior[3]: Korea, then a colony of Japan, as well as from China, the Philippines, Burma and even the Dutch-occupied territories in Southeast Asia. They were sent to "comfort" stations all over East Asia. The soldiers euphemistically called these women "comfort women" because they considered them so-called "playthings." Their sole purpose was to "soothe" the men as they fought on the frontlines.

For many, the slavery lasted as long as eight years; most were raped by as many as 50 men a day. These "women" were merely girls; some were as young as twelve years old (Hicks 233). Young girls were targeted because they were virgins and were free of sexual diseases. They were also mostly from poor families in rural areas, lured away with promises of well-paying jobs. In the comfort stations, where they were confined, they lived in deplorable conditions in tiny cubicles, often as small as three feet by five feet (Coomaraswamy). An army doctor carried out regular health checks to prevent the spread of venereal diseases, but they mostly overlooked the frequent cigarette burns, bruises, bayonet stabs, and even broken bones inflicted on the women by soldiers. The women had very little time off and quite frequently, they barely had time to wash themselves before the next soldier or officer arrived (Coomaraswamy).

Today, there are less than 200 known Japanese military sex slave survivors in East Asia. They are in their 70s and 80s. In Korea alone, only 132 women are alive of the 212 former sex slaves who came forward to testify in 1991, after the first "comfort woman" survivor testified publicly at a press conference in Seoul (see Korean Council).[4] Sadly, these aging survivors are dying before they can hear the apology they have been seeking for some time now from the Japanese government.

Breaking 50 Years of Silence

The first sex slave of Korean descent to publicly bear witness was 68-year-old Kim Hak-Soon. She had seen on TV a Japanese politician deny the military ever used "comfort women" and that a massive sexual slavery system did not exist. After connecting with activists and scholars, Hak-Soon courageously spoke out about her life as a Japanese Imperial Military sex slave, and wept at a press conference on August 14, 1991. She said she was testifying in public because she no longer had any relatives that would be ashamed of her. Soon after, a hotline was opened up for survivors of Japanese military sexual slavery to come forward. In total, 212 women came forward.

Kim Hak-Soon was only 17 when her nightmare began. She'd never had intimate relations with a man before. "The Japanese soldiers came along in a truck, beat us, and then dragged us into the back," she said. "I was told that if I were drafted I could earn lots of money at the textile company, and that it was also the emperor's order. I was taken to China to serve as a comfort woman for Japanese soldiers at military bases. I was raped on that first day, and it never stopped for a single day for the next three months" (Watanabe 2).

Often forced to accommodate dozens of soldiers in a day, Hak-Soon tried to flee three times. Twice she was caught and severely beaten, and finally on the third attempt she escaped with the help of a Korean man. They later married, but she lost her husband and children during the Korean War. In an interview with a Japanese scholar, Hak-Soon explained:

> I was born as a woman but never lived as a woman.... I suffer from a bitterness I do not know how to overcome. I only want to ask the Japanese government not to go to war again. I feel sick when I am close to a man. Not just Japanese men but all men—even my own husband, who saved me from the brothel—have made me feel this way. I shiver when I see the Japanese flag. Because it carried that flag, I hated the airplane I took to come to Japan. I've kept trying to disclose the facts.... Why should I feel ashamed? I don't have to feel ashamed. (Watanabe 2).

The women who made it home returned to lives of isolation and societal rejection, compounded by deeply instilled feelings of guilt and shame. Their lives were destroyed. Further, they were forced into more than 50 years of silence, a second victimization. They experienced even more emotional and psychological suffering because they could not voice their pain (Dolgopol). Many could not marry. As a result of violent physical and sexual abuse, sexually transmitted diseases, and drug addictions arising from their war-time experiences, many women bear serious health effects, including permanent damage to their reproductive organs and urinary tracts. Many of the women also found themselves unable to bear children as a result of their mistreatment.

Hak-Soon and other survivors who came forward launched a class action suit at the Tokyo District Court on December 6, 1991. In the suit, they were demanding: 1) an official apology; 2) compensatory payment to survivors in lieu of full reparation—each plaintiff asked for ¥20 million ($172,549 Cdn); 3) a thorough investigation of their cases; 4) the revision of Japanese school textbooks identifying this issue as part of the colonial oppression of the Korean people; and 5) the building of a memorial museum (see "Comfort Women").

The Japanese government initially denied Hak-Soon's story. But in 1992, Japan's Chief Cabinet Secretary expressed "deep remorse," admitting for the first time that the Japanese Imperial Military was in some way involved in the running of comfort station facilities. Later that year, the Japanese government released 127 documents implicating the Japanese military in the use of "comfort stations." However, the government continued to deny an official role in "recruiting" the women (McDougall 2000).

On March 26, 2001, the Tokyo District Court dismissed the compensation demand of the late Kim Hak-Soon[5] and her fellow plaintiffs. Presiding Judge Shoichi Maruyama admitted the plaintiffs had suffered, but stated that individual victims' claims for damages against the victimizer country were not thought to be acceptable under international law. He said that individuals could not be compensated for wartime damage because the redress issue was settled by a 1965 bilateral agreement between Japan and South Korea.

Meeting *Halmonis*

Motivated in part because of the lack of public awareness of this issue in North America and the seeming indifference to their experiences not only by the Japanese and Korean government, but also by the Korean Canadian community, I have spent the last six years trying to find out more about Korean, Asian and Dutch Japanese military sexual slavery survivors.

In 2001, I traveled to Washington, D.C. and San Francisco to meet the late Kim Soon-Duk *halmoni*. Soon-Duk had to travel to New York that afternoon, therefore I only had 30 minutes to interview her. I was disappointed about the short time we had together having flown to Washington from Victoria, British Columbia expressly to meet with her. For the most part, I asked her questions about her life before she was forced to become a sex slave. I was surprised to discover that she fell in love with a Japanese military officer and she didn't seem to harbour any bitterness.

On March 21, 2003, I met Hwang Geum-Joo at a conference on Preventing Crimes against Humanity that was held at the University of British Columbia in Vancouver. I was Hwang *halmoni's* chauffeur for a few days. I asked her several questions about her experiences during the war over several Korean meals at local restaurants and she told me matter-of-factly about her late parents and that the Japanese military had tricked her into sexual slavery.

Then in the fall of 2004, I set out for a month-long trip to Korea, China, and Japan to speak with other comfort women survivors, activists, lawyers, and writers. I met some determined *halmonis* in two locations in Seoul, Korea. These elderly women want nothing more than an apology before they die. Many survivors have passed away within the last five years, making their current struggle especially urgent.

That fall, my friend Helen Kim and I traveled for two hours south of Seoul by subway, bus, and taxi to The House of Sharing, a home that was set up by Buddhist organizations for impoverished survivors who were stranded in China in 1992, a year after Kim Hak-Soon testified. The taxi carried us up a winding road on a hill where driveways of homes had sedans and chicken coops, and trees with rich green leaves leaning against the skyline. The House of Sharing consists of two dormitories for the *halmonis* with a few rooms for overnight guests, a temple, and an office building with a lounge. In front of these buildings, visitors are greeted by a haunting statue of a young girl with her hair pulled back in a bun, wearing a traditional *hanbok*. Beside the dormitories for the elderly women is the "History Museum of Japanese Military Comfort Women," which was established on August 14, 1998. The museum has two floors with five different sections each depicting various experiences of the military sex slaves as well as multimedia presentations of survivors' testimonies. In the "experience room," one can stand in a model of a bare room in a comfort station. Nine women in their late 70s and 80s live at The House of Sharing. They are some of the most interesting women I've ever met.

The first day at the house, I met several of the women. I called one woman the "ghost grandma" because of her habit of suddenly appearing, seemingly from out of nowhere, at a doorway or in the corner of a room. Ji Dol-Yee is 82 years old and quite striking with her snow white hair and powdery white skin. Ji *halmoni* only converses in Mandarin because she was stuck in China after the war ended. Another *halmoni* at the house, Bae Choon-Hee, 80, had an identity crisis and wished she was Japanese. She married a Chinese man after the war ended, and her daughter and son live in China.

One of the volunteers at the House of Sharing told me the *halmonis* feel like "animals in a zoo" and they are disappointed when visitors who promise to return don't come back. Their morale is low; they're aging. They hear the same questions all the time and they are expected to repeatedly share their entire life stories. The volunteer joked that the house should be called "house of quarrels" because the *halmonis* have stubborn streaks and aren't afraid to voice their opinions.

I was afraid to ask the *halmonis* personal questions on that first day. I was hugely excited—after all I had waited for this opportunity to speak with them in person for many years. I wanted a chance to build trust and rapport before asking any questions. Mee-Hyang Yoon, the General Secretary of The Korean Council for the Women Drafted for Military Sexual Slavery by Japan, later admonished me. She said I should have encouraged them to share their stories from my first day because it is good for their healing.

Seventy-nine-year-old Kang Il-Chulwa was the first survivor I spoke with at length. She was very warm toward me for the first few days. One evening, Kang *halmoni* ushered me into her room on the second floor and shared stories of her life in China after she was freed from the comfort station. She was animated and spoke with passion.

> *Seven years ago I came here. I was living in China before then. I had married a North Korean man who died during the Chinese war [during the Communist takeover in 1949]. I had a hard time with my mother-in-law. I hate North Koreans and I hate the Japanese. I worked as a support staff person at an Eye and Ear clinic, not as a nurse but I did similar work. I can speak Mandarin fluently. I can turn it on at will. I have two sons, two granddaughters, two grandsons. My sons both work in companies in China. I went to a Full Gospel church and became a Christian when I was 73 years old. I like Pastor Yong-Gi Cho.*[6]

Many photos of Kang *halmoni* adorn her room along with a picture of Jesus that has a verse of scripture beneath it. The most striking photo is a large eight by ten of Kang *halmoni* standing pretty in a wedding dress and holding a bouquet of scarlet roses. Her large red lips, her most prominent feature, stand out. This photo was taken recently and more than anything she had shared, it made me feel a deep sense of loss. She still longed to wear pretty things like a beautiful white gown. Her youth was stolen from her and she was claiming it back with the wedding photograph. Noticeably, the photo doesn't include a husband, perhaps to suggest she doesn't need a man. Not surprisingly, a few *halmonis* have told me they hate men and they hate sex.

"Do you pray," I asked, looking around at the many Christian pictures.

"Yes," she said, closing her eyes and folding her hands in front of her. With a hushed voice she prayed:

Why, O God was Korea under Japanese oppression for 35 years? And why were we taken and made to suffer so much? God, why did you allow me to be a wianbu *[sex slave]? We still suffer and hurt. Why? God, in scripture you said you bring justice. I know you will bring justice to this situation. I trust you and put my faith in you. Because we are poor and pitiful [Sylvia] came here. Thank you for this day trip celebrating ancient Korean history and culture.*

That was the last time Kang *halmoni* would say a word to me. For some reason unknown to me she stopped talking to me, and began avoiding my eyes. I literally stopped existing in her world. Once, as I snapped a photo of her at a group event, she blocked her face with a piece of paper. I have come to understand her reaction as evidence of her past trauma.

A few days later, my friend and I accompanied the *halmonis* to their weekly demonstration in front of the Japanese embassy. The women were seated in chairs, while younger activists gave impassioned speeches with the aid of a megaphone. I gave a short angry speech on how the Japanese government shouldn't treat these elderly survivors as violent protesters by having armed guards stationed in front of the embassy, but that they should apologize sincerely and allow them to have closure. I asked the many Japanese tourists in the crowd to go back to Japan and tell others about this shameful chapter of Japanese history. This weekly event was launched on January 8, 1992 and more than 50 groups affiliated with the Korean Council organize it. Several activists and these *halmonis* have resolved to rally every Wednesday until the Japanese government officially apologizes and grants compensation to survivors. So far, they've been involved in more than 700 protests through four seasons of rain, snow, and oppressive heat.

After I left the House of Sharing, I visited a second house in Seoul sponsored by the Korean Council. That's where I got to know Hwang Geum-Joo better. At first, Hwang *halmoni*, 84, didn't remember me from our Vancouver meeting; then her memory was jogged. "I have no uterus," Hwang tells me with a flippancy I would expect from someone who was discussing the weather. She was wearing shimmering copper-gold pants that flared out and narrowed at the ankles, with a denim button-down shirt, over which she had placed a beige embroidered vest. Her black and white hair was tucked into a bun. Her feet are tiny.

Hwang *halmoni* is a straight-shooter. She doesn't mince words or waste time when it comes to sharing her opinions. "That Kim Dae Jung ... promised first thing he would do as president was to resolve the comfort women issue. That son-of-a-bitch didn't do anything. I've had lunch with him. He had promised," she spat out.

Though she shared her story of being raped by up to 40 men a day, Hwang didn't seemed depressed about her life. I spent one night sleeping on the floor of her room and we talked all night. She said that she even forgives the Japanese and doesn't blame the younger generation for what she experienced. While her story seemed rehearsed at times, I enjoyed listening to her recount travels to different countries to bear witness. "I've had operations on my uterus and for the missing bone in my back. I've met so many people who call me *halmoni*," she said. "They all know me. I've traveled to so many cities and I wear my *hanbok*. People go crazy over my dress. I once touched Abraham Lincoln's statue [in Washington, D.C.]. No one else could. Just me." She beamed when she told me she met President Bill Clinton once and shook his hand. One day, out of the blue, she asked me "Do you know how big a man is?" My face flushed with embarrassment and shock that she'd ask such a question.

As a young girl, because her family was poor, Hwang was sent away to be a foster daughter for a family. When she was 20 years old, she volunteered to work in a military supplies factory believing she was going to make a lot more money for her parents. This happened after her father fell ill and the family became destitute. Instead of working in a factory, however, she was placed in a "comfort station" in what was then known as Manchuria, in northern China. "The comfort women in the military unit were not treated like human beings," she said.

We were beaten almost every day. I was particularly rebellious and earned more beatings than the other girls. Even now, my ears sometimes go fuzzy and I can't hear anything for a while. I have strong magnetic strips attached to my knees and hips. If I take these off to have a bath and forget to put them back on, then my knees and hips swell up within five or six hours, and I am unable to sit down.

Hwang was the only one of the girls at her station to attempt to return to Korea. She walked home. "It took four months to get to Seoul. I begged for food and slept on the streets. It was a very painful time," she said. "When I returned, I learned my father had passed away. [Then] I had no desire to go home. I didn't try to find my family. I couldn't tell anyone what happened as I was so ashamed, but when I saw Kim Hak-Soon's interview, I decided to come out, too."

For the next decade, Hwang *halmoni* endured sharp pain and discomfort as a result of contracting a venereal disease. After the Korean War, Hwang remained single and adopted three orphans. One child died. She supported her remaining son and daughter through school by running a small restaurant near Seoul University. Her children have families of their own and still visit her. I was sad to say goodbye to Hwang *halmoni*. The other activists have grown very close to her and I can see why. She's gruff outwardly, but she has a soft heart and a lot of *jeong*.[7]

Recently, I called a survivor I met in Seoul, Lee Yong-Soo, to see how she was doing. A few months after that call, she testified about her experiences before a U.S. House of Representatives subcommittee in February 2007. That subcommittee was investigating Resolution 121,[8] which was introduced in January 2007 by Representative Mike Honda, a Japanese-American democrat from California. This resolution calls on the government of Japan to issue a formal apology to the comfort women. To date, the Japanese government, with the backing of the U. S. Bush administration, has lobbied aggressively against it (Onishi).

In March 2007, the Japanese Prime Minister, Shinzo Abe, denied that military sex slaves were systematically raped by Japanese soldiers in the Imperial Military. The international furor his denial caused has buoyed the redress movement for these elderly survivors with a momentum that has surprised even the most hardened Comfort women activists and perhaps the survivors themselves.

I plan to return to Seoul to visit the *halmonis* and support their ongoing weekly Wednesday demonstration in front of the Japanese embassy. At first, I was interested in the "comfort women" story because I wanted to know more of the history of the homeland my parents left to immigrate to Canada. I began this journey with a fair amount of outrage, unanswered questions, and a curiosity about how these women survived their ordeals. After meeting these elderly women survivors, I have indeed learned about a sad part of Korean history that includes the systematic rape of young women from impoverished families during a time of war and the Japanese occupation. Over the years, I have been inspired by dozens of activists, lawyers, academics and students who are Japanese, Chinese, Dutch, Canadian, and American. They continue to labour selflessly on behalf of the *halmonis* despite the Japanese government's persistent stonewalling and unwillingness to issue an apology.

If I had to choose an image to describe the *halmonis,* it would be the pine tree in Korea known as the *sonamu*. The *sonamu* stands dignified and green throughout all seasons, through harsh winds, hot sun, and blustery monsoons, sprouting up in impossibly craggy landscapes, and because of its resilience it carries great significance as a national symbol of the Korean people who have endured attacks from invading forces over the centuries. The *halmonis'* sheer strong will to survive reminds me of these pine trees. As they've shared their pain, they have also raised awareness internationally about the horrors of sexual violence against women and children in war zones. They deserve an apology, and much more.

[1] No definitive number of Japanese Military sex slaves exists, but researchers from the Republic of Korea suggest that 200,000 women were forced into the comfort women system. In an interview conducted with Su Zhiliang, a Professor from Shanghai Normal University and Director of the China Comfort Women Research Centre, on August 2004, he said the number is 400,000. Of that number, he said, 200,000 women were from China.

[2] Coomaraswamy's report states, "the consistency of the accounts of women from quite different parts of South-East Asia of the manner in which they were recruited and the clear involvement of the military and Government at different levels is indisputable. It is wholly implausible that so many women could have created such similar stories about the extent of official involvement solely for their own purposes."

[3] United States District Court District of Columbia. Plaintiffs Hwang Geum Joo et al. versus defendant Japan, Minister Yohei Kono, Minister of Foreign Affairs (2000). Comfort Women class action lawsuit launched September 18, 2000 in Washington, D.C.

[4] Including Kim Hak-Soon.

[5] Kim Hak-Soon died on December 16, 1997.

[6] David Yong-Gi Cho pastors the largest church in the world, called the Korean Full Gospel church.

[7] The Korean word, *jeong*, is difficult to define but could be translated as deep affection, feeling, and sentiment.

[8] Online: www.govtrack.us/congress/bill.xpd?bill=hr110-121.

References

Chung, Chin Sung. "The Origin and Development of the Military Sexual Slavery Problem in Imperial Japan." *Positions East Asia Cultures Critique* (Special Issue on the Comfort Women: Colonialism, War and Sex). Ed. Chungmoo Choi. Durham: Duke University Press, 1997.

"Comfort Women: Japan, Korean Victims of the Asia-Pacific War." *Memory and Reconciliation in the Asia-Pacific*. December 1991. George Washington University. Online: <http://www.gwu.edu/~memory/yang/new/data/judicial/comfortwomen_japan/haksun.html>.

Coomaraswamy, Radhika. "Report on the Mission to the Democratic People's Republic of Korea, the Republic of Korea and Japan on the Issues of Military

Sexual Slavery in Wartime UN Commission on Human Rights." At the 52nd Session of the UN Commission on Human Rights, New York, 1996.

Dolgopol, Ustinia. "Women's Voices, Women's Pain." The Peace Research Center. Working Paper No. 152 (1994).

Hicks, George. *The Comfort Women: Japan's Brutal Regime of Enforced Prostitution in the Second World War.* New York: W.W. Norton and Company, Inc., 1994.

The Korean Council for the Women Drafted for Military Sexual Slavery. 30 August 2006. Online: <http://www.womenandwar.net/english/menu_04.php>.

McDougall, Gay J. "Contemporary Forms of Slavery: Systematic Rape, Sexual Slavery and Slavery-like Practices During Armed Conflict." At the 50th Session of the United Nations Commission on Human Rights, Sub-Commission on Prevention of Discrimination and Protection of Minorities, New York, 1998.

McDougall, Gay J. Personal interview, November 2000.

Onishi, Norimitsu. "A Congressman faces foe in Japan as he seeks an apology." The Saturday Profile. *New York Times* May 12, 2007.

Watanabe, Kazuko. "Militarism, Colonialism, and the Trafficking of Women: 'Comfort Women' Forced into Sexual Labor for Japanese Soldiers." *The Bulletin of Concerned Asian Scholars* 26 (1994): 3-15.

Yoshiaki, Yoshimi. *Comfort Women: Sexual Slavery in the Japanese Military During World War II*. New York: Columbia University Press, 2000.

GLORIA U. Y. KIM

Madwoman

In Korea, there's a long tradition of shaman-priestesses. They live a life of tremendous suffering in devotion to their calling, and it is believed that they are possessed by ten thousand spirits, *mansin*. The shaman-priestesses, like witches everywhere, are the symbols of power, suffering, life, and death. They are the doorway between this world and the next, and their gift is in recognizing and being able to communicate with the spirits. But I believe that all women are magic and power, whether we can recognize it or not. Madwoman is my homage to the shaman-priestess in all of us.

MADWOMAN

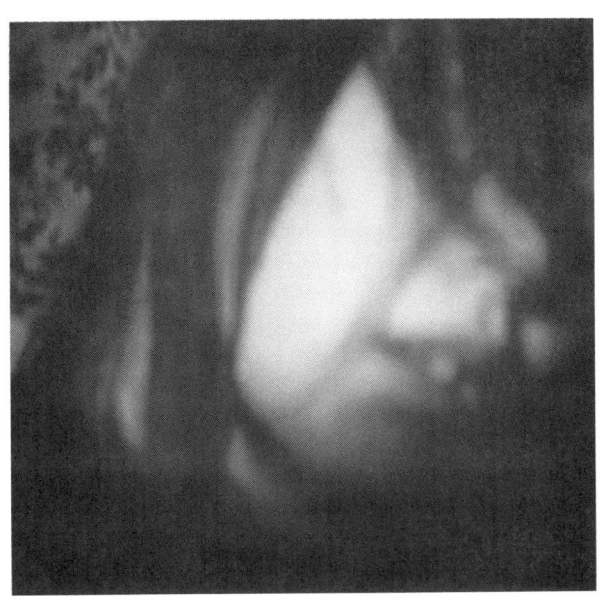

HANA KIM

You

Haven't we met before? Somewhere? ... Yes! You gave me the joy of my life. You gave me the pain of my life. Don't you still remember me? Oh, please don't tell me you don't know me! Liar! Liar! Liar! I gave myself to you. But one day ... I saw your feebleness. Oh, I remember now. I left you because you couldn't satisfy me. But I realized nobody could satisfy me. Both of us know we cannot be separated. I'll learn to love you. Please don't hide.

그대
김하나
번역 김하나

우리 어디에서 만난적 없나요? 어디선가? …… 맞아요! 내 인생에 기쁨을 주었잖아요. 내 인생에 아픔을 주었잖아요. 날 아직도 기억 못 해요? 제발 날 모른다고는 말하지 마세요! 거짓말쟁이! 거짓말쟁이! 거짓말쟁이! 당신께 날 드렸었잖아요. 그러다가 어느 날 …… 당신의 박약함을 보았었죠. 아, 이제 기억나요. 날 만족시키지 못하는 이유로 당신을 떠났었다는 것을요. 누구도 날 만족시킬 수 없다는 것을 알았어요. 당신과 나, 우린 헤어질 수 없어요. 당신을 사랑하는 법을 배울께요. 제발, 숨지마세요.

JENNY J. H. AHN

Breaking Boundaries
Bringing Communities and Unions Together

I was born in Seoul, Korea into a family that did not discuss politics or social justice issues. But, fighting against inequality and oppression has been a part of my life ever since I can remember. From challenging stereotypical gender roles in the home at the age of three, to tackling racism in school from other students, to advocating for children and adults with disabilities, I have been compelled to change the status quo—to make socially progressive changes.

However, it was not until I was had finished school and in my first year of full-time work that I became acutely aware of labour issues at a very personal level. I was completely unaware of the inequalities and problems that can exist in the workplace until I experienced them myself first-hand.

During the Social Contract[1] days, I worked full-time for an organization that provided services for children and adults with developmental disabilities. It was a contract job with no benefits. I soon found out that my co-workers, who were doing exactly same job, were earning up to $4.00 an hour more than I was. They were receiving benefits and had job security in a permanent job. These employees were covered under the union's collective agreement. This opened my eyes and I realized I needed to find a union job. I quickly understood that the union plays an integral role in protecting jobs and ensuring that there is respect and dignity in the workplace. I also learned the importance of getting involved in politics and voting as it determines so much in our lives—for example, from what services are provided and funded (like medicare) to what laws, if any, there are to protect workers in the workplace.

At that time, working in the social services field had become highly unstable in terms of wages and job security. I was in a constant state of anxiety about to the possibility of being laid off and when I would receive my next paycheck. Frustrated, I decided to look for another job. I applied for a position that was advertised in the newspaper, which noted that the wages were based on the union's collective agreement. I still didn't know that much about unions, but

I understood that a union would provide more fairness in the workplace.

When I started this job, little did I know that it would take my life in a new direction. I soon found myself approaching management to discuss problems occurring in the workplace. One of the women I worked with encouraged me to run for the position of Union Steward in the Canadian Auto Workers Union (CAW). Since I still was not that familiar with unions, I quickly told her "no." But, her encouragement was ongoing and eventually she convinced me on the agreement that she would run as the Union Steward and I would run as her alternate or backup. I was not aware at the time that she was pregnant and shortly after the elections she went on maternity leave! Thus, I assumed the job as the Union Steward for my workplace and fulfilled my responsibilities accordingly.

My role as Union Steward provided an opportunity for me to bring about positive change that could improve the lives of my co-workers. I was able to negotiate improved working conditions that included hours of work, more fairness in scheduling, solutions for an array of health and safety concerns, as well as increases in wages and benefits.

As I continued to represent my members in the workplace, my Local Union, CAW Local 40, suggested I become more involved. This time I didn't need much encouragement. I had become so much more aware of the many injustices that exist for workers and I was eager to do whatever I could to address those issues. I believed that becoming more involved in the local union was necessary for me to do what needed to be done for workers on a broader level, including political action.

In 1996, ten workers of colour, including myself, all ran for positions on the Local Union Executive Board. We were all successfully elected, making history for both the Local Union and for the CAW National Union. In addition, this election represented to the labour movement that change is possible and some barriers can be overcome.

CAW Local 40 has a geographical, cultural, and sectoral diverse membership, representing members at that time from Stoney Creek to the downtown core of Toronto, and all the way east to the borders of Scarborough/Markham. I began working for the Local Union on a full-time basis as the Recording Secretary. But my job was no ordinary Recording Secretary job. In fact, I was the full-time Officer responsible for the servicing of the membership. This meant that I was responsible for resolving the grievances and negotiations for 17 different collective agreements, Workers' Compensation cases and appeals, health and safety issues, and anything else that affected workers' lives such as engaging in electoral politics and doing equity work in the community. Shortly after being elected to the Executive Board as Recording Secretary, I was elected and acclaimed as the Local Union President.

Being an activist in the community and doing trade union work blended into each other. I was encouraged to take my union's Workers of Colour Leadership course. It really helped me to understand anti-racism work and what the trade union movement is about, and how we can advocate not only workers' rights, but human rights as well. I learned so much from this course that it inspired me to become even more involved. Which is what I exactly did.

Working with a number of dedicated Asian trade unionists and community activists and leaders during Asian Heritage Month in May 2000, the Asian Canadian Labour Alliance (ACLA) was launched. ACLA was formed because we recognized that the face and culture of Canada has been transformed. Over the last 30 years, we have seen an increase in the movement of people to Canada from Asia and many other parts of the world, and the great majority of these workers have no union. ACLA began sending out a wake-up call to our communities, and to the labour movement, that it was time to learn about the union and to become organized.

ACLA provides a space where Asian Canadian members can begin to feel a part of their union. We reach out and educate our different communities about their rights, and get them involved, encouraging them to become leaders in their communities as well as in their unions, supporting them in their efforts to organize more workers so that they will not be discriminated against and so we can improve their standard of living. The ACLA also helps to strengthen the Canadian labour movement by bringing all workers together.

For me, ACLA and the work that I do in the CAW is about going back to my parents and all generations of Korean-Canadians and trying to help them understand why I'm a trade unionist, why it's important to me, and why it should also be important to them. It is showing by my actions that I have not forgotten about my roots. My roots are more than just being Korean. I am also a worker, a woman, and a person of colour.

A few years ago, I was fortunate to work with a group of Korean-Canadian community organizations that brought an art exhibition to Toronto about the Korean "comfort women" — women who were forced by the Japanese government to serve as sex slaves for Japanese soldiers during the Second World War. The exhibition, "A Quest for Justice," was intended to expose the horrendous exploitation of Korean women that took place in our history. But it was an example of how one community can work collaboratively with unions. This is how we link the social justice work with the human rights work the labour movement does. For me, this is an important part of what I believe is so important to do — building coalitions among different communities and cultures and sharing with them possibilities that working together with unions can offer.

The Korean community in Canada has its own unique history and labour needs. Ten to twelve years ago in Toronto, many of the Asian communities were doing quite well, and prospering. Many Korean families immigrated to Canada in the 1970s, and started their own small businesses. They did not perceive themselves as working-class. Then, with globalization, free trade agreements, and the election of a conservative government, vast numbers of the small businesses, including many Korean Canadian owned businesses, went bankrupt.

All of a sudden, the Korean Canadians affected by this felt that their class, or "social status" as they might call it, was no longer what they believed it to be. Currently, there is an increase in the numbers of Korean Canadians living in poverty, but because of their pride, and other cultural factors, they are very quiet about it and do not seek help. It may be that they don't know how to access the services, or it may be a result of language barriers, but regardless of the reasons, we need to break through this silence and reach out and assist our community because many of them are alone and isolated.

Not only is it important to reach out to the Korean Canadian community, as well as the other communities of colour, it is also important to educate the broader labour movement of the necessity to include workers of colour in every aspect of their union structure. Racism and sexism have an impact on unions as well, and it weakens and robs the labour movement of energies, ideas, and skills.

In 2002, I was involved with a community research project entitled "No Hijab Is Permitted Here." The study was sponsored by Women Working with Immigrant Women, with a host of community partners including my CAW Local 40. Through community-based action research, the study identified the barriers and types of discrimination experienced by Muslim women who wear *hijab*, or a head cover, when seeking employment in the manufacturing, sales, and services sectors in Toronto. This groundbreaking and very timely project, as it was conducted just after 9/11 in the United States, began a powerful working relationship between community and labour organizations that continues beyond this single project.

Another annual community event that we have been involved with for as long as I can remember is International Women's Day. This is an event very close to my heart. Often I am involved in organizing events not only within my local and national union, but I am also working with community groups such as Women Working with Immigrant Women on events planned for that day. While women have overcome many barriers and inequities throughout the last decades, particularly here in Canada, both at home and abroad, women around the world continue to be subject to deplorable inequities, living each day in fear and oppression. International Women's Day recognizes the extensive inequity women face throughout the world and the need to constantly keep up the fight against the oppression.

My political activism is not about working only with the Korean Canadian community, or only with the labour movement. Working with other communities of colour continues to be an enormous part of my life. We all need to help one another and reach out to other communities who also suffer from the injustices of race, class, and gender inequities.

As I have challenged these interlocking oppressions over the years, my union has been supportive of my work and this was recognized in April 2001 when I was elected to the CAW National Executive Board (NEB), which is the union's highest governing body. This represented progressive change, as I was the first woman of colour as well as the youngest person ever elected to the NEB. I was subsequently elected as the Vice-President of the NEB and then appointed to join the staff of my National Union.

The labour movement must and will continue to play a leadership role not only in the Korean Canadian community but for all workers. It is important to acknowledge the gains that have been made so that we can gain strength from the successes to continue to effect progressive change for each person, for each community, and for each workplace. Solidarity forever.

[1] The Social Contract refers to a 1993 initiative of the provincial New Democratic Party in Ontario, implemented by the then Premier of Ontario, Bob Rae, which was an unpopular deficit-reducing tactic that imposed a wage freeze and mandatory unpaid days of leave for civil service employees.

V.
Junctures

HELEN H. KANG

Ajuma
The Third Gender

Several years ago, a female cousin came from Korea to stay with my family in Toronto and study English for eight months. She was quick at the tongue and most of her jokes in Korean challenged my proficiency in the language. But there was one joke she told that was especially memorable because of how much it shocked me. "There are three genders," she said: "Man, woman and *ajuma*." The punch line was *ajuma*, a perplexing word that literally means "aunt," but is used to casually address older women, or poke fun at married women for no longer being virginal and attractive (two qualities that seem to go hand-in-hand). In her joke, the word *ajuma* implied sexlessness, and the subsequent elaboration of her story led the meaning of the word to include stubborn tenacity and an in-your-face manner attributed to older women. This particular joke has stayed with me years after my cousin returned to Korea. I didn't approve of this joke about older women because it denies their sexuality and demeans their strength and wisdom, mocking them in ways that are gendered, sexist, and ageist. I considered myself to have moved far beyond these anti-feminist perceptions, but in the summer of 2005 I realized I may not be entirely innocent myself.

The two opposing terms of my cousin's joke, *ajuma* and sex, came crashing together in unexpected ways that summer when I conducted two sexuality workshops for Korean-speaking women as an outreach worker at an organization called Asian Community AIDS Services. The project was intended to outreach to Korean-speaking women from their teens to their twenties on issues of sexually-transmitted infections and HIV. In order to attract more participants and to reduce potential cultural barriers, I decided to omit the word "sexual" from "sexual health," simply calling them Health Workshops for Women. What ultimately happened, however, was that I twice found myself in a room full of *ajumas*: 40-, 50- and occasionally 60-something Korean women, who had come to gain information on menopause and uterine cancer. Needless to say, ten minutes into the workshop the women seemed hesitant to listen to a 26-year-old, who could very well be their daughter or even granddaughter, speak to them about the ins and outs of sexual hygiene, contraception, and sexually-transmitted infections. There were smiles and giggles, but they nevertheless politely remained in the workshop, claiming: "I can teach some of this to my niece or daughter."

Interestingly, the women came to address me as *sonsengnim*: teacher. The teacher-student relationship in mainland Korea, especially during the time when these women would have gone to to school, is an explicitly hierarchical relationship, where the teacher is upheld with reverence. Hence, this little word the women used to address me was highly symbolic of the kind of relationship I was to have with them. Despite being much younger than they were, through the semi-formal structure of the educational workshop and my command of the English language, I was suddenly perceived a *sonsengnim* with status beyond that which is associated with its direct English translation.

Against this backdrop of highly unconventional circumstances, I began the four-part workshop: reproductive anatomy, hygiene, contraception, and sexually-transmitted infections. The first sessions were generally uneventful. We went over the anatomical parts of the female and male reproductive systems, and the women were particularly drawn to English terms for particular parts of the female body. Their questions centered around those parts of the female anatomy that were prone to infections or cancer, such as the ovaries, fallopian tubes, bladder, and uterus. Cysts, menstruation, menopause, ovulation were also popular terms that the women eagerly wrote down in their notepads. Interestingly, all the terms were medical, or what the women could point out to a non-Korean speaking gynecologist. The vagina and clitoris, however, stirred less interest. Were the women, perhaps, too embarrassed to talk about these parts of a woman's body because they are too closely associated with sex and pleasure? Were the women simply not interested because they don't necessarily cause medical concerns? Perhaps the "education" part of my workshop had already set the tone for a medical information session without hinting, in any way, at the pleasures of "sexual" health. Perhaps it was my own "sanitizing" of the workshop in the advertisements I came up with by omitting "sex" from "sexual health."

In the latter half of the workshops came the dreaded part: the condom demonstration. But it's more accurate to say that *I* dreaded it because the thought of showing *ajumas*, women who reminded me of my own mother, how to put a condom on a wooden phallus was more than slightly unnerving. Why was this the case when I am normally very open about sex? Was it the same kind of dread that children feel when they think of their parents having sex? What kinds of assumptions was I making about these women's sexual lives? That they've had enough sex to know what it's about, that they don't have enough sex to know what it's about, or that they've only had sex for procreation so they wouldn't know how to use a condom? Still today I don't know what I was thinking exactly, and though I suspected what was going through my head would yield some curious analysis, the important thing was that I was more than pleasantly surprised by the reactions of the women in the room.

When I nervously—and somewhat dramatically—pulled out the wooden penis from my plastic bag of workshop goodies, there were some smiles and surprised faces, but mostly the women were very attentive. What was going through their minds as they watched my hands pull a latex condom over the wooden penis? Did they witness something informative? Or did they imagine their daughter, their niece, their friend's daughter—some young Korean woman or girl—doing the same thing? There was some nervous laughter when I asked someone to come up and try the demonstration themselves, but no squeamishness. I had one volunteer in one of the workshops but no-one in the other. I was expecting someone to storm out at any moment and wondered what I would do if such an occasion arose, but the women were genuinely interested and even enjoying themselves.

While the male condom was coolly received, the female condom raised some eyebrows. The women were particularly keen on receiving a sample of the female condom. When I explained how one would insert a female condom into a vagina, some women were appalled by its awkward size, while others were intrigued. More so than the demonstration with the male condom, the women wanted detailed instructions on how to use the female condom. When I passed around a female condom in its original package, the speed at which the condom moved down the line of women was much slower than when I passed around a male condom. The women touched it very carefully, feeling the double-rimmed latex, turning the package in their hands. They discussed with one another how practical or awkward the female condom would be, laughing and grimacing as they did so. It was a marvelous communal moment that stays with me to this day.

Both workshops ended on a high note, with women engaged in active and animated conversations with each other. Throughout the sessions, the women—individually and as a group—fluctuated between high excitement and laughter, and reluctance and hesitance. I attribute the excitement to the surprising frankness that everyone brought to the discussion. I wondered if they had ever talked about sex with complete strangers in a room like this before, and whether the conversation was actually easier because they were strangers. I also wondered whether the secular and pseudo-medical context of the workshop helped them to objectify and neutralize sex, creating some distance from moral contexts of the church and the gendered heteronormative family.

The workshops yielded interesting insights into the lack of services available for Korean-speaking women. When I presented the symptoms of some common sexually-transmitted infections, for example, one woman, who had been relatively quiet during the entire workshop, suddenly became animated and asked numerous questions. She asked whether sexually-ransmitted infections (STIs) can simply appear from a vacuum. I reminded her that these are "infections," and thus require both a host carrier and a vector, such as sexual fluids and skin-to-skin contact. Her face grew grim, and she spoke to me after the workshop about the specific symptoms of common STIs. I discussed this with a friend who had attended the workshop and observed the woman's anxious questioning, and we guessed that this woman may have suspected her partner of marital infidelity. However, this workshop provided no means for us to suggest that she seek counselling. I was neither equipped nor trained to offer her counseling or to connect her with a counsellor. Christian churches and church-driven service organizations provide the primary means of social support for many Korean-Canadians in Toronto, and I wonder still whether they are able to provide marital counselling that takes into consideration STIs and gendered dynamics when it comes to negotiating safer sex. The Korean-Canadian communities are so small and so closely knit that often such intimate problems are very difficult to discuss without the danger of exposure and shame.

The women in the workshops were also curious about access to free or low-cost health care without the Ontario Health Insurance Plan. Unfortunately, I was not trained to answer this question. This is specific to small and relatively new diasporas, such as Korean-Canadian communities, which lack institutional completeness. These communities require support and educational services specific to their social and linguistic needs, and further study is necessary to determine what other services and support are lacking in these communities due to institutional and cultural barriers in the mainstream Canadian society.

After the two workshops, I was surrounded by women curious about my proficiency in Korean. Suddenly, I was brought down from the pedestal of *sonsengnim* and put back in my place as the curious youngster. "How can you speak Korean so well?" This is a question I am often posed by Korean-Canadian communities. It is a question I have always found perplexing and I have always been uncertain about other connotations associated with this query. As I smile in thanks, a small part of me fears whether these *ajumas* and *ajussis*[1] assume that, by speaking the language, I share with them certain "cultural" values, including the value placed on the heteronormative family, heterosexual relationships, and gender roles; I suddenly feel like an imposter. Facing the same questions after the workshops, I wondered whether the women held onto my proficiency in the Korean lanuage as a way to neutralize the unexpected honesty with which I spoke about sex. During the workshop I was their *sonsengnim*, but afterwards I was an unmarried young woman, or a *chonyo*, who knew too much about sex for comfort. One much older woman, laughing, asked outright how a *chonyo* could know so much. The words *ajuma* and *chonyo* stand at opposite poles of the heteronormative spectrum for women: the former married and thus "tainted," the latter unmarried and therefore "virginal." While these words are so deeply absorbed into the cultural fabric of the language that the connotations are glossed over without question, they are nonetheless limiting terms for women. In my case, I was the closeted queer standing before the *ajuma*, who mistook me for a *chonyo*. There is no room for me along that heteronormative spectrum of female identity. I thus resorted to the gender-neutral position of *sonsengnim* while passing for a scandalous *chonyo* in their eyes.

Overall, the fifteen *ajumas* who attended my workshops greatly surprised me with their generous honesty. I was able to confront my own pre-conceptions and fears about the sexuality of older Korean women. Hence, I wonder: When I speak of sex and sexuality as a woman, as a feminist and as a queer woman, who am I excluding in this discussion? I may very well be committing the same error as my cousin, creating a third sexless gender of *ajuma*. Perhaps my internalized racism joined with my fear of parental sexuality so that I inadvertently omitted Korean women when considering the sexuality of older women. Just as the *ajumas* were uncomfortable with the fact that I, a *chonyo* in their eyes, knew too much about sex, perhaps I also felt uneasy with the fact that *ajumas* have sexuality beyond their roles as mothers, wives, and aunts. The women and I occupy spaces on the gender spectrum that are neither *ajuma* nor *chonyo*, two predominant identifiers for women in the Korean language that echo the "virgin/whore" dichotomy. In the workshop room, we were all third or impossible female genders in each other's eyes and in the eyes of heteronormative cultures that surround us in our diasporic experience.

---

[1]Male equivalent of *ajuma*, but interestingly with less of the negative connotations associated with the female term.

FAR-SAN

Mom's Dream and Ginger Man

A routine phone call once in a while has been the medium of sustaining my relationship with mom since I left South Korea ten years ago. That's about the same amount of time that I've spent processing both the pain and joy of my queer life. The Pacific Ocean between mom and me helps to create distance from my family. And yes, I have carried guilt for doing so especially because mom, being a single parent in Korean society, has gone through enough shitty things. I don't want to add another social stigma on her. Doesn't she deserve my support? But how is it possible to give her my full-hearted support without letting her know about an important part of who I am?

In the meanwhile, without mom having any clue about my queer self, I met someone. Our relationship grew meaningful despite all the hurtful experiences I carry from past relationships and flashbacks. I came to ponder how to introduce my lover to my mom within my long-term plan to "come-out" to her. I was inspired by reading *Fall on Your Knees,* a novel by Ann-Marie MacDonald, through meanings associated with Ginger, a character in the novel, and my lover's favourite spice. In the novel, "Ginger Man" is a secret code between lovers to indicate the desire to make love. My lover, who is a great cook, uses ginger in her cooking. Until I got used to my lover's food, I did not like the taste of ginger. Now, I love it. Liking ginger is a big change in my eating habits that mom would be really surprised to know about. During one of our regular phone conversations, I decided to tell my mom how I came to enjoy the taste of ginger thanks to a friend "very close" to me.

I had phoned her, as usual, on a weekend evening in her time zone, asked her regards, and assured her that I was doing well. There was a phone static barking throughout the phone connection. She complained about it. So I called her back, but the static was still there. I was persistent as I really wanted to talk to mom, to tell her about my Ginger Man, my "very close" friend. Mom was also persistent about something she wanted to talk about.

MOM'S DREAM AND GINGER MAN

This is how our conversation went:

I dreamt of....

What did you dream of? By the way, mom....

What did you say?
Far-San, I dreamt a strange dream. (chuckle)
You were ... with a guy in my dream.

What did I do with a guy?
You know I'm not interested in. What a strange dream!
Mom, can you believe that I began to eat ginger?
Because ... cooks so well.

I know you aren't interested in marriage,
but the dream felt so real.
You and the guy seemed serious about each other.
You were hesitant to ...
while the man was waiting for your words.

Mom, did you hear about what I said?
I am now eating GINGER.
I have a CLOSE FRIEND who changed my taste of ginger.

Ginger? You are eating ginger? (chuckle)
Who is [the friend]? Korean?
Another stubborn ... like you?
Anyhow, are you by any chance dating a guy
in reality without me knowing?

Mom, you know me.
I don't have time to [meet a guy].
My friend is not Korean ... someone like your daughter.

I thought so.
But my dream ... so vivid.
I ... it is an epiphany.

You aren't listening to what I said, mom.
I hope you meet my friend when you visit me.

I can't hear you ... this phone....
Can't you buy a better phone card?
You want me to meet your friend? I'm too shy.
Anyway, this phone connection is really annoying.

Both of us were frustrated by not being able to properly communicate with each other when we hung up the phone. Not only were we disjointed by the static on the phone, but our selfish urgency to speak also prevented us from hearing each other's story. At first, I felt the phone call was a good example of how mom and I don't communicate, not only because of the geographical distance, but also because of the social distance between us.

But my second thought was that maybe this phone call was a sign that mom and I *can* communicate intuitively or subconsciously. Perhaps we were talking about the same person. Was my "Ginger Man" the one who was in my mom's dream? If so, mom's dream may be an encouraging sign that she may actually meet my lover in the near future and gradually come to accept my queer life. I want her to know about my life as a queer activist, about my serious relationship and devastating break-up, and how only now I've begun to feel alive in a new relationship. Does she still think of her daughter as an ambitious single woman who has yet to find a right man? Can she move beyond this? I like to imagine that mom and I can make a new connection where our communication is animated, where I can be fully myself, and where we give each other our full-hearted support.

YOUNG-HWA HONG

Skilled Korean Women on the Move
Becoming Transnational Migrants

Globalization has led to the rapid increase in cross-border flows of capital, goods, ideas, media, information, services, and people. Along with global capital, the new immigrant workforce is a major component of transnational categories that have unifying properties across borders (Castles; Sassen). By 2001, it was estimated that approximately 150 million people were living outside the country of their birth, and that there were 1.5 million professionals from developing countries working in the industrial world (Iredale; Stalker). One example of the global migration of skilled workers is a recent trend for South Korean professionals to immigrate to Canada. Yet, there is inadequate research on Korean immigrants to Canada in general and on Korean immigrant women with higher education and job skills in particular.

This paper examines recent migration patterns among skilled Korean immigrant women to Canada and also explores the multilayered reasons for Korean women's decisions to migrate, especially as they are related to gender-specific issues. Using in-depth interviews with eight skilled immigrant women who recently arrived in Canada from South Korea,[1] this paper suggests that migration is a series of gendered processes that develop within the context of global neoliberal hegemony. By examining two particular groups of Korean migrants—*kirŏgi* families and single women—I argue that post-International Monetary Fund (IMF) neo-liberalism and globalization are are leading to transnational migration and reshaping the structure of Korean families in South Korea.

The first section of this paper begins with a brief introduction of Korean immigration to Canada including the characteristics of the participants in this study. The second section will focus on two emerging patterns of migration, which are well represented by the women in my study: that of *kirŏgi* mothers, who live in Canada with their children while their husbands remain in Korea, and of single woman migrants. I show how both *kirŏgi* mothers and single women represent different cases of migration being shaped by the dominant neo-liberal social ethos. In the case of *kirŏgi* mothers, they chose to live in Canada in order to allow their children to gain fluency in English—a vital form of cultural capital in South Korean society. At the same time, they are generally forced to live in Canada separately from their husbands, and are prevented from engaging in professional employment due to the racialized and genderized labour market structure in Canada. The single women in this study exemplify such neo-liberal values as individualism, economic success, and personal initiative—they are therefore much more independent than is usually considered acceptable in South Korea families. As is often the case among transnational migrants,[2] the experiences of the participants in this study are highly complicated and even contradictory.

Korean Immigrants in Canada

The history of South Korean immigration to Canada is relatively short compared to that of other Asian ethnic groups such as Chinese, Japanese, and South Asians. Although the Korean diaspora is found throughout the world, historically, Koreans have migrated mainly to China, Japan, the U.S. (including Hawaii), and Russian Siberia (Yoon). Recently, the number of skilled Korean immigrants has increased enormously due to the social, economic, and political devastation caused by the 1997 Asian financial crisis.

The 1997 Asian financial crisis, generally referred to in South Korea as the IMF crisis, caused enormous damage to the fabric of South Korean society. Due to the crisis, the South Korean government ultimately received a $58 billion loan and rescue package from the International Monetary Fund (IMF). According to the terms of the IMF bailout and rescue package, South Korea was required to follow a Structural Adjustment Program (SAP). The SAP, which is based on neo-liberal ideology, demanded the reduction of state intervention into the economy. It resulted in mass layoffs, bankruptcies, unstable employment, early retirement, declining wages, and an increase in outsourcing. In 1998, approximately 1.6 million workers[3] lost their jobs. The traditional concept of life-long employment in Korea was challenged, and the work environment became very unstable—contract work and temporary employment became the norm. Consequently, the poverty rate rose, the number of homeless increased, and the economic gap between the rich and the poor grew much larger than had previously been the case (Park, H.J.; Seo; Song 2003).

The SAP was not gender-neutral. Without question, women were disproportionately affected, as has been established through extensive literature concerning the impact of the crisis, especially on the labour market. Women were among the first to lose their jobs and the last to be rehired, resulting in the feminization of poverty (Kim and Finch; Seo). Furthermore, as reported in several studies, employers preferred to lay off women based on the gendered notion that women are only a secondary income source (Kim and Finch; Park, H.J.).[4]

Studies suggest that South Korean skilled and professional workers choose Canada as their destination in order to escape the unstable socio-economic situation of their home country (Kwak; Yoon). For instance, South Korea was the fifth largest source of immigrants to Canada in 2001 (Statistics Canada). Compared to South Korean immigrants prior to 1997, the new immigrant group brought rich resources—skills, professional work experiences, and financial capital (Kwak; Yoon). The transformation of the nature of Korean migrants is also a result of changes in Canada's immigration policy, which since 1999 has increasingly encouraged the immigration of skilled independent migrants who are seen to be well-suited to the new knowledge-based economy.

While South Korean immigrants during the 1960s and '70s arrived from a relatively poor country with only several hundred dollars in their pockets, Korean immigrants since the '90s are able to bring rich financial resources from South Korea, now a developed industrial nation. Injin Yoon's study confirms that most recent South Korean immigrants in Toronto had middle-class backgrounds prior to their immigration to Canada. Approximately two-thirds of his research participants had completed post-secondary education and held professional and white-collar jobs in South Korea.

The eight women discussed in this paper were also skilled professionals in South Korea, having worked as teachers, researchers, counsellors, occupational therapists, social workers, music editors, and computer programmers. They immigrated mainly under the independent class. Some used migration agencies to facilitate the process, to which they paid between $1,200 and $12,000 for their services, sums that reflect the growing boom in the migration industry in South Korea. This is to say, while transnational movement is not readily available to all Korean women, the study participants' capability for global mobility is a result of their relatively privileged middle-class status in South Korea.[5]

The women's motivations for immigrating to Canada are varied and complicated. Although many of them mentioned the IMF crisis as the general cause of the migration boom to Canada, their reasons for migrating are not exclusively driven by economic factors. Rather, they are often combined with other factors such as gender discrimination in South Korea, conflicts with mothers-in-law, concern for their children's education, and aspiration toward the promise of a "better life" in the West. For many, gender relations and conflict stemming from patriarchal social and family systems are the hidden reasons behind their decision to leave Korea.

After immigrating to Canada, however, many Korean immigrants experience downward mobility due to racism, negative accreditation of foreign credentials, lack of language proficiency, accent discrimination in use of the English language, and the loss of social and cultural capital. Some of the women I intereviewed survived by setting up small family businesses. Others were forced to return to school to pursue Canadian education in order to have their qualifications as teachers or health professionals recognized. As most of these women were extremely well educated in Korea, this re-education seemed redundant and a waste of time to many participants. Many of these women found employment in part-time, temporary, and contract-based jobs, and reported experiences of racism and sexism in their workplaces. Ironically, although one motive for migration was to escape gender discrimination in the workplace, they continue in many cases to experience gender discrimination at their places of employment in Canada, often in a particularly racialized form. Their employment experiences demonstrate that patriarchal oppression does not stop at the Pacific, and that it is too often combined with other forms of oppression, including class and racial discrimination.

Becoming Transnational Migrants

In this section, two particular groups of women, the focus of my study, will be discussed, as they represent emerging, yet little studied, trends among recent Korean immigrants:[6] *kirŏgi* mothers — mothers in long-distance relationships — and single Korean women who migrated to Canada on their own.

Flexible Family: "Kirŏgi Kajok" Phenomenon

> *My sister spent more than 1,000,000 won [1,200 CDN] per month on private tutoring for her children, even when my sister was in Korea. That is the reason why my sister chose to come to Toronto as a* kirŏgi *mom. It was for her children's sake.* (Maria)

> *I have met some mothers considering immigration for their children's education. If they come as immigrants [and] not as visa students, they can be more stable. These days, Koreans immigrate not because of economic benefits but because of their children's education. So, they first compare the status of visa students and immigrant status. After the comparison, they carefully choose immigration over a visiting visa.* (Meehi)

South Korean society has been struck by excessive "education fever." As English has become an important source of cultural capital not only in Korea, but also globally, particular emphasis is placed on English education. In this study, many mothers explained that their desire to come to Canada was for the sake of their children's education. Especially after the IMF crisis, the high costs of private education in Korea, along with the strong need for English education in order to complete globally,[7] has caused many Korean families to attempt to cope by becoming multinational households, the so-called *kirŏgi kajok*.[8]

Un Cho (2005) interprets the middle-class families' response to the shaky economy of South Korea caused by globalization and the neo-liberal economy as representing the weak and insecure position of the Korean white-collar middle class within the world capitalist economy. After coming to Canada, however, Korean immigrant families face downward mobility and the families thus choose to become separated as a survival strategy, with the father and husband returning to Korea to find more gainful employment.

This model of family separation is becoming more and more common among recent Korean immigrants, although it is not a completely new phenomenon. In the 1960s and '70s, Korean males travelled to the Middle East as construction workers and to Germany as miners (Cho 2004; Kim), leaving their families behind in pursuit of economic opportunities. In recent years, however, family separation has occurred in the opposite way, men are now staying at home in Korea (or returning home) and women with children are living abroad in order to provide their children with an English education. This family separation used to be found mostly among high- and upper middle-class families with rich financial resources who aim to maximize their resources and opportunities in the global economy (Cho 2004). However, more recently, middle-class families who feel their economic status is threatened and are concerned about the dismantling of the Korean economy have been joining this wave in order to secure this powerful form of cultural capital (Cho 2002; 2005). While *kirŏgi* mothers from high- and upper middle-classes do not appear to suffer from financial problems, less wealthy *kirŏgi* mothers often take jobs wherever they can after coming to Canada. One interviewee confirmed that *kirŏgi* families cannot be generalized as a wealthy group; although all *kirŏgi* families can be described as middle-class, the polarization among middle-class Korean families has become extremely severe since the IMF crisis:

> Kirŏgi *mothers with lots of money can play golf while taking care of their children. But,* kirŏgi *mothers who just barely make ends meet work as waitresses or store helpers. There are such poor* kirŏgi *mothers in my church.* (Eunju)

This calls for another approach to investigating the *kirŏgi* family phenomenon in Canada: it is important to consider who is able to participate actively in transnational mothering and who is not, in terms of equity in the sending country, South Korea. As transnational mothering requires a considerable amount of financial resources, low-income, working-class families, in particular, are blocked from participation, and even financially stable one-income families have to suffer considerable economic and social hardship as a result of their choice to migrate. Thus, critical analysis along class lines is essential.

The *kirŏgi* families in my study reflect not only the current socio-economic and cultural changes in South Korea, but also demonstrate that skilled immigrant families cope with their downward mobility in Canada by choosing family separation. Difficulties in obtaining jobs for which they are highly qualified (due to unrecognized credentials), the language barrier, lack of Canadian experience, and lack of social networks, often force male partners to return to Korea to support their family in Canada. This situation reveals a different aspect of *kirŏgi* families, who are most often viewed as rich transnational households without financial worries. In reality, however, *kirŏgi* families have no choice but to separate due to the financial distress that they suffer as newcomers to Canada. The *kirŏgi* families interviewed in this study thus have different contexts for separation, compared to those who are are able to migrate with substantial resources that allow them to be competitive in the global world economy. None of the *kirŏgi* families I interviewed wanted to be separated from one another, but were forced to do so because of their failure to find adequate employment. Family separation can thus be seen as a strategic response to the inequities of Canadian society.

Maria, Hakyung, Eunsu, Sookja, and Meehi all experienced family separation because their husbands could not find employment in Canada, but could instead hold a well-paying job back in Korea. Eunsu and her husband, for example, lived separately for three years before they decided to reunite in Canada for the sake of their family. Since coming to Canada, however, Eunsu's husband has been depressed and he therefore returns to Korea once every two years.

Maria explains how her family became a *kirŏgi* family:

In the beginning, he [husband] was still working on a big project after we landed in Canada. He was working on a project that he used to do in Korea. He took care of the project work for six months after we arrived, and then he did nothing for one year. He tried to search for employment that year and during that time we fought a lot ... because of his unemployment. I asked him to do even simple physical labour work. But he couldn't. Perhaps, it is hard for men. I was even thinking of working as a waitress. But, it was impossible for him. So, we searched for information about running a business like a dry cleaners or a bakery. But my husband is 45 years old. He was told by other Koreans, "why do you do this kind of hard work.... Why don't you go to Korea for a better job opportunity?" We have tried everything we could do [to make our lives here in Canada]

Sookja commented that she and her husband had strategically planned to be apart in order to reduce the stress caused by the early settlement period. They were apart for three years before her husband rejoined the family in Toronto to keep his immigrant status. Similarly, Meehi and her husband were also apart for three years to reduce their risk factors as newcomers, but were able to reunite in Canada afterward. Currently, they run a small family business together as an alternative to blue-collar employment. Meehi explains:

It was too risky for both of us come to Canada at the start. After the IMF crisis, my husband could get another job, though. His company was sold and merged with another company. My husband ended up working for a French firm and the working conditions were good. So, I came to Canada first and my husband remained in Korea for his job. Both of us thought of a strategic way of dealing with our immigration adjustment. If we just quit our jobs at the same time and left for Canada, it would be too risky.... So, we initially made a decision that I would remain in Korea and my husband would come to Canada with our kids. However, it turned out to be the reverse. My husband's working conditions were getting better than mine. So, my husband suggested that I come to Canada with our children while my husband made money in Korea. And then we could live together again at some point. We thought of it as an ideal situation. But, I don't want to recommend this to other people. It is not good to be apart. My children missed their father a lot.... And then, with time, I also began to feel a mental gap between Korea and Canada. He was doing great in Korea while I was miserable in Canada.... After one year of living apart, I wanted to go back to Korea. I finally recognized what it is like living as an immigrant in Canada. I told him that I wanted to go back to Korea and he disagreed. I didn't much worry about my daughter's education.... I didn't necessarily feel that they needed to receive education abroad. My husband still says to me that if I hadn't asked him to join us in Canada, he wouldn't have come. He would rather have stayed in Korea.

While the men often respond to employment barriers by returning to Korea for better employment opportunities, they also have to deal with the bureaucratic hurdle of residing in Canada for the required period in order to maintain their landed-immigrant status. Maria worried about this, and so too did Sookja. Sookja's husband eventually decided to settle down in Toronto after being out of the country for three years. In fear of the potential loss of their immigrant status, both Maria and Sookja applied for Canadian citizenship; in this way there was at least one family member who could secure residency regardless of lengthy periods of domicile abroad. Maria comments:

After he finished the project work, he came back to Toronto. He had no choice, because he was always stopped and questioned by the Canadian immigration officer at the airport. As a kirŏgi *father, he was under suspicion, because he rarely stayed in Canada.... He always got detained by the officer.... I was afraid of that situation. That's why I applied for Canadian citizenship.*

Although the women are in Canada alone for the most part, the *kirŏgi* family model still restricts the identity of the woman to her traditional roles of mother, wife, and caregiver. Cho (2005) argues that the *kirŏgi* family is a result of global economic restructuring and Korea's patriarchal society in which family prosperity relies on what she calls, "instrumental motherhood" (Cho 2004, 2005). Cho argues that middle-class Korean mothers are expected to sacrifice themselves. For example, some mothers migrate and become *kirŏgi* in order to give birth to their children in the U.S. or Canada so that their children can gain citizenship in North America.[9] Furthermore, in North America they are also able to have their foetuses tested for gender, privileging male offspring.[10]

Overall, it can be argued that the *kirŏgi* family relationship heavily reinforces traditional gender roles in families that are already established on a distinctly heterosexual and patriarchal ideological basis. The roles of males as breadwinners and females as housewives/caregivers are defined transnationally. There are extreme gender divisions in the *kirŏgi* family, because Korean patriarch demands that only men should pursue careers. To a certain extent, this phenomenon leads to a "transnational separation of spheres," with women in the "private" sphere maintaining the role of caregiving mothers in Canada while their husbands in the "public" sphere pursue their careers in South Korea.

In the South Korean media, *kirŏgi* mothers are praised for their attention to their children's education and at the same time blamed for abdicating their responsibility to take "proper" care of their husbands. The mass media in Korea often portray *kirŏgi* mothers and fathers in distorted, black-and-white terms, suggesting the mothers are having affairs and enjoying a comfortable life abroad while the fathers work hard, feel lonely, and even suffer from malnutrition due to the lack of their wives' attention. Major newspapers have regularly reinforced this perception *kirŏgi* mothers, describing especially sympathetically the hardship of *kirŏgi* fathers,[11] while entirely ignoring the responsibilitie these women bear while living abroad with their children. The fact that these women are caring for their children and maintaining homes under different and often difficult cultural circumstances is not considered by the newspapers as worthy of comment. The newspapers' purportedly impartial reports take for granted the women's role as caregivers to their husbands in Korea, and completely disregard the fact that these women continue to be burdened heavily by domestic duties abroad. Indeed, the fact that many of these women living abroad must also engage in paid employment is completely ignored as well. Consider the titles of the following newspaper articles, each showing an extremely binary view of *kirŏgi* mothers and fathers: "The Death of *Kirŏgi* Father: Found Five Days Later" (*Joongang ilbo*, October, 10, 2005), "*Kirŏgi* Father's Lonely Death" (*Segye ilbo*, October 19, 2005), "Even if I sell my body, I can support you to study abroad. You just study hard" (*Kukmin ilbo*, March 29, 2006), "Extravagant *Kirŏgi* Mothers" (MBC TV News, August 14, 2006). "The *kirŏgi* father had a hard time supporting his family abroad. Since there was no one to fix his meals, he often drank alcohol alone at night" (*Segye ilbo*, October 19, 2005).

> Experts warn that *kirŏgi* fathers tend to become vulnerable mentally and physically as they literally sell their bodies for their children's education. The fathers send money to their families abroad, but are in danger of losing their health due to irregular life styles and innutritious meals.... According to Jinsu Yang, a medical professor, "*kirŏgi* fathers often suffer from depression due to loneliness and job stress. They also often have sleep disorders and other mental problems." (*Kukmin Ilbo*, March 29, 2006)

> Reporter: I am standing in a golf field just outside of Los Angeles. Only members are allowed to play golf here. Although it is only a morning of a weekday, the parking lot is already full. All the cars are expensive brands and cost about one-hundred thousand dollars each. All the golf-players are women.

> Interviewee: *Kirŏgi* mothers do nothing but play golf there, after sending their children to school. They spend too much money on playing golf. They are even better than men, because they play every day.

> Reporter: It is known that some extravagant *kirŏgi* mothers purchase expensive houses, golf memberships and expensive cars. But other *kirŏgi* mothers are good mothers, taking good care of their children *with their husbands' money*. (MBC News, August 14, 2006; emphasis added)[12]

To date, I have found no reports in the mass media which discuss the hardships of living abroad among the *kirŏgi* mothers, who are burdened by the responsibility of managing their children's education and supporting their households, and who often give up successful careers in Korea to live in a foreign country where they face difficulties such as isolation, culture shock, and language barriers. Maria is an example. She is attending night school at a community college in order to become a certified accountant and works full-time at a Korean broadcasting firm as a secretary, while taking care of her two children and maintaining their home.

Those who view *kirŏgi* mothers more positively often see them as women making big sacrifices for their children's education. The media in Korea thus focuses on these two extremes of *kirŏgi* mothers as either admirable, self-sacrificing individuals or delinquent wives. The portrayal of *kirŏgi* mothers in South Korean media is thus marred by false assumptions that deny their reproductive labour and the reality of immigrant families' downward mobility in Canada, and its impact on family life.

But, is their children's education the only reason these women move globally? The narratives obtained from the women I interviewed suggest that this is too simplistic an answer. Their motives are rather often intermingled with other factors such as a desire to escape the patriarchal family structure, especially the conflict between mothers-in-law and daughters-in-law, and also to look for new opportunities for themselves, and their families. For instance, Eunsu, who initially spoke of her children's education as the migration motive, and who later also persuaded her husband to join her in Canada, said:

> *I feel comfortable here. I don't need to take care of all the family's small and big events. As the eldest daughter-in-law, I endured ten years of* sijipsari....[13] *Sometimes I couldn't find time to wash my face in the morning. I was that busy. That's how I lived in Korea. For my mother-in-law's birthday, I had to be in her house one week before her birthday, preparing everything. My husband was raised in such a family. He is always obedient to his mother too. It made my life very hard. But since I immigrated to Canada, I now can just give her a call [once in a while] to say "hi."*

Thus, for many *kirŏgi* mothers, the motivations for migration include the desire to avoid the ideology and practice of gender discrimination in South Korea, particularly as represented by patriarchal famialism.

Autonomous Single Women

Recently in South Korea, the age at which women marry has risen; therefore, the proportion of unmarried women has increased and the birthrate has fallen drastically. The divorce rate has also jumped, especially during and after the IMF period. Described as "marriage sabotage" and "birth strike" (Cho 2005), South Korea is currently experiencing a more rapidly aging population than ever before. Gender discriminatory practices, especially prevalent during the IMF crisis, result in married women being laid off before men and discourage working women from marrying and having children. The high cost of raising children and the lack of affordable childcare also play a major role in discouraging marriage and having children. Also, young Korean women who witnessed and experienced the neo-liberal work ethics accelerated by the IMF crisis tend to embrace independence, productivity, cosmopolitanism, and individuality. They often choose career success over traditional family norms such as taking care of husband and family and assuming the double burden of housework and employment. More women choose to be single and delay marriage, forging alternative life styles for themselves which challenge patriarchal social systems and resist gender oppression.

Not surprisingly, the three single women I interviewed as part of this study—Ellen, Hyunju, and Sunhwa—all revealed that they considered their professional lives to be more important than marriage. Sunhwa explains: "For now, my career is more important than anything else. If things happen, then I can get married. But, I don't purposefully pursue marriage."

These single women immigrated to Canada as the primary applicant under the independent class. This was possible due to their relatively privileged status, as represented by degrees from well-respected universities and employment as professionals.[14] Before immigrating to Canada, these independent single women had strategically planned their career paths in advance and career development is their major reason for migration. All three succeeded in finding employment in their desired fields: computer programmer, occupational therapist, and music editor. However, it should be noted that two of them had to complete additional education in Canada due to a lack of recognition of their Korean credentials. The exception was the computer programmer, Sunhwa.

Focusing on their career mobility, Ellen and Hyunju discussed in length gender discrimination and the hierarchical structure of the workplace in Korea as critical factors motivating their migration.

Since I have been working in the field of modern music, it was better for me to go to North America or Europe. I heard that Canada was a good place especially for immigrants and women because Canada treats them well. Also, a friend of mine was studying in Toronto at that time, as an international student, so, I had a good impression of Canada. Personally, [I also immigrated] because of gender discrimination. It was a big deal for me. After graduation, I was so stressed out at work because of gender discrimination. It was such a huge issue for me. School, work, and education are reasons for coming to Canada. But mostly, [to get away from] discrimination against women in Korea. (Ellen)

When I asked Ellen for specific examples of the kind of discrimination she faced at her job in Korea, she responded:

First of all, the wage gap. Secondly, women are forced to do a lot of extra tasks.... For instance, I was forced to clean things up at work, even other people's things, and I was forced to drink alcohol after work. Personally I enjoy drinking but the pressure bothered me. I also don't like wearing make-up, but if I don't do it, people give me lots of stress (laughs). Some people just adjust well at work, but not me. I didn't like it. I had difficulties with things like that. So, I searched for information about immigration and jobs while I worked in Korea.

Ellen was a very politically active student when she attended university in Seoul in the late 1980s. She changed her major several times because she was kicked out of that university as a result of her involvement in radical student demonstrations against the U.S. Due to her political beliefs, she chose to immigrate to Canada rather than the U.S. Although she had a prearranged employment contract before coming to Canada, to her surprise, her job came to an end before the completion of her contract. This experience alerted her to consider her new identity as a minority immigrant woman. To make ends meet, she took on various jobs such as lawn care assistant, private tutor, window cleaner, church piano-player, and cashier until she decided to pursue graduate study.

I also asked Ellen whether she felt she had successfully left gender discrimination behind in Korea:

When I started my TA-ship [teaching assistant], it was rough. My accent was obvious and my English was not good. So students ignored me ... teased me, like picking my mistakes in English or in pronunciation. It was hurtful.... I've pondered about it a lot. It is not something to boast about to speak a mother tongue well. If that is the only reason that students are proud, then it is very pathetic. They have a pathetic life (laughs loudly). I thought so and said so. But if people do tease me for that reason, then well, what can I do? It is their problem. If they challenge me in public, I challenge them in public. Otherwise, I just ignore them.... But there was one rude male student. For example, one day, I was smoking outside the school building and the student said out loud, "you fucking smell, I don't understand why those women smoke."... So, I asked the previous TA about the student and he [the TA] was quite surprised. The student was decent in his class.... Ah ha! I think it's probably the case! Then, it is very clear. The student didn't make any troubles in the male TA's class....

Ellen has noted how racialized women instructors who speak English with an accent are viewed and treated by their male students. Crossing the border did not free her from the sexism she also experienced in Korea.

The intersection of gender and race plays a vital role in Ellen's experience as a Korean woman in Canada. Donald Rubin's study on the perceptions of undergraduate students towards their non-native English speaking teaching assistants found that students' language attitudes act as a filter, mediating perceptions of speakers and their message. Thus, undergraduates' ratings are more closely related to their pre-existing stereotypes, which is unrelated to instructors' actual language proficiency (1990: 339-340).

Hyunju had spent a year in Australia studying English before she came to Canada. Her experience of living in Australia encouraged her to think of immigrating to other English-speaking countries. She searched for all the necessary information through the Internet. After extensive research regarding the regulation of professional associations of occupational therapists in various countries and the immigration policies of the U.S., Australia, New Zealand, and Canada, she chose Canada due to the relatively easy process of the point-system, which evaluates applicants' education, skilled work experiences, and official language proficiency. Her comfort with the English language made this possible. When I asked her why she decided to immigrate, she stated:

I really loved my job in Korea. I am still doing the same work. [But] when I was in Korea, I always wanted to get a better compensation for the work I do. My salary wasn't good. The working environment in the hospital where I worked was very authoritarian and hierarchical. Doctors were always at the center while the opinions of nurses and therapists were not taken seriously. I felt that my competency gained through my four years of university education wasn't counted in the workplace. Also, the compensation was not good enough compared to the work I did. Well, it is the overall atmosphere there. I worked at a hospital and my job was professional, which means the gender discrimination is minor. However, you know, those things our female friends often say—for instance, I should attend a dinner meeting after work because of the extremely hierarchal structure in the hospital. I was forced to work voluntarily, even on weekends, if there were events happening in the hospital. They took me for granted ... [I] always had to read my boss' face first to get permission to go home after 6:00 P.M. I can't go home before my boss leaves the workplace. Also, I had to work during weekends: the norm of sacrificing my time for the whole organization... [I] liked my job and I wanted to develop my job skills for my career. However, my needs were ignored and I was forced to sacrifice myself for the organization.

Hyunju strongly desired to build up her career but also wanted to respect, proper compensation, and equal opportunity at work. She perceived the Canadian workplace as less hierarchical. However, her expectations have been only partially fulfilled as she encounters another form of discrimination—accent discrimination—against which she struggles in her everyday life.

Hyunju, like Ellen, is very conscious of her Korean accent and purchased a tape-recorder in order to practice her Canadian accent. When I interviewed Hyunju in her apartment, I noticed a memo on which she had written "practice your accent" placed in front of her computer. The note was intended to encourage her to practice speaking without a Korean accent so that she will be treated better when working with her clients and employers. Hyunju firmly believes that once she is able to speak without an accent, she will not feel marginal.

Accent discrimination—which is experienced disproportionately by people from Asia, Latin America, and Africa regardless of English language proficiency—has been exposed as racism in another guise (Lindemann, 2005, 2003; Rubin 1992). Studies on accent discrimination commonly find that Asian accented-English is the most negatively perceived, and this negative perception is not related to comprehensibility but is driven by racial and ethnic hostility (Lindemann, 2005, 2003; Rubin 1992). A subtle and sophisticated form of racism is thus mediated through accent discrimination. If an accent is defined by Canadian norms to be a problematic, it becomes a serious barrier to participation in the Canadian workplace. Despite her comfort with the English language, Hyunju felt discriminated against in Canada because of her accent.

Sunhwa, a computer programmer, was swept up by the "emigration fever" prevalent after the IMF crisis, and was also driven by worry concerning the unpredictable, constantly changing, sexist and ageist work environment in South Korea. Sunhwa explains:

*When I started working in the company [in Korea] I was very happy, because I could work in the company for the rest of my life.... I didn't need to worry about my future because my job was for life. After the IMF crisis, the concept of lifelong employment was challenged. My company became very unstable.... Immigration was one alternative..... I thought if I didn't immigrate, I would regret it in the end.... [W]hen I applied for immigration to Canada, it was already very popular in Korea. So, I had lots of interest and at the same time my company's business went bad. The atmosphere at work was not good and the company wasn't stable.... I started thinking whether or not to move to another company, and I heard of stories of immigrating to Canada. It was the trigger for me to apply for the immigration and I got [accepted]. That's why I came to Canada (laughs)....
Also, [in Korea] there is a problem of early retirement. People in their late 30s or early 40s are forced to retire. I felt that there is an obstacle for*

employment due to one's age in Korea too. Because of age discrimination, I thought immigration to Canada could give me more freedom. I definitely don't see any discrimination based on one's age in Canada.

Their motives for migrating are strongly gendered—gender discrimination at work and an age-driven life course that strictly limits women's careers. These young women in their middle- and late-30s have also been exposed to gender sensitivity and democratic political awareness since they attended university during or after the peak of the South Korean students' movements of the late '80s. In many ways, these women are the products of the successful pro-democracy demonstrations of 1987; partly as a result of the generally leftist ideologies, which they imbibed during or after this period, they are more likely than older generations to focus on individual achievement and gender equity in their migration decisions. Also, these young Korean women, who experienced the IMF crisis, grapple with neoliberal human values such as independence, productivity, cosmopolitanism, and individuality.[15] The influences of both the leftist ideologies of the 1980s democracy movement and of the neoliberalism of the 1990s encouraged these women to choose to be single and delay their marriage, forging alternative lifestyles and professional careers for themselves.

However, their status as single women is the source of family conflict around their decision to migrate. Each of their their parents objected to them, as unmarried women, immigrating alone. Ellen's case was extreme. Her mother tore up her passport several times in order to prevent Ellen's departure to Canada. None of her siblings saw her off on the day when she left for Canada, because she left without her mother's acceptance. As a result, she did not contact her family for several years after migration. As Parvati Raghram Raghruam similarly observed in other countries, decision-making power concerning migration is rooted in the gender and generational hierarchies within households; this can limit the ability of young women to migrate. In my study, the only socially acceptable way for women to migrate on their own was when—as in the case of *kirŏgi* mothers—they accompanied their children for the sake of their children's education and were thus acting on behalf of the family unit and within the confines of their traditional role as caregiver.

Single women's independence from their families in the crossing of borders is a largely untouched topic. There are some studies on Filipino single women who immigrate as live-in caregivers or nurses. Their decision is mostly conceptualized within the context of supporting their families back home. It mirrors the Korean nurses who immigrated to Germany in the early 1960s to support their families at home and to contribute to Korea's national economic growth. As Paula Saukko points out, a methodological problem present in such research is that women are usually either viewed as victims of globalization in the host countries or as national heroines of their home states due to the remittances they send back to their families. Overall, it is rare to find research on Korean single women who cross borders to pursue their careers and generally do not do so to support financially their family back home. The three single women in this study, Ellen, Hyunju and Sunhwa, in fact, do not feel the need to support their families financially.[16] Instead, they are focused on career development and individual achievement.

Yet, while their actual immigration to Canada often occurs, at the financial level, relatively independently, without support from their families and without remittances to their families playing a significant role, it would not be true to say that they are isolated individuals. Indeed, their family relationships continue, for the most part, post-migration, not financially, but culturally and socially. They become a transnational link to their extended families, acting as a bridge between Korea and Canada. Their settlement becomes a base for possible chain migration among relatives and friends. For example, they are often asked by relatives in Korea to help younger family members studying English. Sunhwa explains: "I have nieces. I have one sister and two brothers. My sister and brother have two children each of them. I think it is necessary for them to come to Canada to learn [English] more. I want to be a helpful person for them, in fact." When I asked Sunhwa what her sister thought of sending her children to Canada to study English, Sunhwa laughed and stated, "of course, everyone likes it."

Sunhwa's extended family takes advantage of her global mobility in order to gain global capital, in the form of the English language proficiency, which helps to secure middle-class mobility for the entire family, including Sunhwa. In this way, English education plays the role of class reproduction. Similarly, Hyunju is well-known among her university seniors (*sonbae*) and juniors (*hubae*)[17] because she was the first person from her university to pass the Canadian Occupational Therapist licensing exam. Hyunju made a trip to her university in Korea a couple of years ago in order to participate at a seminar in which she explained how to become an occupational therapist in Canada. In doing so, she helped young students who want to immigrate to Canada understand the licensing processes and the advanced preparation that is necessary. Through such transnational connections to Canada—studying English, travelling or visiting their extended families—it seems likely that a growing number of single women in Korea will choose to immigrate.

Overall, the gendered motivations and migration processes of the single women in this study are highly complicated. Their mobility was possible due to their relatively privileged status in Korean society. They make linkages with their middle-class families and friends by helping them learn English. This provides them with cultural/global capital in the neoliberal labour market as competent and independent individuals. It also places them at a higher class level than working-class families who continue to struggle with a lack of resources. Yet, these single women's migrations are clearly also acts of resistance against gendered social structures, and part of the same trend that is reflected in the falling birthrate and delayed age of marriage in contemporary South Korean society. Instead of marrying into a middle-class family, which is typically the only option for advancement given to South Korean women, these single women were determined to create alternative opportunities for themselves by resisting the hostile workplace structures and marital pressure based on age-driven life courses. The three single women's migration narratives thus illustrate complex dynamics of agency and subordination as well as interwoven empowerment and disempowerment in their lives. On the one hand, they exercise agency and are empowered by living in Canada, relative to what their lives were like in South Korea. On the other hand, they experience racialized gender oppression as visible minority immigrant women.

Conclusion

This paper highlighted emerging patterns in the recent migration of women from South Korea to Canada, and examined their gendered motivations. This paper also illustrated the fact that migration is constantly changing and negotiable through transnational space as is shown by the fact that both the *kirŏgi* families and single women became the basis for chain migration for their families and friends.

Many of the women in this study used their global mobility to find alternative ways for dealing with the negative impacts of the post-IMF crisis, oppressive family structures, sexist workplace ideology, and ageism. No one single motive is salient over other motives for migrating; rather multiple and gender specific motives are intertwined in the decision-making processes. Many women seek liberation from gender discrimination and oppressive family relations in South Korea by deciding to migrate to Canada.

However, it should be noted that while women's agency in choosing migration is revealed as resistance against gender discrimination and oppressive family structure in South Korea, it does not mean that their choice to come to Canada is necessarily "liberating," as women experience systemic barriers in the Canadian labour market after migration. Their imagined utopia in Canada is greatly challenged post-migration. Considering women's oppressed positions in the gendered, racialized, and colonized social systems, women's resistance and survival strategies always involve contradictory aspects which Deniz Kandyoti terms the "patriarchal bargain." In other words, subordination and agency, as well as empowerment and disempowerment, in the transnational space are continuously interwoven and constantly changing in the lives of immigrant women.

[1] I follow Statistics Canada in defining recent immigrants as those who have been in Canada for less than five years. I recruited participants through various channels such as community centres, Korean business stores, Korean churches, internet websites, and word-of-mouth. For their privacy and confidentiality, all people mentioned by the interviewees, including the interviewees themselves, are referred to by pseudonyms. For those who have taken English names as part of their strategy to integrate into the Canadian job market, I use English pseudonyms. This essay is part of a larger study in which I interviewed 25 women. The eight women discussed in this essay were selected from among those 25.

[2] Scholars in migration studies use the term "transnational migrants" in order to describe the emergence of social processes in which migrants build social ties across geographic, cultural, and political borders. Transnational migrants develop and maintain multiple ties spanning borders, including familial, social, economic, organizational, religious, and political relations. The multiplicity of migrants' involvement in both "home" and "host societies" is considered a central element of Transnationalism (Schiler, Basch and Blanc-Szanton).

[3] The total population of South Korea is slightly over 40 million and the work force was about ten million before the IMF crisis (Song 2003).

[4] For instance, in 1999, 61.3 percent of employed men were permanent workers, but the same was true for only 30.9 percent of female workers. It is also reported that in August 2002, temporary contract workers made up 70.7 percent of the female labour force, while accounting for about 40 percent of the male labour force (Korean Women's Development Institute).

[5] While the hardship of IMF-imposed SAP dismantled the economic status of many middle class families during the crisis, they were generally better positioned to take advantage of economic opportunities in comparison to working class people. It took more time and more difficulties for working class people to recover from their economic hardship (Kim and Finch).

[6] It should be noted that these categorizations are only used in order to highlight the diversity of the participants in the migration process and not to place these women into inflexible categories that purport to define the totality of their identities.

[7] The major area of competition by which one gains university entrance, graduation, and social and academic status is determined by fluency in English, especially North American English. A big portion of family income in Korea

is often spent on private tutoring, of which English instruction is a major part. While Koreans with English skills also provide instruction, North Americans, especially white North Americans, are most in demand and generally the most expensive.

[8] *Kirŏgi* family refers to a family in which the father works in Korea to support his wife and children who live abroad. This term, the Korean version of the phrase "astronaut family," (Ong) is now widely used in mass media and academic writings as well. In 2005, the first Ph.D. dissertation on *kirŏgi* fathers was published in South Korea and the work received great attention in the media and from academics. There are three different types of *kirŏgi* family: (1) A family moves abroad accompanying the husband/father who had been transferred to a foreign location by the government or a multinational company. The family then stays, despite the fact that the husband/father has been transferred back to Korea; (2) The whole family migrates together. Then the mother and children stay and the father returns to Korea due to better employment opportunities; (3) From the beginning, the family plans for the father to stay in Korea and the mother to go abroad with the children. Some *kirŏgi* families are permanent residents and others are on student visas, visiting visas, or working visas.

[9] Some intend to avoid military service by obtaining foreign citizenship.

[10] In Korea, the emphasis on male offspring that has been especially characteristic of society since the entrenchment of Neo-Confucian values in the sixteenth, seventeenth and eighteenth centuries has resulted, since the late twentieth century, in many women aborting female offspring, often under pressure from their parents-in-law. The South Korean government responded to the increasingly dangerous imbalance between male and female children by banning gender testing of foetuses. Women who go to North American for such tests are attempting to circumvent this restriction—as a general rule, then, it can be assumed that if the foetus is discovered to be female under these circumstances, it will be aborted.

[11] Furthermore, while *kirŏgi* fathers are regarded as lonely "single" fathers, the increasing number of "single" mothers in poverty in South Korea does not receive enough public attention. It is estimated that there are about 1,000,000 single mothers, which is four times higher than the number of single fathers in South Korea (Hankyoreh).

[12] The news transcript can be found at http://tvnews.media.daum.net/part/foreigntv/200608/14/imbc/v13690988.html. The phrase "with their husbands' money" is especially striking. With one quick phrase the interviewer informs viewers that, while the childcare preformed by the women needs no compensation, the money sent by the men to achieve educational goals for their children, presumably after careful consultation between husband and wife, is solely the

husbands' money. The interviewer also seems to suggest that wives can barely be considered adults when it comes to managing finances.

[13]This is a Korean term that cannot be translated easily into English. It literally means the life of daughters-in-law living in the same house as their mothers-in-law. There is a saying concerning *sijipsari*, that following marriage, women are expected to endure three years of being blind and another three years of being deaf-mute.

[14]The success of these three women should not be generalized and used to support Eurocentric discourses of Canadian nationalism by which oppressed "third world" women of colour are seen as being saved by their acceptance into a multicultural, liberal and non-sexist Canada. It is very clear that Canada's immigration policy is based on its economic benefits, pushing immigrants into the lower rung of the labour market despite their skills and professional work experiences. Visible minority immigrant women thus generally experience racialization and gendered oppression in the Canadian labour market, and not liberation from gender discrimination in their home countries. These three women are in many ways exceptional, as the preceding section on *kirŏgi* mothers makes clear.

[15]Song (2006) discusses how neoliberalism works not only as macroeconomic doctrine of state policy but also as a social ethos in which social actors participate in the construction of neoliberal governance. She is critically engaged with Foucault's notion of technology of governance to explain why and how the neoliberal ethos spreads.

[16]None of the single women in this study send remittances home. They migrated with their own savings accumulated during their previous employment in South Korea.

[17]Korean universities were (and still often are) very hierarchical. While there was and is always considerable difference between individuals, students would often think of themselves not as individuals studying on their own, but as members of a group. This group would often encompass their particular academic department, but could also be a club of which they were a member. These smaller groups would often be organized hierarchically, with age and university year being taken into account for defining students as either seniors (*sonbae*) or juniors (*hubae*), with juniors being required to show some level of deference and respect to their seniors, and seniors being expected to be responsible for their juniors even after graduation. Such relationships are a vital element of networking in South Korean society.

References

Castles, S. *International Migration at the Beginning of the Twenty-first Cen-*

tury: Global Trends and Issues. 2000. Online: http://students.washington.edu/rogersj/globintermig.pdf.

Cho, U. "The Encroachment of Globalization into Intimate Life: The Flexible Korean Family in 'Economic Crisis.'" *Korea Journal* (Autumn 2005): 8-35.

Cho, U. "Han'guk ŭi kabujangje wa mosŏng: Togujŏk mosŏng e taehan kyebo ch'atki" (Korean Patriarchy and Motherhood: Searching for a Genealogy of Instrumental Motherhood). *Gender, Experience and History*. Eds. O. R. Cho and J. Y. Chung. Seoul: Sogang University Press, 2004. 205-213.

Cho, U. "Global Capital and Local Patriarchy: The Financial Crisis and Women Workers in South Korea." *Women and Work in Globalising Asia*. Eds. D. S. Gills and N. Piper. New York: Routledge, 2002. 52-69.

Choi, H. "Emancipation or Oppression in Diaspora? Korean Women Academics and Their Diasporic Experience." *Asian Women: Interconnections*. Eds. T. Hellwig and S. Thobani. Toronto: Women's Press, 2006. 67-91.

Hankyoreh. *O chipchung il kot honja sanda (One Out of Five, Living Alone)*. July 26th, 2006. Online: http://www.hani.co.kr/arti/society/society_general/144365.html.

Iredale, R. "The Migration of Professionals: Theories and Typologies." *International Migration* 39 (5) (2001): 7-24.

Kandyoti, D. (1988). "Bargaining with Patriarchy." *Gender and Society* 2 (3) (September): 274-290.

Kim, S. C. "'Weekend Couples' Among Korean Professionals: An Ethnography of Living Apart on Weekdays." *Korea Journal* 41 (4) (2001): 28-47.

Kim, S. and J. Finch. "Living with Rhetoric, Living Against Rhetoric: Korean Families and the IMF Economic Crisis." *Korea Studies* 26 (1) (2002): 120-139.

Korean Women's Development Institute. *Che 4 ch'a yŏsŏng ch'wiŏp silt'ae chosa (The 4th Report on Women's Employment Trends)*. Seoul: Korean Women's Development Institute, 2002.

Kwak, M. "Work in Family Businesses and Gender Relations: A Case Study of Recent Korean Immigrant Women." Unpublished MA thesis: York University, Toronto, 2002.

Lindemann, S. "'Who Speaks Broken English?' U.S. Undergraduates' Perceptions of Non-native English." *International Journal of Applied Linguistics* 15 (2) (2005):187-212.

Lindemann, S. "Koreans, Chinese or Indians? Attitudes and Ideologies About Non-native English Speakers in the United States." *Journal of Sociolinguistics* 7 (2003): 348-64.

Ong, A. *Flexible Citizenship: The Cultural Logics of Transnationality*. Durham, NC: Duke University Press, 1999.

Park, H. J. "Sŏngbyŏlhwa doen nodong sijang, chubyŏnhwa doen yŏsŏng nodongja" (The Gendered Labour Market: Marginalized Female Worker). *Wigi ŭi nodong: han'guk minjujuŭi ŭi ch'wiyakhan sahoe kyŏngjejŏk kiban* (*Korean Labour in Crisis: The Weakness of Social Base for Democracy*). Ed. J. J. Choi. Seoul: Humanitas, 2005. 95-136.

Park, K. *In Our Different Names: Korean Immigrant Women and the Challenges of Post-Migration Identity Renegotiation.* Unpublished Ph.D. dissertation, State University of New Jersey, Brunswick, NJ, 2005.

Rubin, D. L. "Non-language Factors Affecting Undergraduates' Judgments of Non-Native English-Speaking Teaching Assistants." *Research in Higher Education* 33 (4) (1992): 511-531.

Rubin, D. L. "Effects of Accent, Ethnicity and Lecture Topic on Undergraduates' Perceptions of Non-native English Speaking Teaching Assistants." *International Journal of Intercultural Relations* 14 (1990): 337-353.

Raghuram, P. R. "Gendering Skilled Migratory Streams: Implications for Conceptualizations of Migration." *Asian and Pacific Migration Journal* 9 (4) (2000): 429-457.

Sassen, S. "Immigration and Local Labour Markets." *Economic Sociology of Immigration: Essays on Networks, Ethnicity and Entrepreneurship.* Ed. A. Portes. New York: Russell Sage Foundation, 1995.

Saukko, P. *Doing Research in Cultural Studies: An Introduction to Classical and New Methodological Approaches.* Thousand Oaks, CA: Sage, 2003.

Schiler, N. G., L. G. Basch and C. Blanc-Szanton. "Towards a Definition of Transnationalism: Introductory Remarks and Research Questions." *Towards a Definition of Transnationalism: Race, Class, Ethnicity and Nationalism.* Eds. N. G. Schiler, L. G. Basch and C. Blanc-Szanton. New York: New York Academy of Science, 1992. ix-xv.

Song, J. *Shifting Technologies: Neoliberalization of the Welfare State in South Korea, 1997-2001.* Unpublished Ph.D. dissertation, University of Illinois, 2003.

Song, J. "Family Breakdown and Invisible Homeless Women: Neoliberal Governance during the Asian Debt Crisis in South Korea, 1997-2001." *Positions* 14 (1) (2006): 37-65.

Stalker, P. *International Migration.* London: Verso, 2001.

Statistics Canada. "100 Years of Education." *Education Quarterly Review* 7 (3) (2001): 18-23.

Yoon, I. J. "T'oront'o chiyŏk hanin ŭi saenghwal kwa ŭisik" (The Study of Koreans in Toronto). Paper presented at the annual meeting of the Association of Koreans Abroad, Seoul, November, 2001.

JULIANNA CHOI

1997

Three days into the new year
I meet Joe for coffee
had a crush on him at school
we go to Sneaky Dee's
(grungy and smoky)
to drink beer
and sexual tension.

I don't want to give any pieces of myself away.
I will not be a receptacle for someone else's misery.

Jim's moved in with his new girlfriend:
fucked up — weak stupid pathetic scum sucking no excuse loser

weak people who don't give a shit about anyone else but themselves,
thinking they're such martyrs all of them the world has no sympathy for me.

I am so stressed out
it's the same refrain I know
I've lost and recovered my purse
three times in the last two weeks
luckily three different people have found it
so no one person has been a witness to
my complete unawareness of my environment.

I'm unhappy, so unhappy
that I felt like crying in class today
and apologizing for my existence to Mary K.

am chain smoking and can't get any work done
almost a year since break up —
anniversary anxiety
I don't know I wish I was still in therapy.

Home from assembly meeting
people are so narrow minded
I am completely justified
in my endeavour to change this constitution
was definitely not in muckraking
silenced by G. Hunt who is abusing his power
he dug his own goddamn grave.

I think I am suffering from a low grade depression
I'm making a resolution to learn to meditate and make lists of
why I am so angry and depressed
what do I want to do and what do I have to do
why do I hate myself and why do I love myself.
I hate the open endedness of my life.

My cat loves me.
Not going to Korea after all.

My heart hurts.
I am agitated by feelings of responsibility toward my parents.

I stroke my cat.
I wish I could stroke myself.

I am committed to self love and self communication.

JULIANNA CHOI

Fallen

Dear Mother:
(The therapist said this would be good for me.)
So there's a question I've been meaning to ask:

Where did you go wrong?

You told me that your father died early,
You were the youngest of six and
An accident of birth
Your sister told me (confidentially) that
You were always the serious one.

Your house is a museum and
your floors are cleaned on your hands and knees
every other day.
Your chairs have been covered in plastic
for thirty years.

When I was six,
I was afraid to drink milk.
What if I spilled it?
Your anger was quick and your words drew blood.

You raged.
I swallowed tears.
Just wait till I'm old enough.
You'll see.

You asked,
Is that the best that you can do?

Yes, you are
A proud mother,
A paragon of virtue, and
A chastising wife.

Ten years later,
The therapist said,
Your mother is the source of your self-critical voice
it's okay to hate your mother.
I said
That's blasphemous.

And then,
I catch us walking,
(Your idea after free cocktails)
Somewhere uptown alone.

You say,
Let's walk.
You are drunk but hardly know it
your eyes are open
I am holding your arm
I want to say,
I will catch you when you fall and
Then you catch me by surprise:
You know I love you.

I know this is true.

ISABELLE KIM

Dear X

July 7, 2006

Dear X,

It all began when I received the 2006 Canadian census form. The long one. Somewhere between pages one and forty-one, there was a question I could not answer. There are many versions and iterations of this question. It goes something like this:

"What are you?" or, "Where are you from?"

My response has changed over time, and still does, depending on my mood. When I was a very little girl, it went something like this:

"I am a girl; I'm from Ottawa, Canada."

When I was a teenager, it went something like this:

"A human being; my mother's womb, you?" (As a teenager, my brother would say that he was "from North Korea"—maybe it was easier somehow, or it felt right, or, as I suspect, because of its exotic appeal.)

My responses, never satisfactory, inevitably lead to further probing:

"Oh ... Where are your parents from?"

I have never been able to talk about "what" I am or where I am from without talking about where my parents are from and *what* they are.

Sometime between being very little and less little, I learned to say (cheerily/warily): "Half-Korean and half-White," with my hand drawing a vertical line down the centre of my face, tracing the halves. (Actually, if you look closely, the right side of my face is definitely the Korean one. The cheekbone is more prominent; the eye is narrower; the skin is more taut because it is slightly fuller than its White counterpart.)

This answer worked for me until the day my brother met a Korean boy for the first time in his life. This boy corrected my brother: "You cannot be "half" Korean. You are Korean. Period. *And* Canadian." The idea of being "half-and-half" suddenly seemed absurd. The problem with this idea has to do with mathematics. Mathematics is an exact science. Or is it? For people who love mathematics, it is both art and science; mathematics requires the imagination. If this is true, for every mathematical problem, there may be an exact answer but often more than one possible solution.

So far, I have heard the following solutions to the equation:

Korean + (White) French-Canadian = ?

Mexican, Japanese-Peruvian, East Indian, West Indian, South American, Spanish, Italian, Jewish, Icelandic, Hawaiian, Métis, "American-Indian," Japanese, Chinese, Xinjiangese, Western Asian, Persian.

Therein lies the beauty of math: the creativity and individuality expressed in the explanation.

There are two expressions that belong to a different school of Mathematics, *the School of Exactitude*:

"What you see is what you get," and "You have to see it to believe it."

These expressions are derived from the A/not A type of logic. Following this logic, there is only one correct answer to the question, "What are you?" When I was younger than 13 years old, the standard response from those who belong to the *School of Exactitude* went something like this:

"But you don't look French-Canadian."

When I was older than 13 years old:

"But you don't look Korean."

Just like that, during my thirteenth summer, the left side of my face decided to take over. My hair became wild and curly. Freckles made their appearance. It is debatable whether the freckles should be attributed to the effects of the ozone layer or to my late maternal grandmother's genes finally making themselves known. It was like receiving a stealthily gradual identity makeover that one did not pay nor ask for. The only remaining vestiges of my Korean identity, the only "proof" were my last name, the shape and colour of my eyes and the colour of my hair. No longer "seeing" much Koreanness, the kind of people who like to vote for a winning candidate chose the left side, clearly the majority party. They ceased to recognize the existence of the right side. Slowly, but surely, with every single "but" that rejected the "and" in my standard "Korean *and* French-Canadian" response, the hand drew an ever increasing rift down the centre of my face. How does one respond to a statement uttered as fact such as "But you don't look Korean?"

The term "banana" is used to describe Asians who are "yellow-on-the-outside-white-on-the-inside." Following this logic, I am a reverse banana: my "White" phenotype betrays its 50 percent "Yellow" genotype. I wonder if "banana," "half-breed," and other such ridiculous terms will still be around when we become old and grey, dear X.

Some people give me the benefit of the doubt despite my predominantly "White" appearance, trying to measure Koreanness in other ways:

Do you speak Korean?
"No."
Do you have family in Korea or in Canada?
"They are all in North Korea, and therefore either incommunicado or dead," (my creative response).
Oh (uncomfortable pause)... *That's so sad.*
"Hmmm... Yes." (bowing my head, nodding gravely).
Do you eat Korean food at home?
My exact response: "Extremely rarely but I love Korean food."
Have you ever been to Korea?

Yes. (This response is 100 percent true). In 1994, I went to Korea. In fact, 1994 was officially declared *Visit Korea Year* by the South Korean government. I was barely seventeen years old and my family was broke. My savings from part-time jobs over the years paid for the ticket. There was not much money left over but it would have to do. My father said that the language barrier would make things difficult. Without showing it, my mother worried about the kinds of things mothers worry about. No one could deter me once I had made up my mind about going to Korea—you know how stubborn I can be, dear X. I declared that at seventeen I was old enough to go to Korea. Seventeen is not old enough to realize that one requires equal parts folly and courage to embark on such a marvellous adventure.

That is how I came to spend five weeks backpacking throughout South Korea searching for clues to the enigma, *How was I, partially or fully*—depending on where one draws the line—*"Korean?"* Possessing only the faintest and most nebulous of clues, in the summer of 1994, I finally decided to find concrete answers. It all began at the airport in Seoul, at the "Visit Korea Year" booth, where I went to inquire about affordable accommodation in the city. The official-looking woman behind the booth produced a list of hotels with three-digit prices. I made the universal hand signal for "too expensive." A second list appeared followed by another hand signal, and so on, until she gave up with the lists altogether. With a disgusted look on her face, she wrote the name of a $US15/night "youth hostel" in Korean on a piece of paper. She escorted me outside, practically shoved me into a taxi, barked the address of the youth hostel to the driver, and slammed the door shut.

It was the middle of the night. July is a muggy, sticky time of year in Seoul. As the taxi wound through the torturous narrow streets of Seoul's red light district and stopped at a place with a very obvious identity two feelings occurred to me at the exact same time: 1) fear that the inside of the "hotel" would be what it promised on the outside; 2) hilarity that my first "cultural" lesson should be to learn the meaning of "youth hostel." Did the damn travel agent at the airport not see the Canadian flag sewn onto my backpack, the running shoes, the sturdy, asexual clothes? Exhausted after a nearly 24-hour journey, would I have the wit and strength to defend the case of my mistaken identity? A very short, very old woman came scurrying out to meet the taxi driver. She paid him off and ushered me in, "You pay me later. Come inside." As I attempted to pay her back immediately, and stay outside, she gripped my arm fiercely and shouted at me to get inside. "I get French man for you." I felt nauseous. "Calm down," I told myself. "There is an upside to this story: you speak French. You will simply explain to this man that there has been a grave misunderstanding.

A short, all-Korean looking man appeared. He introduced himself as "Didier" in perfect French. He was, in fact, Swiss. He explained that he had been adopted into a White, Swiss family and that he had located his birth family and was here to visit them. "Someone in search of his roots," he said. Talking with Didier, I realized that I could not have picked a better and worst year to travel in Korea. In 1994, the *won* was excessively high compared to the Canadian dollar and I possessed excessively limited travel funds. But, 1994 being "Visit Korea Year," the government gave all "gambling" and other shady operations a choice to either shut down or convert into affordable inns for travellers on a shoestring. Didier explained that the current incarnation of this ex-gambling/prostitution-house was "youth hostel," pointing to the Korean and English words posted by the front desk. It had been too dark or I had been too scared to see the sign upon entering the building. What you see is not always what you get. For that first week in Seoul, Didier became my guide and friend. We were traveling companions on different missions. His: to connect with his birth family and find an all-Korean girlfriend. Mine: to search for clues as to the whereabouts of the Korean pieces of me that were missing.

A week passed, my jet-lag passed, and I itched to leave Seoul and see the rest of the country. My father had told me how beautiful Korea was but that was not obvious in Seoul. In the four weeks that followed, I climbed as many mountains as I could. It will not surprise you, X – you know me so well – that on one of these mountains, I got lost. My utter lack of sense of direction is both curse and blessing. On many a times it has led me to interesting places I would not have found had I not been lost. On this particular occasion, I was rescued by a monk on a moped, who took me to a Buddhist monastery nestled in the mountains. Upon arrival, he took me to see the head monk, who happened to be a Harvard graduate who spoke fluent English.

I went as far South as I could: Cheju-Do Island, where there are statues that look like the ones on Easter Island. A trio of Korean women: a cook, a computer analyst and a teacher "adopted me" for the trek and would not let me out their sight. It was during this trip to Korea that I met Ms. L and her family.

The L connection started in Ottawa at the store where my mother was buying my birthday present, a big backpack for my Korea trip. A white man overheard my mother explaining the purpose of the gift to the saleswoman. He gave my mom the name of a Korean woman who lived in Seoul, Ms. L.

"Ms. L. is an old friend. She works as a Korean-English translator in Seoul. Her son is half-Canadian (White) and half-Korean, like your daughter. She would be happy to have your daughter stay with her for a few days I am sure of it."

I did end up calling Ms. L., and staying at her place for a few days. Ms. L's son told me Koreans had bad B.O. but at least he was only 50 percent Korean, which made him not 100 percent stinky. I was too sad to respond. I learned the acronym "B.O." from him. He learned it from school: the American School in Seoul, which is mostly attended by the children of American soldiers stationed in Korea, rich Koreans, and diplomats. When I left Ms. L.'s house, she told me to go visit her brother in Pohang, who in turn referred me to people he knew in Pusan.

While in Korea, I felt a kind of kinship. The kind where you can say your name once without having to repeat it, hear it grossly mispronounced, or have someone ask "what it means." For however brief, however fleeting moments, I *made* family with Ms. L and her family, the trio of women, even the grumpy monks. What did they make of me? Did they take me in out of some sense of pity or hospitality? For the sake of "Korean kinship?" At 17, I was naïve enough and not yet too proud to accept offers from strangers; too hungry for kinship and too broke to refuse their hospitality. Had I postponed my trip to Korea, I might never have "made" Korean family.

A year after Korea, I left Ottawa to begin studies at the University of Toronto at Scarborough. One day, feeling lost and isolated in Scarberia, I made the trek to "Little Korea" in search of kinship and comfort food. My trip to Korea had left me with far more questions than answers about "being Korean." In 1999, the year I met your father, I enrolled in a Korean history class taught by a 100 percent white professor, Dr. S., who spoke fluent Korean. That year, dear X, I forced your father to watch many Korean films. I learned about Korean throat singing from one of these films. The sound moved me. I nearly enrolled in Korean drumming lessons but did not. As you know, I was trained in classical piano, like so many Korean children. I would like to contradict myself. Can one learn to be Korean? In Little Korea and in the Korean history class, I felt like an impostor whose guise could be exposed with a single question: *What are you?*

"You can be whatever you want!" (My parents' standard refrain.)

"You are so lucky! You have the best of both worlds!" (A refrain I hear from other people).

But I have never felt "lucky." "Lucky" is not the right word. The prospect of inventing a new hybridized identity is not as liberating as it appears. It conjures images of genetic agricultural experiments. But agricultural science is not exact. It does not explain my desire, at times, to be mono-culture.

Eleven years have passed since I moved to Toronto. During that time, so much has happened. I am not sure when, how or where it happened, but I realized that the most sensible and realistic option for me was to learn how to become comfortable with ambiguity. It is one of those things that are a lot easier to *say* than to *do*. Looking at life through the lens of ambiguity requires constant readjustments. Optics too, is far from an exact science. You know how the prescription for my eye glasses is never quite right? I find it difficult to remember among the many successive options presented to me which version of the same set of letters and numbers is most clear. Sitting on the chair with my eyes pressed against a lens, the optometrist flips back and forth, asking "Is this one clearer or this one, or this one?" I lose track. My dear X, you who are so young yet have more cultures and history in your little body than both your father's and mother's combined to keep track of, how will you see the world? Perhaps you will draw inspiration from your father, who seems far more comfortable with being Chinese-African-Portuguese. He comes from

Guyana, a place where mixed heritage is the norm. Will you see yourself as "Korean?" What will you want to know about your Korean part?

I will not teach you Korean. I cannot. In 1998, I worked for nine months in Tianjin, a city in North-East China, where there is a large Korean community. Before leaving, I gave my father a piece of paper and asked him to write the names of my favourite Korean dishes in Korean. A few months later, I met university students from Korea who were in Tianjin to study Mandarin. The piece of paper always seemed to generate a strangely emotional response from Korean readers. As embarrassing as it was, I finally asked someone to translate my father's words:

Dear Reader,
I am extremely ashamed to admit that my daughter does not speak Korean. She speaks English and French. She was born in Canada. Her mother is Canadian. Her Korean name is Kim Kyong-Hee. It is my fault if Kyong-Hee does not speak Korean because I did not teach her. I tried to but did not try hard enough. I should have. She is working here for a year. My daughter loves Korean food. These are her favourite Korean foods. If you have any of these dishes, would you be as so kind as to bring her one of them or something similar? I would be eternally grateful.
Thank-you so much.
Her father.

Perhaps you will try to learn Korean on your own, as I did. Perhaps you will not give up, as I did.

Visions of the mountainous Korean landscape and cravings for Korean food haunted me after I returned from Korea. They still do. Perhaps there is an addictive ingredient in *kimchee*. I will probably never cook Korean food just like I will never cook French-Canadian food because I do not like cooking. But I can promise you this: I will take you to Little Korea. We will travel by subway. We will get off at the Bloor and Christie subway station and we will eat to our hearts' content. Possibly, hopefully, when you are old enough to remember, we will go to South Korea. You might even be able to visit North Korea in your lifetime and visit your *harahbeoji*'s birthplace.

Or perhaps, by then we will not have to choose which half. We will simply go to Korea. Period. Korea is a country currently divided in two halves by ideology. Canada is a country that was nearly divided by language not so long ago. Dear X, your father's land, Guyana, was also divided by colonialism. You were born June 8, 2005, 12:16 A.M. That makes you a Gemini. It is said that geminis are two-faced. I say what you see is rarely, if ever, what you get. The whole is greater than the sum of its parts.

My mother, your grand-maman, is fond of a saying she read in a cookbook: "You are what you eat." Are we, dear X, by virtue of our genes, 50 percent and 25 percent respectively, "Korean?" Nutrition and genetics are not exact sciences. Neither is statistics, obviously. A great example can be found in the Canada 2006 census form, the long one. I cannot remember the exact page but you will recognize the question the moment you read it. Among the possible answers proposed for the equation: Korean + French-Canadian + Chinese + African + Portuguese, I could not find the only answer I know is true: "my son."

Whole-heartedly yours,
Mum.

I would like to thank Ruthann Lee for inviting and encouraging me to write. It is a great joy and honour to have my piece in the company of Korean-Canadian women.

ANN SHIN

Korean Drummers

arms flailing against drums slung on their hips
they pound with fury, blue tassels spinning
around red lacquered drums. the housewives
have stepped out of their homes for a night,
slipping into their own skins, drumming
rhythms of who they're meant to be
freed from one tradition

distilled into another:
bom bada bom, bom bom bom
rhythms learned from their mothers
and revised along the way, lift their hands
and reverberate within our breasts.

my mother no longer dances
but my veins are still thrumming
with every move, she is the premonition,
the signal light before the action. I am the left turn
my hands spinning the wheel

though the roads and the roles
in the dance have changed,
on stage or in the kitchen
our mothers drum the bloodbeat
of who I am. they are in me
though I am not them
the way the heart of poetry is
and is something other than the collective meaning of words.

Contributor Notes

Jenny J. H. Ahn is currently working in the Education Department as a National Representative with the Canadian Auto Workers Union (CAW). She was also elected President of CAW Local 40 and Vice-President of the CAW National Executive Board (NEB) — the first women of colour and the youngest member ever elected. She has been involved in a number of social justice issues and is committed to fighting ableism and racism. She is a founding member and Co-President of the Asian Canadian Labour Alliance (ACLA), a community based organization of progressive trade unionists of Asian descent and their allies. In 2003, Jenny received the Social Activist Award from the Metro Network for Social Justice. She continues her work with her union as well as with ACLA, the *Our Times* magazine Advisory Board, and as a Toronto and York Region Labour Council Executive Board Member (Jenny.Ahn@caw.ca).

Elaine K. Chang was born in Vancouver, and received her BA (Hon.) in English at the University of British Columbia and her MA and Ph.D. in Modern Thought and Literature at Stanford University. Her experimental film work premiered at the Tenth Annual Toronto Reel Asian International Film Festival in November, 2006, and she is currently editing a book on independent Asian Canadian film and video, *Reel Asian: Asian Canada on Screen* (forthcoming 2007). She has published essays in the areas of feminist and postcolonial theory, Asian North American fiction and autobiography, film and popular culture, and critical studies of race and ethnicity, as well as poetic and dramatic work. She has been awarded fellowships from the Mellon Foundation, Social Sciences and Humanities Research Council, and the Center for the Critical Analysis of Contemporary Culture, and also the 2004 Central Student Association Teaching Excellence Award at the University of Guelph, where she currently teaches contemporary literary and cultural studies.

CONTRIBUTOR NOTES

Michelle Cho is a 29-year-old Korean-Canadian woman. She is an organizer and researcher with the Urban Alliance on Race Relations, where she organized the Toronto Coalition for Equity in Education, working to address systemic racism in public education. She has also organized political leadership training for youth and women of colour interested in electoral politics. She is a member of Han Kŭt, a Korean women's collective committed to anti-racist, feminist and queer organizing. She has extensive anti-racist organizing, public education, research, and community development experience.

Julianna Choi: I became a reader first: as a child, I would hide in my closet reading Nancy Drew mysteries by flashlight. As an adolescent, I believed my pen was my voice and so I woke up in the middle of the night to write about snowstorms and angels. Today, I practice both fiction and poetry, prodded on by my fellow writers in our group, *Inconceivable Writings*. Currently, Kazuo Ishiguro and Miriam Toews keep me up at night. For the last decade, I've been a teacher helping reluctant teenagers enjoy books and the sounds of their voices on paper. And in order to recuperate from that effort, I occasionally paint abstract images but most often, you'll find me in the kitchen, cooking with voluminous amounts of garlic and wine for my loved ones.

Far-San (far mountain) likes storytelling, visualizing, humming and improvisational piano playing. She has a good memory of context, especially scent, background sound, image of people, emotive signs and ambience, whereas she has a terrible memory of numbers, such as birthday of her best friends or memorial day of her father, and verbatim titles of songs and books. She studies, thinks, interprets, analyzes, critiques of power dynamics in micro and macro human-social relationships in mostly academic space at the risk of losing her capacity of feeling and intuition.

Young-Hwa Hong is a doctoral student in the Department of Sociology and Equity Studies in Education at Ontario Institute for Studies in Education of the University of Toronto. Her research looks at how skilled immigrant women are racialized and gendered in the Canadian labour market. She has also been involved in community work serving as a cultural interpreter, Korean seniors' program facilitator, and HIV/AIDS outreach worker for Korean youth.

Jin Huh (Collective Member) was born in Seoul, South Korea and grew up in northwest Toronto near Jane and Finch and then later in suburban Scarborough, Ontario. She is an educator, community worker, writer, ex-grad student, and closet karaoke superstar who has been involved in political struggles related to anti-racist feminism, anti-imperialism, the environment, and sexual health.

Merose Hwang is a Ph.D. candidate and lecturer of Modern Korean History at the Department of East Asian Studies, University of Toronto. She wrote her BA thesis in Native American Shamanism through the Religious Studies Department at the University of Colorado, Boulder and attended the MA program on Korean Indigenous Religions at Yonsei University. She has held positions as a research fellow at the Institute for Korean Studies (IKS), Yonsei University in Seoul and as a visiting scholar in Seoul for Korea Foundation. She has worked as a freelance translator for the Academy of Korean Studies at Seoul National University and IKS. Merose continually aspires to learn and teach in ways that can help Korean diasporic women combat the daily violence we face through our shared histories of colonial racism, classism, and sexism.

Helen H. Kang was born in Korea and moved to Toronto 20 years ago. She is fluent in both Korean and English. She is currently pursuing a doctorate degree in Sociology at Simon Fraser University, focusing on cultural studies and HIV/AIDS.

Julie Kang was raised in a variety of communities in Ontario, and now resides in Toronto. In sharing stories from her life and in gathering and sketching stories drawn from the lives of people around her, she hopes to spark recognition of what is common and contribute to understanding of what is different, between people. She enjoys unearthing truth and beauty in the details of life in her writing, and is a student hoping to work in advocacy for equity in community health and literacy in the future.

Gloria U. Y. Kim is a Toronto-based filmmaker, writer and photographer. Her writing has appeared in *Maclean's, FilmPrint, Canadian Business* and *Fireweed*. Her series of six Polaroids, Madwoman, appeared at the Christmas Group Show at Engine Gallery in 2004. Her films have screened at the Toronto Reel Asian International Film Festival, the Women of Colour Film Festival, Inside Out Film Festival, POW! Film Fest, and most recently at the 2006 Female Eye National Day of Remembrance and Action on Violence Against Women. Her experimental documentary, *Partial Selves* (9 min., 2000), won runner up for the Best Experimental Film at the 2003 International Festival of Cinema and Technology. Gloria is currently working on her newest short film, *Rock Garden: A Love Story*, for which she has received support from the Canada Council for the Arts, Ontario Arts Council, Toronto Arts Council, as well as the WIFT/ CBC Canadian Reflections Award, Bravo! FACT and NFB FAP. Born in Seoul, Korea, Gloria emigrated to Canada when she was three years old. Gloria works as a reporter for *Maclean's* magazine and spends her free time writing.

CONTRIBUTOR NOTES

Hana Kim is presently the Korea Studies Librarian at the Cheng Yu Tung East Asian Library of the University of Toronto. She is responsible for collection management and development and services relating to Korean Studies. She holds a B.Ed. in Education (German Language and English Language) from the Korea National University of Education, South Korea and an MLIS from McGill University, Canada. Previous to this, she obtained National Accreditation Authority for Translators and Interpreters (NAATI) from the Royal Melbourne Institute of Technology (RMIT) in Melbourne, Australia. She is also an active translator and won The First Annual Min Chapbook Competition for her translation of poems by Cheonhak Kwon. The translations were published in a book entitled *$2H_2 + O_2 = 2H_2O$*.

Isabelle Kim: Isabelle/Kyong-Hee is an avid letter-writer and aspiring video-maker. She recently defended her Ph.D. thesis, "Youth Videomaking Projects: A Spoken Word Study" at the Ontario Institute for Studies in Education at the University of Toronto (OISE/UT). Isabelle has been working in community arts and education over the last several years. She currently lives in Toronto with her son and husband.

Jane G. Kim graduated from York University, receiving Honours in her double Bachelor of Arts degrees in English and Communications. Always harboring the love to write poetry and prose inspired Jane to take her work out of the classroom and into the literary world. Upon graduating from university, Jane held various support positions in the entertainment industry. Her ultimate goals are to write and produce screenplays in addition to penning short stories and young adult novels. "The Funny Looking Dress," her first short story to be published, represents her attraction to the combination of autobiographical pieces with fictive anecdotes. She is thrilled to contribute to this anthology, and she looks forward to sharing her work with readers who can appreciate a light-hearted, hopeful coming-of-age story. Jane currently resides in Toronto.

Nuri Kim was born and lived in Busan and Seoul Korea until 1998 when, at thge age of 26, she moved to Toronto for a break and change. She went to graduate school and worked for a women's non-profit NGO against violence and discrimination. She was also part of community initiatives for peace, justice, and community art. Feeling that it was time to live in Korea for a while, she returned to Korea to participate in the 2005 Women's World Congress held in Seoul and stayed. Since then, she divides her time between Toronto and Seoul, often crossing the fourteen-hour time difference.

Melissa Kim is completing her double major in Criminology and Sociology at the University of Toronto. Planning to attend law school next year, she aims to focus on immigration and refugee law in order to address the numerous barriers that immigrants and refugees face in the Canadian legal system. After a few years of practicing, she hopes to work in policy, feeling that this is the most effective way to implement change within society.

Helen Lee is an independent filmmaker whose films include: *The Art of Woo; Subrosa; Prey; My Niagara;* and *Sally's Beauty Spot*. She is a graduate of the University of Toronto, New York University, Whitney Independent Study Program, and the Canadian Film Centre. Helen was a recipient of a 2002 DAAD Artist Fellowship, 2004 Chalmers Award and Korea Foundation Fellowship (2004/05). She serves on the advisory boards of the Toronto Reel Asian Festival and Cinematheque Ontario. Helen was born in Seoul, Korea, where she currently makes her home, with frequent trips to her other home in Toronto. And she wants you to know that she's the eldest of three siblings—because birth order is everything.

Min Sook Lee is an award-winning documentary director/producer. Her documentary, *El Contrato*, which examines at the lives of migrant farm workers in Canada was nominated for a Gemini Award for Best Social/Political Documentary in 2005. *Hogtown,* which looked at the politics of policing in the city of Toronto garnered the Best Feature-Length Canadian Documentary prize at the 2005 Hot Docs film festival. In 2006 she completed *Borderless*, a docu-poem on the lives of undocumented workers in Canada, which has screened in festivals across Canada and internationally. She is currently working on a documentary, *Tiger Spirit,* which focuses on the reunification of the two Koreas.

Patricia Lee (Collective Member) is a second generation Korean-Canadian writer and media artist working in the fields of film, video and interactive design. She has worked as an Educator and Manager in various social justice, community arts, and violence against women organizations in Toronto.

Ruthann Lee (Collective Member) was born and raised in Toronto. She completed her Master's thesis on "coming out" narratives in 2003 and is currently a doctoral student at York University in the Graduate Programme in Sociology. She has published in *Women & Environments* and guest edited a special journal issue on "Lesbian, Bisexual, Queer, Transgender and Transsexual Sexualities" for *Canadian Woman Studies/les cahiers de la femme*. Her more recent work examines representations of Asian North American masculinities in popular culture. Among other things, she identifies as a radical queer Korean Canadian writer, theorist, artist and activist.

CONTRIBUTOR NOTES

Una Lee's writing has appeared in the *Toronto Star, Fireweed,* and *Rice Paper.* She founded and edited *big boots*, an internationally distributed zine about the experiences of women and trans people of colour. As a graphic designer, she has helped craft social movement campaigns at local and national levels. Her design work has been recognized by Applied Arts Magazine and the Advertising and Design Club of Canada. Una lives in Toronto (una@unalee.net).

Jane Park grew up in Edmonton and Vancouver, Canada. She studied English Literature at Queen's University. Currently, she lives in New York. She has been previously published in *Echoes Upon Echoes: New Korean American Writings*, and *The Queen's Undergraduate Journal* (janezpark@gmail.com).

Hijin Park (Collective Member) was born in Korea and raised in Edmonton, Alberta. She is a Ph.D. candidate in the Department of Sociology and Equity Studies in Education and an Instructor in the Equity Studies Program at the University of Toronto. She has published articles on racialized sexual violence, Canadian immigration and refugee policy and the Los Angeles "riots." Her current work examines how discourses of multiculturalism and globalization operate to erase Canadian imperialism.

Ann Shin's writing has been published in anthologies and magazines in Canada and the U.S., including *On a Bed of Rice* (Anchor Books) and *Geography of Encounters* (Rowman and Little Press). Her latest book of poetry is *The Last Thing Standing* (Mansfield Press). Her award-winning documentaries have screened at festivals around the world. Titles include: *Westerneyes; Four Seasons: A Mosaic; Incident at Roswell; Almost Real.* She lives in Toronto, currently working as a television producer and writing a novel.

Suzy Yim, a.k.a "Titty-Titty Bang-Bang," is a gender-performing, sex-positive, queer activist, advocate, and ally. In her academic life, Suzy is researching the social epidemiology of HIV and is managing a project in Thailand looking at HIV vaccine acceptability by commercial sex workers, men who have sex with men, and injection drug users. Suzy is currently doing her Masters of Social Work at the University of Toronto, specializing in mental health.

Jean Yoon is an actor, writer, and theatre artist. Born in Illinois and raised in Toronto, Jean has lived and worked in Vancouver, Edmonton, Harbin City and Yanji City in North Eastern China, and makes Toronto her home. Jean has published poetry, short fiction, essays and articles in a number of journals, magazines and anthologies. A pioneer in the Asian Canadian theatre community, Jean is best known as the writer/creator of *The Yoko Ono Project*, a multimedia performance art comedy, produced by Loud Mouth Asian Babes/Theatre Passe Muraille in Toronto 2000, by the Firehall Arts Centre in Vancouver 2001 and published by Broken Jaw Press in 2002. Her comical adaptation of a classic Korean folktale *Hongbu and Nolbu: The Tale of the Magic Pumpkins* premiered at the Lorraine Kimsa Theatre for Young People to great response in spring 2005.

Sylvia Yu Chao is a journalist based in Beijing, China. She has worked in Victoria and Vancouver as news reporter for Global TV and CBC radio, and as a TV producer for a national current affairs show in Toronto. She is the author of a biography published in 2002, *Heart and Soul: The Life Story of Pastor Augustus Chao*. Her work has appeared in *The Toronto Sun, The Globe and Mail, Elle Magazine, Vancouver Magazine* and *The Halifax Herald*. Currently she is writing her second book, which focuses on the stories of the survivors of Japanese Military sexual slavery. She lives in Beijing with her husband, Steve.

MEMBER OF SCABRINI GROUP

Québec, Canada
2007